WITHOUT CONSENT

Also by Georgie Hale

TREAD SOFTLY

WITHOUT CONSENT

Georgie Hale

Hodder & Stoughton

Copyright © 2001 Georgie Hale

First published in Great Britain in 2001
by Hodder and Stoughton
A division of Hodder Headline

The right of Georgie Hale to be identified as the Author of
the Work has been asserted by her in accordance with the Copyright,
Designs and Patents Act 1988.

10 9 8 7 6 5 4 3 2 1

A CIP catalogue record for this title is available
from the British Library

ISBN 0 340 76853 3

Typeset by
Phoenix Typesetting, Ilkley, West Yorkshire
Printed and bound in Great Britain by
Mackays of Chatham plc, Chatham, Kent

Hodder and Stoughton
A division of Hodder Headline
338 Euston Road
London NW1 3BH

For Katie and Lucy, who light up my life.

ACKNOWLEDGEMENTS

With grateful thanks to Graeme Mearns of the Royal Shakespeare Company for his assistance, and to Tim and Lucy for their hospitality.

Prologue

Hunter's Wood.

A perfect summer's night, balmy and still.

A badger, heavily pregnant, pads into the moonlit clearing, then stops, like a nervous actor about to take the stage. She senses first, then sees; freezes in fear, as the gleaming alien roars towards her, uprooting tender saplings in its path. It hurtles past, so close the churning air lifts her fur, towards the trees beyond. She feels the shuddering impact as it smashes into a giant oak. Birds clatter off in terror. Then all is still, save for the groan of settling metal.

For a long moment, she eyes it warily. No noise or movement comes from it. Then, prompted by the unborn lives inside her, she continues her endless search for food, moving towards it in anxious, snuffling circles. Clouds dart across the moon and extinguish the floodlights. Somewhere deep in the tangle of trees a fox shrieks.

A sudden muted roar, and the oak is alight, not moon silver now, but hottest amber. Flames lick the overhanging boughs. Inside the glowing skeleton at its base, hair frizzles, smooth hands tighten to shrivelled, blackened claws.

It's over in minutes. The tree breathes in the final spiralling sparks, and sighs. Slowly, the secret woodland nightlife is resumed. From the safety of the undergrowth, the fox lifts its nose hungrily to the aroma of roasting human flesh that fills the air.

A single intruder creeps through the busy peace, stealthily seeking the sanctuary of his urban world, cursing as he stumbles over an obstacle in his path, recoiling as its solid, furry warmth brushes against his leg.

Chapter One

Detective Inspector Ray Whitelaw looked at the rows of faces in front of him, and wondered if maybe he had gone too far.

The whispers and sniggers from the back row had long since ceased. A couple of girls were crying. Even the hard-looking lad who had placed himself provocatively, arms folded, in the centre of the front row had stopped chewing gum. Danny Nolan, Whitelaw presumed.

'Taking without owner's consent. Twocking. Otherwise known as joy-riding. Doesn't bring much joy, though, does it?' Whitelaw addressed the comment directly to the boy at the front. 'Not when you end up like that.' He glanced back at the projected image on the screen: a snapshot of a lad about the same age as Nolan, smirking and cocky in his baseball cap and shades, alongside a lab shot of the blackened, twisted torso to which one too many car thefts had reduced him.

Whitelaw had his reservations about the new 'shock-tactic' campaign. Pictures like those turned even his strong stomach; God alone knew what they must be doing to a bunch of thirteen- and fourteen-year-olds, even ones who thought they knew it all already. And in truth, it seemed a bit of a con. There had been more than six hundred TWOCs in Blackport in the previous year, and bloody frustrating they were too, but not a single one, thank God, had resulted in a fatality; the nameless victim on the screen was courtesy of a training pack borrowed from the

Met. He glanced across at the young community worker who was leaning, arms folded, by the door, and tried to read his expression. Again, Whitelaw wondered if he had come on a bit too strong.

'There you go, then.' The Manchester accent was as strong as ever, as Kieran Henshall levered himself from the wall and walked over to the OHP. 'Don't take my word for it. Or Nicholas Perotti's, for that matter.' He jerked his head towards the screen. 'That's where nicking cars could get you.'

The boy on the front row had coloured, and was shifting uncomfortably in his seat. If the graphic slide show had done no more than give him pause for thought, then the afternoon hadn't been wasted, Whitelaw decided.

As if reading his thoughts, Kieran went on, 'I'm sure you all want to thank Inspector Whitelaw for sparing us some of his valuable time.' He grinned across suddenly at Whitelaw. Whitelaw grinned back in acknowledgement that the piss was now being taken out of him.

They walked back together across the deserted playground — if that were the appropriate name for the litter-strewn stretch of asphalt that separated one stark, graffiti-covered block of buildings from another. St Saviour's Community College was bottom of every educational league table in the town. And in a grim northern town like Blackport, that was saying something.

Kieran was describing, with typical enthusiasm, the drama project that he was running. Whitelaw couldn't help thinking that if a body wanted to run a drama project, there must be easier places than St Saviour's to do it. But he had to admit that Kieran seemed to have managed to infect the kids with some of his own passion; he'd had them eating out of his hand. And not just the kids, by the sound of things. Kieran was now talking about the play they were due to perform at the Freddie Denstone Memorial Gala.

'*Grab and Smash.*' Kieran pulled a face. 'Naff title, and the rest of it's pretty crap too, unfortunately, but beggars can't be choosers. We're not likely to get a more high-profile chance to show what we can do than the gala. Nicholas Perotti's script was part of the deal.' He bent down to pick up a discarded polythene bag, shook his head as he sniffed it warily, then threw it in a bin. 'The lead character comes to a sticky end in the play. No pun intended,' he added, jerking his head towards the bin. 'Well, he would, wouldn't he? The whole play's a cliché. The trouble is, however much the Perottis of this world try to moralise, most of those kids are still going to think that charging around in a stolen car's sexy.'

And if they realised that their charismatic young leader had more convictions for car theft, and worse, than many of them had had hot dinners, they'd think it even more sexy, Whitelaw replied silently, as Kieran went on, 'So Danny's now a folk hero, which isn't exactly what I had in mind when I invited him along. Hence my request to the boys in blue.'

'Danny Nolan? The cocky little git on the front row?'

Kieran roared with laughter. 'That was Wayne Edwards, but he'd be chuffed to bits you noticed him. All attitude, our Wayne. He'd be too frightened of his mum to pinch a Mars bar. No, I hoped Danny would be along this evening, but I guess he was working. Only stacking shelves at Kost Kutter, but it's a start. He's dead set on going straight this time.'

Whitelaw raised an eyebrow.

'He's really good, you know. Really bright.' Kieran sounded defensive.

'So how did you come across him?' Whitelaw tried to appear more interested than he was. He'd heard too many claims about 'going straight' during his thirty years in the force to take anything other than the jaundiced view.

'I was running a workshop at Ripley Grange. Danny stood out straight away.'

Whitelaw didn't say that anyone who could read and write

would probably have stood out at Ripley Grange, one of the North's tougher young offenders' institutions.

Kieran threw his things into the back of a battered, ageing VW, locked it up, then turned back to Whitelaw. 'This project's been the best thing that could have happened to him, made him see there are other ways to get a buzz. I'm encouraging him to apply for one of the Denstone bursaries, so he can get himself out of all that crap for good.' The animated face was suddenly fiercely earnest. Then just as suddenly, it was transformed by another disarming grin. 'Have you got time for a pint, or should you be out nicking people?'

Whitelaw had forgotten, in the three years since they had last met, just how much he liked this young bloke. 'A pint sounds good,' he said. 'How's Flora, by the way?' He hoped he wasn't putting his foot in anything, as he added, 'You two still in touch?'

Kieran nodded. 'We've just bought a place together. Sephton Street.'

The words were spoken casually, but Whitelaw could see the pride in the younger man's face. 'I'm glad,' he said, and meant it.

They walked along for a couple of minutes in companionable silence.

'I could get you some tickets, if you like. For the gala,' Kieran said, as they crossed the road to the Cottage Tavern, a bleak sixties brick box that couldn't have looked less like a cottage if it tried. 'Greg Farrell's going to be there. The kids are beside themselves.'

Whitelaw looked doubtful. 'Friday, did you say?' It didn't sound his sort of do at all, but Val would kill him if she found out he'd turned down a chance to see her heart-throb on the flesh.

'They're fifty quid a throw, mind.'

'*How* much?'

Kieran grinned. 'Didn't think you would.'

Whitelaw had just got the drinks in when his mobile went. He swore, took a long swig of his beer, then looked around and lowered his voice as he spoke into it. The Cottage was not a pub in which to advertise the fact that he was a copper.

'Well, bugger me,' he muttered, as he tucked the phone back in his jacket.

Kieran looked up enquiringly.

'You remember I said we'd never had a joy-riding fatality?' Whitelaw took another swig and got to his feet. 'Well, it looks like we've got one now.'

Forensic were already at the scene, by the time Whitelaw got to Hunter's Wood. He negotiated his way under the fluttering striped tape and plastic sheeting surrounding the burnt-out wreck and stuck his head inside the car. Swallowing down the hot bile that rose instantly in his throat at the stench, he glanced at he charcoaled remains still hunched over the steering wheel.

'I prefer mine medium rare, personally,' the police cameraman commented from behind his lens.

'And they forgot the garlic mushrooms, and all,' DC Lightowler grinned, as he looked up from his fingertip search of the scorched grass surrounding the car.

Whitelaw forced a grim answering smile. He knew that Val would be horrified to hear them joking like this over what was left of someone's brother, someone's son. Few wives would recognise the men that he and his colleagues became in situations like these, nor understand the sick humour that saw them through.

He nodded at the passenger door, hanging from one hinge. 'I assume you got some shots of the vehicle before that was opened?'

'That's how we found it,' Lightowler said. 'Both front doors hanging open. What d'you reckon, Guv? Impact?'

Whitelaw shook his head; the damage to the bodywork didn't suggest sufficient force for that. 'Passenger, more like. Legged it, presumably.'

'Must have been wearing his St Christopher, then. Unlike

this poor devil,' the police surgeon observed, as he joined them. 'Young Medlock's got your uniformed boys searching the area.'

Lightowler snorted.

Whitelaw shot him a warning glance. Thirteen years a constable and only just made it out of uniform, there was no reason for there to be any love lost between Terry Lightowler and the likes of Medlock, but Whitelaw could do without the idiot sounding off in front of all and sundry.

He turned his attention back to the car. The passenger side had taken the greater impact. 'I'd have thought anyone would be bloody lucky to come out of that uninjured, wouldn't you?' He ran his hand over the battered nearside wing. 'Nice motor.'

'BMW 328,' Lightowler said. 'We've already run a check on the chassis number. It was reported stolen from the Oultonshaw area Monday evening.'

'There's a surprise. There's not many outside Oultonshaw could afford to run a BMW. SOCO making any guesses as to how long it's been here?'

Lightowler shrugged. 'Kids found it when they came up here after school. Said it wasn't here yesterday.'

'So last night sometime.' Whitelaw touched the bodywork again. It would have taken time for the metal to cool, especially as the weather had been unseasonably warm that day. 'What else have we got?'

'We're going to have to rely on dental records for an ID, I fear,' the police surgeon said, pulling on a pair of latex gloves as he prepared to make an initial examination of the body.

'Or wait for some distraught mother to report her little darling missing,' Lightowler added with a smirk.

Whitelaw glanced at the corpse and gave an involuntary shudder. Was some poor woman staring out of a window somewhere, wondering where he'd spent last night? Telling herself not to worry? Working herself into a state of righteous indignation as she waited for his return?

Following his gaze, the doctor shook his head. 'Impossible at this stage even to be certain of the gender, although had you noticed these?' He indicated the charred bangles, still encircling one twisted wrist.

Whitelaw hadn't. 'Female?' He blew out his cheeks. That really would be a first, although Medlock would undoubtedly point out that girls were just as entitled to burn themselves to a crisp in these enlightened times as lads. Come to that, 'girl' wouldn't be a word likely to stray into Medlock's university-trained vocabulary either, Whitelaw thought wryly. They were all 'women' these days. He wondered sometimes where it had all gone wrong.

As if on cue, DS Neville Medlock appeared from the far side of the clearing, brushing a stray twig from his sleek blond hair, and disentangling a bramble from the sleeve of his jacket.

'Nothing yet,' he said. 'Undergrowth's flattened over there.' He pointed back towards the path. 'But that could have been the kids. I've left some uniforms searching the ditch, in case the passenger was too badly hurt to make it away from the scene.'

'Should have worn your wellies,' Lightowler observed, eyeing his colleague's expensive, mud-caked shoes.

Medlock glanced down, then wiped them clean on the singed, furry rump of the dead badger that lay a few feet from the wreck. Whitelaw looked away in disgust. He suspected that Medlock would just as casually wipe his shoes on any officer at Blackport Central who got in the way of his relentless rise to the top. Graduate fast-tracker, Superintendent Lambert's blue-eyed boy, he'd taken his sergeant's exam in record time; Inspector would be his next step, God help them all.

'*He's the future, Ray. Get used to it . . .*' The words came back to Whitelaw as clear as if their speaker were standing next to him. He rubbed an impatient hand across his face. Seeing Kieran Henshall again had raised old ghosts.

'Right. I think I've seen all I need to,' he said briskly. 'I'll get back to the station and leave you to your ditch-dredging.'

'Sounds just up his street,' murmured Lightowler, as Medlock strode away.

'What are you going to wear?'

Flora Castledine was sitting beside the crate of as yet unpacked possessions that doubled as a dressing table in the little bedroom in Sephton Street, brushing her hair.

'Eh?' Kieran, sprawled across the bed, wondering if he would ever tire of watching this nightly ritual; Flora's slender arm raised to her head, revealing just a glimpse of swelling breast beneath the thin fabric of her nightdress, as the brush floated a glowing coppery mist of hair around her shoulders and halfway down her back. He felt his heart would melt with the intensity of his love, and the incredulous wonder, undiminished after more than three years, that she seemed to love him too.

'What are you wearing to the gala?' She smiled at him through the speckled mirror. 'You need to think about these things, you know. It's only the day after tomorrow.'

He pulled a face. 'Don't remind me.'

'You want to make an impact, don't you?'

He glanced at the heap of his clothes piled onto a chair in the corner. 'Jeans? I hadn't thought.' He shrugged, then added suspiciously. 'Does it matter?'

He could tell by the expression on her face that she was up to something as she put down the brush and pulled open the wardrobe door. With a flourish, she produced the kind of carrier bag that trumpeted, with the utmost discretion, that it didn't come from a chain store.

'Simon sent a cheque. To wish you luck.' She tipped out the contents of the bag: a pair of pale grey chinos, and a soft silk shirt the colour of a stormy sea. Even Kieran could see they must have cost a fortune; not that that would matter to a man as wealthy as Simon Castledine. He stared at them wordlessly, feeling the familiar knot of anxiety beginning to form in the pit of his stomach. He couldn't take generosity. He wasn't used to it. It made him wonder how long all of it could last.

'I know,' she grinned, misreading his silence. 'I should have bought pots and pans or something useful. But I thought, what the hell! Pots and pans are *so* boring. And Friday's important for you. You need to look good.'

'They're great.' With effort, he smiled and added, 'I'll ring your dad and thank him.'

Pushing the new clothes aside, she climbed into bed next to him. 'I just hope Danny Nolan realises how important it is.'

'Danny?' Kieran ran his fingers through her hair. 'Why shouldn't he?'

She sat up, her arms around her knees, her nightdress tucked firmly under her feet in a manner that told him they were going to talk, whether he wanted to or not, and frowned. 'I'd feel happier if he'd bothered to turn up this afternoon, for a start.'

'Give over,' he groaned. It was not the first time they had had such conversations about Danny. 'He probably thinks he's had enough of the police for a bit.'

Flora's expression spoke volumes.

'Listen,' Kieran said, 'Danny's never going to be one to toe lines. He doesn't trust any kind of authority, for the very good reason that he's never had any cause to.' With tentative finger-tips, he began to massage her back. 'Trust me. I understand the criminal mind.' He gave her his most wolfish grin, making her smile, despite herself.

'Come on, I'm serious,' she said, attempting to keep to the point. She arched her back as he traced the delicate ridge of her spine through her nightdress. 'You've put your neck on the line to give him a chance. The least he could have done was to make the effort to—'

'I told you, he was working. He's always there when it matters. He gave up the whole day last Sunday, helping do the scenery plan out at Oultonshaw Manor, didn't he? If that didn't put him off, nothing will.' He rolled towards her, nuzzling against her hip.

'Don't change the subject.'

'What subject was that, then?'

She pushed him off, but gently, her fingers lingering against his cheek, and he took her hand in his, kissing each finger as he pulled her down into the rumpled sheets.

'Forget about Danny Nolan,' he murmured as he teased the hem of her nightdress up over her slim thighs. 'Trust me, everything's going to be fine.'

Chapter Two

Superintendent Lambert flung a copy of the *Blackport Daily Echo* down on Whitelaw's desk in the CID office and stood over him, glowering. 'You do realise the Chief Constable lives in Oultonshaw?'

Whitelaw, guessing that the question was rhetorical, offered no reply.

'A twenty per cent increase in car thefts in the last six months?' Lambert's voice rose an octave. 'What happened to Operation Hand Brake? And how the hell did Sid Barker get hold of these figures before I did, anyway?'

Whitelaw wondered briefly how it was that any adverse publicity always appeared to take Lambert by complete, enraged surprise, whereas the occasional success was inevitably a result of his own good management. 'With respect, sir, if the budget hadn't been pulled on the CCTV cameras round the Eden Rise Estate—'

'They would have picked up a stolen car between Oultonshaw and Hunter's Wood, would they?' Lambert snapped. 'And don't try that "with respect" routine on me, Whitelaw. A little more in the way of proactivity around this station, and fewer whinges about budget cuts, and we might just give the *Echo* less opportunity to pillory us.'

Lambert was big on proactivity. He was big on all the buzz words. That was why he got on so well with Medlock.

'Do we have an ID on the twocker yet?'

'No, sir.' Whitelaw eyed Lambert's immaculate uniform and added maliciously, 'There wasn't much left to identify. The flesh had all been—'

'Yes, yes.' Lambert's squeamishness was legendary. 'I'm sure all the details will be in the pathologist's report, thank you. Has it arrived?'

'No, sir.'

'Well, tell him to get a bloody move on. And in the meantime, I suggest you get round all the local health centres and hospitals, and find the accomplice, instead of sitting around here on your backside, waiting for something to happen.'

'Never thought of that, sir,' Whitelaw muttered as Lambert slammed out of the office. He put his feet up on the desk, yawned and picked up the paper. He started at the back, checking the lunchtime county cricket scores, which provoked a disbelieving groan, before moving towards the cover story that had had Lambert's hair off, via births, marriages and deaths (another Fenton in the world – more work for the Youth Courts in twelve or so years' time, no doubt), his horoscope (not that he ever read that sort of tripe) and the local three-day forecast (he should be able to get round the allotment at the weekend, with any luck). He stopped at page four. Each Friday, the *Echo* ran an article on the forthcoming weekend's social events; usually a couple of columns consisting of the programme at the town's two cinemas, together with a listing of whichever pubs were hosting live bands. This week's issue ran to a full-page spread on the Freddie Denstone Memorial Gala, which the report described fulsomely as 'the social function of the year'.

Three photographs accompanied the article. One showed the still-smoking ruins of a large house. 'Denstone Park in 1990: The Mysterious Arson Attack that Baffled Police', the caption read. Sounded like one of Sid Barker's, Whitelaw thought, examining the picture. He had been one of the investigating officers. That the fire was nonaccidental had been clear from the start.

Insurance scam, everyone had reckoned, until the family's wealth had become so abundantly clear. The investigation had failed to turn up any motive, still less a perpetrator. The building had been unoccupied and apparently well guarded by a local security firm. Every line of inquiry had petered out, and the file had eventually been closed. The memory rankled; Whitelaw didn't like loose ends.

With an irritable flap of the paper, he turned to the next photograph. Clearly a publicity shot, the dramatically lit profile of a young man in period costume was captioned more prosaically, 'Greg Farrell as Sydney Carton'. Whitelaw studied it, then pulled a face. What was it with women? Why did they have to go mooning after some pansy actor, instead of being satisfied with what they'd got? He caught sight of his own balding reflection in the blank screen of the computer he never used, and gave it a wry grin.

The third photograph described itself as 'Sixties film star Tricia Denstone, with her husband, Henry, Chairman of Denstone Automotive Engineering, and their daughter, Penelope'. It showed a woman of about fifty; attractive, Whitelaw supposed, in a flashy, over-made-up way. Tricia Denstone always made news in Blackport, which was not noted for its wealth of celebrities. Even so, 'film star' was pushing it a bit in Whitelaw's opinion. She'd had a couple of minor hits as the love interest obligatory in the type of action movies that were popular at the time, before retiring to take on the less glamorous role of wife and mother. Dolly birds – that was what they'd called actresses like Tricia Taylor, as she'd been in those days.

Whitelaw wondered what Medlock and his politically correct cronies would make of that.

Tricia Denstone was flanked on one side by a plump, much younger woman, who beamed self-consciously at the camera from behind thick spectacles. On the other side of her stood a tall, angular man whose pinched, unsmiling face Whitelaw recognised both from the time of the arson investigation and, more recently, from his occasional visits to the magistrates' courts to request a search warrant or the like. Henry Denstone, chairman not only of the Blackport Bench, but also of one of the town's oldest and biggest employers, was what would in less cynical days have been described as a pillar of the local community. As as sour-faced and self-righteous as he looked, by all accounts. No wonder marriage had marked the end of Tricia's show-biz career, Whitelaw thought, looking from one of them to the other. It was only her charity work that kept her in the papers these days.

'Reading the society page?' Medlock strolled into the office and glanced at the picture with a supercilious smile. He took a hanger from the back of the door and, removing his jacket, hung it up with elaborate care, before sitting at his desk. Anyone else would have chucked it over the back of a chair, Whitelaw thought, as he regarded the younger man with dislike. Of all the officers in the station, Medlock was the last man with whom he would have chosen to share his office. He suspected Lambert had done it on purpose, simply to spite him.

'Hardly your sort of do,' Medlock went on. 'I'd have put you down as more of a mushy peas and pie man, myself.' As always, the 'Guv' he added fractionally too late was made to sound as if he was taking the piss. He switched on his computer, and added, 'Not that you'd have got tickets if you'd wanted them. Gold dust, as soon as they announced Greg Farrell was going to be there. Friend of mine from the squash club is a personal acquaintance of Penelope Denstone, and even he failed to get his hands on any.' He looked up from his keyboard. 'Quite a coup for a dump like Blackport.'

Whitelaw didn't rise to the bait. 'Greg Farrell?' he repeated innocently.

Medlock gave a snort of amused contempt. 'He's only the hottest property since Hugh Grant. Sydney Carton in *A Tale of Two Cities* last year, and now JC Himself, no less. Seems to be carving out quite a niche for himself as the archetypal suffering hero.' He shook his head at the deliberately blank expression Whitelaw had adopted. '*God's Only Son?*'

'Also known as the *Gospel According to the Box Office*. Yes, I do read the Sunday papers.' Whitelaw got to his feet. Winding Medlock up was so simple it quickly got boring. 'Well, can't stop here exchanging social chit-chat with you, sunshine, tempting as the idea is. I'll leave you to play with your computer. Shame I didn't realise you were so keen on this Greg Farrell bloke,' he threw over his shoulder as he left the office. 'A friend of mine offered me some tickets only the other day.'

Ray Whitelaw was whistling, as he went off down the corridor.

Flora could feel tears of frustration welling up in her eyes. They had been standing in the car park for almost an hour, everyone loaded into the minibus and ready to go, and still Danny Nolan hadn't shown up.

'What in God's name are we going to do now? We should have been there half an hour ago,' she said, her voice sharper than she had intended. It was hardly Kieran's fault, after all.

He was scanning the empty car park as if hoping he could make Danny appear by sheer force of will. He turned to her, real anguish in his expression. 'Christ, Flora. I'm so sorry. If I've put your job on the line—'

'Oh, damn the job,' she said angrily. 'It's you I'm thinking about.' She knew how much the St Saviour's project meant to him. Bringing it to the attention of the Denstones was one of the few things that almost made her soulless job at Denstone Automotive Engineering worthwhile. She swallowed back the 'I told you so' that was clamouring to be said; Kieran's expression told her it was unnecessary in any event. He had been so certain about Danny bloody Nolan from the first minute he had come across him. Flora knew she'd disappointed him by not sharing his faith in the boy. But try as she might, all she could see was a cocky, arrogant yob who was using the gala as no more than a chance to show off when it suited him. She would kill him, personally wring his neck, if he let them down now.

Kieran stood gnawing at his fingernails, then said decisively, 'You'll have to go ahead. I'll take the car and go to look for him.'

'I can't drive that!' Flora stared at the St Saviour's minibus, which was lurching and shuddering under the combined activities of its impatient and overexcited cargo.

'It's the same as the car, love. Same gears and everything.'

'But—'

'Just bigger. See you.' With a quick kiss on the cheek, he was off.

'Thanks, Kieran. Thanks a lot,' she muttered after the VW, as it backfired its way out of the car park and disappeared up the road in a haze of exhaust fumes.

She turned back to the minibus. Yanking open the door, she negotiated the high step and hauled herself aboard. Ignoring the clamorous questioning that greeted her from the back, she checked her trousers for oil and tested the steering wheel. '*Same gears, just bigger.*' Her feet barely reached the pedals. She turned around and bellowed for some quiet, switched on the ignition and crashed around the gearbox until she found first. At least the damned thing was pointing in the right direction. Cautiously, she let her foot off the clutch. The minibus leapt forward, then stalled, to a chorus of cheers and catcalls.

'Damn you, Danny Nolan,' she muttered, as they kangaroo-hopped out into the street. The evening was turning into a disaster, and it was only likely to get worse.

'Very nice.'

Whitelaw dragged his eyes from the closing minutes of the one-day match, as his wife pirouetted in front of him.

She did look nice too. More than nice. It was years since she'd worn her hair that short, and the hairdresser had done something to the colour as well.

He ought to make the effort to take her out more, he told himself, only too aware that it was no more than guilty conscience that had prompted him to suggest a meal at the new Italian. Not that Val could seriously have expected him to part with a hundred quid for a couple of tickets. Anyone would have to be out of their mind to shell out that much for a glass of champagne, a bunch of kids cavorting around and a fireworks display, just for a chance to rub shoulders with a few celebrities. She'd enjoy a night at Mario's just as much, he persuaded himself. Even with a bottle of wine and a pudding, they wouldn't run up a bill for more than half that much. At least he hoped not.

'You'll knock them dead, love,' he said. 'Now why don't you go up and have a nice long soak in the bath. The table's not booked till eight.' His gaze slid back to the final over. Which was, of course, the cue for his mobile.

'Bugger,' he muttered, fumbling in his jacket, his eyes still glued to the screen.

'Pathologist's report, Guv. Thought you'd want to be first to hear it.'

Reluctantly, Whitelaw grabbed the remote and turned off the sound, as Terry Lightowler went on, 'Our corpse is male, probably in his twenties.'

'Male? What about the bracelets?'

'Only one mystery among many.' Lightowler was always one to milk a situation. 'He apparently carked it some hours before the crash took place. Battered to death, the doc reckons. Nasty. Fractured skull, both legs shattered . . . Says it reminds him more than anything else of an IRA punishment beating. Far more extensive injuries than the impact of the crash would warrant, at any rate. You there, Guv?'

Whitelaw closed his eyes in disbelief as the opposition's eleventh man silently belted a six to win the match on the last ball.

'Got that.' He banged off the mobile and scowled at the television.

'Anything wrong?' Val, now in her dressing gown, came in carrying a mug of tea.

'Leicestershire won by three runs.' Whitelaw took a morose gulp of the tea. 'And unless a corpse can drive a car, our missing twocker is prime suspect in a murder inquiry, so bang go my chances of getting the tomatoes planted tomorrow.'

Chapter Three

'Fucking hell!' Wayne's exhaled whisper reflected Flora's reaction, if more colourfully. Kieran had said Oultonshaw Manor was impressive. She hadn't realised just how impressive.

The journey out through the leafy suburbs had taken the best part of half an hour, mainly because Flora had quickly discovered that she lost control of the recalcitrant minibus at anything above twenty miles an hour. By the time they had reached the imposing entrance to their destination, her passengers had been almost hysterical with excitement at the imminent prospect of meeting Greg Farrell. It had taken her a further five minutes to drive from the road and up the gently sloping driveway that led through overarching trees and parkland stretching to either side as far as the eye could see. Now, at the brow of the hill, the drive turned sharply to the right to reveal, in the hollow in front of them, the full magnificence of Oultonshaw Manor. Gabled and turreted, it was built of weathered brick, glowing russet in the evening sun, around a massive half-timbered central section. A battalion of barley-twist chimneys rose from its long, irregular roofline. The peacock that wandered across the manicured lawn looked as if some artistic director straight from Hollywood had planted it there. Simon's house on Scilly was big, but this was something else. The noise level in the back had petered off to stunned silence. Flora felt a great lurch of anxiety. This wasn't some half-empty school gym or draughty church hall; this time their performance would be for real.

A number of cars were already parked in the sweeping circular forecourt: a Rolls, with the number plate DEN 1, a Range Rover – predictably DEN 2 – a long, low-slung estate with tinted windows, and several flashy-looking sports cars, the makes of which were identified in hushed admiration from behind her. Flora chugged down the hill towards them and drew up behind the Rolls.

In an instant, a burly man with a dark suit and shades bore down on them and demanded, in an all but unintelligible Liverpool accent, to know who they were. Flora explained. The man glanced suspiciously into the back of the minibus.

'It's all right, Mr Fieldgate.' A voice that Flora recognised as Tricia Denstone's floated down from an upstairs window. 'Let them through. I'll meet you round there, my dear,' she called, leaning out of the window to wave at Flora.

Reluctantly, Flora waved back. She had hoped that they could slip in and lurk around unnoticed until Kieran joined them.

With a level of politeness Flora suspected he found difficult to maintain, the security man directed her to the 'staff access' at the back. She crunched into reverse and followed a less impressive gravelled path that led down the side of the house. It took her past tennis courts, a newer glass construction that she guessed to be an indoor swimming pool, and a row of kitchen gardens, before opening out into a second courtyard in front of a stable block.

'Flora!'

'Mrs Denstone.' Flora smiled weakly, as she scrambled down from the driving seat.

'Oh, please! Tricia, my dear, Tricia! Mrs Denstone makes me feel positively ancient!' The woman pecked the air behind Flora's left ear, then held her at arm's length, scrutinising the simple linen trouser suit that had been bought with the rest of Simon's cheque. 'You look absolutely marvellous. You didn't get that outfit on what my husband pays you, or if you did, I must take a closer look at the wages bill!'

'Tinkle of laughter' was a phrase Flora had come across in books, but she had never actually heard one before. Tricia Denstone could have walked straight out of one of her own films. She was dressed in an outfit of jet-encrusted black chiffon, her hair and makeup expensive and flawless. Her long painted nails exactly matched the cluster of rubies in her ring. Clearly a woman who paid attention to detail, Flora decided, her heart sinking further. A woman who was hardly likely to miss the fact that neither the director nor the leading man had turned up.

'And where's that gorgeous man of yours?' Tricia immediately confirmed the accuracy of Flora's supposition. She patted her hair and looked expectantly at the troupe of youngsters filing sheep-ishly from the back of the van.

'Last-minute rehearsal.' Flora flashed her a grin that she prayed looked more convincing than it felt. 'He'll be along shortly.'

'No problem, I hope.' Tricia's social smile tightened a little at the corners.

'None at all,' Flora said brightly. And wondered what the hell she was expected to do next.

Kieran drove slowly through the maze of semiderelict streets that led down towards Blackport docks, peering to left and right. It was just after six, that period when the few people with jobs had already come home from work, but too early for the pubs to begin filling up, and the pavements in front of the narrow terraced houses were largely deserted. A heavily pregnant woman, sunbathing on her front step, eyed his slow progress suspiciously from the wooden kitchen stool that served her as a deckchair. A group of lads reluctantly paused the game of football they were playing in the middle of the road to let him pass.

There was no sigh of Danny.

Kieran drove on to the dingy bedsit that had been Danny's home since his release from Ripley Grange. Situated on South Wharf, in what had once been the centre of Blackport's maritime trade and was now the most run-down part of the docks, the Seamen's Rest Home was surrounded by wasteland and disused warehouses. The austere, three-storey building resembled a Victorian workhouse. It had been converted in the fifties; not in the way warehouses in more affluent parts of the country were converted three decades later, but simply plaster-boarded into shoddy post-war flats. Over the years, the flats themselves had been subdivided and sublet into the kind of rooms that housed the desperate; those with nowhere else to go. Only the lettering on the crumbling lintel above the entrance suggested the building's original purpose.

The front door was ajar. Kieran let himself into the hallway, blinking in the sudden gloom as he made his way up the rickety stairs to the top floor. He knocked on Danny's door, shouted his name, and waited. There was no letterbox to look through. Maybe the building's owners assumed the likes of Danny were unlikely to receive much mail. They were probably right. Across the landing a baby's wail competed with the rhythmic thud of a stereo from the floor below. The heat was stifling up here, the air pervaded by the sharp summer stench of unwashed bodies. Kieran knocked again.

'What d'you want?'

He turned to see a huge, elderly man hauling himself asthmatically up the stairs. A cigarette dangled precariously from his lower lip, spilling ash down his mountainous, vest-clad belly. He stopped for breath, squinting at Kieran with milky, distrustful eyes before introducing himself as the 'concierge'.

'Danny around?' Kieran asked neutrally. In other circumstances, the wonderful incongruity of the title would have appealed to his sense of humour.

The man's response was to hawk up a glob of phlegm, which he spat onto the cracked linoleum. Then he pointed a nicotine-stained finger, and wheezed, 'If it's you been banging on his door at all hours, you can fucking pack it in. And when you see him, tell him to get rid of that fucking dog, and all, or he's out.' He turned with difficulty, and lumbered back down the stairs.

Avoiding the glutinous puddle of phlegm, Kieran sat on the top step. There was no way Danny would have missed the performance without good reason; he had put too much into the project simply to walk out on it. He might have been late for a couple of rehearsals, but he was word-perfect, which was more than could be said for anyone else. And he was good. Very good. Kieran had recognised at once the raw energy that had injected an authentic, gritty realism to the script that the sentimental plot, stereotypical characterisations and limp dialogue scarcely merited. Danny had got to be in line for one of the Denstone bursaries, and he knew it.

When Kieran figured the man was out of earshot, he tried the door again, then searched his holdall for a scrap of paper, finally tearing the back page from the script. He hesitated, then wrote simply, 'Call me.' He scribbled his new address and phone number on the bottom of the note, and pushed it under Danny's door.

There was nothing more he could do.

Back in the car, he put his head on the steering wheel for a moment and tried to collect his thoughts. Inside the grim, gloomy boarding house, his concerns for Danny's safety had, for the moment, put everything else out of his head; back out in the sunshine, his more immediate worries came flooding back. He lifted his head and stared at his watch, his fingers drumming nervously against the wheel. The play was due to go on in little more than a couple of hours. Without a leading man.

'My heart aches, and a drowsy numbness pains/My sense . . .' Kieran wondered what had made the words pop up now. Keats' 'Ode to a Nightingale'. He had learnt the poem at school. The discipline of its iambic pentameter had appealed; order amongst chaos. The lines had become a mantra that he would repeat over and over when he had needed to retreat inside his head, which had been often. Through school, and later university, he had devoured literature and poetry voraciously, but it had always been the lines from the Keats that came back to him when he was stressed. He hadn't thought of them for years, until tonight.

He wound down the windows, fruitlessly attempting to get some air into the baking car, and started up the engine. As he retraced his journey, he mentally scanned the rest of the cast. None of them was half as good as Danny, of course, but that was less the point, at this stage, than whether any of them would know, or could ad lib, Danny's lines. He knew he was wasting his time. If he didn't find Danny in the next hour, they could forget the play unless he stepped into the part himself. He shook his head. Amongst other things, Leroy, the lead character, was supposed to be fifteen. Danny himself was pushing it at eighteen; it was only his slight build that had made the casting viable. At twenty-seven, and six feet three, Kieran very much doubted he would convince anyone.

He drove around the sweltering streets for another fifteen minutes, stopping the car and sticking his head into a couple of empty pubs, questioning a listless gang of kids on a street corner. Then grim-faced, a small muscle throbbing in his cheek, he swung the car away from the docks, and headed out for the rural suburbs, and Oultonshaw Manor.

The contrast could not have been more marked. Within ten minutes, he was breathing in air scented not with baked dog excrement but new-mown grass. Birdsong drifted through the car's open windows. The mean, oppressive terraces broadened first to neat roads of identical semis, then to the graceful tree-lined avenues of older, detached houses that formed Blackport's southern outskirts, before meandering eventually into the winding country lane that led into Oultonshaw. The woodland on either side was broken only by an occasional, immaculate sweep of lawn and a fleeting glimpse of weathered brick or basking sandstone. It could have been a different world.

It was as he was passing the edge of Hunter's Wood that Kieran saw Danny's slight figure, head down, stumping along the verge, a large dog in tow.

'Get in.' Instantly furious now he was reassured of the boy's safety, Kieran leapt from the car and grabbed Danny's arm, then dropped it, taking in the expression of terror on his face, the bruising that darkened one cheek and the great ragged gash snaking down his left temple.

'OK. It's OK.' Kieran backed off, holding up his hands to reassure not just the boy but the dog, which had sprung forwards, baring its fangs as it made a lunge at his ankle.

Danny's face relaxed. He clicked his fingers, and the dog reluctantly released its grip on the hem of Kieran's trousers and flattened itself against its master's legs, its lip still curled into a menacing snarl.

'Christ, what have you mean up to, mate?' Kieran kept his tone deliberately casual. 'Are you OK?'

'Fight,' Danny said, the monosyllable more challenge than explanation.

'Have you seen a doctor?' Kieran scanned his face.

'Get real.'

'Who's your friend?' Kieran asked, changing tack.

It was the ugliest dog he had ever seen. Violently orange in colour and as muscular as Danny was slight, it had short, bandy legs, a ludicrously extravagant tail and a sleek, narrow head that seemed to have come from an entirely different animal. The jaunty red and white spotted neckerchief it sported somehow only served to emphasise its singular lack of beauty.

Danny's expression softened. 'Deefer.' He bent and patted its head, and it gazed up at him in manifest admiration. 'Dee for dog. Get it?'

'Felt the sudden need of a bodyguard, did you?'

Danny stiffened. 'Had him since I was a kid, didn't I? When they threw me out, they threw him out with me.' The dog stuck its muzzle into his hand as if it understood what he was saying.

Happy families.

Kieran scanned the boy's face again, then shrugged. Push Danny too hard and he'd simply leg it. It would be a start to get him inside the car, he realised. 'The minibus might have been quicker.' He held open the passenger door and added lightly, 'And if that four-legged offensive weapon wants a lift, I think we should at least be formally introduced, before it has my bloody leg off.'

Danny bundled the dog into the back, where it executed a couple of circles before flopping down on the threadbare uphol-stery and eyeing Kieran balefully.

Kieran eyed it back. 'God knows what we're going to do with it when we get there. What the hell made you bring it with you?'

'He needed the exercise.' Danny's expression was hardly more encouraging than Deefer's. 'You got a problem with that?'

Kieran sighed heavily. 'Get in the car, Danny.'

They drove for a couple of minutes in silence, save for the radio and the dog's malodorous panting. Balanced precariously behind the front seats, it thrust its head between their shoulders, as if to underline the frailty of Kieran's role as taxi driver. Usually, Danny talked nonstop, was never still. Tonight, he hunched in his seat, knees pressed together, fists clenched, every sinew in his slight frame tense.

'OK. Let's cut the crap, shall we?' As they neared Oultonshaw Manor, Kieran reached over and turned off the radio. 'What's going on?'

'Don't know what you're on about.'

Kieran wondered if he might be jumping to conclusions. But the bruising was real enough. 'Is someone after you, Danny?' he asked quietly.

Silence.

'Don't you trust me?'

Danny shot him an anguished glance. Kieran was amazed to see that there were tears in his eyes. He pulled the car into the verge, and turned off the engine. 'Tell me.'

'Nothing to tell.'

'Crap.'

'We're going to be late, man.' The dog bestowed a wet lick on Danny's cheek and he pushed it impatiently away.

'So we are.' Kieran was working on the assumption that the play meant as much to both of them. He glanced at the clock on the dashboard and asked himself what he would do if Danny simply called his bluff. He need not have worried.

'Jesus,' Danny muttered, following Kieran's glance. Then with a long, ostentatious sigh, he said flatly, 'There's this guy, right? He's been leaning on me to help him with some scam. Been following me about.'

Kieran nodded. 'Go on.'

'I told him I wasn't interested, but he's been, like, putting the pressure on, if you know what I mean.'

Kieran could imagine. It would be easy enough for anyone aware of Danny's record to rock his boat, lose him his job and his lodgings. 'What sort of scam?' he asked, trying not to sound as concerned as he felt.

Danny's only reply was a shrug of his shoulders.

'Listen, Danny, you've worked bloody hard to stay away from any strife since you got out. If this guy's giving you a hard time, go to the police.' Kieran said it as firmly as he could, all too aware of how he would have reacted to the same advice when he was Danny's age.

Danny shifted away and muttered, 'Yeah, right.'

'You must.' Kieran put his hand on Danny's shoulder. The dog gave a low rumbling warning.

Danny flinched. 'Forget it.'

'There are things you can't sort out for yourself, believe me. If you're in some sort of—'

'Don't hassle me, man. I don't need it.' Danny stared through the windscreen, biting his lip. 'You're not my fucking probation officer.'

Kieran breathed in hard. The silence lengthened between them, the tension mounting with every second that ticked by. At last, he said, 'So do you still want to do the play, or what?'

'Wasn't me stopped the car, was it?'

Kieran looked across at Danny's mutinous profile and sighed. Whatever was going on, he wasn't going to find out about it this evening. 'Just try to put everything else out of your head for tonight. You're good, Danny,' he said quietly. 'Show everyone how good, yeah? It's your passport out of all this shit.'

Danny glanced at him, and then quickly away, fondling the dog's ear and turning his face into its matted fur so that Kieran could hardly hear his next words as he muttered, 'We're still mates, aren't we?'

'Yeah.' Kieran switched the engine back on. 'Yeah, Danny, we're still mates.'

Chapter Four

It wasn't the bill for eighty-three pounds that the waiter at Mario's had just presented that had ruined the evening. Whitelaw wouldn't have cared quite so much about being ripped off if he'd actually managed to get the criminally overpriced meal inside him before his mobile rang. But they'd only just finished the *affettato di pomodoro* (little more than a cheese and tomato sandwich in Whitelaw's estimation) and his *filetto pepato* had barely touched the table when the call came from Terry Lightowler. One of the local dentists had faxed through an ID on the corpse, and Whitelaw was needed back at Blackport Central to interview the next of kin.

Whitelaw had first come across Jason Morrissey in the days when kids like him were still called juvenile delinquents. He'd been a sad, skinny little runt, no more than eight or nine, done for liberating a large quantity of fags and a bottle of gin from the local off-licence. Whitelaw had given him a ticking off and taken him home. You could do things like that, back then. Not that 'home' had seemed the appropriate description for the shit hole Jason had shared with his alcoholic mother and whoever she was shagging at the time. Whatever, he had been in care within the year, and shortly afterwards had embarked on an escalating career of theft, drug peddling and prostitution. His path had crossed Whitelaw's on a number of occasions over the years. He had grown up into a good-looking lad, for any whose tastes ran to the girlish. Transvestism was his speciality, or had been. Which explained the bracelets.

About the only good thing the years in a children's home had done for Jason was to provide him with regular dental care. Whitelaw couldn't imagine Jason's teeth would have been top of his mum's list of priorities. In which case, they might never have identified him. Whitelaw recalled the charred remains in Hunter's Wood, the pathologist's description of the injuries that had been inflicted before Jason had died, and shuddered. Poor bastard. No one deserved an end like that, he thought as he suppressed a garlicky belch, demanded a cork for the nearly full bottle of wine, and pocketed his change. At eighty-three quid, they could whistle for a tip.

Sunil Doshai was waiting in one of the interview rooms. A squad car had picked him up and taken him in to identify the body. He looked up, his eyes puffy and red, as Whitelaw entered. Rivulets of mascara ran down his fine-boned cheeks. He'd been shacked up with Jason for the last couple of years, in as stable a relation-ship as either of them was likely to manage, and good luck to them, so far as Whitelaw was concerned. As yet, the poor sod knew only that Jason had died in a car accident. No mention had been made, either to Sunil or to the press, of the fact that the death was suspicious. Someone had gone to considerable lengths to make the death appear accidental. Whitelaw had decided to keep things that way for the time being.

Terry Lightowler rolled his eyes and muttered something under his breath that Whitelaw chose to ignore. Sunil might look like a caricature, with his pastel-pink jacket, elaborate jewellery and painted mouth, but his grief was real enough. If he and Jason had brought each other the only affection that either had known, then he deserved the same respect as any other next of kin.

Pushing a packet of cigarettes across the table, Whitelaw listened, nodding encouragingly and jotting notes as Sunil's story unfolded. Jason had been gone since the previous weekend. At first, Sunil hadn't been too concerned; some of Jason's clients expected him to stay the night, or even two. But when, by the third day, he still hadn't got in touch, Sunil had begun to worry.

Lightowler didn't bother to stifle a snigger.

'Go and get Mr Doshai a cup of tea,' Whitelaw snapped, and motioned him out, scowling at the deliberately mincing gait he adopted as he left the room. 'You didn't report him missing?' he said, turning back to Doshai.

Sunil watched Lightowler's departure, his lips trembling. 'You'd have sent out the search parties?'

'Point taken.' Whitelaw lit another cigarette. 'So let's go back to before Jason disappeared.' There was something odd about Sunil's behaviour. He hadn't even queried how Jason's body had come to be in the wreckage of a stolen car. Surely even with lifestyle such as his, he could have been expected to wonder. 'How did he seem? Up? Down?'

'Up.' Sunil didn't meet his eye.

'Any particular reason?'

Sunil shook his head, pulling a black silk handkerchief from the pocket of his jacket and dabbing delicately at his brow. Whitelaw could see there was something more he wanted to say. The interview room was airless and hot, but that wasn't why the line of sweat had broken out on his forehead. Without speaking, Whitelaw slipped the pathologist's report in front of the younger man, then stood up and turned away to stare out, hands clasped behind his back, at the still-shimmering tarmac of the car park below. The only sound was the slight rustle of paper as Sunil turned the pages.

At last he took a deep, shaky breath and said, 'I knew this was no accident, Inspector. As soon as your men told me he was dead, I knew.'

'OK, Sunil.' Whitelaw resumed his seat. 'I think you'd better tell me everything else you know, don't you?'

Jason had apparently been on what Sunil described as a 'high' in the weeks before he disappeared. Not an edgy, drug-induced high; more a contained excitement. He'd met someone, he'd said. Someone from way back. Bumped into him in a shop, as simple as that. Sunil maintained that Jason had told him neither the other man's name, nor why the chance meeting was so important. Just that it provided the missing link in something he'd been planning for a long time.

'You and Jason were close?' Whitelaw interrupted.

Sunil looked wary, as if wondering where the question was leading.

'You really trying to say he didn't tell you what it was he was planning?'

For a moment, Sunil looked down and said nothing. Which answered Whitelaw's question. Then, with an overelaborate shrug and an attempt at cynicism that didn't suit him, he replied that he'd never asked too many questions, had paid little attention. Jason had always been coming up with some scam or other, hadn't he? He'd never been above threatening to tell an unsuspecting wife, a disapproving boss . . . An extra couple of hundred quid here or there . . . Sunil looked up, a touch of defiance in his expression, as if daring his inquisitor to respond.

'I'll go and chase that tea,' Whitelaw said, getting wearily to his feet. 'While I'm gone, why don't you have another look through that report? See if it helps concentrate your mind on which particular unsuspecting wife or disapproving boss smashed most of the bones in your boyfriend's body before setting fire to him, eh?'

Sunil was badly frightened; that much was evident. Whitelaw could only gamble that the revulsion, anger, grief . . . whatever was going on in the other man's head as he reread the catalogue of Jason's injuries, would be stronger than the fear. He went back to his office, waited for five minutes, then went down to the canteen. There was no sign of Lightowler. Nor, when he returned to the interview room, tray in hand, was there any sign of Sunil. Fear had obviously won the fight.

Cursing, Whitelaw took a swig of the tea, then picked up the lab report. As he did so, a photograph fell from between its pages and fluttered to the floor, where it landed face downwards. Whitelaw bent to pick it up.

'What have we got here, then?' he muttered to himself as he turned it over.

Kieran parked next to the minibus, got out of the car and looked around. He could hear a distant hubbub of sound from across the high, clipped hedge that presumably screened them from the house. The dog, with a joyous yelp, bounded out behind Danny, then zigzagged across the courtyard, nose glued to the ground. Finally, it selected it spot, lifted it leg and urinated luxuriously and copiously against the wheel arch of the only other car, a shining, brand-new silver Audi TT convertible.

'Get that creature back in the motor, for God's sake,' Kieran hissed. 'Quickly. We haven't got all night.'

'I need to go, and all,' Danny announced, then shook his head as Kieran nodded towards a secluded bush. 'I need a crap.' He shrugged his shoulders. 'Nerves. The play, that's all,' he added with a sarcastic grin, pre-empting Kieran's question.

'Terrific.' Kieran knew it was a waste of time to pursue their previous conversation. He looked around, noticed a door that stood ajar, and stuck his head into what appeared to be a scullery. 'Come on,' he said, pulling Danny in after him. 'There's bound to be one around here somewhere.'

The scullery opened into a long deserted corridor, chilly after the evening sunshine. Kieran opened a couple of doors, to reveal a laundry, and a storeroom full of gardening equipment. Further along, the corridor split. After a second's hesitation, Kieran chose the right-hand branch that led them further into the house. Above them, they could hear voices, the creak of floorboards and a muffled bellow of laughter that sounded suspiciously like Wayne. Kieran glanced at his watch, wondering guiltily how

Flora had been coping on her own, and quickened his pace.

Eventually, they came to a narrow, spiral staircase. Again, Kieran hesitated.

'I'm getting desperate, man.'

'Great timing,' he muttered, giving Danny a shove and following him up the stairs and into yet another corridor, from which it was simple enough to follow the increasing volume of chatter and laughter until they pushed open a heavy swing door and found themselves behind a barricade of drinks tables at the rear of a vast, oak-panelled hall, already busy with arriving guests.

'Can I help you?' The liveried waiter regarded them as if he very much doubted that he could. Kieran followed the man's gaze down to his chinos, which bore the all-too-clear evidence of Deefer's earlier assault. Flora would kill him. He found himself torn between natural inclination — which was to ask the super-cilious git, in his strongest Manchester, for the location of the nearest bog — and common sense — which told him that this was the home not only of Flora's employer, but possibly Danny's future benefactor.

'Could you direct us to the cloakroom?' Kieran's accent was pure Home Counties. He flashed the man a dazzlingly apologetic smile, ignoring Danny's snigger.

The waiter pointed wordlessly towards a large sign to the left of the hall. Kieran could feel the man's suspicious gaze boring into his back as they negotiated their way from behind the tables and headed for the door he had indicated.

Danny took an age. Kieran stood outside the door of a lava-tory the size of the average living room for a good five minutes, before banging on it and whispering, 'What the hell are you doing in there?'

'What d'you think?' came the muffled reply.

Kieran glanced again at his watch. 'Listen, I'm going to find Flora. They're supposed to have set up the library as a dressing room. On this floor somewhere, I guess. Will you be OK?'

'I have taken a crap before.' Kieran heard the muted thud of a toilet roll being unfurled. 'Shan't be long.'

'Don't be. The show starts in less than half an hour.'

The ballroom was filling up. The advance publicity for the event had ensured that anyone who was anyone, as Tricia had put it, was present. They were an odd assortment. Dress ranged from casual to elaborately formal. One man with a loud voice and a questionable mid-Atlantic accent was sporting a tracksuit, base-ball cap and sunglasses, while others wore dinner jackets. Several women were in ballgowns.

The room itself was stunning, the walls, as in the hall, panelled in intricately carved oak. Glittering chandeliers hung from the high ceiling. A minstrel's gallery ran along one wall. The heady scent from huge arrangements of lilies that flanked the French doors opening on to the lawns was overlaid by the mingled fragrances of expensive perfume and cigar smoke. Blackport society was out in force. Flora looked unhappily at her glass of champagne and wondered how much longer she could allow this charade to continue.

Tricia Denstone had already shown her the vast marquee that loomed menacingly at the far end of the lawn. Rows of chairs were laid out in readiness in front of a raised platform. Heavy curtains, like those in a real theatre, concealed the scenery, which had been collected earlier. It was arranged exactly in accordance with Kieran's diagrams, the mock-up car looking a great deal less convincing in its new surroundings than it had on the stage at St Saviour's. The cast was installed in the library, which was doubling up for the evening as a dressing room. Their costumes had been hanging up waiting for them, carefully pressed. It was obvious that no effort had been spared in getting everything ready. Flora had been wary of leaving her charges to their own devices; they had overcome their initial reticence all too quickly. But Tricia had insisted that she should come and 'mingle', and had fixed each of the cast in turn with a smile of such menacing sweetness that they had instantly and quietly begun to get changed.

The time that Flora had spent 'mingling' had been marginally less enjoyable than driving the minibus, and she had already exhausted her store of polite small talk. Henry Denstone was even more taciturn than usual, standing dourly with Denstone Automotive Engineering's head of finance and another man, whom Flora did not recognise. Henry introduced him as Stanley Brassington, a colleague from the Bench and sales director of Northern Motors. In a booming voice, Brassington, a large, florid figure, asked her how a pretty girl like her came to know a dry old stick like Henry – a description Flora found too accurate to be funny – then turned to his other companions, not waiting for a reply. His loud manner was at odds with his sober but expensively cut suit. Flora could not imagine that he had a great deal in common with her employer.

But even Stanley Brassington was infinitely preferable to the other member of the small group into which Tricia had steered Flora. Nicholas Perotti was the author of the play. A man of at least fifty, with suspiciously jet-black hair, he was dressed in overtight black leather trousers and a white linen jacket, a red silk scarf draped around his neck. As talkative as Henry was silent, he had immediately taken up a position too close to Flora for her liking, and had emphasised each observation with a damp squeeze of her hand.

'Hello. I think we met at Daddy's Christmas do.'

Flora wasn't sure whether she was relieved or not as she turned to see Penelope Denstone standing beside her. The intervention at least allowed Flora to move away from Nicholas Perotti, but she remembered all too clearly how difficult conversation had been with Penelope, who was painfully shy. She was flushing now, her face a bright scarlet that clashed unflatteringly with her dress, which was of puce taffeta, and had a gathered skirt and fitted bodice that did little for the contours of Penelope's lumpy frame.

'Hi!' Flora smiled, feeling a sudden surge of sympathy for her. They must be about the same age, but being with Penelope was like being with a gauche child of eight or nine. 'How are things?'

'Fine, thank you.' Penelope smiled back. They both took a sip of their champagne.

'You've been lucky with the weather,' Flora said desperately. 'Yes.'

This was how it had been at Christmas. Small talk simply didn't work with Penelope. Bat any number of conversational balls across the net, she seemed incapable of hitting one back. Flora cast around for a subject that wasn't even more banal than the weather. 'I . . . I like your dress,' she said at last, feeling all the more guilty at the lie when Penelope, clearly pleased, flushed an even deeper scarlet and answered, 'Mummy chose it.'

Flora could believe it; she suspected that Tricia was not the kind of mother to countenance any competition from her daughter. She looked over to where the older woman was in conversation with Stanley Brassington. Tricia, entirely ignoring her daughter, beckoned Flora to join them. Penelope smiled again, then wandered back to her father where they stood silently gazing into the middle distance, both apparently locked in their own thoughts.

'This young lady and her friend are doing the most marvellous work with just the kind of underprivileged youngsters we are aiming to help,' Tricia beamed, when Flora had been introduced to Stanley Brassington for a second time.

'Is that right?' Brassington made no attempt to disguise his lack of interest, but Tricia was not so easily deterred.

'You'll be able to judge for yourself when you see the play,' she twinkled. 'So if your organisation would like to support the local community by—'

Flora took a deep breath. 'Could we have a word, please?'

Brassington, taking advantage of the diversion, moved smartly off as she drew Tricia aside.

'What is it?' The older woman looked irritated at being inter-rupted in the middle of her sales pitch.

Flora squared her shoulders. The farce was going to have to be brought to an end sooner or later. 'There's something I need to—' she started resolutely, then broke off, relief flooding over her as she saw Kieran standing in the doorway and peering over the heads of the other guests as he searched her out. Spotting her, he grinned broadly and began to make his way across. Swallowing the rest of the sentence, Flora raised a questioning eyebrow towards him. He answered with a wink and a discreet thumbs up.

Catching her expression, Tricia turned. 'Ah, here he is!' she beamed, eyeing Kieran's tall, loose-limbed figure with an undis-guised appreciation that took in the handsome features, the thick dark hair, the amazing black-lashed eyes that so exactly matched his shirt. It was only with evident reluctance that she returned her attention to Flora and asked, 'What was it you were saying?'

'I . . . I just wanted to thank you for giving Kieran the chance to show what St Saviour's could do,' Flora ad-libbed.

'My pleasure.' Tricia instantly lost interest in her as Kieran reached them. Tucking a proprietary arm into his, she thrust a glass of champagne into his other hand and twinkled up at him, 'Now let me show you off to everyone, darling.'

He endured the ensuing introductions with good grace for a full two minutes, then opening his eyes wide in mimed horror over the top of Tricia's head, he looked ostentatiously at his watch and said to Flora, 'Maybe we should check that everyone's ready.'

'Nonsense, my dear. Everything's under control. You must meet Greg before you disappear. I'll just pop up and see where he's got to.' Tricia's laugh was at its most tinkling as she added, 'Flora has told me what a clever boy you are. Although frankly, with looks like yours I would imagine you could find plenty of work in the theatre if you had all the acting ability of a plank of wood.'

Henry Denstone's face was stony. Penelope giggled nervously. Kieran blinked, the corners of his mouth twitching, and downed his champagne as Tricia sailed off across the ballroom in pursuit of Greg Farrell.

After a couple of minutes, a small commotion broke out from the gallery above. A rustled whisper of anticipation ran through the waiting guests and someone close to Flora hissed, 'There he is!'

She looked up, then stared at the object of everyone's attention, momentarily nonplussed. Greg Farrell looked exactly like every image of Christ that she could remember from convent school days: flowing black hair, full black beard, eyes of burningly dark intensity. What unnerved her more, however, were the cigarette, the open-necked shirt and the faded denims. They seemed almost blasphemous.

His entrance via the gallery had been stage-managed for maximum impact. Everyone was gazing upwards. Tricia, clearly delighted, beamed down on her guests. Flora fancied that Greg Farrell himself looked mildly embarrassed, irritated even, as the burly man she had seen earlier appeared at his side, the sunglasses that he was still wearing lending him the appearance of a gangster in a B movie. They made an incongruous couple. With a small frown and a shake of his head, Greg motioned the man away, then made his way down the stairs, Tricia leading the way. Flora thought she could detect the merest hint of strain to his smile as he followed in the woman's bow wave, the crowds parting like the Red Sea, a reverent hush descending as they passed, followed immediately by an excited babble of whispers. She wondered how it must feel to be on the receiving end of so much intense, if admiring, scrutiny.

Henry Denstone moved aside to let the couple through as finally they reached their little group. He did not acknowledge Greg, but stared at him, his fingers clenched around the stem of his glass as if he were about to snap it. Office gossip had it that Tricia would go to bed with anything in trousers, Flora recalled as Henry turned away. And it had to be said that Greg Farrell rated a great deal higher on the scale of sexual attraction than 'anything'.

'Nice to meet you.' The pressure of Greg's hand on hers was firm and warm. Close to, he looked older; middle thirties, Flora guessed, controlling a ridiculous impulse to genuflect.

'Tricia tells me you've done some acting yourself,' he said to Kieran, as they were introduced to each other. 'You've made quite an impression on her.' The observation was made deadpan, but with a glint of wry humour in his eyes that matched Kieran's. Not one of Tricia's trophies after all, Flora decided.

'I've done a bit.' Kieran shook Greg's hand.

'He's done a lot.' Flora knew it sounded pushy, but left to his own devices, Kieran would always play himself down. 'He won the National Student Drama Festival in '98.'

Kieran grinned. 'The Drama Society won it, Flora.'

'They wouldn't have done without you,' she retorted. 'And what about your reviews from the Edinburgh Festival?'

'We must circulate, darling.' Tricia's hand was already on Greg's arm. 'There's someone I want you to meet. I'm sure you'll find time to have a chat later.'

Greg managed a wink at Kieran before he was steered off towards Stanley Brassington. 'See you later.' His eyes travelled to Flora as he added with a smile, 'And your publicity agent, I hope.'

'Right, then,' Kieran said, when they had gone. 'I'd better go and make sure the kids are all set.'

'I'll come with you.' Flora gulped down the last of her champagne and looked around for somewhere to put her empty glass.

'Before you disappear . . .' Tricia, who seemed to have eyes in the back of her head, caught Kieran's arm as they moved off. 'I'd like you to say a few words before the play starts. Introduce that boy you brought along with you on Sunday. I want cynics like Stanley here to understand just what we're aiming at with this venture.'

'I'm not so sure that's a good idea,' Kieran frowned.

Flora could not have agreed more; the last thing any of them needed was Danny being his usual charmless self. 'He's probably very nervous,' she said hastily.

As if sensing they were in need of support, Greg added, 'Come on, Tricia. You of all people know what it's like just before you go on . . .'

A faint flush fought its way up through Tricia's makeup. She sounded pleased as she said to Kieran, 'Well, just do your best, darling.'

Kieran nodded, rather more curtly than Flora would have preferred. She prayed she was the only one to hear his muttered, 'We're not a bunch of performing monkeys,' as he headed for the door. She went to follow him, but Tricia was already speaking again, her expression hardening as she turned back to Stanley Brassington.

'I want Stanley to meet one of the . . . What was your phrase, Stanley?' Her eyes were steely. '"Undeserving young layabouts", wasn't it? I'd like you to hear what Kieran has to say on the subject before you make up your mind about the value of the Denstone bursaries.'

'I just said that if you were hellbent on playing lady bountiful, you'd be better off providing a few textbooks, so they could learn to read and write, instead of encouraging young hooligans with no prospects to walk round with their heads in the clouds.' Stanley Brassington didn't look as if he were used to anyone, least of all a woman, challenging his opinions.

With an acid smile, Tricia moved off, clearly expecting Greg to follow, but instead he moved back to Flora's side.

'Brave man.' He pulled a face.

Flora nodded, hoping the reference was not to Kieran. She was relieved that it was towards Brassington that Greg glanced as he dropped his voice and added, 'You don't mess with Tricia. She may come across as a bit of an airhead, but she's as sharp as a knife about things that matter to her. And Denstone Park really does matter to her.' He looked up at the painting above the fireplace and added, 'Anything to do with Freddie matters to her.'

Flora followed his gaze. She had noticed the portrait as soon as she'd entered the room; it was difficult not to, as it measured a good two metres square. But it was more than its sheer size that had caught her attention. It depicted a man of about her own age. The face was both attractive and faintly disturbing. It was fine-boned, the high forehead and long, straight nose ummistakably reminiscent of Henry Denstone, although the wide, smiling mouth owed nothing to him. The brilliant blue stare that seemed to fix her had the same steely determination Flora had seen only moments before in Tricia's eyes. The portrait was dated 1989. Flora shivered involuntarily. It was hard to imagine that within a year of the artist putting the finishing touches to that vibrant face, its owner would be dead.

'You were at drama school together, weren't you?' She wondered if she should ask. Although the gala was named after him, she had the distinct impression that any mention of Freddie Denstone should be avoided. Cautiously, she added, 'What happened to him?'

'Hit and run.' Greg watched the bubbles swirling in the glass of champagne he had barely touched.

'Sorry.' Flora could feel herself blushing.

'No.' Greg downed his drink, then looked up at her and smiled. 'No, not at all.'

He wasn't in the least what she had expected. There was no affectation to him, no 'side', as Mrs Menheniott, Simon's housekeeper, would say. Chatting to him was easy, as they discussed student drama, and the difficulties of moving on from there to the professional stage. He suggested the names of a couple of theatrical agents Kieran might try, seeming genuinely interested. He had a fascinating, disconcerting way of focusing on whomever he was speaking to as if only they existed. Which couldn't be easy, Flora thought, with the number of admiring onlookers who were drifting close by, attempting to eavesdrop.

Nicholas Perotti joined them briefly. Flora noticed how Greg handled the other man, managing to blank him out with great charm, so that Nicholas went away looking as pleased with himself as when he had descended on them.

Greg pulled a face. 'I hope that wasn't too obvious, but the man's an absolute pest. I met him once, years ago. Ever since I'd had a bit of publicity, he's been sending me the most appalling scripts to read.' He flushed suddenly. 'Christ, that was tactless. He wrote your piece, didn't he?' He gazed at her anxiously, then mirrored the smile already twitching the corners of Flora's mouth. 'I suppose you're going to tell me he's a bosom friend, or something equally embarrassing.'

'If the play's a success this evening, it will be down to Kieran, not the playwright,' she grinned, unable to resist the plug.

Greg laughed, and shook his head admiringly. 'My God, why on earth am I suggesting agents? You couldn't fit another actor on to your books, could you?'

Flora was amazed to realise, when Tricia suddenly appeared beside them and announced that everybody was moving outside to the marquee, that she had Greg had been talking for a full fifteen minutes.

They walked across the lawn together, and into the marquee. Seats had been reserved for Tricia's party behind the front two rows, which had been set aside for the acts that comprised the first half of the performance. Flora hung back, not wishing to assume that she was included, but Greg touched her elbow and patted the seat next to him.

The rest of the audience took their places and the primary school choir that was to open the proceedings shuffled onto the stage, grinning nervously. Each of them was wearing a tee shirt bearing the legend 'Freddie Denstone Memorial Gala', with the date, below a print of the portrait from the ballroom. The movements of their bodies seemed to give the twenty or so identical images a bizarre life of their own. Flora saw Tricia's hand fly to her mouth and felt an unexpected wave of sympathy. The spontaneity of the gesture was so at odds with Tricia's studied public manner that to glimpse it seemed intrusive, like catching her naked, or without her makeup. Flora looked quickly away. She heard Henry clear his throat and shift in his seat on the far side of his wife. He was not a man Flora could easily associate with strong emotions. But Freddie had been his son.

She attempted to focus on the choir. They sang several songs, conducted from the side of the stage by a plump woman, whose ample frame quivered vigorously as she waved her arms, a fact not missed by two small boys in the middle of the row, who began to nudge each other and giggle. The woman responded with ever-more energetic arm-waving as she attempted to retrieve their attention. The boys' mirth was infectious in the emotion-charged atmosphere. Flora bit her lip to stop herself from joining in. Beside her, Greg's discreet cough told her that he was having difficulty too.

Finally, the choir took their bows, greeted by applause louder with relief than appreciation, and filed into their allotted seats on the front row. Other acts followed: a jazz quartet from Blackport's Youth Orchestra; a teenage girl with a voice that made up in amplification what it lacked in tunefulness; a number of dance routines from tap to classical ballet, some better than others. Flora counted them off on her programme, the butterflies in her stomach getting stronger and stronger as applause, polite or enthusiastic, followed applause, and the interval drew inexorably closer. Kieran was to come on immediately before the break to introduce the St Saviour's project. *Grab and Smash* was to take up the entire second half of the show.

Turning in her seat, Flora could see, through the open flaps of the marquee, that waiters were gathering on the lawn, their trays loaded with glasses of champagne. As the diminutive flautist who rounded off the first half took her bow to a standing ovation prompted as much by the arrival of the champagne as the little girl's considerable musical talent, Kieran appeared in the wings.

To anyone who did not know him, he looked relaxed as he stepped forward to join Tricia on the stage. Flora knew only from the tell-tale throb of the muscle in his cheek just how nervous he was. Inside a role, he forgot the audience entirely. Appearing without the armour of a character was an altogether different matter; especially as the light within the marquee meant that the audience was clearly visible. Flora found herself holding her breath as, prompted by Tricia, he began to talk about the project.

He grew in confidence as he went along. After a couple of minutes, he gestured to Danny, who was still in the wings, to join them. The boy walked hesitantly into the spotlight. Then, halfway across the stage, he froze. His gaze fixed on the rows of faces in front of him, his own face tightened into a rictus of panic. Kieran glanced out into the audience and back to Danny, them moved towards him, his hand outstretched as if he were dealing with a startled pony.

'Oh, no,' Flora breathed as, without a word, Danny shoved past Tricia and launched himself from the stage. Head down, he ran between the rows of astonished onlookers and out of the marquee, crashing the tray of a passing waiter to the ground, as he hurtled back towards the house, Kieran in hot pursuit.

Flora, her face burning, mumbled apologies as she scrambled along the row and ran after them. Together, she and Kieran raced across the lawn.

They were just in time to watch Danny scale the high, clipped hedge and disappear from view.

Chapter Five

Whitelaw put his hands behind his head, stared up at the dingy ceiling of his office, went back over what Sunil Doshai had told him earlier and asked himself whether it was safe to believe a word of it. Or more to the point, what he should be reading into what Sunil had *not* told him.

There had got to be more to it than the half-baked blackmail theory. Someone had wanted Jason Morrissey dead. Someone had seen him as threat enough to steal a car, beat him to death and then set fire to his body. For a couple of hundred quid? It didn't make sense. Any more than the photograph Sunil had left between the pages of the pathologist's file made sense. And not just the photograph itself. Unconsciously Whitelaw shook his head as for the hundredth time he examined what was written on the back. He stared at the words, willing them to reveal their meaning. The handwriting was Jason's. Whitelaw had recognised at once the flourish of the M; he'd seen it often enough over the years, and he had checked it against the signature on Jason's last charge sheet, just to be certain. But what did it mean – 'MARIO, 14', heavily underscored?

Whitelaw had rung the restaurant immediately, telling himself it had to be pure chance, but none the less unnerved that he had been eating in a place bearing the same name less than an hour before. No one at Mario's had been able to suggest any significance to the number. There was no table fourteen; the fourteenth of the month had fallen the previous Monday, when the restaurant had, as always at the beginning of the week, been closed.

Coincidence, Whitelaw had decided.

He turned the photograph over again to study its subject. Jason, aged about twelve or thirteen, his eyes screwed up against the sun, gazed back. Just an ordinary, summer-holiday snap. Blue sky, wide lawns, kids playing in the background. Some school trip? A stately home somewhere, judging by the ornate wall and formal garden that could just be made out in the distance. Jason had his arm around the shoulder of another boy, as dark as he himself was fair. They were both wearing swimming trunks, their slight torsos thin as flower stalks. For a moment, Whitelaw had thought it was Sunil, but the boy in the photograph was darker-skinned, curly-haired; more West Indian than Asian. Mario, presumably, although the '14' clearly didn't apply to his age; the child looked much younger than Jason. Five or six at most, he smiled shyly into the camera, all gap teeth and dimples.

And that was it.

Whitelaw rummaged in a drawer of his desk until he found the reading glasses Val swore he needed, and peered at the photograph again. True, the fuzziness he'd taken for poor focus had disappeared, but nothing extra was revealed. It was just a snap of two little boys. He couldn't even be completely sure that it hadn't simply fallen out of Sunil's pocket when he pulled out his handkerchief to wipe his eyes.

On impulse, he decided to fax a copy to Millie D'Sousa. Millie and Val had been friends from the time they had worked in the same residential school twenty years before, which was probably the only reason that Millie, now a senior caseworker with Blackport Social Services, didn't regard Whitelaw as the enemy. In his experience, social workers viewed anyone with a warrant card with approximately the same degree of trust that a coop of chickens might show towards a fox, and the antagonism tended to be mutual. Millie and he had long ago decided to take the radical step of regarding each other as fellow members of the human race. It hadn't prevented some monumental crossings of philosophical swords down the years, but by and large they had agreed to respect their differences and had helped each other out on a number of occasions in the past with a bantering ill-grace that concealed a genuine mutual liking.

'Don't suppose a part-timer like you will get this till Monday . . .' Whitelaw scribbled as his opening gambit. It was worth a try. Millie had a memory that made elephants look amnesiac. If she had ever come across either Jason or the black lad in the photograph, she would be able to provide more information than any file in the Social Services archive. Telling himself he was probably clutching at straws, Whitelaw got to his feet, stretched, and went off in search of anyone who knew how to operate the fax machine without putting it out of action for the following fortnight.

Mission accomplished, thanks to a new PC whose name Whitelaw had already forgotten and who didn't look old enough to be in long trousers, he returned to the office and stood by the open window. The searing heat of the day had softened to a pleasant warmth; there was not a breath of wind. A perfect night for the Memorial Gala, Whitelaw thought guiltily. Val could have ben enjoying herself there now, celebrity-spotting, instead of stuck on her own at home.

He tried to force his mind back to the matter in hand. If all he was going to do was stare out of the window thinking about Val, he might as well be at home himself. The idea was tempting. His stomach was beginning to complain in earnest at being deprived of the *filetto pepato*. Maybe he'd pick up some fish and chips on the way. They'd got that nearly full bottle of wine to finish. It was only half-past nine; they could still make an evening of it. Sit out in the garden maybe . . .

Concentrate.

He went back to the desk. Sat down. Tried to evaluate the notes he had made of what Sunil had told him. A possible meeting with a nameless bloke in a shop somewhere, and a perfectly inno-cent-looking photograph. It didn't amount to much. And it didn't amount to as much as Jason's boyfriend knew, Whitelaw would stake his pension on it. Shaking his head, he slipped the notes into the top drawer of his desk, along with the photograph, and yawned. He might just as well retrieve what he could of the evening with Val.

He'd deal with Sunil Doshai in the morning.

'And most of all, I would like to thank St Saviour's Community College drama group, and especially their very talented young director and leading man, Kieran Henshall, for his magnificent performance.' Tricia Denstone beamed around at the guests packed into the sweltering marquee, then turned to the cast, standing behind her on the stage, as she led the thunderous applause. Finally, she held up a hand and continued, 'I think we would all agree that the little incident they staged before the interval was a masterstroke in whetting our appetites for what was to come. I suspect that without it, some of us might have been tempted to give *Grab and Smash* a miss, and stay out in the sun with another glass of champagne!'

An acknowledging ripple of laughter ran through the audience.

'But before we adjourn outside for the fireworks display, I would like us to remember for a moment why we are all here tonight.' The smile left her face, and a respectful hush fell amongst her guests. 'As you know, my late son, Freddie, was a passionate supporter of the arts, and it is in his name that we tonight launch our appeal to rebuild Denstone Park as the Freddie Denstone School for the Performing and Creative Arts. And before I continue I would like to express my sincere grati-tude to Freddie's dearest friend, Greg Farrell, for breaking into his busy schedule to be here with us this evening.'

Heads craned as Greg got to his feet, smiled and bowed awkwardly to acknowledge the applause.

'Most of you here tonight are aware of the work done at Denstone Park in the seventies and eighties,' Tricia went on, 'and the enormous benefits it provided for some of our region's most deprived young people, introducing them to drama, music, art and literature. Civilising influences to which, I feel sure you will agree, all too little of today's youth is exposed.'

'Hear, hear!' a voice from the wings called loudly, over a fresh round of applause.

'I do believe I forgot to mention the author of this evening's play, and one of Denstone Park's original tutors, Mr Nicholas Perotti.' Tricia inclined her head in the direction of the voice. 'Thank you, Nicholas.'

He took a step forward, as if to join her in the spotlight, but she had already turned back to the audience. 'It is our aim that the school will continue to enable less privileged youngsters to make the most of their talents by offering, each year, a number of bursaries. Many of you have already pledged your most generous support, and I am pleased to announce that, including the proceeds from this evening's gala, the rebuilding fund has already reached the magnificent total of two hundred and thirty thousand pounds.'

Yet more applause.

'But of course there is still a long way to go, so if any individual or business groups who have not so far . . .'

Behind her, Kieran shifted impatiently from one foot to the other as she finally wound her speech to a close. In the role of Leroy, he had been forced to put all thought of Danny out of his head, but now the play was over, he was desperate to get away.

'A close call, my dear,' Tricia murmured, as the lights went back up inside the marquee, and the audience began to drift back into the garden. 'I'm so glad your little friend didn't manage to ruin the entire evening. I would have hated us to fall out.'

'Yeah. Me too.' Without attempt at further conversation, he jumped off the stage and went to find Flora.

It had only been her intervention before the interval that had prevented him from going after Danny there and then, her idea to suggest to Tricia Denstone that Danny's abrupt departure was planned, although Tricia hadn't fallen for that any more than either of them had imagined she would. Flora had been as decisive, supportive, positive as she always was. She had also been spitting feathers both at Danny, for what he had landed them in, and at Kieran, who had made the mistake of disclosing his intention to go after the boy as soon as the show was over, to find out what was wrong.

'What's wrong with Danny Nolan is that he's a selfish, unreliable little—' Flora had bitten the words back. Before the interval, she had managed to keep her fury under control. Now the performance was over, Kieran knew he could expect the worst.

She was standing on her own at the entrance to the marquee, arms folded, watching as the rest of the audience streamed towards the cordoned-off area where the fireworks display was to take place.

'You sure you'll be OK with the kids?' He felt her stiffen ominously as he put his hand on her shoulder.

'I'll have to be, won't I?' She kept her back to him.

'Come on, Flora. You saw the look on his face. I can't just leave it.'

'Yes, you could, actually.' Her voice was calm, but her eyes were blazing, as she wheeled round to face him. 'You could realise you can't take responsibility for every delinquent teenager on God's earth, because some of them will just take everything you give and then turn round and spit in your eye. Yes, I saw his face, and I heard what that man Brassington said during the interval, as well. He was the magistrate who sent Danny down last time he was in court. It's obvious what happened, or at least it's obvious to everyone but you. Brassington was sitting at the front. Danny recognised him and lost it. Maybe he's been up to something else while he's been out on licence; maybe he thought Brassington was going to show him up. I don't know. And quite frankly, after the way he's dropped everyone in it tonight, I don't care. For God's sake, Kieran, stop spending all your time worrying about scumbags like Danny Nolan and think about your own future, for a change.'

'You just don't get it, do you?' He could feel his own temper rising again. Easy for her, easy for the adored only daughter of filthy-rich Simon Castledine to pass judgement. Easy, when she'd never had to shelter behind a wall of belligerence, just to survive. Never had to blot out the present with booze, or drugs, or what-ever else it might take to numb the pain. Easy for her to talk about the future, when the past wasn't ambushing her at every turn.

It was as if she read his mind. She said quietly, 'Danny's not you, Kieran.'

He looked down at his clenched fists, forcing them to relax. Would it always be like this? Would it always be there, ready to pounce; a silent, poisonous obstacle between them? He cleared his throat, trying to control the tremor in his voice. 'Maybe you're right about Brassington, but surely someone should care about Danny enough to go and find out?'

'OK.' Her voice was weary. She held his gaze, then bit her lip on whatever it was she was about to say, and nodded. 'Do what-ever you need to. I'll be fine.'

'Congratulations!' Kieran turned round as a hand was laid on his shoulder. Greg was standing behind them. 'Or maybe I should have said, "You're nicked!" That was a knock-out performance.' He gestured at Kieran's borrowed trainers, baggy trousers and baseball cap. 'Even without that lot, I don't reckon there's a copper in the country who wouldn't take you for the real thing!'

There was a moment's awkward pause, then Kieran said, 'I'm glad you enjoyed it.' He pulled off the baseball cap and ran his fingers through his damp hair with a grimace. 'Listen, I can't stop right now . . .' He glanced across at Flora.

Greg nodded. He seemed to hesitate, before saying, 'You know, I feel partly responsible for what happened back there.'

Kieran and Flora both stared at him.

'The lad . . . Danny, did you say his name was?'

Kieran nodded warily.

'I saw him earlier, before I came down to the ballroom. Wandering around the bedrooms.'

Flora glanced accusingly at Kieran. 'What the hell could he have been doing in the . . . ?'

'He nearly jumped out of his skin when I spoke to him.' Greg frowned. 'I took it for pre-performance nerves when he told me who he was. Maybe I should have—'

Kieran shook his head. 'He was fine before we came on the stage. No more than normal jitters, at any rate. He was chuffed to bits you gave him your autograph.'

'Still, at least you managed to pull it out of the fire,' Greg said more cheerfully. He slapped Kieran on the shoulder. 'Christ, if that was you stepping in at the last moment, what are you like when you've prepared for the part?' His face became earnest. 'Look, where are you parked? I don't want to hold you up, but I'd really like to have a quick chat. You coming, Flora? In your capacity as theatrical agent, that is,' he added with a grin.

'The kids'll be fine for a bit.' Kieran risked taking her hand. 'You won't get them away while the fireworks are on the go, anyway.'

It took them several minutes to get back to the house, by the time Greg had signed endless programmes and Kieran had been complimented on his performance.

'You'd better start practising your autograph,' Greg murmured, as they were hijacked by yet another gushing admirer and her elderly, perspiring partner. Flora squeezed Kieran's hand so tightly she almost dislocated his fingers.

It took Kieran, still trying to contain his elation, a moment to realise that something was missing when they got back to the courtyard. Then, looking slowly around him, he breathed, 'Oh, Danny. You haven't.'

Greg looked at him uncomprehendingly.

Flora said flatly, 'The VW.'

'He must have hot-wired it.' Kieran banged his fist against the side of the minibus. 'Shit.'

'After everything you've done for him.' Flora had dropped his hand. 'All the effort you've put in, this is how he—'

'Yeah, yeah.' Kieran turned away from her, his hands thrust into his pockets, and breathed hard. He wasn't even sure at whom the resentment that was welling up inside him again was directed.

'If I could just . . .' Greg's voice was apologetic. Kieran had almost forgotten he was there.

'I'm sorry.' It was Flora who spoke. 'You don't want to hear us carrying on like this. It seems that Danny . . .' She gestured angrily at the empty space.

'I think I get the picture. Listen,' Greg pulled at his beard and looked from one of them to the other, 'why don't I give you a lift home? I think I've done my bit for the gala. To be honest, I'd be glad of the break.'

Kieran could see Flora was making a big effort to keep calm because Greg was there, but the hot pink spot on each cheek left him in no doubt about what she would be saying if they were alone. 'Tell you what,' he said, by way of a compromise, 'you go back with Greg – if that's OK with him,' he glanced questioningly at the other man – 'and I'll go round to Danny's when I've dropped the others back at St Saviour's.'

'I'd be only too delighted. But I'm just wondering . . .' Greg paused. 'Might it be more sensible if I ran you straight round to wherever this kid lives, Kieran? Make sure your car's OK? By the time you've rounded the others up and got them back . . .' He paused again, then smiled at Flora, clearly anxious not to make things worse. 'Does that make sense? I don't want to . . .'

'Fine, whatever,' she said in a tone that belied the words, then flushed. 'Sorry. That sounds spectacularly ungracious. It's very kind of you to offer to help.' She gave Greg a tight smile, and Kieran a look that said he hadn't heard that last of it.

'I'll get it sorted, love.' He risked pecking her on the cheek; it was like kissing an ironing board. 'Danny'll only have used the car to get home. I'll probably be back before you are.'

Concerned as he was, Kieran couldn't help but enjoy the ride, sitting back in the Audi TT convertible's leather seats, feeling the powerful throb of the engine each time Greg put his foot down. He was disconcerted to realise just what a buzz the speed still gave him.

As they reached the outskirts of Blackport, Greg slowed down. For a while, conversation was limited to Kieran's instructions, as he directed the other man onto the new ring road that led by a longer but circuitous route to the docks. Easier to follow, he explained, and safer than drawing attention to themselves by driving a motor as flashy as the TT through the streets in that part of town.

Once on the dual carriageway, Greg turned to him and said, 'Flora was telling me that she met you at university. I'd have thought you'd have chosen drama school.'

'That was the way you went?'

'Not a hard choice, in my case,' Greg grinned. 'Let's just say I didn't exactly shine at school. Although I could probably scrape through on Theology now, with all the research I've put in over the past year.'

'What's it like, playing Christ?' Kieran had been dying to ask, but realised it must be a question Greg had answered a thousand times before.

He was pleased when, instead of trotting out some glib, rehearsed response, Greg paused, seeming to give it serious consideration before saying, 'Unnerving. I've never been a religious person. Probably just as well, because if I had, I'd have been hopelessly daunted by the task. When I landed the part, I was delighted, of course, but that's all it was – just a part. But then I read the New Testament, went to the Holy Land, spent some time with an order of monks in the north of Scotland . . . You'd have to be pretty shallow for all of that not to have an effect. I'm not talking Road to Damascus here, you understand,' he laughed a touch self-consciously. 'Not quite ready to renounce the sins of the flesh, or not all of them. But yes, it's given me a different perspective, which is no bad thing in this game.'

He drove for a short while in pensive silence, before going on, 'The hardest part is that people tend to blur the distinction, confuse me with the role. There have even been some threats – just religious cranks – but enough to make me a bit nervous about public appearances. Hence the ape of a security man you probably saw back at Oultonshaw Manor. Perhaps you didn't notice, but he got mighty twitchy when your young friend leapt down from the stage. I'm just relieved he didn't try to get him in a half-nelson.'

'I wish he had.' Kieran gave a wry grin. 'At least that way I'd still have a car. Bloody hell, though. Do you really think anyone would try to—'

'To be honest, I doubt they're anything serious. Most rambling, ill-spelt rantings about blasphemy and hellfire – you can imagine.' Greg pulled a face. 'I suspect Tricia dreamt up the idea of the guard more for the extra publicity than through any concern for my wellbeing, frankly.' He grinned. 'I should warn you, you get cynical very quickly.' His face became more serious as he went on, 'I don't find the odd bit of hate mail as disturbing as the letters from people who seem to believe I can help them. They're the ones that really get to you – parents telling me about their sick children, asking for miracles, that sort of thing.'

'Christ!' Kieran hadn't meant the exclamation as a joke, but after a second's pause they both began to laugh.

'Sorry. That was all getting a big heavy,' Greg said, still smiling. 'So tell me about this lad Danny. I take it you don't buy Brassington's theory?'

'Left down here.' Kieran directed him onto the slip road, then shook his head, feeling the knot of muscles at the back of his neck beginning to tense again as he recalled the look of terror on the boy's face. 'I doubt Danny'd even have recognised the bloke. When you're in court, all you're interested in is what you're going to get. You don't really notice who's—' He checked himself, as Greg glanced across, surprise on his face. 'Anyway,' he shrugged, 'something rattled his cage. I just want to make sure he's OK.' He nodded his head at the road in front of them. 'Down there.'

They drove along to the end of South Wharf, past rusting cranes and derelict warehouses that loomed against the darkening sky like the prows of enormous, ghostly ships, until they reached the Seamen's Rest Home. It was as Kieran had thought: the VW was dumped on some adjacent waste ground, headlights full on. Greg drew up next to it, and they both got out.

'Thanks, Danny.' Kieran leaned in and switched off the lights, then examined the ignition barrel, now hanging, a mass of wires, below the fascia panel that had been levered away from behind the steering wheel.

Greg gave a low whistle. 'That's going to take some fixing! Do you want me to give you a hand?'

Kieran looked at him in surprise. 'You know a bit about cars, then?'

Greg was examining the damage. 'You couldn't share a flat with Freddie Denstone for twelve months and *not* know a bit about cars. He was fanatical about them.' He straightened up. 'This is going to take us a while. I'd better ring in to base before that damned minder comes looking for me.'

'Listen, I've put you out enough already,' Kieran interjected as Greg started to punch numbers into his mobile. 'I can easily fix it up enough to get me home. Anyway,' he peered up at the shabby frontage of the Seamen's Rest, trying to make out which was Danny's room, 'if anyone's going to help me sort it, it should be that little bugger.'

Greg followed his gaze. A couple of windows were lit up, one half concealed by thin, sagging nets, the other uncurtained, two of its panes broken and stuffed with old newspapers. The rest of the place was in darkness. 'You think he'll be up there?' he asked.

Kieran shrugged. 'Only one way to find out. Probably wasting my time, but I'd like to get to the bottom of it. Quite apart from giving him a bollocking about the car.' He held out his hand. 'Thanks for the lift. And thanks for your interest. I appreciate it.'

Greg got back into his car and started the engine, then lowered the window and said, 'Perhaps we could meet up sometime?' He fished a piece of paper from the glove compartment and scribbled down a number. 'Why don't you give me a ring?'

Kieran watched the TT's taillights diminish in the gloom as the car roared off up the street. He raised an arm in answering salute as Greg tooted the horn and disappeared. Then, asking himself what he would have said if anyone had told him before the gala that, by the end of the evening, one of the country's most celebrated actors would be offering him his mobile number, he turned back to the Seamen's Rest.

For the second time that day, he made his way up the narrow stairs, his elation already beginning to drain away as the dismal atmosphere of the place settled around him like a drab, familiar veil. The racket from the stereo had been replaced by canned laughter, coming at deafening volume from behind one of the closed doors. The baby was still wailing. Somebody had been eating chips; the smell of vinegar made Kieran remember he'd had nothing to eat since breakfast.

There was no light coming from under Danny's door.

He knocked.

Silence.

If Danny were inside, Deefer would be there too. Kieran knocked again then rattled the knob, already realising the futility of the exercise.

'You there, Danny?' he shouted, just in case. Half-heartedly, he added, 'You could at least apologise for taking the bloody car.'

Suddenly, the door opposite crashed open to reveal a thin, exhausted-looking girl with a filthy, half-naked toddler hanging on to her skirt and a purple-faced baby under her arm. Over their combined wailing, she yelled at Kieran to fuck off before she called the police.

It seemed as good a moment as any to admit defeat.

'*Thou wast not born for death . . .*' The words sprang into his mind unbidden as he reached the bottom of the stairs. The Keats again. Kieran shivered involuntarily in the heat as he stepped back onto the pavement. It was as if someone had trodden on his grave.

He walked back towards the wasteland where he could just about make out the shape of the car in the gathering darkness, and tried to focus on how he was going to get the damned thing started. The VW's interior light was long gone, which wasn't going to help. He sat in the driver's seat, deciding not to risk further deadening the battery by switching the headlights on. He reached under the dashboard for the ignition barrel, wondering, in passing, if picking up a curry on the way home might provide him with an appropriate olive branch to offer Flora, but deciding it would take more than a chicken tikka and a garlic naan to win her round, if her face when he'd driven off with Greg was anything to go by. He felt for the loose wires, working by a mixture of touch and guesswork as he selected which ones to bring into contact.

He was concentrating so hard that he didn't hear the foot-steps until they were right on top of him. A torch was shone into his face, temporarily blinding him. As he put up his arms to shield his eyes, a strong hand grasped his elbow.

Frozen in the seat, he felt a moment of utter panic.

Then a voice said quietly, 'Excuse me, sir, is this your car?'

Chapter Six

Whitelaw negotiated the Saturday morning traffic in Blackport High Street and reminded himself sourly that today was supposed to be the start of his weekend off. The morning was bright, the sun already strong, with a slight breeze promising to alleviate the unpleasant heat of the previous day. A perfect morning for the allotment. But as the Jason Morrissey case was now a full-blown murder enquiry, the tomatoes were going to have to wait.

Hooting irritably at the driver of the car in front as the lights turned to green, and asking himself why he'd chosen red wine when he knew it always gave him a headache, he turned right past the Town Hall, away from the shopping centre. Park Street housed the council offices, the magistrates' courts and, at the very end, at the intersection with the ring road, Blackport Central police station.

He parked around the back, and made his way up the steps and through the custody suite, stopping for a couple of minutes to pass the time of day with Cyril Turner, the duty sergeant, who informed him that Lambert had been looking for him.

'Better see what he wants, I suppose,' Whitelaw said without enthusiasm when, after a further ten minutes, they had covered Lancashire's chances in the Nat West trophy, the relative merits of organic and chemical fertilisers, and the latest guest beer at the Feathers. He looked into the office on his way along, disgruntled to see how many bits of paper were already littering the desk he'd cleared the night before. Deciding that as Lambert had waited this long he could wait a bit longer, he sat down and glanced through them. Yes, he did realise he was two months behind with his expenses claim. He screwed up the memo and lobbed it in the bin. Next was the invitation to Lambert's summer social the following weekend. That was more difficult, the thickness of the card making it impossible to crumple satisfactorily. Whitelaw opted for folding it into a paper plane instead – a futile gesture, attendance being obligatory, but enjoyable none the less, even if the plane did miss its target by a couple of inches. He looked through the rest of the messages, filing them, in just about equal numbers, between his already overflowing 'pending' tray and the bin.

Paperwork dealt with, he turned to the phone. His answering machine was flashing that it had three messages. Whitelaw was of the opinion that if capital punishment were ever reintroduced, the inventor of the answering machine should be the first customer. Irritably, he jabbed the 'play' button. The first two were Lambert, demanding Whitelaw's immediate presence in his office, the latter with a pointed reference to the time. The third was Millie D'Sousa.

Thirty years in Blackport hadn't entirely robbed Millie of her native Caribbean lilt, and Whitelaw recognised the voice as soon as she spoke. With an economy of words he found both admirable and rare in one of her profession, she said that she might be able to help him with the photograph. He caught the chuckle in her voice as she timed the message, with the addendum that she would be in the office until about six that evening; the argument as to whether police or social workers worked the longer hours was a long-running one between them.

Whitelaw tried her number, which was, predictably, engaged. He was just getting to his feet to go along to Lambert's office, when Terry Lightowler stuck his head around the door.

'Had a report of a suspected break-in, Guv,' he said with the air of one who knew more about the relevance of the statement than he was currently letting on.

'Break-in? In Blackport? On a Friday night? Surely not.' Had anything but an interview with Lambert been the alternative to Lightowler's tiresome method of providing information, Whitelaw would have been less willing to play along.

'Thought the address might interest you.'

Whitelaw made to put his jacket on, changed his mind – it was too hot for anything but shirtsleeves, Lambert or no Lambert – and glared irritably at his sergeant. It was getting painful, even by Lightowler's standards. 'Spit it out, for God's sake. I haven't got all day.'

Lightowler looked aggrieved. 'That Indian poofter's place. Neighbour spotted the door's been forced. Do you want me to—'

'No.' Whitelaw reached into the drawer for his car keys; saw the photograph. 'I'll go. There's something I need to ask him about anyway.'

Break-ins were not exactly an uncommon occurrence round Heckton Fields, the just-becoming-fashionable district that separated the red-light area of the old docks from the sprawling campus of Blackport University. But that Jason and Sunil's place had been targeted so soon after Jason's death seemed too much of a coincidence to overlook. Ignoring Lightowler's injunction to keep his back to the wall and avoid bending down to look through keyholes, Whitelaw headed into the corridor, where he was almost immediately stopped in his tracks by a bellow from Lambert.

Medlock was already in the Superintendent's office. He didn't get up, but shot Whitelaw the sort of smug grin that told him his lateness had been noted and commented on.

'Don't bother to sit down,' Lambert barked as Whitelaw went to do so. 'Oultonshaw Manor. Theft. Last night. You were due there fifteen minutes ago. Medlock will fill you in on the details.

And remember who you're dealing with, Whitelaw, if you please.'

'Theft?' Whitelaw echoed. He hadn't missed out on his only lie-in of the week and abandoned his tomatoes to go holding the hand of some bigwig who had had his video recorder nicked. It was only with considerable restraint that he said, 'I'm in the middle of a murder inquiry, sir.'

'Oultonshaw Manor,' Lambert snapped. 'Do you have no sense of priority at all?' He was already turning his attention to his in-tray as he added, 'And let's see if you can get this one cleared up more successfully than you did that bloody arson attack, shall we?'

Flora promised herself she would keep calm. After the night Kieran had had, she told herself, the last thing he would need was her having hysterics, even if she had been awake half the night herself, frantic.

She had known it would be a long shot that he would be back by the time she'd dropped the kids off at St Saviour's. She had driven back to Sephton Street telling herself not to expect him to be there. But she had been disappointed when she arrived to find the house in darkness.

For the first hour she had nursed her anger. How dare he leave her to pick up the pieces while he went off on some wild-goose chase around Blackport in Greg Farrell's flash sports car? She had fanned the embers of her resentment with memories of the horrendous journey in the minibus, during which she had been forced to stop three times to allow Wayne Edwards, who had somehow managed to access the Denstones' champagne, to be sick. The fourth time, she had failed to stop quickly enough. It had taken her a good half-hour to clean up the back of the van when they'd reached the school.

When it had got towards midnight, and still Kieran hadn't returned, Flora had begun to cheer herself by constructing a variety of scenarios centred on him in a pub somewhere, being offered a part in Greg Farrell's next film. Temporarily, her resentment had faded.

By half-past two, she had admitted to herself that she was seriously worried. Not only the pubs, but also Blackport's unimpressive selection of clubs would have been shut by then. In the three years they'd been together, Kieran had never stayed out all night. She had gone over the angry words they had exchanged back at Oultonshaw Manor, wondering if he could be sulking. But Kieran didn't sulk. He could retreat inside himself sometimes, put up the barriers that she still found so frustratingly difficult to penetrate, but he wasn't a sulker, and he wouldn't stay out deliberately to make a point.

She had paced around the house, peering out at the deserted street, turning the late film on, then off again. She had taken a shower and put on her nightdress, had even got into bed for a few minutes and tried to sleep, until a squeal of brakes from further down the street had propelled her swiftly out again. She had heard raised voices. A dog yelping. She had wondered if she should go out and see if there had been an accident, but when she had pulled back the curtain, all was still. Telling herself to get a grip, she'd gone back downstairs and made herself a piece of toast, carefully buttering it, then throwing it in the bin, where it had been joined several minutes later by the magazine she had picked up. She had wondered whether to ring the hospitals, or the police, but could imagine the response she would get, reporting a twenty-seven-year-old missing at two thirty on a Saturday morning. She had wished, suddenly and to her own surprise, that she could get hold of Greg Farrell. Maybe it was simply the fact that he reminded her so much of the Gentle Jesus of her childhood, but she had felt instinctively that he would be able to sort everything out.

By five, she had been beside herself. She had just decided to contact the police, whatever they might say, when the phone rang. Heart in mouth, she had picked it up, a hundred different emotions flooding into her at the sound of Kieran's voice.

'I'm at Blackport Central, love,' he'd said, as if it were the most natural thing in the world. 'I've been arrested.'

She had wanted to go straight down to the police station. She had asked him if he wanted her to get a solicitor, because that was the sort of thing people said on the TV, but Kieran had reckoned everything was under control. Not that she would have had the first idea where to get hold of a solicitor at five o'clock in the morning.

That was four hours ago.

The table was set, had been set for over an hour, ready for Kieran's return. She had taken another shower, washed her hair, dressed. Decided she would be too hot in what she was wearing. Changed. Wondered whether to risk missing his return by running down to the end of the road for the papers. Dismissed the idea. Fished the magazine out of the bin. Threw it back in again.

She checked her watch, glanced out into the street that was just beginning to come alive, saw that the sky was clouding over, and went upstairs to change for a second time. She was pulling clothes out of a drawer and searching for a tee shirt she *knew* she had put in there only the day before, when the doorbell rang. Had Kieran forgotten his key? Half naked, she wrapped a towel around her and ran to the window, disappointed to see Norah Bateman, known to all the neighbourhood as Batty-Norah-from-the-wool-shop, standing on the doorstep, gazing fixedly at the front door as if hoping to open it by sheer force of will.

Norah was dressed in a low-cut purple cocktail dress of indeterminate age. In the interests of modesty, she had fastened the dress's gaping neckline over her skinny chest with a number of large nappy pins. Over it, she wore a heavy Aran cardigan with a cable design sufficiently erratic to suggest its marker had not been entirely accurate in following the pattern. The ensemble was completed by black ankle socks, and a pair of fluorescent yellow trainers.

Flora ducked behind the curtain. After three more rings, the old woman moved on to the house next door, her manic expression suggesting she was on one of her missions.

It was not much more than six weeks since Flora and Kieran had moved to Sephton Street, but they had already come to understand how Norah had earned her nickname, and what to expect from her frequent calls. Each one saw her with a different collection tin: Cats' Protection League, NCDL, Bangladeshi donkeys. Angry petitions of one sort or another were a regular alternative to the collection tins. Norah threw herself tirelessly into any cause designed to aid what she described as 'God's helpless creatures'. The Almighty's human creations, helpless or otherwise, she appeared to have less time for. Potential customers seldom visited her wool shop twice.

Offering a prayer of thanks that she had looked out before opening the door, Flora watched Norah's progress as far as the corner. Then throwing on the dress she had just discarded, she returned to the kitchen. She'd make meatballs, she decided. An odd choice for breakfast, possibly, but they were Kieran's favourite. It would at least give her something to do.

At last, she heard his key in the front door. Gripping the edge of the sink, she promised herself she would neither fuss, nor lose her temper. She'd finish making his breakfast as if nothing had happened, give him some space, allow him to tell her in his own good time just what was going on. No tantrums, no recrimination.

'In here,' she called brightly.

He came in through the kitchen door, whereupon Flora threw the frying pan at his head, herself into his arms, and burst into tears.

Whitelaw had insisted that he and Medlock went in separate cars to Oultonshaw Manor. Lightowler had been dispatched to check out the break-in at Heckton Fields, with strict instructions to ring through as soon as he had anything to report, and to leave interviewing Sunil Doshai until Whitelaw arrived.

He hadn't bothered to ask Medlock for the details. Probably one of the Memorial Gala guests liberating a few crates of champagne; nothing that the younger officer couldn't have handled perfectly well on his own. Had the complainant been anyone but Henry Denstone, Whitelaw thought ill-temperedly as he turned between the high wrought-iron gates leading to Oultonshaw Manor, there was no way two CID officers would have been sent to deal with a theft.

By the time he reached the house, Medlock's car was already there; a yellow MX5, its hood down to reveal a dashboard like a flight deck, and black leather bucket seats. So much for political correctness, Whitelaw thought as he parked his Metro next to it. Medlock might insist on calling girls 'women', but it didn't stop him going for a bird-puller when he chose a car. Despite the day's early promise, the sky was now banked with cloud, the air still and heavy with the threat of thunder. Whitelaw had the unworthy hope that it might start to rain while they were inside.

He was locking the driver's door, more through habit than because he expected his car to get nicked with such an impressive array of motors to choose from, when he felt a tap on his shoulder. He turned to confront a heavily set man, who, despite the sunglasses, was vaguely familiar.

'If you're with the contract cleaners, they're parked round the back, pal,' the man said, eyeing the Metro with ill-concealed contempt. His Liverpool accent was so strong it was nearly impenetrable. Again, there was something elusively recognisable about it.

Whitelaw bridled, and flashed his warrant card.

'Your mate's already gone in.' The man jerked his head towards the front door. Then, apparently finding detectives of even less interest than contract cleaners, he went back to polishing the already shining Volvo estate that was parked further along the drive, its tinted windows glinting in the sun.

The door was ajar, so Whitelaw pushed it open and went inside, still trying and failing to remember where he had seen the bloke before. The entrance hall bore the evidence of the previous night's festivities; the large sign pointing to the cloakroom was presumably no more a permanent feature than were the empty champagne glasses planted at the base of a potted hydrangea. Two aproned women, who were in the process of half lifting, half dragging a long table towards the stairs at the rear of the hall, turned to look at him. Whitelaw identified himself, to avoid being handed a duster, and was asked to wait.

After a couple of minutes, an elderly man appeared. His manner of patronising obsequiousness suggested he might be the butler. He showed Whitelaw into the living room, where Medlock was already installed, drinking coffee. As Whitelaw entered, a plain young woman, easily recognisable as the Denstones' daughter from her photograph in the *Echo*, got to her feet. For the second time that morning, Medlock didn't.

'Miss Denstone has kindly provided some preliminary details,' he announced, gracing her with a predatory smile, before introducing Whitelaw to her almost as an afterthought.

Penelope Denstone blushed furiously.

Whitelaw fancied he knew exactly what calculations were going on in Medlock's brain; he'd be asking himself whether the kudos of dating the Denstones' daughter would outweigh the embarrassment of being seen in his flashy sports car with a partner so unlike the leggy, undeniably classy types he normally favoured. And it wasn't taking him long to reach a decision, by the looks of things.

Adopting an expression of boyish earnestness, Medlock offered the girl a biscuit that in Whitelaw's opinion she could well have done without eating, and said, 'I hope I don't appear out of line by saying how much I admire your family's support of the performing arts, Miss Denstone.'

Whitelaw was still trying not to choke on his coffee as the girl's parents entered the room.

To say that Tricia and Henry Denstone came in together would have suggested a harmony of purpose that it quickly became clear was entirely lacking. Rather, they came in simultaneously. Whitelaw didn't wait for Medlock to do the honours. 'We've met before, as a matter of fact, sir,' he said as he showed his warrant card. 'At the time of the arson attack on Denstone Park.'

'Really?' Henry Denstone held out his hand. 'I'm afraid the police investigation made little impression, Inspector.'

It was impossible to glean from his frosty expression whether he was being sarcastic.

Medlock had jumped to his feet. 'Your daughter was just telling us a little about last night's function, sir,' he said. 'A tremendous success, by all accounts.'

'I suppose one could describe it as such if one calls opening one's home to the public in order to have a wallet and an apparently extremely valuable watch removed from the premises a success,' Denstone replied acidly.

Tricia did not so much as glance at her husband. Flashing a brilliant smile that encompassed both police officers, she said, 'Unfortunately, gentlemen, I fear we've wasted your time in dragging you out here. Mr Farrell made it absolutely clear before he left that he didn't wish to press charges.'

Whitelaw said briskly, 'Maybe you could tell us exactly what happened last night.' As it was as yet unclear which of the Denstones was calling the shots, he addressed the comment at a point on the wall between them.

It was Henry Denstone who answered. 'That was my purpose in calling you out here.' He made it sound as if he'd summoned a plumber to fix a dripping tap. He took a seat and gestured to Whitelaw and Medlock to do likewise. 'Perhaps you would bring some fresh coffee, Penelope', he added dismissively to his daughter, who left the room, looking chastened.

Tricia, with a sigh of dramatic resignation, arranged herself elegantly on one of the deep brocade sofas and took out a cigarette. Denstone glanced at her, his mouth turned down in disapproval.

Whitelaw cleared his throat. 'If we could have a list of the stolen items, sir . . .'

It didn't take Denstone long to fill them in on the facts. When Greg Farrell had returned to his room shortly after midnight, he had apparently discovered that his wallet and a gold watch were missing, having earlier noticed one of the performers acting suspiciously in the vicinity. Whitelaw considered asking why anyone would leave valuables lying around when the place was full of strangers, but horses and stable doors came to mind and he dismissed the question.

'Why would Mr Farrell choose not to press charges?' he asked instead.

'Because he has no wish to jeopardise the success of the gala with adverse publicity, Inspector.' Tricia spoke at last. 'Greg understands the importance of what I am seeking to achieve.' The look she shot her husband would have reduced most men to a very small pile of ash. She leant forward and stubbing out the cigarette with deliberate care, lit another. Whitelaw saw the stub crumple between her scarlet nails and felt a fleeting sympathy for her husband. He looked from one to the other expectantly. A full-scale domestic would be worth witnessing, and Whitelaw was momentarily tempted to make one of any number of comments that would kick it off. But as Medlock was no doubt making mental notes that would in due course be relayed back to Lambert, he opted instead for a diplomatic request to Denstone to elaborate on the substantive, if less controversial element of his statement.

'So am I to understand that there is reason to believe one of last night's participants was responsible for the alleged theft?' he asked, choosing his words carefully and gratified to see that he had managed to irritate both Denstones to an equal degree. Couldn't be more diplomatic than that, could he?

Denstone snapped, 'There is nothing *alleged* about it, Inspector. And there is every reason to believe—'

Tricia let out an exasperated exhalation of smoke and stubbed out her second cigarette with even greater viciousness than her first as she cut across him. 'Greg saw one of the St Saviour's boys upstairs before the performance. The poor child was in all probability simply lost.'

'The youth subsequently took to his heels on catching sight of one of my colleagues on the Bench who had sentenced him to a period of custody some months ago,' Denstone retorted. 'The implication is obvious, wouldn't you think, Inspector?'

Whitelaw was thinking nothing of the sort. What he was thinking was *shit*. He could take an educated guess at which of the St Saviour's kids they were talking about. Having the leading man legging it couldn't have done much for Kieran Henshall's plans for the evening.

'What happened about the play?' he asked, realising that Denstone was waiting for a reply.

'*The play?*' Denstone stared at him.

It was Tricia who answered. 'Thank you for your interest, Inspector,' she said. 'Fortunately, the situation was retrieved.' Judging by her tone, they would have noticed small pieces of Kieran scattered across the driveway otherwise, thought Whitelaw. But it was an ill wind . . . Unnerving as the incident must have been for the young community worker, it presented Whitelaw with an unmissable opportunity to put one over on Medlock. 'Would the name of the boy in question be Danny Nolan, by any chance?' he asked as casually as he was able.

Even Denstone appeared momentarily impressed. 'That is correct,' he answered.

'Allow me to make a few discreet enquiries, sir.' Whitelaw nodded sagely.

'You have the boy's identity, Inspector,' Denstone snapped. 'I trust we can achieve a speedy resolution. Justice delayed is justice denied, as you are no doubt aware the Lord Chancellor has made clear to both the police and the magistracy on many occasions.'

If there was one thing Whitelaw disliked above everything, it was being told how to do his job. And he was buggered if he was going to be used as the shuttlecock in the Denstones' game of domestic badminton. 'In my experience, justice requires appropriate investigation before any conclusion can be reached about a suspect's guilt. Or otherwise,' he said stiffly.

Denstone ignored the heavy sarcasm. 'I want Nolan found, Inspector, and found quickly.' He stood up, clearly deciding the interview was over.

Medlock was instantly on his feet. Whitelaw stayed where he was, leaving both men looking down at him. He allowed a full thirty seconds to pass before he too got up. 'I'll bear that in mind, sir.'

'We can rely on your discretion, Inspector?' Tricia took his hand and squeezed it, clearly imagining she had made a conquest.

'As I said, madam, I'll make some enquiries about Nolan.' Whitelaw withdrew his hand. 'Sergeant Medlock will take a look round here, with your permission. We shall, of course, keep you informed of any development. Please apologise to your daughter about the coffee, but I do have a couple of other matters to clear up this morning,' he smiled politely. 'A murder, for example.'

Two murders, as it happened.

The message came through as soon as Whitelaw got back to his car. Terry Lightowler had gone to investigate the break-in as instructed and had discovered Sunil Doshai's body. The constable, unused to being the first on the scene of a crime of such magnitude, was so pleased with himself that he managed to get the facts out without the benefit of his usual embroidery. Fearing a relapse, Whitelaw didn't ask him for details. He slammed the car into gear and drove.

Sunil and Jason's flat – Whitelaw remembered with an unexpected wave of sadness the way that Sunil had insisted on

referring to it as an 'apartment' – was on the first floor of a dilap-
idated villa in what had once been one of Blackport's more
prosperous areas. Just close enough to the docks to make it con-
venient to the newly wealthy Victorian traders, but far enough
away to make it an acceptable environment for their families, the
property had reached its heyday in the late nineteenth century.
A hundred and odd years later, the rural delights from which
Heckton Fields had derived its name were long gone. It was
a very far cry from Oultonshaw Manor, Whitelaw thought as
he parked his car, nodded to the uniform guarding the door,
and followed Lightowler into the house and up the communal
staircase.

The usual paraphernalia of SOCO and Forensic had yet to
arrive. Whitelaw had been relieved to note that only a single
police vehicle was parked outside; it could be hard to get an accurate first impression when the place was crawling with white
overalls and done up with tape like a building site.

Despite the run-down appearance of the exterior, the apartment itself was immaculate. Whitelaw glanced into the living
room, the tiny kitchen and the front bedroom which, judging by
the clutter of toiletries on the dressing table, had been the one
Jason and Sunil had slept in. The décor was conservative, pretty
in an *Ideal Home*-ish style that he found surprising. It was touch-
ingly obvious that the two, despite their lifestyle, had been
striving for their idea of middle-class normality.

'In here, Guv.' Lightowler was standing on front of another
door at the end of the hall.

The second bedroom was a very different story. But then this
had been their workplace, Whitelaw thought as he stepped inside.
Presumably no more a part of their off-duty lives together than
was the greengrocery on the corner to the Chinese family who ran
it and lived in the rooms behind.

The bedroom was done up like some cut-price maharajah's
palace: all red silk, incense burners and stylised drawings of sloe-
eyed Asian boys engaging each other in erotic activities

sufficiently acrobatic to make Whitelaw wince as he leant forward to peer at one of the more eye-catching of them.

'Bugger me,' he muttered, immediately regretting his choice of words.

Lightowler, unusually, had the grace not to comment. Instead he indicated a folding door on the right of the bed that Whitelaw, his attention otherwise engaged, had failed to notice. In more affluent times, the small, windowless chamber into which it led would most probably have served as a dressing room. In its present existence, it was painted black from ceiling to skirting board, the only illumination coming from a single low-watt candle bulb in the mock sconce on the wall above the bed. The room was stuffed with enough equipment to convince even the most seasoned sado-masochist that he had died and gone to heaven. Masks, chains, whips and any number of rubber gadgets, the function of which Whitelaw could only surmise, festooned the walls. Getting dressed was not what the average punter would have had in mind.

Not what this particular punter had had in mind, at any rate.

On the black silk-draped bed, Sunil's slender body lay face down and naked, his wrists and ankles bound to the wrought-iron bedstead, his long black hair flowing around his shoulders so that it was impossible, in the dim light, to make out where he finished and the bed began.

The only colour in the room was the crimson bloodstain that spread flower-like from the shattered pulp that had been his skull.

Chapter Seven

'Sunny side up, or easy over?' Kieran flashed a cheesy all-American smile to match the accent.

It had taken him a while to calm Flora down after he had returned from the police station. He was doing his best to make a joke of things, make light of his arrest, as together they scraped the remains of the meatballs from the kitchen wall and set about cooking an alternative breakfast. About Danny he had said nothing, and she hadn't asked.

'There I was, sat in the pitch-dark with an ignition barrel in one hand, a bunch of wires in the other, and no documents.' He broke eggs into the frying pan, testing its weight as he added with mock severity, 'You know, it's a good job you're such a lousy shot. You could have given me concussion with this bloody thing.'

Flora looked up from the bread that she was buttering. Pushing back her curtain of hair, she gave him a crooked grin and said, 'I was worried about you.'

'Right. And knocking my head off, not to mention splattering me with bolognese sauce, made you feel better, did it? I'll bear that in mind.' He watched the translucent whites solidify around the perfect domes of the yolks as he tipped the pan, listened to the splutter of the hot oil, and considered how it was that Flora's presence made even the most mundane of activities special. The luxury of coming back to her, of coming back to a home, almost made the night in the cells worthwhile.

'Anyway, like I was saying,' he said, returning to his original theme, 'you could hardly blame the poor sods for being suspicious.'

'They didn't have to arrest you.' Flora plonked the plate of bread and butter on the table. Having slung the pan, she had transferred her wrath to the Blackport constabulary. 'They'd know you were the owner, once they'd run the PNC check.'

Kieran shrugged, trying to keep the bitterness from his tone as he said, 'Yeah, but that wasn't the only thing a PNC check would have told them, was it?' He looked down at the pan. The eggs were beginning to burn, the whites darkening and curling in on themselves at the edges. 'Anyway,' he yawned hugely as he shovelled them onto a couple of plates, 'it's all sorted now, so you can relax. I don't know about you, but I'm knackered. I think I'll catch up on a few hours' sleep after breakfast.'

'Poor you. You must be tired out.' She came and stood behind him, moulding her body into his back as she put her arms around his waist.

'Well . . .' He felt his body stir as her fingers found their way inside his tomato-stained shirt and strayed down towards his jeans, 'maybe not *that* tired.'

It was nearly dark when he woke up, and he could hear rain rattling against the window. Cautiously twisting his head to look at the alarm clock, he realised that they had slept for almost twelve hours. Flora was still spark out, one arm flung across her face, a strand of coppery hair sticking damply to her cheek, the sheet kicked down to reveal the matching triangle of her pubic hair.

Kieran trailed his fingers lightly towards it, circling one pink, shell-like nipple, tracing the slope of her hip, the flat plane of her stomach. She sighed, her lips curving into a smile, but did not wake. Gently, he kissed the top of her head, then slipped out of bed, pulled on a pair of boxer shorts, and padded downstairs. He turned the light on in the hall, frowning as he noticed that the phone was off the hook. Flora must have disconnected it while he had been having a shower after breakfast, so that they wouldn't be disturbed. He replaced the receiver, wondering, as he did so, if Danny had attempted to get through, hating the thought of him trying to make contact only to get the engaged tone, hour after hour.

He went into the kitchen and made a pot of tea, rummaging through the cupboards until he found some biscuits. He felt guilty that, until five minutes before, he hadn't given Danny a thought since the previous night. What had been going on in the intervening hours? Danny had said he had severed his links with the mad, bad crowd he'd hung around with on the Eden Rise estate. And his family seemed an even more unlikely port of call. So where would he have gone once he'd dumped the car?

'Ring me, you silly sod,' Kieran murmured. What would Danny be doing at that moment, he wondered, while he himself was pottering around the cheerful, cluttered kitchen making tea, eating chocolate digestives, part of his mind still harbouring lustful thoughts of Flora asleep upstairs in the bed they shared? Would he be holed up alone in that cheerless, wharfside dosshouse? Or, if he were really frightened, already busy losing himself somewhere he wasn't known, Manchester? London? He could be anywhere.

A flash of lightning briefly illuminated the back garden. Kieran put the teapot, biscuits and two mugs on the tray. Please God he had found a dry doorway, if he were out on the streets somewhere. A low rumble of thunder followed the lightning like the growl of an angry dog.

At least Danny had his psychopathic canine sidekick to protect him, Kieran reassured himself as he took the tray back up to bed.

If Kieran and Flora's Saturday was mainly horizontal, Whitelaw's was decidedly vertical. Minutes after his arrival at Sunil and Jason's apartment, the rest of the travelling circus turned up, and within half an hour it was almost impossible to move without tripping over someone investigating something.

Whitelaw supervised the sealing off and initial search of the premises. First indications ruled out robbery as the killer's motive. Nothing appeared to have been disturbed. Whitelaw wasn't so sure. True, none of the meticulously tidy cupboards and drawers seemed to have been touched, but if the search had been a professional one, that was only to be expected. The top drawer of the dressing table was a fraction out of line with the others, he noticed. An ornament on the sideboard was facing the wrong way. The fingerprint boys soon had every surface plastered with clinging grey dust, just in case. The place looked like the scene of a recent fire. The irony was not lost on Whitelaw.

With so many people working in such a confined space, it quickly became stifling. Not wishing to disturb potential evidence by opening a window, Whitelaw pulled off his tie and unbuttoned his collar, leaving a long streak of fingerprint powder down the front of his shirt.

'That'll please the missus,' Lightowler observed as he handed Whitelaw a mug of tea.

'Yeah, well, It's been that sort of a day, hasn't it?' Whitelaw muttered, taking a swig and wincing at the tea's strength. Walking on water might be classed as a miracle, but Lightowler's tea would take any bugger's weight, he decided as he dabbed at the front of the shirt, making things worse. It would have to be his best one, the one Val had bought him specially for their trip to Mario's, the one he'd only put back on that morning to save her the washing. He was still fiddling with it when the police surgeon turned up; immaculate, of course.

Lightowler directed the men to the corpse. Whitelaw had no desire to follow them back into the black, airless chamber. In his job, the sordid became commonplace, but now and then the squalor of the lives with which he came into contact could still depress him. Jason and Sunil had been hardly more than kids. And now they were both dead.

Leaving Lightowler and the surgeon to get on with it, Whitelaw set about interviewing the neighbours. They were a motley collection. A muscular, bare-chested man with a shaven head, skull and crossbones tattoo, and a ring through his left nipple opened the door directly opposite. When informed of the nature of the inquiry, the man launched into an immediate and vicious tirade. He didn't know what that pair of bloody queers got up to in there, and he didn't want to know, he snarled. Medlock, who with his psychology degree regarded himself as the constabulary's resident trick cyclist, would undoubtedly have taken the vehemence of the response as indication that the bloke was a closet gay, Whitelaw thought as he thanked the man politely for his assistance and moved on.

Students occupied one of the ground-floor flats, a young West Indian couple the other. No one, predictably, had seen anything; too wary, too truculent or, in the case of at least two of the students, too spaced to provide information of any value. Whitelaw, his nostrils so filled with the sickly sweet fog of the latter's pigsty living room that he was surprised he wasn't high as a kite himself, considered running them in, but decided he couldn't be bothered.

In contrast, the old lady on the top floor was only too willing to help; so painfully grateful for Whitelaw's company that he felt obliged to drink two glasses of sweet sherry and consume a slice of chocolate Swiss roll well past its sell-by date before he could drag himself away. But being deaf, and as near blind as made little difference, she was able to throw no light on Sunil's comings and goings, nor that of his clients. Not that the poor old soul was remotely aware of the trade being plied in the rooms below, Whitelaw realised. Eventually he managed to get away by promising to come back for another chat next time he was passing. He suspected she hadn't even really grasped the fact that he was a policeman, let alone why he had come. He hadn't had the heart to tell her Sunil was dead.

Stuffing a mint into his mouth to alleviate the cake's musty aftertaste, he made his way back down the stairs. Sunil's body was being removed. So far, Whitelaw thought as he stood at the top of the stairwell and watched as the body bag was loaded into the back of the black coroner's van waiting in the street outside, his investigations had come up with the square root of sweet f.a. But there was one thing of which he was absolutely certain. Whatever Jason, and apparently Sunil too, had been involved in, it was a hell of a lot more serious than tapping up some hapless punter with a guilty conscience. Drugs? Whitelaw sucked thoughtfully on his mint. Some sort of organised porn ring? In the shadowy world Jason and Sunil had inhabited, you could probably take your pick. He raised his hand in an unconscious half-wave, as the van moved off. Whatever they'd been into, they'd messed up big time. And paid the price.

Whitelaw's mind was still working along the same lines when, several hours later and none the wiser, he drove back to the station. The earlier storm had done nothing to alleviate the day's heat, if anything only adding to the oppressive humidity. The promised rain had come to no more than a couple of short, sharp showers that had evaporated almost as soon as they had hit the baking pavements. A spatter of drops smacked the windscreen as Whitelaw drove. He wound down the window, and let the tepid rain sprinkle him.

If it turned out that the two killings were tied into something out of Blackport's league, the case would be handed over to one of the specialist metropolitan squads. There had been a time, he realised, turning his face to the last of the fat, cooling drops of water as he waited at the traffic lights at the top of the High Street, when he would have resented any intervention from another force – fought for his patch, the way coppers always did in detective stories on the telly. These days, he'd opt for the quiet life any day. If the big boys from Drugs or Vice wanted to pick up the pieces, then as far as he was concerned they were welcome.

He was relieved, on entering the office, to discover that Medlock had already gone home. Listening to his junior officer's account of his social conquests at Oultonshaw Manor was more than Whitelaw felt he could have stomached at that hour of the evening. He found a typed résumé propped up against his computer monitor instead. Without so much as a glance, he shoved it into his 'pending' tray, along with the rest of the clutter that had accumulated in his absence.

A glance at his watch told him he had long since missed Millie D'Sousa. He wrote a reminder to himself to call her first thing Monday, adding a mental note to get a dig in by phoning before she'd be at the office. It was the only reason to ring at all, he thought to himself; by Monday, the case would most likely be off his hands, and he could concentrate on something undemanding, like the Denstone theft.

He reached into the top drawer of his desk for the photograph. MARIO, 14. Was it significant? He stared at it hard, willing it to give up any clue it might hold.

But all it showed were two little boys, smiling into the sun.

Chapter Eight

Kieran threw down the notes he'd been going through for a workshop at Ripley Grange the following day and stared out of the window. A brilliant sun had already dried the vestiges of the previous night's rain as if it had never been. It was Sunday morning, the time of the week he usually liked the best. Sunday meant no alarm clock. A drowsy ascent into consciousness. Leisurely love-making and a breakfast so late it was dinner was well.

But not this Sunday.

He had found it impossible to sleep again after he'd taken the tea back up to bed. Unsurprising, he'd told himself as he tossed and turned, in view of the fact they had slept the day away. Flora's capacity for serious, round-the-clock dormancy had long been a source of amazement to him, and last night had been no exception; she'd drunk her mug of tea, planted a drowsy kiss on his cheek, turned onto her side and within thirty seconds was once more unconscious. The most Kieran had managed was a fitful, restless doze, punctuated by jumbled, anxious dreams, then a nightmare of such vivid intensity that at three o'clock he had got up rather than risk its repetition. He had watched the dawn break, choosing neither to recall nor analyse the images that had wrenched him back to wakefulness. He had wondered if Danny and Deefer were somewhere watching the sunrise too. For the past four hours, he had struggled to concentrate on the workshop, knowing he was only marking time until the rest of the world began to surface, and he could begin his search.

At last, he heard the creak of the floorboards above his head that told him that Flora, at least, was up, then water running in the bathroom.

'You should have woken me.' She appeared in the doorway wearing one of his tee shirts. 'I've run you a bath. Do you want something to eat?'

Her face was still flushed with sleep, her hair tousled. For a wistful moment, Kieran contemplated breakfast in bed. Then he shook his head. 'I'm going out for a bit.'

She sat down, tucked her feet under her, and looked at him without comment. Her voice was resigned when finally she uttered the single word, 'Danny.' It was more statement than question.

'Danny,' he replied.

Eden Rise, situated a mile or so from the town centre, was a typical sixties high-rise development: a maze of wind tunnels and forbidding alleyways stinking of stale urine. The concrete paths leading from block to block of flats were littered with aerosol cans, empty glue containers and used condoms. Packs of half-wild dogs roamed the patches of scrubby grass that were the council's only stab at horticulture. Although Kieran had never visited the area before, it was as if he were stepping back a dozen years in time.

He hadn't taken the car. With its ignition barrel still out, a child of five would have been able to hot-wire it in a district like this. As he walked between the blocks he could feel his guts knotting, his fingers tightening into fists. Unconsciously, he began to recite the Keats under his breath.

Number ninety-three Alpha House was situated at the top of a block right in the centre of the estate. Kieran didn't even bother to try the lift. Fit though he was, by the time he made it up five flights he was breathing hard. Pausing to look up the stairwell, he wondered how the old woman who he'd passed negotiating her way cautiously down the echoing concrete steps would manage her return journey.

The old woman excepted, Alpha House appeared largely deserted, although it was after nine. Kieran's search had lasted over two hours already. He had started at the Seaman's Rest, risking the concierge's wrath by knocking him up, and wasting a fiver he could ill-afford to bribe his way into Danny's bedsit. It had been unoccupied. The note that Kieran had written on Friday evening lay crumpled on the table. He had pocketed it, telling himself that at least it had been read. He had been touched to see a poster for *Grab and Smash* blu-tacked to the peeling plaster above the bed, the room's only adornment. The only hint that Danny had ever lived there.

After the Seaman's Rest, he had scoured the train station, the parks, the shop doorways of the empty city centre, all the places that swallowed youngsters who wanted to disappear. Only Danny's family was left. With most kids, it would have been the obvious starting point, Kieran thought, as, finally reaching the top of the steps, he stopped to catch his breath while he got his bearings.

The flat he was looking for was adjacent to the stairwell, its front door opening, as did all the other flats, on to the draughty open walkway on which he stood. A low brick wall topped with head-high mesh prevented anyone drunk or desperate enough from toppling the eight storeys to the concrete pavement below. The area outside the flat was strewn with the evidence of Danny's younger brothers and sisters: a child's sandal, a pink plastic hair slide, an Action Man with its head missing.

Kieran took a step towards the door, then hesitated for a moment. Maybe it was too early. His reception was likely to be hostile enough, without dragging Danny's mother from her bed. But the younger kids would have ensured that she was up. Still Kieran hesitated, knowing that it wasn't fear of disturbing anyone that held him back.

At last, he knocked. After a minute or so, a curtain twitched at the front window. A small, pale face appeared, then vanished. After a further wait, the door was opened by a girl of seven or eight. She hung back, half-hidden by the door, her eyes watchful. The smell of neglect seeped from the flat behind her.

'Is your mam in?' Kieran asked.

The girl stared at him.

'I need to speak to your mam.' Kieran peered beyond her into the dark hallway. A television screen flickered in the room at the other end of the hall. He could make out another, much younger child sitting cross-legged inches from the screen, naked but for a vest, a baby's bottle dangling from its mouth. 'About Danny,' he added.

The girl glanced nervously towards the closed door on the right of the hall leading to what Kieran presumed to be a bedroom.

'It's important,' Kieran pressed, his eyes following hers. Could Danny have come back here after all?

Suddenly, the door swung open. A woman appeared, wrapping a grubby dressing gown around her and tugging at the rollers in her long, peroxided hair. Closing the door behind her with a caution that suggested someone else was still sleeping in there, she shuffled to the front door, pushing the girl behind her. Before she spoke, she slipped the chain on. Regarding Kieran from behind it with a mixture of hostility and apprehension, she said in a low voice, 'What d'you want?'

Kieran noted the similarity of the woman's reaction to that of the little girl, as soon as he mentioned Danny's name. 'I'm not the law,' he added quickly, as she glanced back into the flat. 'I'm just a mate.'

'He's not here.' She shut the door on him.

Kieran hesitated, momentarily tempted to give up. Then he banged the letterbox as hard as he could, estimating that the last thing the woman wanted was for whoever was asleep in the bedroom to be woken. He was right. Before he could bang a second time, he heard the chain being slipped off.

This time, she stepped out onto the walkway, shutting the front door behind her and hissed, 'Leave us alone.'

'Is he here?' Kieran found himself lowering his own voice in response. Encouraged by the 'us' that suggested Danny's presence, he smiled at her and added, 'I only wanted to check he was OK.'

'No, he's not here.' His smile went unanswered. 'I don't know where he is, and I don't want to know. He's been nothing but bloody trouble from the day he was born. Now just piss off.'

'You're his mother,' Kieran said as neutrally as he was able, trying to make it sound more a query than a recrimination.

The woman reached into her dressing gown pocket and pulled out a cigarette and a box of matches. Kieran noticed that her hand was trembling as she struck a match.

'Danny knows the score, or if he doesn't he bloody well should do by now,' she said. 'I've got myself to think of. And the other kids.' She swallowed, still not meeting Kieran's eye. 'Listen, just tell him—'

'I can't tell him anything, can I? He's disappeared.' This time Kieran made less effort to keep the accusation from his tone. 'I'm trying to find out what's happened to him.'

'Who are you, anyway?' the woman spat. 'His sodding social worker or what?'

'What the fuck's going on?' The front door suddenly opened. In the doorway stood a man of about forty. His tone was quiet, conversational. He wasn't tall, nor particularly well-built, but he had an air of coiled, wiry aggression about him that Kieran recognised instantly as far more dangerous than sheer brawn. The woman shrank back into herself as she drew her dressing gown around her.

For a split second, Kieran felt an almost overwhelming desire to run. The old, familiar terror hit his stomach like a physical blow. He was hardly able to believe the calm, confident voice was his own as he said conversationally, 'Sorry to disturb you, mate. I was just asking when Danny was last here.'

'Who wants to know?'

Kieran looked him up and down before answering, 'I do.' He could tell by the way the other man stared at him that he was sizing him up, wondering whether to take him on.

Danny's mother looked from one of them to the other, then muttered, 'Steady, Mick.'

The man swivelled his stare in her direction, and she lowered her eyes. Then he sneered, 'Thursday. Not that it's any business of yours. Came round to see his mummy when he thought I was out. Only I got back early, didn't I? And as I'm not that keen on having some other bloke's bastard hanging around the place, I beat the shit out of him.' He took a step forwards. 'Same as I do out of anyone who upsets my family. Anything else you want to know?'

'He was here Friday night too.' The woman's voice was barely audible. 'I didn't let him in, Mick. I told him—' She already had her arm up to protect her face as he swung round on her, his fist raised.

Kieran moved by instinct. Without thought or word, he leapt at the man, grabbing him by the throat and pinning him back against the wire mesh. The man's fingers were scrabbling at Kieran's hands as they tightened. His eyes began to bulge. Kieran was vaguely aware that behind him, the woman was screaming and trying to drag him away, but he was focused on the purpling face. The veins were standing out on the man's temples like ropes. How much pressure would it take to burst them? How much pressure before those popping eyes popped right out of his head?

'Dad, Dad!' The little girl's screams scythed through Kieran's brain to bring him back to his senses. Abruptly, he released his grip, and the man slumped to the ground, gurgling and gasping for breath.

'*To cease upon the midnight with no pain . . . no pain . . . no . . .*' The words followed Kieran's echoing footsteps down the steps. When he emerged into the light, he leant against the doorway and was violently sick.

It was almost two o'clock as he walked the last couple of hundred yards down Sephton Street, hot, tired and footsore. He had done another trawl of the parks, telling himself he was double-checking. But he knew in his heart that his reason for not going home had nothing to do with his search, and everything to do with his need to compose himself. Flora could read him too well. A scab had been ripped from the raw place deep inside him, and he was frightened she would see it in his face.

He stopped at the newsagent on the corner and picked up a paper, and a bag of pear drops: Flora's favourite. He glanced at his reflection in the chiller cabinet as he took out a pint of milk. He looked the same as normal.

As he went back out into the street, he was stopped in his tracks by a reedy, 'Yoo-hoo!' from the shop next door. He turned to see Batty Norah, a violently striped woolly hat pulled down over her ears despite the afternoon heat, leaning at an alarming angle from an upper window.

'Wait there,' she commanded, and disappeared from view.

Kieran stood on the pavement, shifting from foot to foot. No point in making a run for it: Norah would simply turn up on his doorstep two minutes later. He took what change he had left from the shopping out of his pocket and counted it: thirty-seven pence. She'd have to make do with that. To pass the time, he examined the fly-blown window of her shop. At some stage of the past, it had been papered on the inside with heavy yellow Cellophane to prevent the sun from fading the stock; a measure that had long outlived its purpose. All that the window displayed were several bluebottles in varying stages of desiccation and an untidy pile of knitting patterns. The top one, Kieran noticed, bore the black and white picture of an overweight baby in a woolly romper suit, and was priced at 1/3d.

Norah wasn't brandishing a collecting tin when she re-appeared, dressed in fluffy slippers, tracksuit bottoms and a strapless pink sun top designed for someone at least forty years her junior. Instead, glancing at the flawless blue sky, then pulling her hat down further over her ears as if expecting snow, she beckoned Kieran over to her front door. Grasping his arm with a skinny hand as though fearing he might make a bolt for freedom if she didn't hang on to him, she said confidentially, 'Is he yours?'

Kieran was unsure how to respond.

'I've tried the couple at number twenty-six, and that lot at thirty. Not that you'd get any sense out of them.'

Pots and kettles sprang to Kieran's mind, but he knew better from past experience than to attempt an interruption.

'He must have come from somewhere around here,' she added truculently. 'He's too well cared for to be a stray.'

'Right.' Disengaging his arm, Kieran edged away from the door. Rehoming strays was another of Norah's passions; mainly small wild animals whose only misfortune was to have found themselves in Norah's back yard. She had already tried to talk Kieran and Flora into adopting a hedgehog, a fox cub and an elderly pigeon. 'Listen,' he said, 'I've really got to—'

'And *someone* put that lovely red and white hankie round his neck, didn't they?' Norah jabbed an arthritic finger at him to emphasise her point.

'What?' Kieran stopped. He felt his stomach lurch.

Norah, gratified to have finally captured his full attention, was only too willing to fill in the details of the poor dog she had found wandering the street in the early hours, dazed and bleeding from a head wound. Yes, she nodded energetically in answer to Kieran's urgent question, the dog's coat *was* ginger. Well yes, she agreed with rather more reluctance, anyone who wasn't a dog-lover *could*, she supposed, describe him as ugly, but as one of God's helpless creatures—

'Where is it now?' Kieran cut across her.

Norah looked distressed. She would have loved to have kept

him, she explained. Even if he was a bit grumpy, although that was only to be expected after what he had been through. But it was Albert. Norah shook her head. Albert still got so possessive if another dog came into the house. Even though she'd had him tidied up behind, she added coyly.

Finally, Kieran managed to get out of her that 'Hank' as she had christened the dog on account of its neckwear, had been taken to the Animal Rescue Centre. Norah gave him directions, insisting on writing them down for him on a grubby, crumpled envelope she fished from her pocket.

She squeezed Kieran's arm as she handed the envelope to him. 'You're a good boy. I knew you'd sort it out.'

Kieran was already halfway down the street, as she called after him, 'He'll make a lovely pet.'

Flora was reading, sitting out in their tiny, unkempt patch of back garden, her rickety deckchair surrounded by weeds, when Kieran returned an hour or so later. He watched her for a moment from the kitchen step, before he called her name.

'Hi!' she said, waving over her shoulder. 'How did you get on with . . . ?' She put down her book and removed her sunglasses as she got up, then stopped dead. '*What* is that?'

Kieran glanced down at his companion, and frowned. 'Meet Deefer,' he said. His hand tightened on the lead, as he added, 'Dee for dog, get it?'

Chapter Nine

Whitelaw did not stop for his usual chat with Cyril Turner when he arrived at Blackport Central on Monday morning. Instead, he headed straight for his office, intent on leaving a message for Millie D'Sousa before she got in to work. It was one of the few tasks of the day he viewed with any enthusiasm.

An interview with the duty officer at the community drugs centre the previous afternoon, together with the information Medlock had pulled off the computer, made it clear that both Jason Morrissey and Sunil Doshai had been involved in the local drugs scene. There was even a whisper, via a mate of a mate, that the young Asian's name had cropped up from time to time in a big investigation already underway in Manchester.

Medlock had wanted to know what it was all about; Whitelaw had told him it was none of his business. Information was only ever given to the opportunity-hungry Medlock on a need-to-know basis, as far as Whitelaw was concerned; and in this instance, Medlock needed to know nothing. He had the distinct feeling that the younger man would be less than delighted at the prospect of losing a murder investigation to the heavy brigade, and there seemed very little doubt that that was the way things were heading. Whitelaw was pretty sure that his Monday was going to be spent getting the sparse details of Jason and Sunil's deaths into something like working files, so that Lambert could hand them over, and he didn't need Medlock complicating things.

They'd wasted enough time already acting as glorified filing clerks for Drugs, he thought as he dialled Millie's number and glared at the interview notes, computer printouts and general garbage that covered his desk. He might just as well have spent the bloody weekend on his tomatoes.

Two rings into the call, and he realised that even the one small anticipated triumph of the day was to be frustrated. A brisk voice on the other end of the phone said, 'Millie D'Sousa,' the words rising interrogatively as if to save the 'Can I help you?' that might have been expected to follow.

The answer being that yes, she could.

After a couple of minutes' conversation, Whitelaw replaced the receiver thoughtfully, and went to the pile of newspapers that topped the filing cabinet behind his desk. It was a habit that had developed over the years; his personal, short-term archive. Each copy of the *Blackport Daily Echo* was saved for two weeks. Not thirteen days, not fifteen; the back issues folded and stacked in date order, and woe betide any unschooled cleaner who threw them out or re-arranged them. Whitelaw had lost count of the number of times some incident had sparked off a recollection of something or someone he had read about the previous week . . .

He took down Friday's copy and turned to the entertainments page. He examined the picture of the ruins of Denstone Park, its roof off like a doll's house, the chimney stacks incongruously intact, its blackened, glassless windows staring out at the world in wide-eyed, blank surprise. He compared it to the background in the snap of Jason and his unknown companion. Millie was right. The same ornamental garden wall was visible in both. His eyes travelled over the page to the *Echo*'s adjacent picture: 'Tricia Denstone and her husband . . .' He decided maybe it was time to take a look at Medlock's report on the theft.

Most of it was stuff Whitelaw already knew, but one section caught his eye. Tricia Denstone had noticed that Danny Nolan was heavily bruised about the face, and had what had appeared to be a recent cut to the forehead. Whitelaw reread the statement, his mind leaping back to the car in Hunter's Wood, its passenger door lolling from its hinges . . . He picked up the phone again, this time to summon Lightowler into his office.

Lightowler, at thirty-five, still lived at home with his mother; which, according to Medlock, was probably of significance in explaining the constable's 'regrettably homophobic tendencies'. Whitelaw fully intended to kick things off between the two of them in the pub one evening, by divulging Medlock's theory that Lightowler was a closet pouf. But for the moment he was more interested in the remembered fact that Lightowler's mother was a secretary at Denstone Automotive Engineering. With any luck, Lightowler had inherited from her his talent for gossip. In which case, he might be able to provide something a bit more useful in the way of background information on the Denstone family than what Whitelaw could recall from the arson investigation, or was likely to glean from the obsequious stuff in Medlock's report.

Lightowler was only too happy to oblige, and within ten minutes Whitelaw had been filled in on Freddie Denstone's death in a hit-and-run accident, reputedly just minutes after a violent argument with his father at the factory. Freddie had been a frequent visitor there, during his college vacations. Young, handsome and as affable towards the workers as his father was remote, he had been popular, particularly with the female employees. According to Lightowler's mum, there had been rumours of an affair with a typist from—

'That was a few months before the fire, wasn't it?' Whitelaw strove to bring him back to the point, if point there was.

Lightowler nodded. The destruction of Denstone Park, the family seat since the early eighteen hundreds, was considered by many to have been divine retribution, and no more than Henry Denstone deserved. Tricia Denstone apparently hadn't been the only one who blamed Henry for their son's death.

'You could tell there was no love lost between the two of them,' Whitelaw commented.

'Ah well . . .' Lightowler looked knowing.

Whitelaw glanced up at the clock. 'See if you can do this in under ten volumes, will you? I'm supposed to be in with Lambert.'

Freddie had always been Tricia's favourite, his constable went on, unabashed. The daughter, eclipsed even when her brother was alive, didn't get a look-in once he was dead. 'Of course, being an actress, looks would be important to Tricia, wouldn't they?' Lightowler said sagely. 'And it has to be said, Penelope Denstone's got a face that would frighten one of the police horses.'

Whitelaw thought back to Medlock's predatory leer and prayed the girl had more sense than looks; enough, at least, to see through Neville Medlock.

'Happy as anything, they were, before Freddie died, mind.' Lightowler was warming to his theme. 'Take Denstone Park, for instance.'

Whitelaw refrained from pointing out that that was precisely what he had been attempting to do for the last ten minutes, as the other man went on, 'Tricia never wanted to live there. And what Tricia wanted, Tricia got, especially in those days. Henry bought Oultonshaw Manor for her when Freddie was born. She didn't do any more acting, of course, once they were married, but it would still be in her blood, wouldn't it? That's why she turned Denstone Park into a stage school. She could have turned it into a brothel, if she'd wanted to. Henry was besotted, see. But after Freddie died . . .' Lightowler shook his head knowingly.

'Well, he certainly doesn't seem very besotted with her now,' Whitelaw observed briskly. He'd got the picture. All he'd wanted was a bit of background, not a double-page feature out of *Hello!* He had a sudden, vivid picture of Lightowler and his mum. The two of them, sat together of an evening, chewing over the lives that clearly struck them as so much more colourful than their own, when Lightowler should have been down the pub, or out with his mates on the pull. Maybe Medlock had a point.

Fortunately, the phone saved him the necessity of attempting to convince the man, who was once more in full flow, that further detail, however fascinating, was unnecessary. Having listened to the ring to check that it wasn't an internal call – Lambert would have worked up quite a head of steam by now – Whitelaw answered it.

A mistake. The call might temporarily have silenced Lightowler, but the voice that assaulted Whitelaw's eardrums was not an improvement. 'Sid Barker here,' it bawled, with the unnecessary addendum, *'Daily Echo.'*

Whitelaw closed his eyes and motioned Lightowler, who was not unknown to keep up his monologue over the top of phone calls, from the room.

So far, all that had been released to the press about Jason's death was that the body of an as yet unidentified male had been found in the wreckage of a burnt-out car. Sunil's murder was going to be more difficult to play down. A rent boy with his skull caved in was not easy to pass off as accidental, but Whitelaw had managed temporarily to fob Sid off with phrases such as 'suspicious circumstances' and 'until the results of the post mortem are known . . .'

Not any longer. Sid, never one for social foreplay, followed up his self-introduction with, 'A little bird tells me your Hunter's Wood stiff was another arse-bandit. What's going on?'

'No comment. A press release will be issued in due course.' The standard response cut about as much ice as Whitelaw had known it would.

'Don't give me that bollocks. Come on, Ray, old son. What's the angle?'

The *Echo*'s offices were less than a quarter of a mile away from Blackport Central. Whitelaw considered suggesting Sid cut down on expenses by dispensing with a telephone altogether.

Receiving no response, the other man went on, 'Don't tell me there isn't something going down . . .' A bellow of mirth at his own pun had Whitelaw holding the phone at arm's length, from where the raucous tones were still clearly audible. 'Going down, get it?'

Reluctantly, Whitelaw put the receiver back to his ear.

Evidently feeling the need to elaborate, Sid chortled, 'I bet they've both gone down on a few punters in their time, eh?' Had he been able to see Whitelaw's expression he would have realised that his joke was not being shared. As it was, he gave another shout of laughter. 'So what d'you reckon? Two paid-up members of rent-a-bum in under a week? Queer-bashing, is it?'

Whitelaw sighed. 'I can see how you got into journalism, Sid. It's a gift, your way with words. Listen . . .' He knew he would have to give him something soon, or Barker would simply invent it as he went along, and God knew what he'd end up sparking off. 'I'm just off to see Lambert about it now. Give me a call this afternoon and I might have something for you.' He put the phone down before Sid could reply, tore out the entertainments page from the back copy of the *Echo*, and headed for Lambert's office.

'You'll never guess who's been trying to get hold of you!'

Flora looked up from a pile of depressingly badly written CVs for the post of switchboard operator, to find Thelma Lightowler, personal assistant to Henry Denstone, standing in front of the desk. Thelma's shorthand pad, so habitually clutched that it seemed like a surgical extension to her right arm, was poised as though she were about to take notes.

'Who?' Flora put her hand over the mouthpiece of her phone and forced an expression of polite interest. A good part of her Monday morning had so far been spent on hold, as she tried vainly to establish contact with the Personnel department at the town hall to check a dodgy-looking reference; her ears were already ringing with electronic Mozart. She did not need Thelma.

'You're a dark horse, aren't you?' Thelma gave a knowing

smile. She was of indeterminate late middle age and given to wearing hand-knitted angora cardigans in pastel colours. But the myopic baby-blue eyes and mildly scatty manner were deceptive, Flora had been warned by the younger secretaries. Beneath her fluffy blonde hair, Thelma carried the entire history of Denstone Automotive Engineering, administrative, commercial and personal; the more personal the better. Her memory had more bytes than the most powerful IBM computer. If anyone in any office at Denstone Automotive Engineering dropped a paper clip, Thelma Lightowler knew about it before it hit the floor. And would still know about it six months later.

'*I* saw you making eyes at him the other night, you madam,' Thelma added with a wink.

'Sorry?' Flora, exasperated by both the Mozart and Thelma, put the phone down. It immediately began to ring.

Thelma nodded at it triumphantly. 'That'll be him now.'

Flora picked up the receiver again. 'Can I help you?' Her voice was more irritable than she'd intended as she swivelled her chair away from Thelma's expectant gaze.

'Sorry. Bad timing?' She recognised the voice instantly, and swivelled the chair still further, feeling the colour rush to her cheeks, as Greg Farrell went on, 'I did try to ring on Saturday, but your phone was engaged all day. I think you must have a fault.'

Flora tried to sound less flustered than she felt. 'Sorry. It was off the hook.'

'No problem. Tricia mentioned you worked at Denstones.'

'How are you?' They both said the words at once. Greg laughed. 'I'm fine.' He paused, then said, 'Listen, I'm really sorry if I've made things worse. With Danny, I·mean.'

Flora had no idea what he was talking about.

Greg must have sensed her hesitation, because he added, 'Look, I've obviously caught you at a bad time . . .'

'No,' she said quickly. 'No, not at all. I've got someone with me, but she's just going. Thanks, Thelma.' She smiled brightly, and added, 'Would you mind shutting the door?'

Even Thelma Lightowler was unable to ignore so pointed a dismissal. She went huffily, leaving the door ajar.

Tucking the receiver under her chin, Flora got up from the desk and kicked it shut. 'Sorry about that. Where were we?'

She listened, her heart sinking. Bloody, *bloody* Danny Nolan.

'I thought maybe Kieran could have a quiet word with him and get it back,' Greg was saying. 'I'm not worried about the money, but the watch means a lot to me. It was a present.' Flora found herself wondering from whom, as he went on, 'Even so, I'd never have said anything to the Denstones if I'd realised they were going to get the police involved.'

'Oh God. Listen, I'm so sorry. We didn't know anything about it. Kieran's been trying to get in touch with Danny all weekend, but he seems to have taken off. I can see why now.'

'Looks like that guy Brassington's theory was right all along.' Greg's voice was sober as he added, 'Poor Kieran. He'd put so much trust in that youngster, hadn't he? This is going to seem like a real slap in the face to him.'

'If he can bring himself to believe it, it will.'

'How do you mean?' Greg sounded puzzled.

'It's a long story.' Flora hesitated, pushing to the back of her mind the vague sense that she was betraying Kieran, as she added, 'I'm worried about him, to be honest . . .'

It was only the sound of the factory hooter announcing the end of the morning shift as she finally put down the phone that made her realise how long she had been talking. Greg's gentle, noncommittal responses to her concerns had been comforting in the same way that unburdening her worries on the priest at confession had been comforting when she was younger and still believed in such things. She had told him of Danny's disappearance. Of the dog, and Kieran's absolute conviction that Danny wouldn't have left Blackport without it. Of Kieran's irrational and growing obsession that Danny was in danger. She had confided how disturbed he had seemed when he had come back from seeing Danny's mother. How he had woken crying out in the night from a nightmare that had nothing to do with Danny.

She had told him too much.

She ran her hands through her hair, and watched the factory workers stream out into the sunshine. She was dreading breaking the news of the theft to Kieran, but there was no point in putting it off. Resolutely, she dialled the number of Ripley Grange. Kieran wasn't there, she was told when she finally got through to the Education Unit. The woman in charge sounded concerned. He hadn't stayed for lunch as he usually did; had seemed a bit distracted. Said he had to see a man about a dog. Did that make any sense to Flora?

'No,' she said wearily, 'no sense at all. But I know what he meant.'

Chapter Ten

By mid-afternoon, Whitelaw's headache had returned with a vengeance, both in the literal and metaphorical sense. His forehead felt as if it were in a vice, and the Denstone theft, which on Saturday he had regarded as no more than a trivial inconvenience, had taken centre stage of his workload.

The meeting with Lambert had gone much as he had thought it would; one mention of a potential link, however tenuous, between Denstone Park and the Morrissey/Doshai inquiries had been enough to light the blue touchpaper. The murder investigations were to remain in house. Lambert had made it clear he wasn't having some bunch of Drugs Squad heavies from another force piling in on the act. In the meantime, he had suggested to Whitelaw in no uncertain terms that a speedy resolution to the theft inquiry was Highly Desirable. Maintaining a Successful Working Relationship with Blackport's leading family was, Whitelaw had been reminded, Imperative. Lambert always talked in upper case when he was trying simultaneously to make a point and be sarcastic. He had ended the homily by enquiring, at a decibel level of which Sid Barker would have been proud, just what the hell Whitelaw had thought he was doing, trying to patronise the Denstones in their own home? And why the Nolan kid hadn't been pulled on Saturday morning, when Henry Denstone had provided such cogent evidence against him. If there was not a Significant Upturn in the inquiry, Lambert had rounded off the rant, he might be forced to consider a Reallocation of Resources. Other officers were More than Competent to Succeed where Whitelaw had so far Signally Failed.

Whitelaw suspected that Medlock had already had the Superintendent's ear.

Duly bollocked, he was dispatched to bring Nolan in for questioning. Immediately, if not sooner. He decided to pop down to the canteen on the way. Nolan had been on the loose since Friday night; an extra half-hour, in Whitelaw's estimation, was unlikely to be crucial. But any hope of lifting his mood with a good, unhealthy fry-up was quickly dispelled. The first person he spotted was Medlock, sitting not alone as he normally did, but with Lightowler. The sight bothered Whitelaw. Medlock was dangerous; always had been. The only possible chink in his armour was that he was also the most unpopular officer in living memory. It meant no one told him more than they had to. But get him cosying up with some gormless, big-mouthed idiot like Lightowler . . .

'Thought I might get one for home,' Lightowler explained, tapping the computer magazine that lay open on the table between them as Whitelaw joined them. 'Neville reckons it might help with my sergeant's exam if I was computer literate. He's giving me a bit of advice about what to buy.'

Whitelaw, thinking that any sort of literacy would be a start, looked from one to the other. Neville, was it, now?

Medlock read his expression. Raising a sardonic eyebrow, he murmured, 'Always willing to help a fellow officer.'

'Very admirable.' Whitelaw looked at Lightowler despondently. Anyone with more than Neanderthal brainpower could have worked what Medlock's game was. 'Right,' he said resignedly, 'you can pull me a copy of Nolan's previous, if you want some practice on the computer. And you,' he glared down at Medlock, who was still sipping his coffee, 'if it's not too much trouble, you can put your talents to the test by getting hold of Probation to find out Nolan's current address.'

Which, naturally, was out of date.

Whitelaw wasted the best part of what was left of the after-noon at Eden Rise, where Mick McTeer, Nolan's stepfather, took the opportunity to put in an official accusation of assault against one of Nolan's acquaintances whose description sounded worry-ingly like Kieran Henshall. Whitelaw, with a civility he found hard to maintain, promised to look into it. Getting information was like drawing teeth. The mother, a blowsy blonde, claimed to have no idea where Nolan had been since he'd got out. Whitelaw wasn't sure he believed her, but quickly realised he was wasting his time leaning on her, at least while McTeer was around. The woman's heavy mask of makeup didn't disguise her fear any more than it did her bruises. Whitelaw just hoped Kieran had thumped as hard the weaselly little bastard who had inflicted them.

It was Kieran that Whitelaw visited next, in the hope that he might be able to shed rather more light on the boy's whereabouts. By the time he reached St Saviour's it was well after five and the site was largely deserted. Through the open windows of the gym, Whitelaw could see a bunch of plump, sweating women doing keep fit, and in one of the classrooms, a group sitting in a semi-circle, peering earnestly at some old bloke standing in front of a blackboard. Continuing Education, Val called it. A bloody daft way to spend a summer's evening was what Whitelaw would have called it.

He wandered about for a bit, looking into empty classrooms, trying locked doors, thinking to himself that it was no wonder there was so much vandalism at the place, if any Joe Bloggs could come in off the streets and roam as freely as he was doing. He said as much to the elderly caretaker who finally ambled out of one of the buildings and across the playground to ask if he could help. Unoffended, the man shook his head and laughed, 'Bit long in the tooth for vandalism, you and me, mate.'

Whitelaw, nettled that the bloke seemed to think they were much of an age, said who he had come to see, and was directed towards a low, concrete building beyond the bicycle sheds on the far side of the site. The building was clearly used for storage. An up-and-over door at one end was partly open. From behind it, Whitelaw could hear what sounded like furniture being dragged around. He ducked under the door and went inside, blinking as his eyes adjusted from the sunlight.

Kieran was at the back of the storeroom, hauling a large section of painted scenery board towards a stack already leaning precariously against the far wall. He hadn't heard Whitelaw come in. Grunting with effort, he manoeuvred the board into place. His tee shirt was dark with sweat, his hair plastered to his skull. His profiled face was grim, the mouth drawn into a tight, down-turned line. He wiped his forehead with the back of his arm, then let the arm drop heavily to his side and bowed his head. Whitelaw sensed that there was more to the gesture than mere physical exhaustion.

'How did it go?'

At Whitelaw's words, Kieran wheeled round.

'The play? How was it?' Whitelaw repeated as the younger man, with a final glance at the stack of boards, walked towards him.

'OK.' Again, Kieran ran his arm across his face.

'I hear you had a bit of bother with Danny Nolan.'

Whitelaw was good at sensing hostility. In his job, he'd had plenty of practice. Kieran was trying to keep it under control, but it was there anyway, as he asked, 'Was there anything in partic-ular? Only I've still got all this lot . . .' He gestured to the jumble of props just inside the door.

'I'll give you a hand.' Whitelaw picked up a mock-up lamp-post. 'Where's it got to go?'

They worked together in silence for a couple of minutes. Kieran didn't ask why Whitelaw was there, which meant he already knew. Finally, he said, 'I'm not pressing charges, if that's what you're after. I told Danny he could borrow the car, OK?'

'Car?' Whitelaw echoed. Abruptly, he put down his end of the box they were lifting. Of the possible responses he had envisaged to his presence, this wasn't one. His mind was straight back to Hunter's Wood again as he asked sharply, 'What car?'

'What car do you think?' Kieran heaved the box onto his shoulder, the hostility now coming off him in waves. 'My car. The one I spent Friday night trying to convince your mates I hadn't nicked. And Danny didn't nick it either, all right?'

The reason for Kieran's hostility soon became clear; as did the fact that he was in no mood to be mollified.

'Listen, I'll have a word when I get back to the station,' Whitelaw said. 'Find out which pillock was responsible for holding you overnight, OK?'

Kieran looked unimpressed.

Whitelaw shook his head. 'No, I mean it. It was way over the top.'

'So you'd have done any differently, if you hadn't known me?' Kieran gave a mirthless laugh. 'Sure. Face it, Whitelaw. Dogs don't lose their bad names, for all the fancy talk of fresh starts.'

Whitelaw suspected Kieran might be right. 'Aren't many make so much of a fresh start as you've done, though,' he said. 'A university degree, and everything.'

'Yeah?' As an olive branch, it was too obvious and Kieran saw straight through it. 'You think announcing I've got a first in English Literature might have helped, is that what you're saying? Come off it! Most of your mates trust students about as much as they trust ex-cons.'

Again, Whitelaw couldn't disagree.

'Anyway,' Kieran went on, 'now we've established I didn't nick my car and Danny didn't nick it either, is there anything else I can help you with? Only I'd like to get home somewhere this side of midnight.'

'It wasn't your car I came here about, as a matter of fact,' Whitelaw said, wishing they had got off to a better start. He suspected that Kieran was unaware of the theft at Oultonshaw Manor. He also suspected that the young community worker wouldn't buy Nolan's involvement in it, and he was quickly proved right on both counts. In Kieran's eyes, it was simply another case of the police going for an easy target: Nolan had a record, therefore Nolan must be the culprit. It was only with obvious reluctance that he provided an address, making it clear his co-operation was going to stretch no further than that.

The two men had been working as they talked, and the props were all back in place. Whitelaw waited while Kieran locked up the storeroom, and they walked back across the yard together.

'Listen, I know you're concerned about him,' Whitelaw said, breaking the prickly silence as they reached the car park. 'Just back off a bit, OK?'

'That's an official warning, is it?' Kieran said coldly. 'I'm sorry, I didn't realise there was a law against being concerned with the welfare of a missing teenager.'

'There's a difference between missing and scarpered,' Whitelaw snapped back. 'And there *is* a law against assaulting a member of his family. You talk about bad names. What do you think the CPS would make of someone with your previous, if Nolan's stepfather decides to press charges?'

Kieran coloured and stared down at his clenched fists, saying nothing.

'Just do yourself a favour, will you?' Whitelaw softened his tone. 'Go easy. Leave the job of finding Danny Nolan to us, OK?'

He watched Kieran stride off towards the gate without

another word, asked himself what were the odds on having his advice heeded, and was glad he wasn't a betting man.

As Whitelaw pulled up outside the address Kieran had given him, the evening sun was still strong, the breeze light; which was more than could be said for the bacon sandwich he had snatched before leaving the station. It rested greasily on his stomach, heavy as a cricket ball, adding to his headache-induced queasiness.

Nothing about the Seamen's Rest seemed destined to improve things. The overweight charmer in the string vest who described himself as the concierge confirmed that Nolan had shot in as if the hounds of hell were after him some time after nine the previous Friday, then out again a few minutes later carrying a holdall, and hadn't been back since. Wheezing, the man lumbered up the stairs ahead of Whitelaw, unlocked a door on the top floor, and stood aside.

Home, sweet home, Whitelaw thought. Boasting neither curtains nor carpets, the room contained a sagging armchair, the moquette cover of which was so greasy and worn, its original colour was indiscernible. The remaining furniture comprised a single bed covered in a couple of threadbare grey blankets, and a flimsy plywood coffee table. Apart from a poster above the bed advertising the Memorial Gala, the bedsit bore no trace of its former occupant.

'I knew the little bastard was trouble,' String Vest muttered, as he locked the door again. 'There's been some dodgy-looking character turning up all hours, the last couple of weeks. Drugs, is it?'

Whitelaw stepped backwards just in time to avoid a gob of phlegm landing on his shoe. 'Anyone turned up since Nolan left?' he asked. Kieran Henshall again, he realised with some irritation as the man elaborated. What did the young idiot think he was doing? Setting up a private detective agency? No other callers, String Vest asserted with a truculence defensive enough to make

Whitelaw think he was probably lying. He didn't pursue the subject. As he had no idea at this stage what or who he was looking for, there didn't seem much point. Massaging his temples, he set about the thankless task of interviewing the Seamen's Rest's other residents.

It beat him that so many people were in on such a lovely evening. Door after door revealed seemingly identical rooms, curtains drawn against the sun's slanting rays, TV screens flickering Aussie soaps, air thick with cigarette smoke, or worse. No one knew anything about Danny Nolan.

Well, there was a surprise.

After about a quarter of an hour, Whitelaw had had enough. He had interviewed everyone except the occupant of the room opposite Nolan's; predictably enough, the only person who might have seen something wasn't in. Whitelaw went back up to the top floor to knock on the door again, then glanced at his watch, half relieved when no one answered. Val got in early on Mondays; she often did a bit of baking . . . Suddenly, he felt desperate to be with her, to rid his nostrils of the Seamen's Rest and breathe instead the friendly, familiar smell of chalk and baking and lavender soap. Moving with more enthusiasm than he had all day, he made his way down to the ground floor.

The bottom of the stairs was blocked by a young woman who was attempting to bump a baby buggy up the steps one-handed, while balancing a screaming toddler under her other arm.

'Here, let me.' Whitelaw squeezed past her and took hold of the pushchair's footrest. Its small occupant slept on undisturbed as together they hauled it up the two flights of stairs. The woman went to the door he had just tried.

'Thanks. Hold him, will you?' As soon as Whitelaw, sweating from the exertion, lowered the pushchair to the ground, the woman thrust the toddler into his arms and rummaged in her pockets for her key. The child ceased to bellow. He stuck his thumb in his mouth and observed Whitelaw with solemn saucer eyes.

'You're good with kids.' The woman's wan face lit up briefly as she smiled at Whitelaw and took the little boy back from him. Whitelaw felt ridiculously pleased. He bent down to examine the sleeping baby, which despite the heat was wrapped in a grubby cot blanket. 'Little girl?' he hazarded.

The woman nodded. 'Chantal. And this is Bradley.' She ran her hand through the toddler's sticky hair.

Whitelaw straightened up, reluctant to get back to business. Such moments of uncomplicated friendliness were rare, in his profession. 'I wonder if I could ask you a few questions, Mrs . . . ?'

The woman's smile vanished, replaced by instant wariness, as he had known it would be.

Her relief was revealingly obvious when she realised that it was about her neighbour that Whitelaw had called. Fiddling a bit extra on her benefit, would be his guess. She pushed open the door and went in with Bradley, clearly expecting Whitelaw to follow, so he negotiated the buggy through the narrow doorway.

A rickety cot was jammed up against the single bed and a carrycot stood on the Formica-topped table amongst a clutter of disposable nappies and feeding bottles. A clothes horse crammed with greying babygros and tiny vests stood in front of a sash window that generations of paint had ensured would never open. Whitelaw tried and failed to imagine what kind of nightmare it must be to bring up a young family in such conditions.

She swept some toys from the chair, gestured for Whitelaw to sit down, and perched on the end of the bed. Bradley, thumb still in mouth, observed him from the safety of her lap.

'So,' she said. 'What're you after Danny for?'

'Just routine enquiries.'

'Oh yeah?' She gave a derisive laugh.

Looked at more closely, she couldn't be more than early twenties, although at first sight Whitelaw had taken her for at least ten years older. With a bit more flesh on her bones, she could be quite pretty, he decided. He wondered what kind of life she'd led that had ended her up in this dump.

'You know Mr Nolan then, Miss . . . Mrs . . . ?' he asked, leaning forward to light the cigarette that she'd pulled from a crumpled packet on the bed.

'Sykes. Carlie Sykes.' She turned her face to blow the smoke away from Bradley. 'Why is it coppers always answer a question with another one? Yeah, I know him. He's done a runner, hasn't he? I thought I hadn't heard that bloody dog of his for a bit.'

'Any idea where he might have gone?' Whitelaw suspected she'd be unlikely to tell a copper if she did.

'Lost himself, if he's got any sense.' She exhaled, and looked at him through a curtain of smoke.

'What makes you say that?' Whitelaw tried not to sound too interested.

She shrugged. 'You're not the only one looking for him. Couple of blokes came round Friday night.'

'Together?'

She snorted. 'Why come round together, when they can disturb everyone twice?'

Whitelaw wasn't following. It must have shown.

'Chantal's teething. I'd been trying for hours to get her off and then this guy comes round banging and bawling . . . I really lost it. Shame, really, 'cos we don't get too many like him round here. A real looker, he was.' She broke off and flashed him a wry grin. 'Anyway, don't suppose you're interested in all that.'

'Looker?' Whitelaw repeated, irked but unsurprised to receive a further description of Kieran Henshall. 'You mentioned two visitors,' he said.

She nodded, then looked down at Bradley, twisting a strand of his hair between thin, nicotined fingers. 'About midnight? I heard someone letting themself into Danny's room. Quietly.' She gave the ghost of a smile. 'No one's quiet around here. That's what made me take a look.'

'Did you see anyone?'

She shook her head. 'Danny's door was pushed to. But there was a car. Parked out front.'

'What kind of car?'

'Big. Black, I think. New-looking. Didn't take much notice.'

Whitelaw frowned. 'No idea of the make?'

She rolled her eyes. 'I don't watch *Top Gear* that often.'

The baby, still strapped into the buggy, had woken and was letting out a thin wail of protest. Stubbing out the cigarette, the girl slid Bradley onto the floor and went to fetch her. The toddler began to grizzle. Whitelaw wondered how she managed to keep sane when they were both on the go at once. It was one of the great sadnesses of Val's life that they had been unable to have kids, but Whitelaw wasn't at all sure he would have had the patience. Surreptitiously, he stuffed a tenner down the cushion of the chair. He'd be long gone before she found it. Then he picked up a battered toy car and pushed it towards Bradley, who stopped crying, stared at it for a moment then tentatively pushed it back.

Carlie sat down and without any apparent sign of embarrassment, hitched up her tee shirt and plugged the bawling baby to her breast.

Whitelaw tried to keep his eyes averted from the baby's implacably chomping jaw. Funny how breasts became so much more discomforting when they were being put to their proper use, he thought, shifting in his seat; he scarcely even noticed the page threes plastered all over the locker room back at the station.

'The bloke downstairs said someone had been calling on Danny recently,' he said to a point above Carlie's head.

'That fat scumbag?'

'Said he was round all hours,' Whitelaw persisted. 'Dodgy-looking, he reckoned.'

She let out a snort of laughter that jerked the baby's eyes open. 'That'd be Jace.'

'Jace?' Whitelaw leant forward.

'Jason. Jason Morrissey.' She didn't take her eyes from the baby.

It took Whitelaw a moment to digest what she was saying.

'He's a friend?' He remembered, just in time, to keep to the present tense. If she hadn't heard already what had happened to Jason, telling her was the surest way to make her clam up.

'I know him. Bump into him now and then.' One-handed, she lit another cigarette. 'Used to work the same patch before I had these two.' She looked challengingly at Whitelaw and blew out a plume of smoke before she went on with a sneer that didn't suit her, 'Good address for a retired tom, semen's rest, what d'you reckon?'

Bradley, bored with the car, toddled over to her and buried his head in her lap, leaving a snail's trail of snot across her skirt. Her expression softened. 'Jace is a bit of a dickhead, but he's been good to me. Took care of me when I was expecting, know what I mean? He'd make a lovely dad, if he wasn't bent as a five-bob note. Often drops me a few quid to get the kids something.'

The baby had fallen asleep, its head lolling in the crook of Carlie's arm, its rosebud mouth a puckered, milky O.

'She always does this.' Carlie jiggled a nipple against the baby's lips, which immediately clamped shut. 'As soon as I put her down, she'll start yelling again.'

Whitelaw was mortified to realise that he was blushing. With relief, he watched her pull down her tee shirt and lie the baby in the carrycot. 'Any idea what he was seeing Danny about?' he asked.

'Jace?' She straightened up. 'Isn't seeing him, is he? Danny wasn't having any of it.'

'Any of what?'

'How should I know?' she said, too sharply.

'The bloke downstairs seemed to think it might have been drugs,' Whitelaw pressed.

'Well it wasn't,' she snapped. 'I'd kill anyone bringing that shit near my kids. What's Danny supposed to have done, anyway?'

More than nick a few trinkets, that was for sure, Whitelaw told himself silently. 'At this stage . . .' he began, then stopped. Carlie Sykes was too streetwise to be fobbed off with police-speak. 'I don't know yet. That's what I'm trying to find out.'

She looked at him hard, then sat down heavily on the end of the bed, scooping Bradley into her arms. 'Shit. What's going on?'

She looked very, very young.

'Listen, love,' Whitelaw said gently, handing her a full packet of cigarettes. 'About Jace . . .'

He couldn't get Carlie out of his mind, as he drove home. He'd said merely that Jason had been killed in a car crash, no more. He told himself that he didn't want the full story leaked to the press, but he knew he couldn't have brought himself to tell her anyway. She'd hardly flinched; the barest shrug of her thin shoulders as she'd tightened her face into a mask of blank indifference. Too much pain in her life already was what the mask said. The only give away had been her trembling fingers, as she stroked her son's tousled head.

Remembering the snarl-up of road works at the top of the High Street, Whitelaw decided to cut through the university campus, a route he seldom took. The wide, leafy avenues were, by that stage of the day, nearly emptied of traffic; not too many lectures in progress at getting on for six thirty, he guessed. A more leisurely pace of life. He wound down the car windows and tried, for a few brief moments, to empty his mind and relax. Birds trilled above the muted thud of rock music that drifted from the open windows of one of the halls of residence. The steady 'plop' of ball on racquet came from the tennis courts beyond. Knots of sunbathers lay sprawled on the neat lawns in front of the Student Union building as he passed it; reading, drinking beer, chilling out.

They were all about the same age as Carlie Sykes.

Chapter Eleven

'Simon, I'm going to have to go.' Flora clamped her hand to her ear and strained to catch her father's response over Deefer's frantic barking. She aimed a kick at the animal's flank, but he side-stepped her with a warning snarl, and started barking again. 'Listen, I'll ring you back.'

She put the phone down, shrieked, 'Shut up, you bloody moron,' at the dog, and retreated to the kitchen. Yanking open the fridge, she poured herself a very large glass of wine, thus adding guilt at drinking on a Monday, which was supposed to be strictly alcohol free, to the day's growing list of disasters.

It had started after lunch. No, she corrected herself, it had started before lunch, when Greg rang. Unburdening herself so comprehensively to him had made her feel disloyal to Kieran. So that when Henry Denstone had called her into his office after lunch to interrogate her as to Danny Nolan's whereabouts, and had made a sarcastic comment about Kieran's work at St Saviour's, she had risen to the bait with a lack of restraint unlikely to improve her career prospects. She had followed that up by telling Thelma Lightowler to mind her own damned business when the woman had quizzed her about Greg's call; arguably an even worse career move. Then she had rounded the afternoon off by realising that she had accidentally shredded the entire pile of applications for the switchboard appointment.

Home time had provided no improvement to the working

day. She had missed one bus, the second was full, the third fifteen minutes behind schedule. When she finally accomplished the crowded, sweaty, ill-tempered trip home, she discovered that Deefer had not only urinated all over the kitchen floor, but had also helped himself to the chicken breasts she had left out to defrost for dinner. She had been in the process of mopping the floor and cursing Kieran for forgetting to call in on his way back from Ripley Grange to let the dog out as he had promised he would, when Simon had rung to ask how the gala had gone. She had been so short with him that she'd had to ring back to apologise, and had ended up inviting him to come to stay.

On top of which, she was going to have to break the news of Danny's exploits to Kieran when he did finally put in an appearance.

As if on cue, she heard the front door close, and realised that it must have been his key in the lock that had set the dog off. The barking turned immediately into piercing yelps of welcome; faced with Danny's departure, Deefer seemed to have transferred his affections with remarkable speed and pragmatism.

'In the kitchen,' she yelled over the racket.

Kieran came in, the dog leaping up nearly head-high behind him until he turned and told it, with uncharacteristic sharpness, to get down.

He looked done in, Flora thought, a wave of anxiety sweeping away her other irritations as he dumped his jacket down on the cluttered worktop. He could hardly have slept the previous night. His nightmare, not long after they had gone to bed, had woken them both; after that, each time she had briefly come round, he had been wide awake beside her. The whole business was becoming an obsession with him, and finding the dog had only made him worse. He was convinced beyond any rational argument that Danny would not have gone away and left it behind. Therefore Danny had come to some harm. For which, in some obscure way impossible for Flora to fathom, he held himself responsible. It was rubbish. But one look at the dark shadows under his eyes revealed just how much, rubbish or not, Danny's disappearance was getting to him. Perhaps, Flora told herself with more hope than belief, once he heard about the theft he would finally see sense and recognise Danny Nolan for what he was: trouble.

Without asking if he wanted one, she poured him a glass of wine and handed it to him. Then she said, 'I tried to get hold of you at Ripley Grange this morning. They said you'd left early.'

She knew him too well not to recognise the defensiveness in his tone as he answered, 'There were a couple of hostels I thought I'd try . . .'

She sighed. The last thing she wanted was for it to become an issue between the two of them. 'Greg Farrell rang. There was a burglary at Oultonshaw—'

'The coppers told me.' He downed the glass. 'Thought you were coming to St Saviour's to give me a hand?'

Her first reaction was to apologise. She *had* said she would help him sort out the scenery when it was delivered back from Oultonshaw Manor. She had had such a foul day it had simply slipped her mind.

Her second reaction, when she thought of just how foul the day had been, was to slap in a counterclaim. 'The dog had peed all over the place by the time I got back. You were supposed to let him out.'

Kieran rubbed a hand wearily across his face. 'Yeah, sorry.' He patted the Deefer's head absently. 'Don't worry, I'll clean it up.'

'I already have,' she said irritably. 'Let's face it, Kieran – Danny stole Greg's stuff. That's why he's disappeared. So for goodness' sake stop worrying about him. If anyone's going to find him, it'll be the police.'

Kieran shook his head. 'He'd never have abandoned Deefer.'

Flora could feel her temper rising. How could anyone so bright also be so obstinately stupid? Trying to sound calmer than she felt, she said, 'Think about it. Danny would have been far too conspicuous if he'd tried to hitch a lift or whatever with Deefer in tow.' She attempted a smile. 'He's hardly a dog you wouldn't notice, is he?'

'Don't you think it's peculiar that he was found around here?' It was as if she hadn't spoken. 'I'd left our address, remember. What if Danny was coming round to see me, ask for my help, and—'

'Oh, for God's sake . . .' They'd covered this ground before. They'd covered every inch of every conceivable ground a hundred times, and she had had enough.

'He'd never have left him injured.' Kieran looked down at the dog. 'You don't understand. Deefer's all he's got.'

'Stop telling me I don't understand,' she snapped. 'Just open your eyes, Kieran. Stop fooling yourself that Danny's one of the Babes in the bloody Wood, because he isn't. He saw you coming.' She glared at Deefer, who was up on his hind legs sniffing the plate from which he had liberated the chicken. The surface cut to his head had hardly been life-threatening. It certainly didn't seem to have impaired his appetite. 'Same as that damned dog saw you coming. If he's going to stay here, you're going to have to get something sorted.'

'Like what?'

'Like someone to let the bloody thing out, for a start, if you can't be bothered,' she shouted. 'Ask Batty Norah. She was the one who landed him on us in the first place.'

They both had hot tempers, and Flora, expecting him to shout back, already had her next prong of attack lined up; she hadn't yet told him there was no dinner.

'All Norah did was tell me where Deefer was. Kieran's voice was infuriatingly reasonable as he picked up his jacket and turned towards the door. 'It was theft, anyway. Greg Farrell's stuff. Theft, not burglary. There's a difference.'

She would very much have liked to slap him. 'If you want to try your hand at being a defence lawyer, go and bloody well train to be one. At least you'd be earning a decent living.'

He turned back; looked at her properly for the first time since he'd come in. 'So that's what this is really about, is it?' he said quietly.

'No.' She had wanted to unsay the words before they were out of her mouth, but she wasn't going to apologise for them. 'You know perfectly well it isn't, so you needn't try to—'

'I'm going to have a shower.'

She followed him out into the hall, the frustrations of the day boiling up in her as she yelled, 'Don't you bloody dare walk off when I'm—'

Again, he turned back. He didn't raise his voice. Instead, he repeated quietly, 'I'm going to get changed. We'll talk later.'

Normally, he sang in the shower. All she could hear was the creak of the floorboards, a drawer being opened and shut again, then water gurgling in the pipes. Kieran in a temper she could cope with; she quite enjoyed a good row to clear the air every now and then, after the ultra-civilised restraint of her upbringing.

Kieran quiet meant things were serious.

Deefer was scratching at the door. She bundled him out before he disgraced himself again, then scanned the cupboards, wondering what they could eat. She was tipping baked beans into a pan when the phone rang again. She considered leaving it; Simon had sounded so delighted at the prospect of seeing her that it was probably him to say he'd got his ticket booked.

'Cow,' she muttered ill-temperedly to herself as she threw the can into the bin and went through into the hall.

'Is Kieran there?'

She recognised the gruff mutter instantly. 'Danny! Where the hell have you been?'

'The money'll run out soon. Is he there?'

'Where are you?'

A pause. 'London. Tell him I'm OK, yeah?' Another pause. 'Say I'm sorry, and that.'

'Sorry?' He'd left them in the lurch, driven Kieran half out of his mind with worry, not to mention the small matter of the theft, and he thought he could stuff ten pence in a call box and make everything OK. 'I should bloody well think you are sorry, you selfish—'

The receiver was snatched from her hand. Kieran shouted, 'Danny? Is that you, mate?' as the phone went dead.

He stood, naked and dripping wet, staring into the mouth-piece as if he expected Danny to appear like a genie from a bottle. In any other circumstances, it would have been funny. But there was no humour in his expression as he raised his eyes and said, 'Why didn't you shout me?'

'He was only on the phone two minutes.'

'Did you ask where he was ringing from?'

'London. Now will you believe—'

'Did he sound OK?'

'Of course he sounded OK.' She could feel her mouth twisting into a sneer as she added, 'He said to say sorry.'

Kieran didn't rise to the bait. He ran his hand through his wet hair, his face creased into a frown of concentration. 'What else did he say?'

'What else were you expecting him to say? That he's donating all proceeds from the burglary – sorry, theft – to the Memorial Fund?'

'He didn't mention Deefer?'

Flora shut her eyes. 'Oh, for Christ's sake.'

'He didn't ask about him at all?'

'Get real, Kieran.'

He sat on the bottom step, his head in his hands. He looked so beaten, sitting there, naked, that her heart contracted with pity for him; for the funny, passionate, strong, vulnerable, confident, insecure bundle of contradictions that was Kieran Henshall, the person she loved more than anyone else in the world. 'Listen.' She reached out to touch his hair. 'If you're that worried, go and see Ray Whitelaw. Get Danny registered as a missing person.'

He ducked his head away from her, then stood up. 'And you're telling *me* to get real?'

She realised she wasn't angry any more, just worn out. Kieran was halfway up the stairs when she said, 'I think I might go and stay with Simon for a few days. I've got some holiday left over.'

He turned to face her. Flora felt as though she were looking at him through the wrong end of a telescope; the couple of metres between them seemed to stretch miles.

'I ought to see him. It's his birthday on Thursday, and it's ages since I . . .' She was trying to reach him, bring him back.

He raised his shoulders slightly, his eyes not quite managing to mirror the indifference of the shrug. 'Yeah. Why not?'

'Just for a few days,' she said quickly. 'He gets lonely, down there.'

Kieran nodded, looking away from her. 'Whatever.' Then he turned his back and went on up the stairs.

Chapter Twelve

With Flora's departure, the routine of Kieran's world seemed abruptly to collapse. It was approaching the end of term, and his work at St Saviour's was finished until the autumn. The Education Department at Ripley Grange was similarly slowing down for the summer. Kieran had been looking forward to the break, had ordered a stack of books from the library, planned to get down to writing a proper CV to send off to the list of theatrical agents he had put together. But somehow, with Flora away, none of it seemed worthwhile.

It was beginning, as somewhere in the back of his mind, he had always known it would. Flora was leaving him. If not now, soon. 'Why would she do anything else?' the poisonous, insidious voice inside his head whispered to him.

He couldn't face the prospect of sleeping in the double bed, partly because it made the missing of Flora sharper than ever, partly for fear of waking from the ever more frequent nightmares to find himself alone. Instead, he catnapped on the sofa in the front room, his head on the nightdress she had left under the pillow. The slight, flowery scent of her got fainter as the days went past.

He spent more and more time out of the house. His quest to find Danny was becoming his only focus; as if by doing so he could, in some obscure way, find himself as well. He stood for hours, motionless, outside the bedsit, or staring up at Danny's mother's flat in Alpha House. Each time he moved from one sentry post to the other, he was haunted by the thought that as soon as he had gone, Danny might appear. Unable to sleep, he would go into the town centre, moving stealthily from one shop doorway to the next as he tried to glimpse the faces inside the tattered sleeping bags, knowing, even as he did so, that with the police after him, Blackport was the last place Danny was likely to be.

Kieran wasn't sure, with hindsight, when he first noticed the Volvo T5R. Each time he went outside, it was parked down the street, its expensive, low-slung body and tinted windows strangely out of place against the shabby houses. Once, as he came away from his vigil outside the Seamen's Rest, he was sure he saw the car disappearing around a corner ahead of him. A couple of times when he was driving, he glanced in the rear-view mirror, and there it was again.

Lack of sleep, he knew, was making him jumpy. He had already begun to sense hostile eyes staring back at him from every window. He imagined he could hear furtive footsteps behind him as he paced the midnight streets. He was terrified he was losing his grip. Everyone, everything, seemed to be mocking him.

Flora had called him, once. Desperation had rendered him inarticulate; he could hear how churlish and offhand he sounded. She had put the phone down after a couple of minutes, and hadn't rung again since. He longed to call her back, hear the warm voice that had been his anchor for so long, but he was afraid that he would only make things worse between them.

She had been gone for only three days – though it seemed like months – when Greg Farrell rang on the Friday afternoon, wanting to invite them both out to dinner the following week. Kieran tried to sound enthusiastic, telling himself that Greg could not have known that Flora was away; that it was only his own exhausted brain that imagined mockery behind the other man's easy laughter when he said that she had gone to see her father.

At least the call gave him an excuse to ring her. It took him ten minutes to summon up the courage to pick up the phone, only to be told by Simon's cultured, apologetic voice that Flora was out. Were things really so bad that she was trying to avoid him, Kieran wondered, as he left his message.

It was late afternoon. The shops on the corner were shutting, the street quiet. He paused by the door, glanced up and down the street, but there was no sign of the car; the space that it had occupied earlier in the day was empty.

Kieran walked as far as the park and sat on a bench, watching a group of squealing children playing on the swings and slides, while Deefer raced around, nose to the ground, tracking smells. A small girl came and sat down on the bench, smiling shyly as she said hello and asked Kieran the dog's name. Absently, Kieran smiled back. The child repeated her question, but before he could respond, her mother called over, sharply summoning her back and glaring at Kieran with unconcealed hostility. With a nod of acknowledgement, he whistled Deefer to heel and left, feeling lonelier than ever.

Retracing his steps, he passed a phone box outside the post office at the top of Sephton Street. He paused, searching his pockets for loose change, suddenly overwhelmed by the desire to hear Flora's voice.

He heard the car before he saw it; registered that it was going far too fast. He took an involuntary step back as he looked up and saw the now-familiar gleaming shape speeding up the deserted street, and held his breath, pressing himself against the metal security door of the closed post office as he waited for it to pass. This was paranoia, he told his hammering heart. It was just a car. Maybe one of the neighbours had won the lottery, or something. But as it neared him, it swerved suddenly sideways, the low sun reflected dazzlingly off the tinted windscreen as the car came towards him. Kieran stood mesmerised, watching in fascinated horror as if he were viewing a sequence of film, frame by inevitable frame. The universe seemed, for a moment, to have slowed. Then, after what could in reality have been no more than a split second, Deefer took off with a startled yelp, yanking Kieran's arm, on the other end of the lead, nearly out of its socket, and jerking him out of the car's path.

The car clipped the metal post at the side of the security door where, an instant before, Kieran had been standing, swerved violently as it bounced off the kerb, then accelerated away. His handful of loose change lay scattered across the pavement. He watched as a ten-pence piece rolled lazily into the gutter.

It wasn't until the car was out of sight that he began to shake.

Whatever else Danny Nolan might or might not have done, he had not killed Jason Morrissey. Or Sunil Doshai either, for that matter.

The pathologist's report estimated that in each murder, the considerable force used to inflict the injuries put the perpetrator at over six feet tall, and powerfully built. Not sufficient to confirm conclusively that they were looking for the same man for both crimes, the pathologist, never one to commit himself, had added. But more than enough to remove Nolan from the frame, as the description in Medlock's report on the Denstone theft put Kieran's missing protégé at no more than five feet seven and of slight build.

A week's work had failed to throw up anything new to connect Danny Nolan to the murder victims, other than the fact that all had spent part of their childhood in care. Which was hardly an unusual occurrence amongst young offenders, Whitelaw told himself as he scanned the sorry chronology of failed foster placements that Millie D'Sousa had extracted from Nolan's case notes.

'No help, then?' Millie took the cigarette he offered and leaned across the desk so that he could light it.

It was Friday evening. She and Val were meeting for a drink before going on to the cinema. No trouble to drop the notes in on the way, she'd said. Whitelaw knew she was reluctant to trust confidential material to fax or post, and he admired her for it. But it looked as if her detour had been a waste of time. He dragged on his cigarette, took a final look at the notes, then passed them back to her. 'Thanks all the same.' He massaged the bridge of his nose. Ten days since Jason's death, almost a week since Sunil's, and so far the investigation was going nowhere. 'I hate murder inquiries when they're at this stage,' he said.

Millie flicked ash, nodded sympathetically, but made no comment.

'Press at your heels, powers that be baying for a result, and all you've got is a bunch of loose ends. Some investigations are dead easy: a bloke has a skinful and takes a meat cleaver to his wife; a woman has one too many sleepless nights with a screaming toddler . . .' His mind strayed back momentarily to Carlie Sykes. '. . . It's simple when it's that personal. The rest — it's a case of searching for whatever it is that's going to tie all your loose ends in together. One piece of evidence that'll make all the others fall into place. Trouble is, it can be a long time coming. And until it does, you're left feeling the only choice you've got is between treading water and drowning.'

He stopped abruptly. He wasn't given to such lengthy speeches. There was something about Millie's silence that always invited confidences. A trick of the trade, he supposed. But the fact remained, he *did* feel as if he might be drowning on this one. There was something big going on, of that he was sure. There were signs that Sunil had been tortured before he died — Whitelaw averted his mind from the horrific details in the report — and the very lack of fingerprints, or any other forensic evidence around the apartment, suggested that the place had, as he had suspected, been professionally searched. For what? The only lead he'd had, or had *hoped* he'd had, was Danny Nolan. And that seemed to be going nowhere.

Whitelaw had decided to go public with the information that Jason and Sunil's deaths were linked, were both being treated as murder, in the hope that the press coverage might turn up something. Lightowler had brought in a copy of the *Echo* earlier. Sid Barker had made the most of what he'd been given. 'Rent Boys Butchered', the front page headline trumpeted. 'Police Appeal for Information in Double Vice Slayings.'

Another case of wait and see.

Millie picked up the Denstone Park photograph. 'You still think this is relevant?' she asked.

'The mystery Mario 14?' Whitelaw sighed. 'God knows.' He stared at the photograph upside down as Millie placed it back on the desk. He'd wanted to get that publicised too, certain that they would have achieved a damned sight more support if the public had been reminded that Jason had once been as fresh-faced a teenager as any of their own sons. No one, he suspected, was going to lose too much sleep over the fate of a couple of transvestite rent boys.

Lambert, of course, wouldn't have any of it when Whitelaw had brought up the photograph at the briefing session. Medlock hadn't helped, echoing Lambert's own view that it was 'inad-visable' to risk anyone recognising Denstone Park at such an early stage of the investigation. At the time, Whitelaw had thought Medlock was just creeping. But then he'd started thinking that maybe young Neville might have a more personal agenda. Rumour had it he would be bringing Penelope Denstone to Lambert's summer social. Whitelaw asked himself whether the devious bastard was really ambitious enough to compromise his duty as a police officer for the sake of his social climbing.

It hadn't been a hard question to answer.

He shook his head and gave Millie a wan smile. 'If it hadn't been for the bloody Denstone name, we'd probably have handed the whole lot over to Drugs or Vice a week ago. PR, eh? The curse of modern civilisation.'

'Don't I know it?' Millie snorted.

Lightowler stuck his head round the door. 'Someone to see you, Guv,' he announced. 'Down at the front desk. Are you here?'

'Depends who it is.' Whitelaw grunted, deciding that he

would be wasting his breath by having yet another go at Lightowler for not knocking.

'Looks a bit rough.' The other man grinned. 'Reckons he's a friend of yours.'

'Friend?'

'Bit of a nutter, if you ask me. Probably just come back for a rant.'

'What're you on about?' Whitelaw asked irritably.

'We had him in the other night. Suspected TWOC. Record as long as your arm, so it seemed a good bet. Turned out it was his own vehicle, but—'

'Send him up,' Whitelaw cut him short. 'And he *is* a friend of mine,' he shouted after the constable. 'So make sure you bloody well treat him accordingly.' He stubbed out his cigarette and muttered, 'Prat.'

It was fortunate that he was unable to see the gesture that Lightowler made as he headed back down to the front desk.

Millie stood up. 'I'd better . . .'

'Can you just spare a couple more minutes?' Whitelaw frowned. 'We had a bit of a run-in last time we met. It might help, having you here. Would you mind?'

As they waited for him to be brought up, Whitelaw filled her in on the last conversation he'd had with Kieran Henshall.

'Sounds like you're not the only copper he's had a run-in with in his time,' Millie commented.

'True,' Whitelaw agreed ruefully. 'Trouble is, he's got too personally involved with this kid's disappearance for his own good. There's already been an allegation of assault against him from Nolan's stepfather.'

'Mick McTeer? I've met that man.' Millie's tone was eloquent. She paused, not usually given to judgemental comments about her clients. 'Did you take the allegation seriously?'

Whitelaw glanced towards the door. He could hear two sets of approaching footsteps. He lowered his voice as Lightowler, for once in his life, knocked. 'I'd take it a bloody sight less seriously if Kieran Henshall hadn't done time when he was a lad for stabbing his own mother's boyfriend to death.'

Whitelaw wasn't sure, as Lightowler entered the room, whether the shock on Millie's face resulted from the revelation, or from the demeanour of its subject. Kieran didn't look 'a bit rough', he looked bloody terrible; as if he hadn't slept in the days since Whitelaw had seen him last. His face was drawn, the skin under his eyes so dark it looked bruised. He hadn't shaved, and from the look of his clothes, any sleep he had managed had been taken on a park bench. Whitelaw had realised Nolan's disappearance was getting to Kieran; he hadn't realised how much. He wondered whether to shake the younger man's hand; extended an arm; at the last minute converted the movement to gesture the chair next to Millie's.

Kieran remained standing, his expression suggesting that whatever the conversation was to be about, it wasn't going to involve social niceties. If he had noticed Millie at all, he didn't acknowledge her.

'Something's happened to Danny,' he said without preamble. 'I know it has.'

Keen as he was to know anything new about Nolan's whereabouts, Whitelaw found himself concentrating as much on the fixed intensity of Kieran's face, the tense, jerky movements of his body, as on the urgent, garbled account he was giving them of Nolan's phone call. He forced himself to focus on what was being said. The fact that the call had come from London made sense. They had already had notification from Greg Farrell's bank that someone had tried unsuccessfully to use the stolen cash card in a hole in the wall near King's Cross station earlier in the week.

'You haven't heard from him since?' Whitelaw asked. He glanced at Millie, who had been observing Kieran carefully.

She caught Whitelaw's eye, then picking up on what appeared to be the central thrust of Kieran's argument, said quietly, 'What makes you so certain Danny would worry about his dog?'

She nodded gravely, as Kieran explained.

Whitelaw nodded too; having seen Nolan's family, he could well see how a dog could come to be the lad's only source of affection. He leant back in his chair. 'Let me get this straight. You think someone's after Danny?'

Talking to Millie, Kieran had seemed more relaxed; at Whitelaw's intervention, he tensed again. He paused, eyeing Whitelaw as if trying to weigh up whether it was worth saying more. Then he said slowly, 'I think someone might be after me, as well.'

Whitelaw and Millie exchanged glances again. Then Whitelaw said evenly, 'What makes you think that, son?'

Kieran hesitated. Then, gathering speed as he went on, he told them about the car. 'Don't you see?' he said urgently, when Whitelaw, unsure how to respond, said nothing. 'Whoever's after Danny saw the note I left for him. That's how they know where I live.'

'Right.' Whitelaw didn't ask the obvious questions; i.e., who 'they' might be, and what earthly reason 'they' could have for trying to kill Kieran. Instead, he said, 'And this car . . . did you get the number?'

'W reg.' Kieran shook his head in exasperation. To himself, rather than to Whitelaw, he muttered, 'It all happened so fast. I should have taken it earlier, when it was following me.'

'Following you,' Whitelaw echoed, his heart sinking.

'Everywhere I go, it's there. But it wasn't until it drove at me that I realised . . .' Kieran stopped, took a deep breath; was clearly making an effort to control himself. In a calmer voice, he went on, 'It was a Volvo T5R. Black. Tinted windows.'

Whitelaw frowned. The description rang a bell, but he couldn't for the life of him think from where. 'Any witnesses?' he asked.

Again, Kieran shook his head.

'Not even Flora?' Whitelaw asked gingerly, his heart sinking still further when Kieran looked down and said in a low voice that she'd gone away for a few days.

The poor bloke was falling apart in front of their eyes.

Whitelaw decided to change direction. 'So this phone call . . .' He chose his words carefully. 'You're saying – what? That it *wasn't* Danny?' He tried and failed to keep his scepticism to himself.

'I knew this was a waste of time.' Kieran turned towards the door.

'No,' Whitelaw sighed. 'Sit down, son. Please.'

Millie, he realised, was watching him impassively. He felt obscurely as if he were being assessed; although for what, he was unsure. He was relieved when Kieran hesitated, turned back and sat down next to Millie. 'Listen,' he leant forwards across the desk, 'I'm as keen to get to the bottom of this as you are. I just think maybe you're letting this Danny Nolan business get . . .'

Kieran wasn't listening. He had picked up the photograph. 'Who's that?' he asked.

Whitelaw realised he was pointing at Jason Morrissey.

Kieran looked up. 'Who's the kid with Danny?

Chapter Thirteen

Lambert was not well pleased at being disturbed at home on a Friday evening. He was dressed in shorts and a polo shirt, so well-pressed and immaculate that he contrived to give the impression of still being in uniform.

'It hadn't occurred to you that Nolan might be the other boy?' he snapped when, grudgingly, he had shown Whitelaw into the dining room.

'No, sir.' Whitelaw glanced out at the equally well-pressed and immaculate garden beyond the dining-room window, and pondered on what a wonderful thing hindsight was. It had never dawned on him for a single moment that Danny Nolan was black. The descriptions from Oultonshaw Manor had detailed height, build, hair and eye colour. Presumably Medlock had deemed it politically incorrect to ask about the colour of the boy's skin. Not that he could hold Medlock entirely responsible, much as he would have liked to; he hadn't asked the question either. He'd seen that Nolan's mother was white, and had simply jumped to the wrong conclusion.

'So where in God's name does this "Mario" come in?' Lambert demanded irritably.

'I don't know, sir.' Whitelaw allowed a moment's respectful silence, before he said doggedly, 'That's one reason why we need to publicise the photograph.' He had made the request by telephone as soon as Kieran and Millie had left. Lambert had refused.

Which was why Whitelaw had turned up on his superintendent's doorstep to make the request again.

Lambert exhaled sharply. 'I repeat my earlier question, Inspector. To what purpose? I have no intention of dragging the Denstone name through the papers until you can tell me . . .'

'Morrissey and Nolan are photographed in front of the Denstones' *old* house. Ten or so years later, just as the place is to be rebuilt, Morrissey is murdered. And Nolan disappears following a visit to the Denstones' *new* house. Now, I'm not sure yet just what the link is—'

'Precisely my point!' Lambert snapped. 'You come here with vague talk of some "scam" . . .' the word was heavy with sarcasm, 'that Morrissey may or may not have had in mind. Some liaison with Nolan that may or may not have taken place . . . Correct me if I have this wrong, Inspector.'

'All I'm saying—'

'For God's sake, man! You can't even say with any certainty that the damned photograph didn't simply fall out of Doshai's pocket accidentally! And as for the assertion that Nolan has "disappeared" – it's hardly bloody surprising he disappeared in view of what he'd been up to on the evening in question, is it? Or had you forgotten the slight matter of the theft?'

Whitelaw could feel his headache coming on again. He hated to admit that, to a large extent, what Lambert said was true. Nolan's previous consisted of shoplifting, TWOCs, and a number of domestic burglaries – enough to have put him inside, but there was nothing on it to suggest he was caught up in anything more sinister. No drugs convictions; nothing for vice.

It was like one of those puzzles in a kids' comic: trace the maze, and every time you came to a dead end. Only what Whitelaw came kept coming up with was Denstone Park.

'But you do agree that DS Medlock should come off the case, sir?' he asked, shifting to a topic which he hoped would be of less dispute.

Another sharp exhalation. 'If you consider it absolutely necessary.' Lambert was well aware of the long-standing animosity between Whitelaw and Medlock. His expression, as he glared at his inspector, made it clear where his sympathies lay, but they both knew that he couldn't afford to take the chance.

'I do.' Whitelaw held the other man's gaze. 'We can't risk contaminating the investigation by Medlock's personal involvement with Penelope Denstone. It's a matter of public perception, isn't it, sir?' he added, turning one of Lambert's more favoured phrases to his own advantage. 'And, for the same reason, I think it would be advisable for him to be moved into another office.'

Lambert glared at him, realising he was being outmanoeuvred. 'Don't you think you're being just a touch paranoid, Whitelaw?'

'With respect, sir, it strikes me we're into murky enough water in this investigation without muddying it further.'

'Very well.' Lambert walked across to the window. He gazed out at the military ranks of lobelia, salvia and begonia; the ornamental fish pond; the lawn already close-cropped in readiness for Sunday's summer social, as if hoping to transfer the same sense of order into the conversation he was having with his inspector. Then turning back to Whitelaw, he snapped, 'Well, it's simple, isn't it? We must find this Nolan. And find him fast.'

'Yes, sir.'

A teenage runaway. Probably somewhere around King's Cross. Only contact, a bloke not only hostile to the police, but also quite possibly in the throes of a nervous breakdown.

What, Whitelaw asked himself, could be simpler than that?

Flora sat on the end of St Mary's quay and watched the gigs come in. Every Friday evening during the holiday season the little rowing boats were raced against each other by local teams: fishermen and farmers, shop assistants and teachers. Some of the gigs were new, some well over a hundred years old. Each had its vociferous supporters. *Serica, Bonnet, Nor-Nour*; the tourists, milling on the quay or following in the flotilla of tripper boats, soon learnt the names and bellowed for their chosen team, before retiring to the packed bars of the Mermaid or the Atlantic to celebrate victory or drown their sorrows. There was a carnival atmosphere. Flora glanced at the crowds of laughing, tanned faces and asked herself what on earth she was doing there.

Kieran had taken her to the station, had kissed her, asked her to give Simon his regards. No row, no acrimony. Their politeness towards each other had terrified her. She had been missing him even before the train pulled out of the station, had almost jumped back out onto the platform, but he had already disappeared. She had rung him from Birmingham, where she had changed trains. There had been no reply. She hadn't managed to get hold of him until late the following night.

Her heart had leapt at the sound of the familiar Manchester accent, but somehow the words had come out wrong, so that when she told him how much she had wanted to talk to him the day before, it sounded like an accusation. He had apologised stiffly, but without explanation, for his absence. He hoped she would enjoy the break, he'd said, sounding equally as accusing. She wondered if he had felt as wretched as she did, when he rang off. The conversation had lasted for scarcely five minutes. They hadn't spoken since.

The last of the gigs came in. The crew slumped, exhausted, over their oars. The crowds began to drift off; to the pubs, or back with their tired and overexcited children to their holiday lets. Soon the quay was deserted. Flora stayed where she was, watching the sun set over the off-islands, streaking the sky a fiery red that promised another sunny day. Finally, wearily, she got to her feet and made her way back.

She went via the cliff path. The bustle of the little town was behind her in minutes. In Blackport, she might have felt nervous walking alone as dusk fell, eyes scanning every shadow, ears alerted for stealthy, following footsteps. Here, the only sounds were the lap of the waves, the mew of the gulls, the scuffle of scattering rabbits as she picked her way through the springy heather. She walked slowly, less lonely on the silent, deserted downs than on the crowded quay; less lonely than she knew she would be when she reached the farmhouse that she could never recall thinking of as home. Her mind went back to the previous evening and the expensive, restrained birthday dinner at the island's most exclusive hotel that had been her father's only way of telling her how pleased he was to be sharing the occasion with her.

She could tell from the light in Simon's study, when she got back, that he was still working. She let herself in through the kitchen. Mrs Menheniott, the housekeeper, had already gone. A note informed Flora that a chicken salad was prepared in the fridge; a tray set with a starched linen cloth and shining silver cutlery sat on the table. A wave of homesickness hit her, made her feel physically sick, as she thought of the cluttered little kitchen in Sephton Street, the mismatched assortment of plates and mugs, the orange stain on the wall where the meatballs had landed . . .

'Flora?' At the sound of her father's voice, she blinked hard and blew her nose.

Simon Castledine came slowly into the kitchen, breathing as heavily as if he had walked the steep cliff path to reach her, rather than the few yards from the next room. Each time she saw him, Flora was struck by how much older he seemed; how much frailer he had become, although she knew it was she who had changed, not he.

'Kieran rang.' Simon scanned her face, anxious to know what was happening, too polite to ask.

She filled the kettle, rearranged the cups and saucers on the tray, before asking lightly, 'Did he say what he wanted?'

'Something about an invitation . . .' He frowned. 'Grant? George?' His small lapses of memory irritated him intensely. 'Greg. Greg . . . Farrell.' He nodded, momentarily pleased. It was evident that it was a name he had never heard before.

'Did he say anything else?'

'We didn't speak for long.' The anxiety returned to Simon's eyes. 'He sounded . . . distracted. Will you ring him back, my dear?' He held her gaze. 'I think you should.'

It was the closest he had ever come to interfering. Flora knew how fond, in his own way, Simon had become to Kieran. She wished she could reassure him. She wished he were younger. Wished he were the sort of father she could have confided in; could have told that she was frightened . . .

Briefly, she squeezed his hand, felt it tense at the unexpected intimacy, and was overcome by another wave of homesickness.

She rang straight away. Before she lost her nerve.

Kieran answered at once.

'How's it going?' she asked, hating the banality of the question, when there was so much she wanted to say. It was as if some creeping emotional paralysis overcame her as soon as she heard his voice. Fleetingly, she wondered if she was more her father's daughter than she realised.

'OK. How was the gig race?' His voice was terse.

'Fine.' She swallowed. 'Listen, Kieran—'

'Greg Farrell phoned,' he interrupted, anxious to get on with the conversation, to avoid her questions. 'He's going to be up here next Monday. Something to do with some honorary degree he's been offered. He wants to take us out for dinner.'

'That's brilliant.' The response was automatic. A week ago, she would have been turning cartwheels.

'Yeah, brilliant,' he echoed. A pause, then he said carefully, 'Will you be here?'

'Do you want me to be?' A week ago she would not have thought the question possible.

She could hear him breathing. Could picture him, standing in the hallway, arm laced around the banister, one foot hooked behind the other knee, which was how he always stood when he was answering the phone. Could smell him; soap, the faint citrus smell of his shampoo, underlain by a sharper, muskier scent that filled her with intense longing.

'You know I do,' he replied at last.

She shut her eyes, imagining herself back there beside him, as if sheer force of will could vanish the hundreds of miles that separated them. 'I've missed you,' she said simply.

She heard the long, ragged breath he took before he answered. 'I've missed you too.'

'What are we like, the pair of us?' It was as if a giant bubble had burst inside her chest. She was grinning; could feel the stupid great smile spreading across her face as she made rapid mental calculations. 'I'll get a ticket sorted first thing in the morning. I shan't be able to get back tomorrow. You know what Saturdays in the summer are like. Oh God, it's so frustrating! No flights on Sunday . . . it's going to be Monday, isn't it? I'm counting the hours already.' She was laughing now. 'Why did we ever—'

'I love you, Flora,' he said softly.

'I love you too! Listen, I'll let you know as soon as I find out what time I'll be back. Will you be able to meet me from the station? I mean, it doesn't matter. I can get a bus if—'

'I'll be there.' Another pause. Then, so quietly that she could hardly hear him, 'Everything's going to be all right, isn't it?'

'Oh, sweetheart, of course it is. We'll talk. Properly this time. Hey, I'm so pleased for you about Greg! He must be really interested in you to get back in touch so soon. This could be just the break you need.' She knew she was beginning to babble; unnerved by the anxiety in Kieran's voice. 'It's brilliant! Really exciting.'

'I'll see you Monday, then.'

'Monday.' She wondered whether to ask about Danny. Decided against it. 'Take care of yourself, Kieran,' she added quickly, not quite knowing why, before she rang off.

Chapter Fourteen

Whitelaw had forgotten just how many there were. Hundreds and hundreds of them. He had gone through them before; everyone had, from time to time, when a kid turned up on the street, or in a raided squat, or begging in the shopping precinct or the railway station. A sad catalogue of broken homes, neglect, or sheer bloody-mindedness The Missing Persons file. And for every face in the file, every photograph registered by frantic parent or unsurprised care worker, how many other faces went unregistered? How many kids like Danny Nolan simply ceased to exist?

They had tried the obvious places first. A week's wages waited uncollected at Kost Kutter, where the manager spoke highly of Nolan's reliability. At his bank, the account remained untouched. If he had been involved in any criminal activity since his release from Ripley Grange, it hadn't been very lucrative; his statement showed regular weekly deposits of fifteen pounds, taken directly from his wages, and nothing more. A regular, if modest, saver. The picture Whitelaw was building didn't add up to what he had expected. Maybe Kieran Henshall had been right; maybe Nolan had genuinely been attempting to go straight.

So what had stopped him?

A check with the Benefits Agency had failed to show any record of Nolan signing on since his disappearance; not in his own name, at any rate. Whitelaw and his team, scaled up by the addition of three extra constables on Lambert's orders, had tried the coach and train stations and issued copies of Nolan's description to the local haulage firms; no one remembered anyone who might fit it buying a ticket or hitching a lift. But, more than a week after the disappearance, Whitelaw was all too aware that memories could already be cluttered by too many faces since.

Lambert had personally set up a link with the Met, ensuring, or so he reckoned, both confidentiality and efficiency. But whatever Lambert imagined, Whitelaw knew trying to find Nolan would be like looking for a needle in a haystack. The initial feedback that had been faxed through first thing that Monday morning suggested a blank had been drawn over the weekend in London. Centrepoint, the shelters and hostels around King's Cross and Piccadilly, the late-night cafés – the Met knew the places to look. All negative.

Danny Nolan, like so many others, had simply dropped off the face of the earth.

Whitelaw rubbed his eyes. He'd stared at so many mug shots, his vision was beginning to blur. Putting the faxes and the Missing Persons file aside, he went down to the canteen. He hovered over the steaming aluminium trays of bacon and sausage, hesitating for so long that a young uniform behind him in the queue coughed politely. Whitelaw turned around, glared, then moved along the counter and reluctantly picked up a salad roll and a bottle of mineral water.

He was on a diet.

'Since when?' the cashier laughed, when he went to pay.

'Since I tried to get into my best trousers for Lambert's do yesterday.' He tried not to look at the tray of bread pudding by the till, but he couldn't avoid the smell of cinnamon and sugar.

'I hate thin men.' The cashier, herself of more than ample proportions, winked at him.

'Go on then, you've talked me into it.' Whitelaw helped himself to the biggest slice on the tray.

Cyril Turner looked up from the sports page of his *Telegraph* as Whitelaw approached. He pushed aside the congealing remains of his sausage, egg and chips, and eyed but did not comment upon the contents of Whitelaw's tray. 'Missed a good game yesterday, by the look of things,' he said.

Whitelaw grunted. Lambert's summer social was pain enough in its own right; standing around with a glass of wine and a prawn vol-au-vent and making polite conversation with Lambert's wife about the begonias was not, in his estimation, the most desirable way to spend a precious afternoon off. Clashing, as it had done, with a one-day county match against Surrey, for which he could have got tickets, and which the home team had won by a single run, made it bloody intolerable.

'Young Fancy-Pants was on form,' Turner observed wryly.

The only person, apart from Lambert himself, who had seemed to enjoy the occasion was Medlock, who had turned up with Penelope Denstone in tow, looking as pleased with himself as if she'd been some Hollywood sex symbol. The poor girl had appeared completely mortified as Medlock paraded her around, but if he had been aware of her discomfort, he had chosen to ignore it.

Whitelaw shook his head, 'Brown-nosing Lambert, you mean?'

Turner turned down his mouth in disgusted recollection. 'I'm bloody grateful we'll both be long gone from the force by the time it's Medlock's summer socials, that's for sure.' He took a swig of his tea. 'I tell you something that did surprise me, though. Him and Terry Lightowler getting all chummy.'

Whitelaw had noticed. Lightowler had trailed Medlock and the Denstone girl all afternoon. 'Probably hoping to pick up some gossip for his mum,' he shrugged. 'Medlock reckons he's gay, you know.'

'Wouldn't be surprised.' Turner checked his watch. 'Better get back to it, I suppose. Want to read this and really cheer yourself up?' He pushed the paper across to Whitelaw, then murmured, 'Eh up. Here comes the blue-eyed boy now. Think we ought to curtsy?'

'Good do yesterday, I thought,' Medlock observed, sitting down, uninvited, opposite Whitelaw. 'Penelope thoroughly enjoyed herself.'

'That's all right, then.' Turner stood up, then paused, mid-stretch. 'Eh, your nose, son,' he said with an exaggerated display of concern.

'What about it?' Medlock looked up suspiciously and put a hand to his face.

'It looks very brown. What d'you reckon, Ray? He must have had it turned up to the sun yesterday.' Turner made a show of peering at it, then winked at Whitelaw. 'Or up somewhere, at any rate.'

A couple of uniforms at the next table looked across and sniggered as he sauntered off.

Medlock flushed. 'There's a young woman waiting to see you out in the front office,' he snapped at Whitelaw.

'I take it you asked what it was about?' Whitelaw, still grinning, decided to ignore the younger man's tone.

'I didn't think it was any of my concern any more.' Medlock had been pulled off the murder inquiries earlier that morning and he'd taken it badly; the more so after his efforts the previous day. He didn't realise that by flaunting his new girlfriend in front of not only Lambert but the entire station, he'd hammered the last nail into his own coffin, as far as the Morrissey/Doshai investigation was concerned.

Whitelaw almost felt sorry for him.

Almost.

'Superintendent Lambert's decision, not mine,' he said blandly. 'Reallocation of resources, I think it's called. Oh, by the way,' he added, 'you're moving in with the photocopier at the end of the corridor for the time being. Get your desk cleared, will you? Lightowler can have it for now.'

Medlock gave him a long look. 'Desk sergeant said could you make it snappy? Your visitor seems in a bit of a state.'

Whitelaw made himself swallow the rest of the bread pudding

before he moved, but the words had set off a small spark of anxiety. Once away from the canteen, his pace quickened as he made his way down to the front office. Why was it that Flora Castledine had sprung instantly into his mind?

He could hear a raised female voice as he slipped the catch on the heavy door that led into the public area at the front of the station. He could also hear the wail of a young baby.

Carlie Sykes was leaning across the counter, giving the sergeant some grief, the baby over one shoulder. Bradley had evidently been amusing himself by emptying the racks of information leaflets that lined the waiting area. His mouth was bulging with chocolate, and the screwed-up papers amongst which he sat were streaked with sticky brown dribble. The sergeant, a young chap recently transferred from the Dales and doing his first inner-city stint, was looking hassled.

'Half an hour I've been waiting to see you.' Carlie turned on Whitelaw as soon as she spotted him. She stabbed a finger at the sergeant. 'He told me to come back at eleven o'clock this morning.'

'The young lady came in asking for you yesterday, sir,' the sergeant murmured. 'I said you wouldn't be in until—'

'So I get here at eleven,' she interrupted. 'Which means I have to wake Chantal, pick Bradley up early from nursery . . . for what? So I can sit around here for half a fucking hour waiting for you to get off your fat arse.' Her face was white, stiff with a disproportionate rage that told Whitelaw that she had seen the *Echo*'s report of Jason Morrissey's murder.

'You'd better come up, love,' he said quietly, holding open the door.

He considered using one of the interview rooms, but decided the formality of the setting was unlikely to encourage Carlie to talk. Instead, he led the way to his office, stopping to pick up a Dictaphone on the way.

Medlock was sitting head to head with Lightowler over the computer.

'Thought I told you to get that desk cleared,' Whitelaw snapped.

'Just giving Terry a few tips about the software,' Medlock replied, not lifting his eyes from the screen.

'Not right now, you're not. I've got work to do, if you haven't.' Whitelaw beckoned Carlie into the room.

Medlock turned, then scanned Carlie and her grubby children with a look of undisguised scorn. 'Sorry. Didn't realise you had company.'

Whitelaw's fingers were itching. He felt Carlie tense beside him.

'Out. Now,' he hissed, blanking the screen as he turned the computer off at the mains.

Medlock gazed at him. 'You realise you've just wiped the file?' he said quietly.

'Stick with pencil and paper next time,' Whitelaw snarled. 'Now sod off, both of you.'

He waited until they had gone, then returned his attention to Carlie, who was standing in the middle of the room, arms folded defensively across her chest. He indicated a chair, and was relieved when she sat. Bradley immediately scrambled up onto the seat Medlock had just vacated and started fiddling with the keyboard, leaving a chocolatey trail of saliva across the desk.

'Get down from there!' She slapped the little boy's leg and yanked him, bawling, onto her lap.

'He's all right.' Whitelaw couldn't imagine from what he had seen of them both that she was in the habit of slapping the child. She was wound up as tight as a spring, her thin shoulders trembling as she hugged the sobbing Bradley to her with one arm, the other cradling the still-wailing baby. Whatever it was she'd come here to say, it was important. And whatever it was, they weren't going to get far over the top of that racket.

'Look,' Whitelaw said, sure, even as he asked, that she would never be prepared to let her kids out of her sight. 'Do you want me to get someone in to take care of the two of them for a few minutes? Then you can tell me what this is all about?'

To his amazement, Carlie nodded. Then, burying her face in Bradley's hair, she began to cry.

When a constable from the Child Protection Unit had been summoned, and the children were taken from the room, Whitelaw produced the Dictaphone and went to turn it on.

'Nothing formal.' Carlie was on her feet in a second. 'I'll deny all of it if you try to get me into court.'

'OK,' Whitelaw said evenly, only too aware that if he pushed her too hard, she would be out of the door and after the kids before he could blink. He moved his chair away from the table, leant back, and folded his arms. 'Take your time, Carlie. Tell me what it was you wanted to see me about.'

Hesitantly, she started. She had known Jason Morrissey on and off since she was a kid, she said. Whitelaw listened in silence, well able to imagine the intense, fractured relationship between them, their paths crossing and recrossing as they moved between foster placements and council children's homes; both desperate for a bit of security in their shifting worlds; each trying to pretend the friendship didn't matter.

They had both embarked on their careers as prostitutes young.

Criminally young.

'Jace liked the attention.' Carlie gave a tight smile. 'He must have been twelve or thirteen when he got started. Always was a show-off. Said they used to pay him to dress up as—'

Whitelaw sat forward. 'Who did, Carlie?'

Instant wariness. 'Just blokes.'

Learning from the technique that always had him telling Millie D'Sousa more than he'd meant to, Whitelaw said nothing.

After a moment, Carlie added in a low voice, 'At one of the places he was at.'

Keeping his tone neutral, Whitelaw asked, 'Did he say which place?'

Carlie shook her head quickly, then glanced up. 'I'd tell you if I knew.'

Whitelaw believed her. Too much to hope she was going to come out with those two, magic little words 'Denstone Park'. 'Do you think what happened there could have something to do with Jace's death?' he asked.

She was twisting a soggy ball of tissues between her fingers. 'He'd . . . He'd got some deal lined up,' she said at last. 'Blackmail.' Another quick glance at Whitelaw.

He nodded his encouragement.

'He reckoned he'd be able to make some serious cash if he could get this bloke –' She broke off, and looked nervously around the room. '– I wouldn't be telling you any of this if Jace wasn't dead. I don't want you thinking I'd grass up my mates.'

'I know that, Carlie. Anyway, Jason's partner had already told us . . .' Whitelaw realised he'd said the wrong thing before the words were out of his mouth.

'Yeah, and look what happened to him.' She jumped to her feet, pointing to the notes Whitelaw had begun to take, her voice rising in panic. 'I told you, I'm not signing anything. I've got to go. Where's my kids?' She looked around wildly. 'What have you done with my kids? I shouldn't be here.'

'You're here because you care about Jace.' Whitelaw didn't know how much more she had to tell him, but he couldn't let her slip through his fingers now. 'You care about what those perverts did to him.' Her hands dropped back down by her side as he added quietly, 'Now Sunil's dead as well, you're the only one who does care, aren't you?'

She sat down again. Stuffed the tissues up her sleeve. Took another cigarette from the packet Whitelaw had pushed across at the beginning of the interview. It took her three matches to light it.

'So what did he tell you about this deal?'

She shook her head. 'He was going to blow the lid on what had happened. Said he'd seen some stuff in the papers . . .'

'What stuff?' The Memorial Gala publicity would have been too late, Whitelaw realised regretfully; Jason was already dead by then.

'How should I know? Papers are full of it, aren't they? Abused kids.' She looked up, her face bitter. 'All those nice, respectable old blokes getting a stiffy from reading about it while they're having their toast and marmalade. Cheaper than a porn mag any day.' She shrugged. ''Spect it got him thinking. Anyway, all he told me was he knew someone who would be prepared to pay a load of cash to keep it quiet. Reckoned it would be a pushover.' She gave a harsh laugh. 'Like I said, he always was a dickhead.'

'And was Danny Nolan involved in this blackmail?' Whitelaw asked, carefully.

Carlie bit her lip. 'Jace said he got him into something. Just the once. Years ago, when Danny was little.' A single tear welled up in her eye, and rolled down her cheek unheeded.

'Listen, love,' Whitelaw said, 'this is important. Did either Danny or Jason mention anyone to you called Mario?'

'Mario?' she repeated, her blank expression answering the question for her.

'Never mind,' he said. 'So did Danny go along with it?'

She shook her head. 'Said he didn't remember anything about it.'

'So Jace reminded him?'

'Jace wanted Danny in on the scam. He wanted to make things up to him.'

Or needed him to strengthen the blackmail bid, more like. The word of a rent boy wouldn't have counted for much on its own. But the memories of an innocent, gap-toothed little kid . . . Whitelaw remembered Danny's meagre wages waiting at Kost Kutter. The pathetic little deposit account. The bullying step-father who had beaten him black and blue when he'd sought sanctuary with his mum. Everyone's willingness to write the boy off as a loser. Too easy to feel righteous indignation at the way Jason Morrissey had used him. Too easy, even, to pin it on the perverted bastards who got their kicks by defiling innocence.

The blame fell wider than that.

It was mid-afternoon by the time they finished. Bradley had eaten the canteen out of crisps and chocolate biscuits, the constable from the Child Protection Unit told them with a smile, when he brought the children back. Chantal had slept peacefully. Carlie hugged them both to her.

'No comeback?' she said, over the tops of their heads.

'No comeback,' Whitelaw promised.

He arranged for the family to be taken back to the Seamen's Rest in an unmarked car. He warned Carlie that he might need to speak to her again, but he very much doubted she would still be there next time he called, and he didn't blame her.

He just hoped she'd find the tenner before she went.

Chapter Fifteen

'So you've decided to take Danny's disappearance seriously at last?' Kieran led the way through to the kitchen.

Whitelaw was relieved at how much better the younger man looked; he had showered and shaved and was smartly dressed. He appeared to have extended the spring-clean to the house as well; Whitelaw side-stepped a vacuum cleaner in the narrow hallway. A pile of mugs and dishes were soaking in the kitchen sink.

'Flora's coming home tonight,' Kieran said, as he filled the kettle.

Which explained things.

'Where's this dog, then?' Whitelaw asked, more to make conversation than anything else.

Instant hostility.

'He does exist, if that's what you mean. Same as that car that tried to run me down exists.' Kieran spooned coffee into two mugs, his back to Whitelaw. 'Batty Norah's taken him for a walk.'

'Right.' Whitelaw decided against pursuing the subject further. 'Look, I'll try not to keep you very long. I just need to get a clearer picture of what happened on the night of the play.' He took the mug Kieran was holding out to him, and added, 'I'm trying to establish exactly what it was made Danny take fright.'

'Apart from the magistrate who sent him down, you mean?'

Whitelaw could have spread the scarcasm on a piece of toast. He sighed. 'Listen, Kieran, I'm not sure how we ended up on opposite sides of the fence again, but I wish we hadn't, and if we're going to find Danny, we'd do better co-operating with each other instead of making snide comments.'

Kieran looked down into his coffee for a moment, then nodded. He tipped back his head and shut his eyes as he massaged the back of his neck, then let out his breath in a long sigh and said more briskly, 'So what is it you want to know?'

'Have you got a recent photograph of him, for starters? His mum hasn't been much help.'

'There's a surprise.' Kieran went out into the hall, returning with a large brown envelope. 'We had these done just before the show. Danny's the one in the red bomber jacket.'

The fact was thinner, the eyes warier, but Whitelaw would have recognised him without being told. 'Is this what he was wearing when he took off?' he asked.

Kieran nodded. 'Black baseball cap, denim jeans, white trainers. And the *Chicago Bulls* jacket.' He gave a wry smile. 'Which Wayne Edwards wants back, incidentally. I'm surprised his mum's not reported it stolen, the way she's been kicking up. Danny was only supposed to have borrowed it for the show.'

Whitelaw grinned. 'So tell me again what happened that night.'

Painstakingly, they went over the events leading up to Danny's disappearance, starting with the conversation in the car. Danny had been distressed, Kieran confirmed, but had calmed down before they got to Oultonshaw Manor, and had seemed fine by the time they prepared to go on stage together before the interval.

'Not even nervous?' Whitelaw asked doubtfully. 'I'd have been scared shitless at the prospect of appearing in front of that bunch.'

Kieran shook his head. 'It's funny, but the footlights act like a barrier, once you're on stage. You forget there's an audience out there in the darkness. But of course it wasn't like that at the Denstone do. As soon as I walked on, I was worried about how Danny would handle it.'

'How do you mean?'

'Because we were in a tent, it was quite light; I was very aware of all the people. I thought Danny was too, when I realised he was hanging back.' He shook his head again. 'But when I turned round, and saw his face, I knew it wasn't stage fright. It was a look of . . .' he paused, frowning as he searched for the right word, '. . . horror, is the only way I can describe it. And that's not me being melodramatic, if that's what you're thinking.'

If the last sentence were a challenge, Whitelaw decided not to rise to it. He was relieved that they seemed to be managing a sensible conversation, at last. 'And that's when he ran?'

Kieran nodded.

'You said you were very aware of all the people. How many would you have actually been able to see from the stage? I mean see as in recognise?'

Kieran looked as if he were about to ask a question. Then, staring into the middle distance as if trying mentally to recreate the scene, he said slowly, 'There was a bunch of kids on the front two rows, then behind them were . . . I suppose what you'd call the official party – the Denstones and their mates. Flora was there too, next to Greg Farrell. Behind them . . .' he shrugged. 'It's difficult. I couldn't really see faces beyond that, because the seats were all on the flat. I was just conscious of a lot of people.'

'Go back to what you called the official party,' Whitelaw prompted.

'Danny had already met some of them, either before the show, or on the previous Sunday when we went to measure up for the sets.' He paused, scanning Whitelaw's face. 'Do you still think he stole that stuff?'

'Someone stole it.'

But Kieran was too bright for that. 'What if someone set him up? To explain away why he'd legged it?'

Whitelaw wished some of his own men were as sharp. But they were getting side-tracked.

'How many people would he have seen for the first time from

the stage, do you reckon?' Seeing that Kieran wasn't happy to let it drop, he added, 'Let's try to find out why he ran, first. We can deal with the rest of it later.'

Kieran gave him a long, speculative look, then said, 'OK.'

'Could you make me a list?' Whitelaw produced a notepad. He watched patiently as Kieran scribbled, stared into space, crossed out, and scribbled again. The final list comprised: Henry Denstone, the magistrate Brassington and his wife, an unknown man whom Kieran thought worked at Denstone Automotive Engineering and the playwright Nicholas Perotti.

'Henry Denstone wasn't at the house when you went to measure up, then?' Whitelaw queried.

Kieran shook his head. 'Just Tricia and Penelope. Perotti should have been there too, but he was busy with some last-minute rewrites that we could have well done without.' He handed over the list. 'So what happened to make you so inter-ested in Danny's welfare all of a sudden?'

Whitelaw wondered how much it was safe to tell him. He badly needed Kieran's continued co-operation, and beyond that, he admitted to himself, he valued the younger man's apparent renewed trust.

Maybe it was time to demonstrate some in return.

'I think you were right,' he said. 'I believe something did happen to Danny. I don't mean recently,' he added, as Kieran's face paled. He looked at the younger man, sizing him up; still not sure he was doing the right thing. 'I mean when Danny was a little boy,' he said carefully.

Flora scrambled down from the train and scanned the platform, fighting a childish surge of disappointment as she realised Kieran wasn't amongst the people waiting. She couldn't seriously have expected him to hang around for the two hours and more that the train had been delayed, especially with Greg Farrell due at seven o'clock, she told herself. She checked her watch against the digital clock above the timetables, as a nasal, disembodied voice regretted the delay to passengers travelling on the sixteen ten from Exeter.

'So you bloody well should, as it's now eighteen thirteen,' she muttered as she headed with her grumbling fellow passengers towards the stairway. The delay had been the more frustrating in that they had been no more than five miles away from the station at the time; she had almost felt tempted to get off the damned train and walk.

She wondered whether to go straight for a taxi, or to use some of the little time left before Greg's arrival to ring Kieran and let him know what was going on. She opted for the former; Kieran would have found out about the delay, dismissed glibly as 'a problem on the track', when he had come down earlier. She would barely have time to get changed, as it was.

Everything seemed to be conspiring against her. The delayed Exeter train had arrived at the same time as a packed commuter shuttle from Manchester, and there was a bottleneck at the exit barriers. By the time she had shoved her way out of the station, the queue for taxis reached halfway up the street. She looked at it, hesitated, knowing that a bus would take even longer at this time of day, then dumped her bag behind the elderly woman at the back of the disconsolate snake of commuters. Asking the woman to keep her place for her, Flora ran back into the station to the phone booths, where the queue wasn't much shorter.

'You can borrow my mobile, if you like.'

Under normal circumstances, Flora would have turned down the offer, coming as it did from a leering teenage boy whose eyes were riveted on her braless cleavage.

'Thanks.' She flashed him the briefest smile compatible with politeness, punched in the number, and turned her back on him while she waited for Kieran to answer.

No reply.

Impatiently, she tried the number a second time. She glanced back towards the teenager, who was gazing at her and picking feverishly at a pimple on his chin.

Still no reply.

'D'you fancy a coffee?' the boy asked her cleavage.

'Another time.' She thrust the mobile back at him and hurried back to the taxi rank, where, thankfully, much of the queue had disappeared. Along with her bag, and the elderly woman.

'Did you notice . . . ?' Flora began to a peroxided girl about her own age, who was staring impassively into space and chewing gum. But plugged as she was into a personal stereo, it seemed unlikely that she would have noticed if the St Valentine's Day Massacre had unfolded in front of her.

'Oh, forget it,' Flora muttered, and joined the back of the remaining queue.

At last it was her turn. She jumped into the taxi, all hope of having time to shower and change long gone. It was almost a quarter to seven. She felt grubby, flustered, and unreasonably resentful towards Kieran for not being there to help her out. She was almost crying with rage and frustration by the time the taxi, after a tortuous journey through the rush-hour traffic, drew up in Sephton Street. It was at that point that she remembered that her purse was in her bag. The only money she had left was the handful of coins in her pocket. The fare was six pounds fifty. She had precisely one pound seventy-three.

'Wait here a minute, will you?' she said.

The driver regarded her through the rear-view mirror then winked. 'Your money, sweetheart. I'll wait here all night, if you like.'

She ran to the front door, realised her key was also in her bag, and knocked. A volley of furious barking greeted her. She had forgotten all about the bloody dog. She looked at her watch; five past seven. Surely they wouldn't have gone off without her?

'Hope you're not trying it on with me, darling,' the driver observed from his open window.

'Of course I'm not,' she snapped. She bent down and was greeted by Deefer's halitosis as he pressed his muzzle to the door. 'Go and fetch Kieran, you stupid idiot,' she yelled.

'Can I help?'

The amused voice made her jump nearly out of her skin. Her heart sank. She knew who it belonged to even before she turned round. Blushing furiously, she straightened up, looked, then looked again. The man grinning down at her was for a moment unrecognisable. Clean-shaven and cropped-haired. Only the unmistakably piercing eyes, no longer brown but a startling violet blue behind his wire-rimmed spectacles told her it really was Greg Farrell.

Seeing her confusion, he laughed. '*God's Only Son* yesterday, a World War Two fighter pilot tomorrow. Well, next month, actually, but playing the Almighty gets to be a bit of a strain after a while. Particularly the contact lenses.' He bowed deeply. 'What you see this evening is the real me.'

'You two going to stand there all night, or what?' the taxi driver enquired irritably.

Greg thrust a twenty-pound note through the window, waved the man away, then glanced towards the front door, which was shuddering against Deefer's prolonged onslaught. 'What's the problem?'

Flora was still trying to readjust to his new image. 'I . . . Thanks for . . .' She glanced down the street, where the taxi was disappearing from view. 'I lost my bag. At the station. When I got off the train.' As if it mattered to Greg Farrell where she had lost her bag. She knew she was stalling, as she wondered how she was going to explain Kieran's inexplicable, inexcusable absence.

'And your key was in your bag,' Greg added helpfully.

'Yes. I . . .' She stared at the closed door and asked herself what she should do next.

'Back door?' Greg suggested.

'Yes . . .' Flora made an effort to pull herself together. 'Yes,' she repeated, more decisively. 'You stay here . . . I mean, if that's all right . . .' She knew she was blushing again. 'I'll go round and let you in.'

Without waiting for his reply, she sprinted to the side entry that led to the backs of the houses, noticing Greg's sports car parked further up the street, and dashed down the narrow alleyway. She had to check the houses to make sure she'd got the right one; they never came in this way and the battered, unfamiliar gate was choked with weeds, the latch stiff and rusty. Cursing, and breaking several fingernails in the process, she eventually got it open and ran up the small, overgrown garden to the back door. Deefer had beaten her to it. She could hear him scratching at the paintwork and growling. One bang on the door, and the barking set up again, louder than ever.

'Good boy,' she called insincerely over the noise. She sized up the kitchen window, which was on the latch, and wondered if she could climb through without the creature taking a lump out of her leg. Telling herself she had very few options, she pulled one of the garden chairs to the window and slipped off her shoes. It was only as an afterthought that she tried the door handle.

The door wasn't locked.

Cautiously, she pushed it open, and was sent flying back into the garden as the dog belatedly recognised her as friend, not foe.

Extricating herself from paws, tail and tongue, and slamming the door on Deefer before he could follow her back inside, Flora went into the little kitchen, ignoring his yaps of protest. A stack of washing-up was soaking in the sink. A grease-encrusted chip pan sat on the cooker. Healthy eating clearly hadn't been on Kieran's agenda while she was away. Flora pulled a face at it and called his name.

Silence.

She went into the hall, nearly tripping over the vacuum cleaner that was presumably Kieran's token attempt at cleaning up. Irritably, she threw it back into the cupboard under the stairs. She could see Greg's shadowy form through the glass panel at the top of the front door, and hurried to let him in.

'Kieran's not . . . He must have been . . . held up,' she said, as Greg followed her into the living room. She gathered up an armful of books and papers, nudging a half-eaten pizza under the sofa with her toe as she smiled weakly and said, 'He's probably gone back to the station. My train was delayed, and . . .' She broke off.

They both looked up at the ceiling as a low moan came from the room above.

Flora was up the stairs in a split second, Greg at her heels. The door was ajar. Her heart hammering, she pushed it open, her hand flying to her mouth.

Kieran was spread-eagled on the bed, fully dressed amidst a tangle of sheets. Clutched in his hand was an almost empty bottle of whisky.

Flora stared at him in horror.

'Oh dear,' Greg murmured, stepping round her into the room. At the sound, Kieran opened one eye, lifted his head a fraction from the pillow, then let it fall back with another moan. Greg raised an eyebrow, shrugged, then, hand under Flora's elbow, steered her from the room and shut the door behind them.

'Oh God! Greg, I'm so . . . I can't understand . . .' Mortified, she floundered for words, unable even to begin to express the turmoil of emotions she was feeling. Close to tears, she muttered, 'I've *never* seen him like this . . .'

Greg still had his back to her. When he turned, she was amazed to see that he was trying very hard not to smile.

'He doesn't even like whisky,' she said lamely. At which Greg Farrell threw back his head and laughed out loud.

'He's going to be out cold for hours yet.' Greg handed her a glass of the red wine he'd found in the kitchen and shook his head as once again she began to apologise. 'Listen,' he said, sitting down next to her on the sofa, 'he was probably keyed up about this evening, thought he'd have a quick one to steady his nerves, and then one glass led to another.' He shrugged. 'It happens. It's happened to me once or twice.' He grinned at her, sideways. 'Highly strung bunch, we thespians.'

'But he *never* drinks more than a couple of glasses of anything. I just don't understand . . .'

'Don't worry about it.' Greg grinned again. 'After the hangover he's going to have as the result of this little bender, he'll probably sign the pledge.'

'And in the meantime, you've had a wasted journey.' Flora's emotions were beginning to sort themselves out; anger was coming out on top. 'Greg, I'm so sorry.'

'Forget it.' He raised his glass. 'Anyway, it doesn't have to be a wasted journey. The table's booked. Why don't I just take Kieran's agent out, as the man himself isn't available?'

She could feel herself colouring. 'Oh, I don't—'

His smile softened. 'As a friend, Flora. That's all.'

She gulped her wine, doubly embarrassed at his assumption that she'd imagined he was chatting her up, and tried to think of something to say that didn't make her sound a complete idiot. In the garden, Deefer's barking had subsided to the occasional reproachful whine. Above them, Kieran was snoring loudly.

Greg topped up her glass and said lightly, 'Why don't you stop looking as if you're about to visit the dentist, and just go and get ready?'

'Do you think it's safe to leave him in that state? What if he—'

Another sonorous snore came from above.

Greg raised an eyebrow. 'I don't think he's likely to be going anywhere, do you?'

She showered at record speed, pulled a brush through her hair and grabbed items at random from the wardrobe. She settled for a strappy black top and the linen trousers that she had worn to the gala, and which, she hoped Greg wouldn't notice, could have done with being pressed. Not quite how she would have anticipated preparing to go out for dinner with a national celebrity, she thought as she gave herself a quick, critical glance in the mirror.

She went over to the bed. Kieran had rolled over onto his side, his knees and elbows tucked foetus-like into his body, the empty bottle still clutched to his chest. He looked so vulnerable that Flora felt her anger begin to evaporate.

'You're an idiot,' she whispered, prising the bottle from his grasp and pushing a strand of hair from his face. He flinched from her touch, a fleeting grimace clouding his features as he mumbled something in his sleep. Flora stood looking down on him for a moment and chewing off the lipstick she had just applied. Then, with a sigh, she made her way downstairs.

Greg was reading a magazine. He stood up as she entered the room. Flora was relieved that he offered no compliment on her appearance.

'What do you want to do about the dog?' was all that he said.

Flora hesitated. 'Leave him in the garden,' she said, recalling the mess she had come back to last time he had been left alone.

Greg nodded. 'I've locked the back door.' He grinned. 'Have you got a key, this time?'

'Good point.' She looked on the hook in the cupboard under the stairs, which was where they usually kept the spare, cursing under her breath when she found it empty.

'Problem?' Greg queried.

'No.' She decided that he'd been exposed to enough of their domestic difficulties for one evening, without hearing that the spare key had gone missing. She took Kieran's instead. It seemed unlikely he would be needing it before she got back.

'Shall we go then?' Greg held the front door open for her.

She glanced up the stairs, then said firmly, 'Yep. Let's go.'

Shutting the door behind them, she turned Kieran's key in the lock and followed Greg towards the waiting sports car.

Chapter Sixteen

He heard the front door.

Felt himself tense.

Coming in or going out?

Lay curled in a ball, waiting for the footsteps on the stairs.

Waited for them to stop.

Waited for the creak of the hinge.

Waited for the cream-cheese triangle of light into the darkness.

Waited for the nightmare to begin.

My heart aches, and a drowsy numbness . . .

Must remember the words.

Brain was muddled.

Could smell smoke. Pipe? Cigar?

Bastard must have brought his mates.

Wanted to sit up, but knew he mustn't. Only hope was to feign sleep. Pretend he wasn't there.

To cease upon the midnight with no . . .

Remember. Had to remember the words. Leave his body to face the nightmare; escape into the safety of his head.

Somewhere outside, a sharp, monotonous sound. Slicing through his brain. A dog's bark? He didn't have a dog. Not since . . .

My heart aches . . .

Remember.
Smoke getting thicker. Catching in his throat.
Wished he had the strength to cough.
To cease . . .

Chapter Seventeen

Whitelaw watched the blackbird not six inches away from his spade, and the blackbird watched him.

'Greedy bugger,' he grinned as he turned over another clod of earth and the bird darted forward, then flew up to the fence, a writhing worm in its beak. For the last two hours, Whitelaw had been digging. The bird must be so full of worms, he was surprised it was still able to fly.

Digging, Whitelaw had always found, was the best antidote to worry. And this fine summer evening he had bellyful enough of worries to rival the blackbird's worms. Maybe that was where the phrase 'can of worms' had come from, he mused, as he turned the spade again and watched the hard crust of soil erupt as another one writhed its way to the surface.

He went over the evidence again. That Jason Morrissey and his lover had died as the result of his blackmail attempt was beyond doubt. That the blackmail was aimed at a paedophile, or more likely a ring of paedophiles, seemed equally irrefutable.

And that was where the speculation took over.

Common sense told Whitelaw that the most probable seat of the paedophile ring was Denstone Park. It also told him that the only way to track down other victims after so many years was to go public, put out an appeal for them to come forward. But he didn't need Lambert to remind him that he needed a damned sight more than common sense before he did any such thing. He needed hard evidence. Which didn't exactly look like being a piece of cake, bearing in mind that Jason Morrissey was dead, Danny Nolan in hiding, and Denstone Park, together with all its records, conveniently destroyed more than a decade ago.

Whitelaw didn't like abuse cases. Nobody liked them. He liked old abuse cases even less. Long-buried secrets writhing their way to the surface . . . He shivered involuntarily. It was dusk, too dark, almost, to see what he was doing. The familiar theme tune that floated through the open French windows from the television next door told him it must be nine o'clock. Val would be wondering whether he was ever going to come in. Tossing a final worm to the blackbird, he trudged back up the lawn, his back already beginning to complain now that he had stopped.

His best bet, he was sure, was to approach the case from the other angle, try to piece together what had made Nolan disappear and work backwards from there. Which was why he had gone to see Kieran Henshall. Quickly, he averted his mind from what threatened to be yet another source of anxiety to add to his catalogue.

He tried to pick up the thread of his thoughts as he eased off his wellies. He needed to find out who it was that Nolan had spotted from that stage that had tipped him over the edge. Someone remembered from when he was a little boy? Or had he recognised a face from much more recently? From when Jason was murdered, possibly?

More speculation.

'Supper?' Val queried, looking up from ironing a shirt as he padded into the kitchen in his stockinged feet.

'I'll have a quick bath first,' he said over the babble of the local radio that was Val's habitual accompaniment to housework. He was grateful that she always seemed to know when not to ask questions. He paused at the door, his attention caught by a news report of a multiple pile-up on the southern approach road to the town that had brought the rush-hour traffic to a standstill earlier that evening. A lorry, one of the vehicles at the tail end of the crash, had slewed down an embankment and temporarily blocked the inter-city railway line as well. 'Poor sods on Traffic will have had a busy time of it,' he yawned.

'Yes, well, you're not one of them, so don't start fretting about that, on top of everything else.' Val gave him a gentle shove. 'Go on, get upstairs and run that bath.'

He lay back in the water and closed his eyes, attempting to clear his head of work, knowing that he would be in for another sleepless night if he didn't succeed; knowing that even trying was a waste of time.

He heard the front doorbell go, held his breath in case it was someone from the station, heard Val's voice rise in pleased surprise, a muted conversation which moved into the living room and was then extinguished as the door was shut. He settled back into the water.

He didn't realise he had drifted off until Val tapped on the door and called, 'Millie's downstairs, love.'

For once, Millie didn't make a crack, as he appeared in his dressing gown. She got straight down to business.

As soon as Carlie Sykes had left his office earlier that afternoon, Whitelaw had phoned Social Services and asked Millie if she had ever heard any rumours about Denstone Park. When Millie had enquired what sort of rumours, he had ended up, with an indiscretion that would have him back on the beat if Lambert could have heard him, telling her everything that Carlie had just told him. He had finished the conversation by requesting that she get in touch straight away if she came up with anything.

And here she was.

'I went back over Danny Nolan's foster placements after you called,' she said briskly, taking a list from her briefcase. Whitelaw could see that one of the names on it was highlighted. 'The Bennetts,' she said, following his glance. She handed it across. 'Danny was with them from July to November in 1988.'

'So?' Whitelaw asked cautiously as he took it from her, already calculating that it was the right time-frame for the photograph.

'They also fostered Jason Morrissey. For two years.'

Whitelaw sat forward. 'So we can place both boys in the same foster home at the time that—'

But Millie was shaking her head impatiently. 'The Bennetts only take under-tens.'

Paedophiles? was Whitelaw's first thought. He opened his mouth, but Millie cut him off. 'If you'll stop interrupting, we might get somewhere.'

Val, who had been listening in silence, suppressed a smile as she got to her feet. 'I'll leave you to it for a while.'

Whitelaw looked up apologetically, hating that she felt she had to be turfed out of her own living room. But he knew she was uncomfortable when he was discussing business, even though he would stake his pension that she would never repeat anything confidential that she might hear.

She touched his shoulder as she passed. 'I'll go and make some coffee.'

Millie was so focused on what she had come here to tell him, Whitelaw doubted she had even realised Val had left the room. 'The Bennetts kept in touch with Jason for a number of years,' she went on. 'Birthdays and such. They were devastated to read about his murder. When will the body be released, by the way?'

Whitelaw shook his head.

'I said I'd ask.' Millie flexed the back of her neck briefly. The gesture was the nearest concession to weariness that Whitelaw had ever seen from her. 'Anyway,' she went on, instantly businesslike again, 'they visited him in July 1988, on his thirteenth birthday, and they took Danny with them. Jason was on a summer school at Denstone Park. I crosschecked his file to be sure of the dates.'

'My God, Millie!' Whitelaw looked at her in admiration. 'You don't fancy changing careers, do you?'

She gave a snort that said the question wasn't worth answering. 'As I told you, they kept in touch. Jason sent them a copy of the same photograph you've got.' She reached into her briefcase again. 'And this one as well.'

It showed an almost identical scene. Rather less, if anything, to identify Denstone Park. But this time, there was a third person in the group. A man of about forty; hair immaculate, jeans over-tight, jacket sleeves pushed up his forearms in a fashion that Whitelaw had found intensely irritating even at the time, he stood between the boys, an arm around each. Jason was smiling up at him in a way that Whitelaw could only describe as smug.

'Bennett?' he asked, his mind jumping back to his initial suspicion.

'Hardly.' Millie was dismissive. 'D'you seriously imagine we'd employ a wanker like that as a foster father? Phil Bennett's a lay preacher. And before you say it, I know that doesn't mean anything, but the Bennetts are genuinely good people. I seem to remember that Jason got a serious dose of religion when they first took him on.'

Whitelaw raised a cynical eyebrow, but didn't comment.

'Anyway,' Millie went on, 'to get back to the man on the photograph, the Bennetts thought he might be a member of staff. It shouldn't be hard for you to check out, should it?'

No, it shouldn't, was the answer. For the first time since the investigation had begun nearly two weeks earlier, Whitelaw was really beginning to believe they might be in with a shout. He mouthed a kiss at the photograph, then looked across and grinned. 'If I wasn't already married, Millie, I'd propose to you!'

'I'm glad you can be so flippant.' Millie wasn't smiling. 'You may or may not be able to nail whoever is behind what went on there. I hope to God you can. But that doesn't suddenly make things all right for those two little boys, does it?'

'You're right, of course.' Whitelaw was ashamed that his euphoria had so totally swept everything else from his mind, if only for a moment.

'So do you want to hear the rest?'

He nodded, chastened.

GEORGIE HALE

'A week or so after the visit to Denstone Park, Danny ran off. It was all reported to Social Services at the time. The police picked him up from his mother's a couple of days later. It had happened on a number of occasions before. But this time, Mum insisted he'd only been there a few hours, leaving about thirty-six hours unaccounted for. At the time, no one took her seriously. She'd been in trouble with the courts for not handing him straight back before. But in view of what you've told me . . .' Millie shook her head. 'Over the following months, Danny's behaviour deteriorated dramatically. Bed-wetting, violent temper tantrums, self-harm . . . we're talking about a child of considerably above-average intelligence, despite his social deprivation, and one who had settled into the placement unusually well. The Bennetts said they did their utmost to persevere with him, and I believe them; they're amongst the most committed foster parents we've got. The crunch came when Danny went for their eighteen-year-old natural son with a penknife. The placement was terminated the same day.' She shook her head again. 'The signs were all there. We failed Danny Nolan, Ray. We didn't ask enough questions and we failed him.'

'Well, we'll bloody well be asking them now,' Whitelaw said gruffly, getting to his feet and staring out into the darkness before he drew the curtains. He turned around suddenly and asked, 'You said Jason sent the Bennetts the photograph. So who took it?'

Millie shook her head. 'They didn't know. Quite a few people had cameras, with it being Jason's birthday. Everyone went out of their way to make the kids at Denstone Park feel special, they said.'

The irony of the words silenced them both for a moment.

'So how did you get on talking to Kieran Henshall?' she asked, when Whitelaw sat down again, bringing them both a brandy.

'Potentially useful.' Whitelaw took a grateful swig of the burning liquid and attempted to focus his attention away from what Danny Nolan must have felt when, after everything else that had been done to him, he had been sent back from the Bennetts like an unwanted parcel. He tapped the photograph. 'More so, hopefully, now we've got this.'

'I meant how did he handle what you had to say about Danny?'

Whitelaw frowned into his glass.

As soon as he had started to explain what he suspected had been going on at Denstone Park, he had realised he'd made a big mistake. Kieran had been beside himself. The more Whitelaw had tried to back-pedal, calm him down, the more agitated he had become; claiming that Danny's disappearance was all his fault, that he had been the one who led the boy back to the bastards who had abused him. Whitelaw could see him now, pacing the kitchen in Sephton Street. He'd tried to reassure him, but Kieran had turned on him with eyes so wild that Whitelaw had felt a split second of real fear, remembering that this was a man who had killed once in his life already. Then the face had seemed to collapse in on itself. Without another word, Kieran had pushed past, out of the front door and up the street, leaving Whitelaw standing on the doorstep and wondering whether he should go after him, call a doctor, or simply leave him to cool off.

He had opted for the latter, mainly because he was dog-tired himself. And had been regretting the decision all evening.

'Badly, then.'

Whitelaw had forgotten Millie had asked a question. He looked at her, bemused, as she went on, 'You'll need to be careful with him.'

'*Me* be careful with him? It's a bloody psychiatrist he needs if you ask me.' Guilt made the words come out far more aggressively than he had intended.

'Very possibly.' Millie observed him in the disconcerting way she had. 'But you're the one who has involved him in a sexual abuse investigation with absolutely no idea of what demons you might be raising for him. I'm simply advising you, in my professional capacity, that if you don't go about it gently, you're very likely to push him over the edge.'

'Jesus.' Whitelaw drained his glass, as the implication of her words sank in. In the hall, his mobile began to ring, but he ignored it. 'You think . . . ?'

'A pattern of escalating offending that started from nowhere at eleven, when he was removed from foster parents to go back to his mother? And finished just as abruptly five years later when he stabbed his mother's live-in boyfriend who had, incidentally, a number of convictions for violent sexual offences? It was you who showed me the files, Ray. I'm just amazed it wasn't picked up at the time.' She looked down into her own glass and added quietly, 'Still, who am I to talk?'

'And it was me that went in like a bloody bull in a china shop about Denstone Park this afternoon.' Whitelaw put his head between his hands. 'Shit.'

'Ray, there's a——' Val broke off as she stuck her head around the door, mobile in hand. 'Is everything all right?'

'Yes.' Whitelaw rubbed his face. 'No.' He sighed and got heavily to his feet, holding his hand out for the phone.

'I took a message. One of Terry Lightowler's for-information-only calls.' She looked at him, her face full of concern. 'You look done in, love. Surely it can wait until the morning.'

'She's right, Ray.' Millie was back to her usual no-nonsense self as she snapped her briefcase shut with the air of a GP on a home visit. 'You've had a crap day. Just give yourself a break, or you'll be off sick and Kieran Henshall will have some *real* bull in a china shop riding rough-shod over him.'

Whitelaw could think of several.

'OK,' he said wearily. Lightowler was probably only ringing about the pile-up, anyway; the idiot had a penchant for issuing entirely irrelevant news bulletins when the fancy took him. He attempted a smile at Val. 'I can't fight off a two-pronged attack, seeing as you've brought in the heavy brigade. Let's have that coffee, shall we?'

Still, he couldn't quite resist asking, when an hour later Millie had gone and he and Val were washing the cups, 'What was it Lightowler wanted?'

Val turned from the sink with a smile. 'You're hopeless, you know that? I knew you wouldn't be able to last out until the morning!' She dried her hands on the tea towel, kissed him on the cheek and, reading his mind, said, 'You'll only ring in the minute I'm in the bathroom if I don't tell you, won't you?' She went through to the hall, shaking her head. She took a pad of paper from her bag of school work, pushed her glasses onto her nose, and read, 'Fire at domestic dwelling. Honestly, Ray, anyone would think you were running the emergency services single-handed!'

'Must be a suspicious.' Whitelaw was rummaging around in the fridge; he never had had any supper. 'What's the address?'

'It doesn't sound remotely suspicious. Chip pan fire, according to Terry Lightowler. Sephton Street. Isn't that round by the university somewhere, or am I thinking of . . . ?'

Whitelaw, pork pie in hand, stood stock still. He took a deep breath, surprised that his voice sounded quite calm as he asked, 'Any casualties?'

'The firemen had recovered a body, Terry Lightowler said. Awful, isn't it, to think that while we were having an ordinary Monday evening, some poor soul . . . ?' Val shivered then glancing at Whitelaw, replaced the pad in her bag and said firmly, 'Just go to bed, Ray. You look absolutely terrible.' She caught his arm as he went to pick up the phone. 'Information only, remember?'

'In a minute,' he muttered. 'I just have to find out . . .'

'What's the point, Ray?' Her voice was weary with resignation, 'There's nothing you can do to help the poor devil now, whoever it was.'

Chapter Eighteen

Flora was enjoying the evening more than she felt she should have done.

The restaurant, a half-hour's drive out into the country, was quiet and unpretentious, which had been a pleasant surprise. If any of the waiters recognised Greg, they were discreet enough not to say so. The terrace on to which they had been shown overlooked open countryside. Cows grazed. Birds sang. Blackport could have been a million miles away. Flora had been tempted to ring Kieran when they first arrived, but the chances of rousing him seemed minimal, and she had had no desire to keep reminding Greg of what had happened. As the waiters cleared the plates from the main course, she realised guiltily that she hadn't given Kieran a thought in almost two hours. The food had been delicious, the wine perfect. Flora could feel herself unwinding. Greg was very good company.

'I take it you've heard no more about that lad?' he asked, as he poured her a glass of mineral water. He had been careful, she noticed, to restrict himself to only one glass of the wine, and didn't seem to feel the need to pressure her into drinking the rest.

Flora sighed. Why did every conversation seem to come round to Danny Nolan, sooner or later?

'You knew he rang from London?' she said.

'Kieran mentioned it when I spoke to him the other night.'

Flora gave a wry smile. 'You'll be sick of the sight of

Blackport. Last time you were up here Danny stole your watch, then Kieran lets you down tonight . . .'

'I'm not complaining.' Greg raised his glass to her. 'Not about tonight, at least. So tell me a bit more about yourself. You did some acting yourself at university, didn't you?'

'Some,' she nodded. 'I enjoyed it.'

'You've never thought of pursuing it?'

'What, as a career?' She considered the question for a moment. 'No. Not seriously. I don't think I'm ambitious enough. You have to be, don't you?'

'Yes.' His face darkened momentarily. 'Yes, you do.'

She wondered if he was thinking of Kieran, back in Blackport, spark out, when he should have been here, grabbing this once-in-a-lifetime opportunity.

'So have you got much lined up?' she asked, changing the subject. 'After the World War Two pilot, that is?'

'More than I can cope with, actually.' He pulled a face, then laughed. 'And just how churlish does *that* sound, with two-thirds of the country's actors out of work? But it can be a pressure, believe it or not. You're frightened to turn a part down in case you never get offered another one.'

'That hardly seems likely, surely?'

He shrugged. 'It's a fickle business. People can go out of fashion very fast. It's all too short a drop from leading man to baked bean commercials.' His face brightened. 'I'm really excited about one of the projects, though. *Hamlet*. Next season, with the RSC.'

'Oh brilliant!'

'Yes, it's a part I've always wanted. And it will suit me very well, because I have a cottage in Stratford. I don't get there anything like as much as I'd like to, so it will be a good opportunity to touch base. You must come and stay sometime. There's a chance I might be able to put something Kieran's way there, as a matter of fact. That's what I wanted to talk to him about. I've had a word with a couple of people already, mentioned this talented young guy who's got the world's pushiest publicity agent.' He grinned. 'An audition could be on the cards. Not a big part, probably just one of the courtiers, but it's a start, so tell him to get a couple of soliloquies up his sleeve. In fact, I've got some useful books——'

'Why are you being so kind?' The question popped out of her mouth unbidden; abrupt enough to sound ungrateful.

Greg looked at her thoughtfully, then said, 'You told me Kieran identified with that lad Danny because he'd been in trouble himself. Things can't have come easily to him. In a lesser way, they didn't come easily to me either. Maybe I recognised his hunger. And maybe that's how I can understand why he got plastered this evening. He wants it all too much. You *have* to want it too much.' He picked up his glass of water and watched the bubbles as they spiralled to the surface. 'My background is what would be called solidly working class. Now that I've hit the big time, of course, the publicity machine has tried to glamorise that – ordinary bloke makes good, that sort of stuff – but let me tell you, there was nothing glamorous about it. It was just totally, mind-shatteringly boring. I was brought up in a mediocre town in the Midlands.' He gave a wry smile. 'Not even the North, which has a certain cachet, as Kieran will find out, if he hasn't already. I went to a mediocre comprehensive, where I was a mediocre pupil. Everyone – parents, teachers, even my friends – thought I was completely crazy when I announced I was going to be an actor. I was absolutely bloody determined to prove them wrong.' Flora noticed that his grip had tightened on his glass as he spoke. He was silent for a moment, and she wondered if he were expecting a response. Then he looked up suddenly, and grinned. 'And I did. I sense there's that same streak of bloody-mindedness in Kieran, and I admire him for it. Now, how about pudding?'

It was late, by the time they got back to the outskirts of Blackport. Flora wondered whether Kieran would have sobered up; what he would think when he realised what had happened; how they would be with each other. She wasn't sure that she wanted to find out.

Greg was saying something to her. She realised that she was frowning, and wondered how long she had been lost in her thoughts.

'You were miles away,' Greg said, glancing away from the road to smile at her.

'I was just thinking what a great evening it's been,' she said lightly.

'I enjoyed it too.' He transferred his attention back to the traffic, threading across the lanes of the ring road, before adding, 'It's rare that I can be myself. Most people don't get beyond the looks.' It could have sounded stunningly conceited, but it somehow didn't. 'You must have found that yourself,' he added.

Flora said nothing.

He glanced across again, reading her thoughts. 'That's not a chat-up line, by the way, it's a statement of fact. I see a great many beautiful women in my job, and you are *exceedingly* beautiful, Flora. Kieran's a lucky lad.' He shook his head. 'Not that he's going to feel very lucky when he wakes up to that hangover!'

'No.' Flora found herself laughing with him.

'I expect I shall be up again. For this thing at the university, if not before. Maybe we could try again then? In fact . . .' he hesitated. 'Listen you could always say I cried off this evening, couldn't make it for some reason, if you think it might save Kieran the embarrassment of thinking—'

'Thanks, but I don't think that would be such a good idea.'

'Whatever,' he said quickly. 'I only meant—'

Flora had no wish to offend him. She said, with a small smile, 'It's just that I wouldn't feel comfortable lying to him.'

'No.' He seemed genuinely embarrassed. 'No, of course not. It was crass of me to—'

'I'll cook dinner next time,' she cut across the apology. 'To say thank you for tonight.' In order to fill the silence that suddenly seemed heavy with unsaid words she added, 'Congratulations on the honorary degree, by the way.'

'Thanks. And thank you for the invitation; I shall look forward to it.' Another silence, then he laughed suddenly, and the moment was past. 'My old headmaster must be turning in his grave. CSE woodwork was the pinnacle of my academic success at school, so the thought of— Bloody hell!' He braked sharply as a police car flashed past, siren wailing. 'They're in a rush!'

Barely slowing, the car swerved as it turned left into a side road a couple of hundred yards further on.

'Christ!' Greg blew out his cheeks in relief. 'I thought I was going to get done for speeding again!'

'*Again?*' she asked in mock disapproval.

He grinned sheepishly. 'This car's a magnet to traffic police. I've got six points on my licence already. Doesn't look good when you're supposed to be a member of the Holy Trinity.'

'Not so bad for a fighter pilot.'

'True enough. But all the same . . .' He made the same left turn as the police car, but at a considerably more sedate speed.

Flora stifled a sudden yawn, the length and traumas of the day abruptly catching up with her.

'You must be shattered, after the journey up from Scilly.' Greg took his eyes from the road for long enough to give her a sympathetic smile. 'Why don't you close your eyes and relax. I know the way from here.'

She must have dozed, so that she was momentarily disorientated as the car came to an abrupt halt.

'What the hell . . . ?'

Greg's tone jerked her back to wakefulness.

Two fire engines half blocked the entrance to Sephton Street. The night sky was illuminated with a counterpoint of the flashing lights.

'Oh, no. Oh, please God, no.' Flora was out of the door and

tearing towards the house before Greg had undone his seat belt.

She pushed her way through the small crowd of on-lookers, some in pyjamas and dressing gowns. For a moment, she stood rooted to the pavement, her hands pressed to her mouth as the colour drained from her face. Then screaming Kieran's name, she hurled herself at the smouldering shell of what had been their home.

'Oh no you don't, love.' She was halted almost immediately by a policeman, who grabbed her from behind in an enveloping bear hug.

'Where is he?' She struggled and fought against the implacable embrace. 'What's happened to him?'

'All right, I'll deal with this.' The voice was familiar and its calmness temporarily silenced her. Although it was more than three years since she had seen him, she recognised instantly the portly, middle-aged man who took her arm as the other policeman released his grip. The dreadful events of their last meeting, the rocky outcrop on St Mary's where – incredibly – she had stood only that morning, collided with her present night-mare, and she felt her legs buckle under her. Only Whitelaw's firm grasp stopped her from falling. 'It's Flora, isn't it?' he said, quietly.

She struggled against the blackness that was threatening to engulf her, her mouth forming words that wouldn't come.

'It's all right, love.' He spoke to her as if she were a child, the compassion in his tone telling her that nothing was going to be all right, ever again.

'What's going on?' Greg had caught her up. He slipped his arm around her waist to support her as she bent forward, gulping the acrid air, choking on it, as she fought to remain conscious.

Whitelaw's voice ebbed and flowed above her head, as he established Greg's identity. His words were muttered, as if he hoped she wouldn't hear. '. . . too early to tell . . . could have been a chip pan . . .' The voice dropped even lower. 'One fatality, that's all I know, until I get the chance to speak to . . .'

Grim-faced firemen were dragging the charred and sodden remains of a carpet out onto the street. One of them caught Flora's eye, and looked away. With a supreme effort, she straightened up and forced her gaze to the blistered paintwork, the shards of sooty glass that were all that remained of the windows, the brickwork blackened by the heat. She knew with a terrible, icy certainty that no one could have survived such an inferno.

'Where is he?' she said, her own voice echoing in her ears as though she was in a long tunnel. 'Where have you taken him?'

Chapter Nineteen

Whitelaw negotiated a path between discarded hoses that lay coiled across the flooded pavement. The fire must have been brought under control some time before: all that was left for the firemen was to sift through the debris and try to make some sense of what had happened.

His first reaction when Val gave him the message had been to jump in the car, but she had talked sense into him, reminding him of the second brandy he had just knocked back. So he had rung the station, hoping against hope, as he double-checked the Sephton Street address, that Lightowler had got it wrong; knowing that he hadn't. He had instructed the man to take a couple of uniforms and get over there straight away, and to send a patrol car to pick him up. His urgency must have got through; the car had arrived within minutes. It had driven him across Blackport at speeds that would have given Lambert heart failure, Whitelaw sitting rigid in the passenger seat and refusing to consider what bearing his earlier conversation with Kieran might have on the incident they were travelling to.

Pushing the thought aside again as he stepped round the still-smouldering remains of an armchair, he tapped one of the firemen on the shoulder and asked who was in charge. The man lifted his visor and ran the back of his hand across his forehead in a gesture that reminded Whitelaw sharply of Kieran, the evening he had observed him at St Saviour's. The action spoke of exhaustion, mingled with the unwilling recognition of failure. Whitelaw fought a confessional urge to lay claim himself to any failure that might be going, as the man pointed to one of the engines parked further up the street. If he'd just gone after Kieran earlier . . . Called a doctor . . . If he'd been in less of a hurry to get home, put the day behind him . . .

'Suspicious is it, then?' He was accosted, as he made his way towards the fire engine, by Dean Hollings, photographer on the *Echo*.

'No comment,' Whitelaw snapped.

'You know who's here?' Hollings' tone, normally one of terminal boredom, was gleeful as he pointed back down the street. 'Only Greg Farrell!' When Whitelaw failed to respond, Hollings added with a smirk, 'All over some red-haired chick like a rash.' He tapped his camera. 'The nationals'll be falling over themselves for these. So what's the story?'

Whitelaw tried to tell himself that it was natural for anyone to be excited by the unexpected appearance of a film star. That, in different circumstances, he might have been quite interested himself. He failed. His voice was shaking with emotion as he spat out, 'The story, you gormless bastard, is that a young man died in that fire.'

'Yeah, well . . .' Hollings shrugged, then grinned as he caressed the camera. 'One man's loss and all that?'

Whitelaw would very much have liked to insert Hollings' zoom lens somewhere the sun didn't shine. Instead, he contented himself with shoving the man aside with a force only just the legal side of an assault charge.

'Oi, watch it!' Hollings grabbed at Whitelaw's arm to steady himself.

Whitelaw shook him off. 'Like I said, no comment.' He headed away, only to be halted in his tracks as Hollings called after him, 'Anyway, I thought it was a woman.'

He wheeled around. 'What?'

Hollings jerked his head towards the house. 'Way I heard it, it was some old bird they'd brought out.'

It only took Whitelaw a matter of seconds to confirm with the fire officer that the body inside the premises had indeed been female. As yet, unidentified. The news seemed almost too good to be true. 'But the occupant . . .' he started, refusing to allow himself even a small measure of relief until he was absolutely certain of the facts.

'Jumped from an upstairs window. He's being treated in the ambulance over there. Drunk as a skunk, by the smell of his breath, which is probably why he escaped with no more than minor injuries,' the fire officer added bitterly. 'My men had already spent the afternoon trying to scrape up the remains of that pile-up on the bypass. We could have done without this prat rounding off the shift for us.'

'So what happened?'

'Got pissed, fancied some chips, then nodded off,' the fire officer said, his mouth twisting with scorn. 'If I had a tenner for every time some silly sod did that, I'd have retired years ago. Should be a law against it, if you ask me. Which of course, nobody will, because I'm just here to pick up the pieces,' he muttered, as Whitelaw sprinted away from him.

One glance told Whitelaw that the survivor was Kieran; his face blackened with soot, his left arm in a sling, the younger man sat hunched in the back of one of the ambulances, staring sightlessly ahead of him as Lightowler attempted to question him. He didn't appear to notice Whitelaw, and Whitelaw didn't waste time by stopping to make his presence known. Instead, he hurried back to Flora. She was sitting on a low wall outside the next-door house, Greg Farrell beside her, his arm around her shoulder as he talked quietly into her ear. Someone had brought her a mug of tea, which she clutched, undrunk, in both hands. A blanket had been wrapped around her shoulders, although the night was warm and the residual heat from the fire made it warmer still. Dry-eyed, silent, she was Kieran's mirror image.

'He's over here!' Whitelaw called from across the street, adding hastily, as she looked up, her face tight with fear, 'He's OK!'

It was a phenomenon that he had witnessed many times in his career: during a crisis, those most closely involved managed to hold themselves together. It was when the crisis was resolved that they fell apart. And so it was with Flora. For a second, her eyes widened and her whitening lips moved as if to speak, then the mug crashed to the ground as Farrell caught her.

'That was a bloody stupid way to break it to her!' Farrell's eyes were blazing as Flora began to come round. He cradled her to his shoulder, his hand covering her ear as he hissed, 'What the hell's going on? First you reckon he's dead, then you tell us—' He broke off, murmuring to her as she struggled to sit up.

The force of Farrell's anger took Whitelaw by surprise. He wondered briefly what Dean Hollings would have made of it, and was relieved that the photographer, bent on getting his film developed, had already left the scene.

'I'll go and tell Kieran she's here,' he muttered, hoping with all his heart that he was misreading the situation.

He got back to find that Kieran was still being questioned. More reluctant than he cared to admit to repeat their last confrontation. Whitelaw decided to speak first to the paramedic who was standing some distance away, chatting to one of the firemen. Jerking his head in Kieran's direction, he asked in a low voice, 'How's he doing?'

The man stubbed out his cigarette and, matching his tone to Whitelaw's, murmured, 'Cuts and bruises. Ankle injury from when he jumped. Possible concussion, but that could just be the booze, and some nasty burns to his one hand. He needs treatment, but he's refusing to go to hospital. He's in shock, of course. Your man's in there now, threatening to arrest him if he won't go voluntarily, which I don't think has helped the situation.'

'Sodding idiot,' Whitelaw muttered. He walked back to the ambulance and impatiently beckoned Lightowler outside.

'Here, Guv, it's that same bloke—' he started, as he jumped down.

Whitelaw cut him short. 'I know who it is. What the bloody hell's all this about arresting him?'

'Just trying to get him to co-operate.' Lightowler sounded aggrieved. 'He's still pissed. Either that, or he's missing a few screws. Rambling on about—'

'Keep your voice down, for Christ's sake,' Whitelaw snapped.

At which his constable went on in a penetrating whisper, 'Reckons he's got to wait here for someone. Some bird by the name of—'

'Flora Castledine.' Whitelaw, wondering how the imbecile had ever been allowed to progress beyond traffic duty, finished the sentence for him. 'I know. She'll be over in a minute.'

Lightowler looked intrigued.

'What's he said about the fire?' Whitelaw ignored the unspoken question.

'That he woke up to find the place ablaze. Adamant he never put the chip pan on.' Lightowler rolled his eyes. 'Claims someone's trying to kill him. Again. Like I said—'

'Did anyone notice anything suspicious prior to the fire?'

'Like what?'

'Like anyone hanging around the place, for starters.'

'Are you kidding?' Lightowler sniggered. 'The guy's a nutter.'

'Get the neighbours interviewed first thing in the morning,' Whitelaw snapped. 'Find out if anybody saw anything out of the ordinary – anything at all. See if anyone noticed a Volvo T5R. Tinted glass.' He cut off the other man's incredulous response. 'Now, do we have an ID on—'

He broke off as Flora ran towards them, Greg at her heels.

Her face, which had been ashen, was infused with colour; her eyes sparkling. 'Where is he?' she cried breathlessly.

'In there, love.' Whitelaw gestured to the back of the ambulance, hoping it would be her expression that Kieran noticed and not who she had in tow, as the younger man half rose at the sound of her voice then, his own expression unreadable, looked beyond her to Farrell.

'I can see why he was so keen to wait,' the ambulance man observed appreciatively as he joined them. His eyes travelled to Farrell. 'Now where have I seen that chap before?' he murmured.

'Here, isn't it . . . ?' Lightowler's voice rose in excitement as he followed the man's gaze.

'This isn't the sodding Oscars,' Whitelaw snarled. He had no wish to intrude on the moment, still less to have half the emergency services offering a running commentary. 'The ID on the fatality,' he prompted irritably, as Lightowler dragged his attention back with obvious reluctance.

'Oh, you're just going to love this, Guv.' Lightowler shook his head as he fished for his pocket book. 'About as off the wall as the rest of his story, if you ask me.'

'I *have* asked you,' Whitelaw snapped. 'So stop farting about and just tell me what he said.'

Lightowler found his page. 'You ready for this?' he asked. He seemed to be having some difficulty in suppressing a grin as he glanced at the ambulance man. Then he cleared his throat and read, 'According to our young friend, the victim's name was Batty Norah.' The grin burst its banks. 'Still want me to interview the neighbours, Guv?'

'If I decide to change my plans, Constable, you can be sure you'll know about it.' Whitelaw's sudden flare of temper was no more than a thin disguise for his growing anxiety. He strode back towards the scene of the fire, then turned and snarled, 'And if I want a psychiatric report, I'll ask someone a fucking sight better qualified to give one than you, you half-wit.'

'Blimey, he's on a short fuse, isn't he?' The ambulance attendant watched him go. 'He needs to watch his blood pressure, with a temper like that.'

'He needs to get his fucking head examined,' Lightowler muttered, morosely. 'Strikes me there's more than one round here with a few screws loose.'

Whitelaw followed the ambulance to the hospital. Farrell, after a flurry of calls on his mobile, had gone back to his hotel, having insisted on arranging a room for Flora, and Kieran if he were discharged that night. The fire had left the couple homeless and with no more than the clothes they stood up in, but Whitelaw doubted if either of them had taken the fact on board. Flora was still too overwhelmed with relief to care about anything other than that Kieran was alive, and Kieran . . . Whitelaw gazed out of the window as the patrol car sped towards the General. He'd only spent a couple of minutes with the younger man before they had set off, but that had been enough to force him to agree with Lightowler's crude assessment of Kieran's mental state, although he hadn't been in any mood to admit as much. God help the future of British policing, he thought bitterly as they swung into the hospital car park, if the choice was between moronic plods like Lightowler and devious smart-arses like Medlock. They might as well all pack up and go home.

The General's A and E department was heaving. They had arrived at the post-chucking-out-time period that always saw the place at its busiest. At least Kieran's arrival in an ambulance guaranteed some queue-jumping, and he was taken straight through to be seen by a doctor, Flora by his side.

Whitelaw hovered outside the examination room, trying not to get in everyone's way, and attempting to shut his ears to the piercing screams of a young child in the adjoining cubicle. He wondered what was being done to it. He had never been good at witnessing pain, would have made a lousy nurse despite the gruesome sights he'd experienced during his career. Bodies, he was

OK with; they were past suffering, by the time he got to them. But the living . . . The child's screams set his nerves jangling. He longed for a cigarette. Part of him asked what he imagined he was doing here at all; the fire officer's version of the blaze was straightforward enough.

Finally, Kieran emerged, his hand wrapped in gauze, being pushed in a wheelchair. Whitelaw followed him down to X-ray, fetched three coffees from the machine, one of which was immediately removed by a nurse who glared at him as if to say that he should know better, and took a seat next to Flora. Kieran, unable to keep still, was out of the wheelchair as soon as the nurse left them. He limped jerkily up and down the crowded waiting area, apparently oblivious to his injuries.

'They want to keep him in overnight,' Flora murmured, her eyes following him. 'He doesn't want to stay.'

And leave Flora to go back to Greg Farrell's hotel alone? Whitelaw could imagine. Not that any of it was his business. He knew he was already more personally involved than perhaps he should be, without getting entangled in Kieran's love life.

'No one likes hospitals,' he said noncommittally, glancing over at the younger man. 'He's bound to be in a state after what's happened. Maybe I can just confirm a few things with you before I speak to him?'

He quickly got the picture leading up to the time she had left Kieran upstairs on the bed. She told him of her wait at the railway station, the theft of her bag, her surprise, when she did finally get home, that Kieran was nowhere around. Her shock, when she found him upstairs, dead drunk. No, she said, they didn't usually keep whisky in the house. Which presumably meant he must have drunk almost the whole bottle. She glanced at Kieran, who was standing at the far end of the room gazing at a notice board, his face tense, the fingers of his good hand picking nervously at the gauze dressing on his damaged one. She still couldn't understand what had made him do it, she said.

Whitelaw remained silent.

She told him of the arranged meeting with Greg Farrell, and their decision to go ahead without Kieran.

Again, Whitelaw made no comment.

'That's all I can tell you,' she said. 'When we went out, he was asleep. When we got back . . .' her voice trailed off, her eyes filling with tears.

'You know he's saying someone else started the fire?' Whitelaw said in a neutral voice.

She looked down at her hands. 'Norah was a harmless old woman, who was trying to help. How do you imagine you'd be feeling if you thought you'd caused her death?'

Whitelaw nodded. 'I'll try talking to him again,' he said.

He had a word with the staff nurse on duty first. It took a while to convince her that her patient wasn't a suspect, and that he wasn't about to be dragged, untreated, from the hospital. With a bit more persuasion, Whitelaw managed to wangle an empty office further up the corridor, so that the interview could be conducted in rather more privacy than the waiting room would allow.

'But he'll have to come through as soon as they're ready for him in X-ray,' the nurse said, clearly determined to keep the upper hand as she bustled about, locking papers into the filing cabinet as if expecting Whitelaw to rifle through them the moment her back was turned.

Whitelaw nodded, not even attempting to explain that they were on the same side; that they both had the patient's welfare at heart. When he had first joined the force, he thought with regret, people had still trusted the police. He wasn't even sure when that had changed.

'OK, son,' he said, when Kieran and Flora had been brought in and the nurse had gone. 'Supposing you tell me what you remember of this evening?'

Grudgingly, Kieran repeated what he had already told Lightowler. He hadn't been near a chip pan, he said. Or the kitchen at all, for that matter. He'd been asleep all evening.

Hadn't even been aware of Flora coming in and going out again.

'Asleep,' Whitelaw repeated, deliberately keeping his voice expressionless.

Kieran covered his eyes with his good hand. 'OK, then. Drunk. Pissed. Out of my face. All right?' His head came up. He held Whitelaw's gaze for a moment, before looking away. 'I'd had a bad day.'

Whitelaw noticed that Flora was looking from one of them to the other, as if sensing that there was something she had missed.

He attempted to steer them on to firmer ground. 'Let's just try to establish the sequence of events, shall we?'

Kieran nodded. Leaning his head against the back of the chair and staring at the ceiling, he said in a weary voice, 'I was on the bed. The dog was barking. That's what woke me up. At least . . .' he hesitated; seemed to be reconsidering. 'I think I heard the door,' he said slowly.

'What, someone knocking? Ringing the bell?'

Kieran shook his head. 'Opening. Or closing. I'm not sure which.'

'Front door or back?' Whitelaw pressed him.

'Front.'

'What time would that have been?'

'I don't know.' Kieran shifted irritably in the chair, grimacing as the movement jarred his hand. Whitelaw stayed quiet; allowed the silence to lengthen. After a few moments, Kieran added, 'It was still light.'

'Could it have been Flora going out, do you think?'

'I don't *know*.' He pressed his forehead with the heel of his hand, then ran his fingers through his hair in frustration. 'I thought . . . It could have been a . . . dream. A nightmare. I sometimes . . .' He glanced quickly at Flora. Then turning his attention to Whitelaw, he went on, 'I could hear the dog barking. I lay there for a while, feeling like shit, and then I realised I could smell smoke.' He sat forward. 'What if I'd heard someone breaking in? What if—'

'Let's leave the speculation on one side for a moment,' Whitelaw said firmly. 'You smelt smoke. Then what?'

'I went out onto the landing. I was a bit . . .' Kieran swallowed, '. . . a bit unsteady. 'Everywhere was full of smoke. I got halfway down the stairs. The hall was on fire; I could see flames coming from through the kitchen door. I tried to get out of the front, but the door—'

'I'd locked it. My key was in my bag, and I couldn't find the spare one, so I took yours.' Flora looked at him, stricken. 'Oh God, if I'd thought for one minute—'

'Let me just get this straight,' Whitelaw intervened. 'The front door was locked from the outside?'

Flora nodded. 'It's one of those you have to do yourself.' She fished in her bag and brought out a long silver key.

Whitelaw took it from her and examined it. 'And how many of these are there?'

'Three,' Kieran answered. 'Flora's, mine, and . . .' his voice dropped to a whisper, '. . . and the one I gave Norah.' Again, he glanced at Flora. 'So she could let the dog out.'

They would have to get round to her sooner or later, but Whitelaw was keen to get the incident fixed in his head in the right order first.

'You're in the hall,' he prompted. 'You can't unlock the door. Then what?'

'I tried to kick it down, but I couldn't get a run at it, because of the flames. So I went back upstairs.' Kieran's flat voice entirely failed to convey the terror he must have experienced. 'I could still hear Deefer barking. I couldn't get into the back bedroom — it was already alight — but I caught sight of him through the window. He was down the bottom of the garden, barking his head off, so I knew he was safe.'

Flora took a sharp breath, but didn't speak.

'It mattered, OK?' Kieran turned on her angrily. 'Anyway, if he'd not barked, I'd probably not have woken, so—'

'So you'd satisfied yourself the dog wasn't in danger,' Whitelaw said, evenly.

Kieran dragged his eyes away from Flora. 'Then I smashed a window in the front bedroom, and jumped. That's how I did my ankle in.'

'Why smash the window? Why not just open it?'

'They're painted shut,' Flora explained. 'None of them opens.' Her eyes flicked to Kieran. 'We've been meaning to get round to some decorating, but . . .'

The tension was still there between them. Kieran gave a short, bitter laugh. 'As well we didn't, as things have turned out.'

'So let me get this straight,' Whitelaw brought them back. 'The front door was locked. None of the windows would open . . .'

'So how did anyone get in to start the fire?' Kieran was there before him. 'Only someone did. I'm telling you, I might have been plastered, but there's no way I'd have gone downstairs, found the chip pan—'

Flora cleared her throat. 'The chip pan was already out. I saw it on the cooker when I came in.'

'OK, so it was out,' he said angrily. 'That still means I'd have had to light the gas under it, and then go back to bed. Without remembering any of it.' He looked from one of them to the other. 'For Christ's sake, I've remembered everything else that happened, haven't I?'

No one spoke.

'Anyway, we hadn't even got any potatoes in the house. I'd run out. How could I have been making chips, when there weren't any—'

'How about the back?' Whitelaw cut across him. Kieran was clutching at straws, and they all knew it. It was painful to watch.

'Locked,' Flora said quietly. 'And nobody would have got past the dog, anyway.'

Kieran gave her a long look. The room fell silent. Then reluctantly, Whitelaw said, 'So tell me about Norah.'

There wasn't much to tell. By the time Kieran had jumped, the street was full of people. The dog could still be heard, barking frantically. In the general confusion, no one had taken any notice when Norah had bolted off to the wool shop, then returned a minute later, muttering to herself. Kieran had realised too late what she was doing; had tried to stop her, but his ankle had slowed him down. As soon as she'd opened the front door, she was engulfed in flames. He'd tried to go on in after her, but the neighbours dragged him back. She hadn't stood a chance.

'Poor old girl.' Whitelaw shook his head. 'Bloody brave, though. If only she had realised you were already out.'

'Norah wasn't interested in people.' It was Flora who spoke. 'She wouldn't have been worried about Kieran. She was trying to save the dog.'

'And you tried to save her, son.' Whitelaw said quickly, realising belatedly that his last words would have done nothing but pile on extra guilt. He gestured to Kieran's damaged hand. 'You did everything you could.'

Kieran looked up, his eyes red-rimmed. 'She's dead. So I didn't do enough, did I?'

'I think I've got everything I need,' Whitelaw said quietly, when the staff nurse had taken Kieran off to have the ankle X-rayed. He glanced at his watch and got to his feet, then looked down at Flora, who was slumped in her chair, her face grey with exhaustion. 'Will you be OK?'

She nodded.

'I don't mind waiting, if you want a lift.'

'No.' She got up, flexing her back. 'I'm fine. But thanks.' She followed him out into the corridor. 'Strange, isn't it? This is the second time we've sat waiting in a hospital. Do you remember . . . ?'

'I remember.' It was a case Whitelaw never mentioned. A case he would rather forget.

They walked back to X-ray together in silence.

'What happened to the dog, by the way?' he asked inconsequentially.

'One of the neighbours is looking after it. I thought cats were the ones that had nine lives.' She attempted a smile, but her heart wasn't in it. In a small voice, she asked, 'So do you believe what he said about someone starting the fire deliberately?'

'Do you?'

It was a long time before she responded. 'He's been under a lot of strain. All this business with Danny Nolan . . .'

Whitelaw could sense the resentment. 'Which you think he's blown out of proportion, right?'

'Yes, I do. It's perfectly obvious what Danny's game is. I wouldn't be surprised if he'd decided right from the start that Oultonshaw Manor would be a good place to rob. Kieran really believed in him, you know.' Her voice was bitter. 'God help him, he still does.'

'Maybe he identifies with Nolan, in some way.'

'Maybe.' Flora looked at Whitelaw appraisingly. 'He'd been in enough trouble with the police at the same age.'

'All the lads in Ripley Grange have been in trouble with the police, otherwise they wouldn't be there. What do you think made Danny so special?'

'Kieran reckons he'd got a lot of talent.' She shook her head. 'No, that's not strictly fair. He *does* have a lot of talent. I could see that the first time he turned up to rehearsals. It's just that he's chosen to waste it. What he did the night of the gala was his choice. That's what Kieran refuses to see. I know Danny hasn't had things easy, but . . .'

'No. He had a pretty rough time of it when he was a kid, by all accounts.' Whitelaw made the observation gingerly. He realised that he must feel his way more carefully this time.

'So he's got lousy parents. I feel sorry for him.' She gave

an exasperated sigh. 'I do, truly. But it doesn't give him the right to spit in the eye of anyone who does try to help him, does it?'

The words came back at him so quickly that Whitelaw suspected it was a well-rehearsed argument. 'I'm not just talking about the set-up at home,' he said. He was all too painfully aware of the disastrous consequences of his last bull-in-a-china-shop act. He was also aware that he owed it to Kieran to explain as much to Flora. What he was not aware of was how much she knew, or suspected, of Kieran's own childhood. 'I've found out quite a lot about Danny Nolan recently,' he said. 'Things happened to him when he was a kid.' He watched her reaction carefully as he went on, 'Shocking things. Things that no adult should have to experience, let alone a little boy.'

If Whitelaw had had any residual doubts about the accuracy of Millie D'Sousa's assumptions, they were banished by Flora's reaction.

'Oh God,' she murmured, her eyes widening momentarily in unspoken question. Then her hand went to her throat and she said in an unsteady voice, 'Does Kieran know about this?'

'I went to see him earlier this evening.' Whitelaw nodded to confirm her dawning comprehension. 'So now perhaps you can see what made him hit the bottle.'

It was after two in the morning by the time the squad car dropped Whitelaw off outside his house. The ankle had turned out to be no more than a sprain, but the hand would need further treatment, and the doctor, concerned about the possibility of concussion in view of his behaviour, had with difficulty persuaded Kieran to stay in overnight for observation. Whitelaw had stuck around outside the ward until he was settled, and had insisted on giving Flora a lift back to the hotel; somehow, it had seemed the least he could do. Farrell, he had noticed, was waiting for her in reception, despite the lateness of the hour.

Val had gone up to bed, leaving a note and a plate of sandwiches on the kitchen table. Knowing that he wouldn't sleep anyway, Whitelaw took them into the lounge, along with his briefcase and another generous glass of brandy. No point in wasting what was left of the night; the following day promised to be a busy one. And, with any luck, a productive one, too.

He couldn't remember just what had made him stuff the photograph Millie had unearthed into his wallet before he'd set off for Sephton Street. He wasn't even sure what had made him show it to Flora while Kieran was being taken up to the ward. Maybe it was divine intervention. Maybe the Almighty had finally become so outraged at what had happened to all those young lives that He'd decided to lend Whitelaw a hand. Whitelaw didn't know and he didn't particularly care.

What he did know was that Flora had taken one look at the slimy bastard posing with his arms around Jason and Danny and had identified him without a second's hesitation.

Chapter Twenty

Despite the fact that he had had no more than three hours' sleep, and that taken slumped uncomfortably in an armchair, despite the two further celebratory brandies he'd put away, Whitelaw was raring to go when he got into the station well before seven the following morning.

For the first time in his life, he wished he had come sufficiently to grips with the age of technology to know how to tap into the PNC via the unused computer on his desk. He very badly needed to check a record. And although there were any number of bright young things he could have asked, even taking into account the necessary exclusion of Neville Medlock, the fortuitous way in which he had come by his suspect's identity made him feel obscurely possessive about the information. It took him a full five minutes of arguing with himself over the first cup of tea of the day before he could bring himself to pass the name on to someone with the ability to check it out for him.

Complete waste of time. No hint of form; not so much as a speeding ticket. But then one of the frightening things about paedophiles was that so many of them didn't have any previous. Stolen property seldom went unreported. Stolen lives all too frequently did.

'You'll have something to write on your record before I've finished with you, you pervert,' Whitelaw muttered to the photograph. It wouldn't help Jason Morrissey. It wouldn't help Kieran

Henshall; he'd taken the law into his own hands at the tender age of sixteen, and would carry the burden of a murder conviction around with him for the rest of his life. But it might just help young Danny Nolan to see behind bars the bastard who had ruined his childhood. And Whitelaw intended to raise heaven and earth to make it happen.

He obtained an address by the conventional method of looking in the phone directory, glad that some information, at least, could still be had without the need for gadgetry. Then, scribbling a list of instructions for Lightowler, he headed straight back out to the car park. Early-morning interviews, he had found before, could catch a suspect off guard; without time to dress, to prepare, to adopt whatever façade was presented to colleagues and acquaintances as 'normal'. Guilt was more easily visible without the window dressing.

The pretentiously named Blackport Boulevard turned out to comprise the feeder road into a new estate built on land that had previously accommodated a steel works and that was now attempting, with the assistance of a number of overpriced housing developments, to claw its way towards gentrification. Just about every architectural style, from scaled-down Tudor manor to Victorian artisan's cottage, was represented in the maze of *closes*, *rises* and *avenues*. No *streets*, or even *roads*, as far as Whitelaw could discern. The pocket-handkerchief gardens were uniformly pristine; the middle-range company cars parked on the block-paved driveways shining. Whitelaw would have staked a month's pay that there wasn't an out-of-date tax disc on the entire estate. The very picture of middle-class respectability. He very much hoped that he was about to ripple its tranquil surface.

He had taken a marked vehicle, working on the tried and tested premise that there was nothing like a patrol car outside a house first thing in the morning to get the neighbours talking. He parked next to a red Mercedes convertible, six or seven years old; a car that suggested, to Whitelaw's seasoned eye, that its owner had aspirations to a lifestyle he couldn't quite afford. He examined it, unsure what he was looking for, then walked up to the front door of the house and rang the bell.

He moved back towards the pavement so that he could observe the inevitable twitch of the bedroom curtains. It wasn't long coming. But it was a full three minutes after that before the door was opened. Whitelaw asked himself how many people, confronted by a squad car at their front door before seven thirty in the morning, took three minutes to find out what was up. Unless, of course, they already knew.

The time hadn't been spent in getting dressed; the man who stood in front of Whitelaw had brushed his hair, had applied aftershave, by the smell of him, but he was wearing a kimono-style dressing gown. Whitelaw could see why Flora had had so little trouble in identifying him. Apart from a few extra pounds he looked almost identical to the photograph taken more than a decade before, although the uniform darkness of his hair, a certain puffiness under the eyes, suggested that the ageing process had been slowed more by artifice than a healthy lifestyle.

'Nicholas Perotti?' Whitelaw asked, flashing his warrant card. 'Could we have a word, please?'

Perotti stood aside to let him in. He showed Whitelaw into a living room that seemed unnaturally orderly; no papers, no cups or plates from the night before, no book or videos in evidence. Tidied in those three minutes?

'Nice house, if I might say so, sir,' Whitelaw observed genially, taking a seat. 'I was always led to believe there wasn't much money in writing plays. You know, starving in garrets, and such.'

Perotti smiled thinly.

'Have you had a lot of your stuff put on?' He remembered Kieran Henshall's assessment of the man's talent, or lack of it, and added disingenuously, 'Forgive me for asking, but I'm not a great theatre-goer, and I don't get a lot of time for the telly. I expect the wife . . .'

'I've had a number of works performed.' Perotti didn't elaborate as to where.

'So you would describe yourself as a professional writer?'

He had clearly hit a nerve. Perotti said curtly, 'I also do some teaching.'

'Where would that be, sir?'

'I run several creative writing courses.'

'At the university? I understand the English department there is very—'

'For the local authority.' The words were spoken grudgingly. Whitelaw got the impression it wasn't an image of himself that Perotti was keen to project. As if anxious to get away from the subject, he added, 'May I enquire what this is all about, Inspector?'

Whitelaw had thought he was never going to ask. Now he had, he decided to get straight to the point. 'I'm making some enquiries into the disappearance of a young man. Can you confirm that the man in the centre of the picture is you, sir?' He produced the photograph, watching Perotti's reaction closely as he handed it to him, taking in the slight tremor in his fingers, the merest hint of a grimace as he gazed at it.

Perotti cleared his throat, then said in a low voice, 'Disappearance? Is this some kind of a joke, Inspector?' It was not the response Whitelaw had been expecting. Perotti got to his feet, still holding the photograph, and went on, 'I'm sure you are as aware as I am that he's dead.' He stumbled slightly over the word. 'So why this talk of disappearance?'

'Dead?' Whitelaw echoed. He hadn't expected to do much more in the first interview than rattle the bars of Perotti's cage, get a preliminary impression of the man. And here he was listening to what sounded as if it could be leading to an admission of . . .

But it was at Jason's likeness that Perotti was staring as he went on, 'I assume you read your own press releases. Jason Morrissey was a boy of considerable charm, Inspector. And talent. I very much regret the . . . appalling circumstances of his death.' Perotti cleared his throat again. Steadied his voice. 'Other than that, I can tell you very little, I'm afraid.'

'Do you remember all the boys who passed through Denstone Park as clearly, Mr Perotti?'

'Jason stood out from the others . . .' Perotti was still staring at the photograph; he had barely glanced at Danny Nolan, Whitelaw noticed. As if realising he was being observed, he handed the picture back, and said stiffly, 'I mourn his death as a waste of talent, and for no other reason.'

'From what you've said, I take it that the two of you were . . . close?'

'What exactly do you mean by that?'

'Whatever springs to mind, sir,' Whitelaw replied placidly.

Perotti flushed. 'I accept that in a job like yours, Inspector, misanthropy must be difficult to avoid.'

Whitelaw felt a fleeting gratitude to all the crosswords he and Val had done together in their time; he couldn't help thinking Perotti was deliberately attempting to wrong-foot him with long words. 'It is,' he agreed. 'But I always attempt to look for the best in my fellow man. So if you could tell me a little more about your relationship with Jason Morrissey . . . ?'

Perotti looked at him keenly, then sat down again. 'Let me see if I can explain. The children who came through Denstone Park were like plants that needed water. They were crying out for encouragement. Recognition.'

Whitelaw bit back a response.

'The whole ethos of the place, Tricia Denstone's vision, was to provide those things.' Perotti pressed his hands together earnestly. 'Yes, I was close to Jason. I hope I was close to all the youngsters in my charge. I tried to give them confidence, a sense of self-worth that for most of them was sadly lacking.'

He was good. Whitelaw had to hand him that. But then persuasiveness was the main weapon in the paedophile's armoury.

'Well, sir, you certainly appear to have succeeded in young

Jason's case. From what I've gleaned of his specialities as a rent boy, no one could accuse him of lack of confidence. Quite the extrovert, as I understand it.'

Perotti stared at him in silence for a moment. Then he said stonily, 'Was there anything else I can help you with? Because if not—'

Whitelaw handed him the photograph that Sunil had left at the station the night before his murder. As before, it was on Jason that Perotti's gaze was fixed.

The avidity in the man's expression filled Whitelaw with disgust. 'If you look at the back sir, you will see there is a name,' he said tersely. "Mario, 14." Does that mean anything to you?'

'Nothing at all.'

Whitelaw was inclined to believe him; there had not been the slightest glimmer of recognition as Perotti had turned it over, glanced at it and handed it back. Nevertheless, he said, 'I just wondered, it being an Italian name, like your own . . .'

'My father was born in Blackport, Inspector. He had ambitions to be a singer when he was young. I assume he decided that "Perotti" had a more exotic ring to it than "Parrot". He changed his surname by deed poll before I was born. He never visited Italy in his life.' With a faint smile, Perotti added, 'He was wrong about the name, by the way. He ended up running a chip shop in Wharf Street.'

'And a very nice fish supper he did there, if my memory as a beat bobby serves me correctly,' Whitelaw beamed, getting to his feet. He'd done what he came to do; he'd let the bastard stew for a bit.

'Just to clear up any confusion,' he said, when they got to the front door. 'I wasn't referring to Morrissey when I showed you the photograph. It was the other lad I was talking about. Maybe you didn't recognise him. After all, he was hardly more than a baby, when the picture was taken. Coincidence, though, isn't it?'

Perotti looked at him blankly. Either he was a better actor

than he was a playwright, Whitelaw thought, or he really hadn't recognised Nolan.

'Small world, isn't it? Young Danny was the leading man in the play you put on at the Freddie Denstone Memorial Gala. I expect you recall, he disappeared before the play started. Strange, that, after all the effort he'd put into it.'

He watched the colour recede from the other man's face as quickly as it had appeared.

'Makes you wonder what on earth he could have been thinking about, doesn't it, sir?'

Whitelaw's next task of the day was to visit Danny Nolan's mother.

'Just one or two questions,' he said, when she reluctantly allowed him entry to the cluttered, unkempt flat.

She stared at him truculently through a cloud of cigarette smoke. 'I've already told you everything I know.'

'Why can't you piss off and leave her alone?' McTeer, his mouth so full his words could barely be understood, looked up from his piled plate of bacon and sausage.

Whitelaw would have laid odds that he was the only member of the family who ate so well. Ignoring him, he went on, 'I know how concerned you must be about Danny's disappearance, Mrs Nolan . . .' He doubted that the words sounded any more convincing to her than they did to his own ears.

'McTeer,' she corrected him, glancing nervously at the man.

'Yes, of course.' Whitelaw's gaze followed hers for a moment. 'Danny's the odd one out, isn't he?'

It was the only snide remark he allowed himself. Getting down to business, he asked her to go over what Danny had said when he had turned up on the night of the gala. Which was nothing, because she had refused to let him in. If he'd come to his mother for help, he'd been disappointed; probably not for the first time in his short life. According to Mrs McTeer, he had made no attempt to get in touch with her since.

'He was in care a few times when he was a kid, wasn't he?' Whitelaw tried not to make the question sound like an accusation, but it was met with instant hostility.

'So?'

Whitelaw kept his voice even. 'When he was about six or seven, he spent a period with foster parents?'

'Yeah,' McTeer laughed, and jerked his head at his wife. 'Until the stuck-up wankers found they couldn't handle the little sod any better than she could.'

Get the questioning over quickly, Whitelaw told himself. Before the temptation to commit GBH became irresistible. 'Mrs McTeer, did Danny ever mention anything . . .' he sought a suitable phrase '. . . anything untoward that happened to him at around that time?'

That hit the spot. The woman bent to stub out her cigarette, but not before Whitelaw saw the expression on her face.

'I don't know what you mean,' she said, lighting up another one.

'Did he ever tell you of anyone trying to . . . interfere with him, in any way?'

'Are you saying that bunch of tossers at Social Services let some pervert get their hands on him?' For the first time, McTeer was interested. No doubt he had spotted some mileage in a compensation claim, Whitelaw thought in disgust, or at the very least, a bit of publicity in the local press.

'Danny went missing from his foster home for some days on one occasion, I understand.' He addressed the question to the mother. 'When he came back here, did he—'

'Danny was always making things up when he was a kid. He spent too much time with his head in bloody books, that was his trouble.'

Her aggression told Whitelaw everything he needed to know. 'So he did tell you,' he said quietly.

'Kids make up stories like that all the time,' she said, not meeting his eye.

'Stories like what, Mrs McTeer?'

Whitelaw felt physically sick, as the woman recounted what Danny had confided in her all those years before. How he had been taken on the train by a big boy. How they had gone to a posh hotel to have their pictures taken. And what had happened to him there. The childish terminology, as she repeated it, only served to add to the horror.

'And you did *nothing*?' he said at last, making no attempt to keep the disbelief from his voice. 'Not even try to find out who those animals were?'

'I told you,' she snapped, taking a deep drag on her cigarette. Her eyes were hard, as if daring Whitelaw to challenge her further. 'I know Danny. You don't. He was just trying it on to make me feel bad about not having him here. He was always at it. Still is.'

Inadequate didn't come close, for her brand of parenting. Whitelaw told himself not to judge; told himself that he knew nothing of her early life, and what had made her into what she was. He tried to ask himself what Millie would have had to say about her. But still, all he could feel was contempt.

Chapter Twenty-One

Whitelaw called in at the General on his way back. His warrant card gained him eventual access to the ward, where he found Kieran apparently asleep.

'You've got a visitor!' The young nurse who drew back the screens smiled, then murmured in a less friendly voice to Whitelaw, 'He's had a very disturbed night, so make it quick, please.'

Kieran, his left hand heavily bandaged and in a sling, opened his eyes. His face lit up briefly, until he spotted Whitelaw standing behind her.

'Sorry, son. Too early for anyone except nuisance callers,' Whitelaw said in an overhearty voice. 'How're you doing?'

He'd been cleaned up, but apart from that Kieran looked little better than he had the night before. Whitelaw didn't wait for a reply to the fatuous question. Instead, he said, 'Just came to tell you I've got one of my men interviewing your neighbours. In case anyone spotted anything suspicious before the fire.'

Kieran nodded. Then he said, 'I'm not making it up, you know.'

'No one's said you are.' Not in so many words, at any rate, Whitelaw added silently, aware that he was most probably wasting valuable police time on the interviews for no better motive than that he felt sorry for the young bloke. Not to say responsible. 'Here,' he added quickly. He dumped the carrier bag he'd been clutching on the bed. 'I bought you these. I thought perhaps Flora could take them round.'

'Hospital food's not that bad,' Kieran said with a glimmer of his old humour as, rousing himself, he peered into the bag. He sat up and, one-handed, tipped half a dozen tins of dog food onto the bed. He picked one up and examined the label, not looking at Whitelaw as he added, 'Thanks. I appreciate the thought.'

'I used to have dogs myself, when I was younger.' Whitelaw was pleased that he'd decided grapes or flowers would be naff. 'I reckon I'll get another one when I retire. A Border collie, I've always fancied.'

'Dead bright.' Kieran nodded. 'Need a lot of exercise, though. I had one, once. When I was—' He broke off, as if realising that for a moment he had been in danger of dropping his guard. Whitelaw couldn't help suspecting that the sudden yawn was manufactured, as Kieran slid back down in the bed and murmured, 'Anyway, thanks for the tins.'

'Yeah, well . . .' Whitelaw levered himself to his feet. 'Listen, I'll let you know if . . .' Kieran's eyes were closed. Whitelaw patted him self-consciously on the shoulder. 'Just you take care of your-self, son.'

Flora was coming up the stairs as he made his way down to recep-tion. She looked hardly less exhausted than Kieran.

'Has anything . . . ?' she began anxiously, when she spotted Whitelaw.

He shook his head. 'Social call. How's it going?'

'Oh, you know.' She shrugged, then straightened her shoulders and said with a brightness that didn't quite ring true, 'Could be worse, I suppose. Greg's said we can borrow his cottage in Stratford-on-Avon when Kieran gets out of here, so at least we'll have a roof over our heads.

'Won't be a problem then, being away from Blackport?' Whitelaw knew it was none of his business. 'What about your job?' he added, anyway.

'My boss was great, as a matter of fact.' Flora sounded as though she hadn't expected it. 'I rang him from the hotel just before I came out. Said I could take off as much time as I needed. On full pay.'

'That's Denstone Automotive Engineering, isn't it?'

She nodded. 'I was amazed, to tell you the truth. Henry Denstone's never struck me as being exactly the soul of compassion, but he couldn't have been nicer. Really helpful.' She shrugged her shoulders. 'Just shows how deceptive appearances can be, doesn't it?'

'It does indeed,' Whitelaw said thoughtfully.

'Have you questioned . . . ?' Flora hesitated. Whitelaw had instructed her not to mention her identification of the photograph to anyone; she was clearly taking him at his word.

'It's early days,' he said noncommittally.

'I . . . I didn't mention anything about it to Kieran.'

'I gathered not when he didn't ask.'

She looked troubled. 'I don't like not telling him things.'

Whitelaw nodded sympathetically. 'Best not, for now, eh? Until he's feeling a bit more himself.'

She was silent for a moment. Then she said quietly, 'Don't let that monster get away with what he's done.'

'As God's my witness, Flora, I'm going to do everything in my power to get to the bottom of this bloody business. Lift up every possible stone to see what comes crawling out. Then stamp on it.' Whitelaw realised, to his embarrassment, that his voice was shaking with emotion.

For a moment, neither of them spoke. Then Flora looked into his face and said, 'Do you know why I've always resented Danny so much?'

'Because you thought he was taking Kieran for a ride?' He

could guess why she was asking. 'Listen, love, it was a perfectly understandable reaction. For that matter, you might well still be right. Danny Nolan's no angel, so don't start to feel guilty just because you've found out—'

'I resent him because when I look at him, I see what Kieran used to be.'

'And it's a side of him you find difficult to accept.' Whitelaw nodded. 'I can see that. It must be hard for you to—'

'This isn't about me,' she said fiercely. 'It's Kieran I'm talking about. As soon as he started on about this kid he'd met – dodgy background, really bright – I knew it was bad news. I could almost see him being sucked back into his own past. And then when I met Greg Farrell—' She broke off, her face troubled. Whitelaw wondered what was coming next, as she twisted the silver ring on her little finger, then said angrily, 'I don't know how I can explain it to you.'

He looked at her uncomfortably. 'I don't think it's me you should be worrying about explaining it to, love.'

It was as if he hadn't spoken. 'You see, I thought Greg was what Kieran *could* be, if only he could let go of what happened to him when he was a child. Put it all behind him.' She gave a bitter laugh. 'I really imagined it was as simple as that.'

'Maybe it is.' He could imagine her turmoil. How many girls her age, faced with the choice between a rich, successful heart-throb like Farrell, and a penniless can of emotional worms like Kieran Henshall, would even stick around for long enough to think about it? It could hardly be called a fair contest. He cast around for what he hoped were the right words. 'Ask yourself the question, how many youngsters with Kieran's background could have managed to—'

She wasn't listening to him. 'We were talking. Last night, before I left him on the ward. I found out why Danny's dog's so important to him. I wish he'd explained before. Maybe I wouldn't have been so bloody . . .' She bit her lip; seemed to be having difficulty in going on. 'He had one of his own,' she said at last. 'When he was small.'

'Yes.' Whitelaw still wasn't sure what she was trying to say. 'He was talking about one, just now.'

'His mother's boyfriend killed it. It was trying to protect Kieran from him, so he kicked it to death. Kieran was twelve years old.' Her eyes filled with tears. 'How can anyone be expected to put something like that behind them? Ever?'

'I don't know, love.' Whitelaw felt an almost overwhelming sense of helplessness. Thirty years, he'd been in the job. Thirty years, and he could still be shocked by the wickedness he confronted. But maybe the day he stopped being shocked, he told himself, was the day he should pack it all in. Impulsively, he put his arms around her and gave her a hug. 'You're a good girl, Flora. You'll get him through it.' Then, instantly embarrassed, he stepped back. 'Look, I've got this friend,' he said gruffly, scribbling down Millie's number. 'She's a good listener. Maybe she could help.'

Flora nodded; pushed the scrap of paper into her pocket. Then rubbing her hands across her eyes, she said, 'Anyway, I must go. I've only called in quickly to drop him off some clothes and stuff.' She gestured to the carrier bag she was holding. 'And find out what time he'll be coming out. Then I should get in to work. There's all sorts of loose ends I must tie up if I'm going to be taking a few weeks off.'

'I can imagine.' Whitelaw was relieved to be back on the surer territory of practicalities. 'You run along, then.'

She nodded again; made no move to go. Then she asked suddenly, 'Have you got any children?'

'No.' He felt himself colouring. 'Just never seemed to happen.'

'That's a pity.' She pecked his cheek, then started off up the stairs. 'You'd have made a lovely dad for someone.'

*

Whitelaw had never felt a greater weight of responsibility on his shoulders, as he parked the patrol car and made his way into the station.

'Did we get consent to that application?' he demanded, sticking his head into the incident room.

'Came through from the Crown Court a couple of minutes ago, Guv.' Crutchlow, one of the three new constables on the case, produced a signed warrant.

Whitelaw grabbed it from him. 'Lightowler's over at Sephton Street, I take it? Tell him I want a full report. As soon as he gets back.'

'Don't think he's gone yet, Guv.' Another of the men, whose name Whitelaw knew he should by now have committed to memory, looked up from his computer.

'What? Why the hell not? And who are you, anyway?' Whitelaw added bad-temperedly.

'Don't shoot the messenger, Guv!' The man's grin quickly subsided when he saw the look on Whitelaw's face. 'DC Mason, Guv. Lightowler took a call from the Met while you were out. They've come across some stuff on the Net they thought you should see. I think he's logging on to it now.'

'Speak bloody English, for Christ's sake,' Whitelaw snapped. 'Who's doing the Sephton Street interviews, then?'

Mason shrugged his shoulders. 'Don't know, Guv.'

'Do I have to do everything around this sodding place myself? Crutchlow, get yourself over there. Now. Mason, off your arse. I want you to check out any recent links between Perotti and Jason Morrissey. The rest of you, stop sitting around at those bloody contraptions as if you're the typing pool, and get some fucking work done.'

Crutchlow gave a low whistle as Whitelaw slammed out of the room. 'Bloody hell, what's bitten him this morning?'

'God knows.' Mason shrugged again. An older hand, he was clearly unfazed by the sudden outburst. 'Probably pissed off because everyone except him's moved on from quill pens. Or maybe Lightowler's right, after all.' He stifled a yawn as he turned back to his screen. 'Maybe the miserable old fart really is losing the plot.'

Lightowler was sitting hunched over his computer. He jumped to his feet as Whitelaw came into the office, his back to the screen, his face flushed. His eyes, Whitelaw noticed, seemed unnaturally bright.

'I hope you haven't been playing games on that bloody thing, when you were supposed to be out . . .' Whitelaw's voice tailed off as he glimpsed the image behind Lightowler's back. 'Jesus Christ,' he breathed. 'What in the name of . . . ?'

'From the Met, Guv.' Lightowler's gaze strayed back to the screen, as he resumed his seat. 'They picked them up off the hard drive of some perv they raided over the weekend. Thought one of the kids might be Nolan.' He leant forward, his head on one side, his eyes fixed on the monitor. Then, with an un-convincing show of indifference, he looked up and added, 'Impossible to tell, from what you can see. The cameraman wasn't too interested in faces.'

The slight, dark-skinned body was all but obliterated by the bulkier figure above it. Whitelaw forced himself to examine the image more closely, momentarily unable to speak. He wasn't sure which was the more sickening; the obscenity of what was being done to the child on the screen, or the erection that Lightowler hadn't quite managed to conceal before he had sat down so hastily.

In as even a voice as he could manage, he said, 'OK, I'll deal with it now.'

'There are others.' Lightowler seemed to have regained his composure. He pressed the mouse, and another image appeared. Another click, and the child's head suddenly filled the screen in a blur of black, out-of-focus curls. 'But even if you try magni-fying—'

'I said, I'll deal with it, Constable.'

Lightowler's head came up at the harshness of Whitelaw's tone. For a second, the two men's gazes locked. Then, a dark flush spreading from his collar to the roots of his close-cropped hair, Lightowler got up from the desk and left the room without another word.

Whitelaw's head was still filled with the images as, blinking at the sudden sun after the dimness of his office, he left the station to walk the few hundred yards to the High Street branch of Perotti's bank.

It was lunchtime, and every inch of the meagre lawns in front of the town hall was occupied by sunbathing office workers; sleeves rolled up, ties askew, trying to pretend they were at the seaside. Whitelaw experienced the same sense of dislocation that he had felt as a kid, coming out of the cinema after one of the Saturday morning horror films that had seemed so chilling to his young, uninitiated eyes; of stepping out into a world where everything was suddenly, blessedly, normal again. In the days when he had still been sufficiently naïve to think horror was only make-believe.

A morning spent staring at the flickering computer screen as Crutchlow manipulated the images had done nothing to dull his sense of outrage and disgust; neither had it brought him any closer to deciding whether any of the children could have been Danny Nolan. According to the information from the technical boys at the Met, the images had been scanned from Polaroids, which explained their poor quality; probably ten or so years old, which was why someone had thought of the Blackport inquiry. But it simply wasn't possible to identify any of the victims. As Lightowler had said, it wasn't faces the cameraman had been interested in. Whitelaw asked himself what Nicholas Perotti's reaction would be when he was asked to drop his trousers.

He was still smiling grimly at the thought as he stepped into the coolness of the bank foyer, flashed his warrant card, and demanded to see the manager. The court order swiftly ensured co-operation, and within minutes he found his gaze fixed on another screen. He scrolled through the lists of figures, searching for any recent withdrawals that might confirm that Perotti was being blackmailed. But what he found was something entirely different. Amongst the local authority payments, the standing orders for mortgage, fuel bills and council tax, one entry jumped out at him from the screen. An authorised credit for a thousand pounds, as regular as clockwork on the first Monday of every month.

From Denstone Automotive Engineering.

Chapter Twenty-Two

Much as his first instinct was to wade straight in, Whitelaw decided to let the situation simmer for a few more days before he questioned Henry Denstone.

For one thing, he wanted to allow time for Perotti to contact the other man, as he surely would. He wanted the two of them to work themselves into a lather. The anticipation of being collared, Whitelaw had discovered in his long career, was a marvellous tongue-loosener. Panic in the ranks was what he was after.

For another thing, he needed to prepare his argument for bringing Denstone in; every 'i' dotted, every 't' crossed. Lambert would have his arse for an ashtray if he'd got it wrong. And in the small hours, tossing and turning next to Val, it was easy to convince himself he had got it very wrong indeed. Was he really saying that Henry Denstone, pillar of the local community, had been part of a paedophile ring? Running it, even? It was hard to imagine those icy loins fathering a child, let alone molesting one. But Whitelaw didn't need Medlock's psychology degree to tell him it was precisely that kind of repression that could spill over into perversion. Why else would Denstone have been shelling out twelve thousand a year to a no-hoper like Perotti? Whatever hold the man had over him, it was powerful. And Whitelaw needed to find out exactly what it was.

So, for the rest of the week, he went back over the case, checking and double-checking. Mason's investigations at the

Heckton Fields address revealed that Nicholas Perotti had been a regular visitor to the place right up to the time of Jason Morrissey's death; which hardly confirmed the man's assertion that their only association had been at Denstone Park.

But it was the questioning at Sephton Street that proved most fruitful. Although no one had seen anything out of the ordinary on the night of the fire, Crutchlow had taken it upon himself to widen the inquiry; and to good effect. A resident from further down the road came up with an incident that he had witnessed a couple of weeks previously. A boy in a Chicago Bulls bomber jacket being dragged into a car that sounded similar to the car Carlie Sykes had reported as being parked outside the Seamen's Rest, the night Danny disappeared. And identical to the one Kieran Henshall claimed had tried to run him down.

'Volvo T5R, the witness thought,' Crutchlow said, when he came into Whitelaw's office with the news late on the Thursday afternoon. 'Spoilers, tinted windows. Described it as looking menacing. Said he's seen it around a few times since, as well.'

Whitelaw snorted. 'If it looked so "menacing", why the hell didn't he report it at the time? And can't he be more specific than "about two weeks ago"?'

'I did push him, Guv, but he couldn't remember. Or wouldn't.'

'Christ, what's happening to this bloody country, that a kid can be grabbed off the street and all anyone's interested in is what the bloody car looks like?'

Crutchlow shook his head. 'You can't really blame him for not wanting to get involved. Sephton Street's not that far from the docks, Guv. He thought it was a couple of drugs dealers having a bit of an argy-bargy. And as the car's been hanging around since—'

'All right, all right,' Whitelaw cut him off irritably.

'He assumed it was drugs because Nolan's black, I suppose?' Lightowler looked up from his desk. 'I thought we weren't supposed to be jumping to conclusions like that any more.

Institutionalised racism, it's called,' he added, pompously.

Still cosying up to Medlock then, Whitelaw thought; the devious bastard's influence couldn't have been clearer if he'd been standing by the desk, pulling the strings. 'Just get on with what you're doing,' he snapped, temporarily distracted back to the problem of what he was going to do about Lightowler. Since the incident with the computer, the constable had been restricted to the most basic of paperwork, but it couldn't go on. Whitelaw realised he was going to have to involve Lambert again. He also realised that Lambert wasn't going to like it. One request for the removal of an officer from the case might be deemed cautious; a second could be interpreted as paranoia.

He turned his attention back to Crutchlow. 'Run a list of registered keepers. And check the description against the car Carlie Sykes saw.'

'Already tried, Guv. She's done a moonlight.'

Whitelaw grunted. The investigation must be playing havoc with the landlord's takings, down at the Seamen's Rest; although some other poor bugger had probably already moved into the dump Carlie and her kids had vacated in such a hurry. He wondered if she'd found the tenner.

'So what's happened to Nolan, do you reckon?' Crutchlow asked.

It was a question Whitelaw didn't particularly want to consider. But one thing seemed for sure, in view of this latest piece of evidence: no way had Danny Nolan left Blackport of his own volition. Would it have made any difference, Whitelaw asked himself, if they had taken Kieran Henshall's fears seriously from the beginning? Another question he didn't want to consider.

He stared at the daunting mountain of paperwork in front of him and shook his head. 'God alone knows,' he answered Crutchlow wearily.

Which, at six forty-five the following morning, on what promised to be another scorching day, became God plus the security guard at Chemico, who was patrolling the wharf alongside the disused factory, five miles or so up the estuary from Blackport docks. Spotting a glimpse of sodden red jacket amongst the tangle of discarded shopping trolleys and rusting bicycle frames, the man was later to explain, he waded out to investigate.

And discovered Danny Nolan's decomposing body.

The corpse had already been bagged, by the time Whitelaw got to the scene. A cloud of bluebottles, alerted by the stench, buzzed expectantly above it. Whitelaw flapped them angrily aside, then lowered the zip and glanced reluctantly inside. The time spent in the water had done Nolan's features no favours, but even without the help of the distinctive jacket, identification was beyond dispute.

'Cause of death?' he asked the police surgeon huskily.

If the man noticed the struggle Whitelaw was having with his emotions, he gave no indication of it. 'I think we can rule out suicide,' he said drily, indicating the tape that bound the wrists and ankles.

Whitelaw nodded, biting back the rebuke that sprang to his lips; how many times had he made equally flippant comments over a corpse?

'There's evidence of garrotting, you'll notice.' The surgeon brushed away a fly, and pointed to the deep indentation below the jaw. 'Quite a professional job,' he added dispassionately. 'Someone seems to have opened a contract killing firm in Blackport. This is the third death I've attended in the last two weeks that has all the hallmarks of a hitman.'

'Tell me about it,' Whitelaw muttered, fastening the bag before any more flies had time to settle.

'There are a number of bruises and abrasions, although it's impossible to determine whether they were caused before or after death, until the post-mortem examination is carried out.' The surgeon glanced down at the murky, sluggish waterline. 'Before, would be my guess. There doesn't appear to be much tidal movement round here to explain them.'

'And how long has it . . . he . . . been in the water?'

The surgeon lifted his shoulders. 'Again, I'm only hazarding a guess. Between one and two weeks?'

And the difference between one week and two was huge, Whitelaw realised. He needed a time frame that put the death between the night of the Memorial Gala and the phone call to Kieran Henshall three days later. Beyond then, Nolan would have had time to go to London, try the stolen cards, make the call. But if they could prove that the boy had been killed within those first three days . . . There was little point in trying to push for greater precision, however, no matter how important it might be. The doctor simply couldn't provide it. Nor was it by any means certain that the post mortem would be able to pinpoint the time of death accurately enough to be conclusive either. The water had done its work too well for that.

Next, Whitelaw went to have a word with the uniformed constable who'd been first on the scene. The body had got caught up, he told Whitelaw, which was what had kept it submerged. The jacket sleeve had been entangled in the spokes of a bicycle wheel sunk into the mud a few feet from the shore.

'Normally be about six or seven feet deep out there,' the constable, a local man, nodded out towards it. 'Mind, it's been that hot the past few weeks, the waterline's dropped. Security guard reckons there's all sorts appearing that's usually submerged.'

'So it would seem,' Whitelaw said grimly. 'So where is this bloke?'

He was directed up the bank, to where the security guard was sitting. The man's face was almost the same colour as the scrubby patch of grass on which he was sitting, his uniform caked in evil-smelling mud. He was only young; mid-twenties, Whitelaw guessed, mountainously broad, with a shaven head and biceps that spoke of hours training at the gym. Whitelaw had met the type before; thought they were hot enough to take the police on any day, but there were aspects of the job they weren't so hot on. Like dealing with decomposing corpses.

Whitelaw offered him a cigarette. 'Patrol round here every day, do you?' he asked.

'Yes.'

The response came back too quickly, too defensively. Whitelaw took his time lighting his own cigarette, inhaled deeply, then said, 'Let's try that again, shall we? I didn't ask what you were paid to do. So, when were you last down here?'

The man shifted his meaty buttocks uncomfortably on the grass. 'Few days,' he muttered.

'How many days?'

'I dunno.' He shrugged. 'It's not like anything ever happens.'

'Apart from the odd body being dumped.' Whitelaw's sarcasm reflected his frustration. 'Take a real pride in your job, do you, son?'

'You try patrolling an area the size of the town centre, where fuck-all ever happens, and see how much fucking pride you'd take,' the man retorted, with greater animosity than eloquence.

Whitelaw ignored the outburst. The poor sod was probably in shock, he reminded himself. 'So you didn't notice anything last time you came round?' he asked.

'Water level was a lot higher, wasn't it?'

Whitelaw nodded. 'And this morning?'

The man was still on the defensive. 'Just saw the top of the jacket, didn't I? Never realised . . .' He swallowed hard, and took a deep drag on his cigarette.

'It was very diligent of you to wade out to investigate,' Whitelaw said, neutrally.

'Yeah, well . . .' The man had the grace to flush. 'Chicago Bulls. Those jackets cost a bomb. My kid brother's nuts on Michael Jordan, isn't he? Thought he'd be dead chuffed. It's not like it was stealing, or nothing.' He glared challengingly at his questioner, suddenly very young, despite the muscles.

'OK, son,' Whitelaw nodded wearily.

He asked a few further questions, anticipating correctly that even such a cursory examination was a waste of his time. Then he left the guard to a reinvention of the facts that would most likely have him the hero of the hour by closing time, and walked the ten or so yards down to the waterline. He gazed out across the estuary. Hard to imagine that birds must once have waded in this soup-like slime, fish bred in the littered, murky water beyond. Civilisation hadn't added much. The area was clearly used as an unofficial tip. Further up the bank, a concrete ramp leading down to the water was flanked on one side by a disembowelled sofa, and on the other by a battered, rusted cooker.

'NO TIPPING', a sign attached to the wire-netted compound beyond declared, ineffectually. 'YOU ARE BEING WATCHED.'

Whitelaw read the sign, then read it again, his attention engaged by its final warning: 'CCTV CAMERAS IN USE.'

He hurried back to the guard. 'Your firm operate the cameras?' he demanded.

The man nodded warily.

'Which firm is it?'

'Listen, if they find out I haven't been——' the man started, but Whitelaw cut across him impatiently. 'Just tell me who you work for.'

'Pioneer Security,' he muttered, his expression becoming truculent. 'But I won't be for much longer once they find out——'

'Pioneer?' Whitelaw said sharply. He pulled his mobile from his pocket. 'Get the files on the Denstone Park arson,' he ordered without preamble, when he heard Crutchlow's voice. 'Check the name of the firm that was supposedly guarding the place. Yes, I do know how many files there are. Ring me back.'

He wandered back down to the water, while he waited. He poked the toe of his shoe against an ancient, half-submerged pushchair. Seventeen years ago, Nolan was being wheeled around in something similar, and now he had been snuffed out, his death as squalid as his short life. Whitelaw's mind veered away from what might have happened to the boy after he had been bundled into the car in Sephton Street, to how Kieran Henshall would react when he discovered what had happened. Standing on the litter-strewn shore, Whitelaw made a silent vow to take the time to visit him in Stratford-on-Avon; break the news to him personally before it hit the papers.

Crutchlow's call was several minutes coming. Whitelaw listened, and nodded. 'I thought so. Tell Mason to get over there now. Tell him to check the films from the CCTV cameras for the last two weeks. Frame by frame.' He frowned, then added, 'Tell him to get a list of employees too. Past and present. Right back to the time of the fire.'

Pioneer Security was a firm clearly stronger on administration than it was on recruitment; the list of past employees ran to more than two dozen sheets of A4, Mason reported when he rang in to the incident room a couple of hours later.

'Bring it back with you,' Whitelaw ordered. 'How about the cameras?'

'What do you want first, Guv? The bad news or the good news?' the man asked, in a fashion horribly reminiscent of Lightowler.

'Get on with it,' Whitelaw snapped.

'The camera's range doesn't extend as far as the end of the slip. There's no footage of anything being dumped in the water. Yes, Guv, but listen to this,' Mason went on rapidly when Whitelaw had demanded, with a turn of phrase that would have made the security guard blush, just what, in that case, the good news could be. 'At four twenty-three a.m. the morning after Nolan disappeared, a vehicle can be seen backing down the slip. It reappears at four thirty-one, travelling at speed. Driver too indistinct for possible ID, because of the tinted windscreen.'

'Licence number?' Whitelaw barked.

'Plates so splashed with mud it was impossible to make them out, Guv. But the car definitely fits the description of the one Nolan was seen being bundled into. So unless the post mortem throws a spanner in the works, I'd say Nolan died within hours of his disappearance.'

In which case, Whitelaw asked himself as he put down the phone, just who the hell was it who had rung Flora Castledine three days later?

Chapter Twenty-Three

'Ray Whitelaw's just been on the phone. He's down this way on Sunday, and asked if he could call in.' Flora came out into the sun, carrying two glasses of wine.

The setting was idyllic; the long garden, bordered by weeping willows, its flowerbeds vivid with lavender and foxgloves, hollyhocks and delphinium, was as tranquil and secluded as it must have been when the cottage was built, four centuries before. Yet the Royal Shakespeare Theatre rose majestically from the banks of the Avon, as if springing from the river itself, less than half a mile away. Within a couple of minutes, they could plunge themselves into the bustle of tourists on Waterside and the High Street, mingle with the expectant jostle of theatre-goers queuing for the next performance, celebrity-spot over a pint at the Dirty Duck. Flora had been in Stratford-upon-Avon for only a few days, and already she was in love with the place. She just wished that Kieran could share her enthusiasm.

He seemed reluctant to be there at all; abrupt to the point of rudeness towards Greg when he had driven them down, shown them how everything worked, took them on a whistle-stop tour of the town. Greg had been understanding; Kieran would need time to get over the trauma of the fire, was exhausted, still in pain from his burns . . .

Flora knew that none of Greg's explanations accounted for Kieran's anguish. He was locked in a torment at which she could only guess. The RSC had represented the height of his ambition since she had first known him. She had hoped that being so close to the theatre might have cheered him, but he seemed even more agitated in the rural tranquillity of Greg's cottage than he had in Blackport.

As if to underscore the point, he levered himself up, took the glass she offered him, swallowed most of it in one overquick gulp and asked sharply, 'Why would Whitelaw want to come here?'

'Just a social call, he said.' Flora wasn't sure that she believed Whitelaw any more than Kieran did; there had been something more than a little guarded in his tone. His line that even coppers had the odd day off sometime, and that his wife had always wanted to visit Stratford, hadn't quite rung true. He'd protested too much. And a two-hundred-mile-round trip was a hell of a long way for a day out. But that had been his story and he'd stuck to it. He had mentioned casually, just as he had been about to ring off, that he was bringing a friend as well; the social worker he had talked of at the hospital. Flora suspected that that was the real purpose of his visit. She also suspected that if she said as much to Kieran, he would make some excuse not to be there.

'He didn't say anything about Danny,' she added, before he asked.

He nodded, swallowed the rest of the wine, and then sat staring into space. 'Did he say whether Norah's body had been released yet?' he asked eventually.

'I didn't ask.' Which sounded, she thought, as if she didn't care. 'He would have said, if it had,' she added. 'He knows it's important to you.'

'I want her to have a proper send-off.' He spoke the words into space, his voice emotionless; the throbbing muscle in his cheek the only giveaway.

'I know, love,' she said quietly.

'I owe her that much, at least.'

'Kieran.' Flora knelt down on the grass beside him and took his good hand in her two, partly for the reassurance of physical contact with him, partly to stop his vicious gnawing at his finger-nails. 'It's a nice idea to do Norah's funeral for her, especially as she didn't have any family. But you owe her nothing. You did your best to save her.' She looked into his face and added gently, 'And at the end of the day, what she did was her own decision.'

He withdrew his hand. 'Which she should never have had to make.' He eased himself back down onto the grass and lay staring up at the cornflower sky.

The small silence between them lengthened. Somewhere up in one of the willows, a bird sang out, gloriously indifferent.

At last he whispered, 'I must have done it, mustn't I? Like that police bloke said, it was either me or the tooth fairy.'

'He was an idiot,' Flora said hotly. 'I've never heard a more insensitive—'

Before she could finish the sentence, Kieran pulled her down to him and stopped her mouth with his. It was the first time they had kissed, properly kissed, in almost two weeks, and she responded eagerly, moulding her body against him as the kiss deepened. But even as she felt him harden beneath her, felt the insistent probing of his tongue against her own, she sensed the desperation in his urgency; a hunger for oblivion that she knew neither she, nor anyone else, was able to satisfy. After a moment, he rolled away from her. Then with a muttered, 'I'm sorry,' he pulled himself onto his feet, and walked back into the house, Deefer at his side.

Flora stayed where she was; she didn't have the energy to do anything else. From the house, Deefer's boisterous barking told her that Kieran was preparing to take him for a walk. A minute later, all was quiet.

Kieran didn't reappear for lunch. By tea time, Flora was begin-ning to get seriously concerned. She was just debating whether to embark on the hopeless task of searching the crowded, unfamiliar streets for him when at last she heard the squeak of the front gate.

Running to the door, she threw it open to find Greg Farrell standing on the step.

'You saved me a dilemma.' He gave her a lopsided grin. 'I wasn't quite sure of the etiquette. Do I ring the bell, or use my key?'

Her attention had been so focused on Kieran, that Greg's sudden appearance had disorientated her. Recovering herself, she forced a smile and stood aside. 'It's your house.'

He followed her into the living room. 'I'm up for some meetings.' Evidently sensing her restraint, he added, 'Look, I hope you don't mind me dropping in like this. I can always—'

'No, of course not.' She realised how rude she must be appearing. What right had she to treat him as if he were an unwelcome guest in his own house? 'Have you eaten?' she asked him. 'Can I get you . . . ?'

'I thought we might all go out for something.' He peered out into the garden. 'Where's Kieran?'

'Gone walkabout, I think.' She attempted to keep her tone light, but Greg picked up on it immediately.

'Things are no better, then?'

She shook her head, not trusting her voice.

'Do you think he's still fretting about that Nolan lad?'

Suddenly, the weight of how very much more there was to the story than Greg knew overwhelmed her. Sitting down abruptly, she put her face in her hands and began to cry; great ugly, racking sobs that felt as though they would never stop. She was aware that Greg was standing above her, and vainly attempted to regain some self-control. She blew her nose, tried to speak, but the tears choked her off again before she could find any words.

Greg sat down next to her. He made no move to comfort her, just sat close until she had cried herself out. His nearness was soothing. At last she wiped the back of her hand across her face and managed a watery smile. 'I'm sorry. I don't know what all that was about,' she lied.

He looked at her in compassionate silence. Then he said, 'It must be hard for you.'

'For me?' Automatically, she shook her head; anything else would have been disloyal. 'Why would it be hard for me? It's Kieran . . .' Her voice caught as she said his name. She could feel the tears tightening her throat.

He touched her cheek, and said quietly, 'It doesn't have to be like this, you know.'

She didn't ask him what he meant, because she knew, just as she knew that if she didn't stand up, move away from him, he was going to kiss her. It was as if she had been hanging by her fingertips to a high ledge until her arms were out of their sockets; and now she had no choice but to let go. But with the relief of loosening her grip came the instant knowledge that she was in free fall; and that the outcome of that fall could be nothing but damage. Greg's lips had barely brushed her own before she pulled away from him.

He breathed in sharply, the colour flooding into his face, then stood up, turning away from her as he took off his glasses and made a big show of polishing them.

Flora sat stock-still, horrified by just how much she had wanted, for that split second, to forget that Kieran existed. She cleared her throat, then said in a voice that amazed her with its normality, 'I'm sorry. That was unforgivable of me. I should never have—'

Putting the glasses down, he took both her hands in his. 'You're a very special person, Flora. Be quite sure you're not throwing yourself away.' With a small squeeze, he released his grasp, then said in a brisker voice, 'I think I'd better be getting off.'

'Don't go.' Fearing that the words might sound as ambiguous to him as they did to her own ears, Flora went on quickly, 'How can we possibly turn you out of your own house? Look, we can easily find somewhere else to stay . . .'

'I think that might be a little difficult to explain to him, don't you?' He held her gaze for a moment before she looked away.

'I'll see you out,' she said.

Greg had been gone for less than five minutes when Deefer's excited barks told her that Kieran was back. She wondered if he had seen the car on his way up the lane. Jumping to her feet, she noticed Greg's glasses, still sitting where he had left them on the coffee table. She stuffed them hastily behind a cushion, hating herself for the small deception, and ran out into the hall.

Kieran looked different, somehow. Tired, but not as tired as he had when he had left. When she hugged him to her with a fierceness borne at least partly of guilt, he kissed her with a warmth and a simplicity that she had almost forgotten.

'I've been an idiot, Flora,' he said.

He led her through to the garden, stopping only to collect a couple of glasses for the bottle of wine he had brought in with him. Flora watched him, as he struggled to uncork it, and wondered what they were drinking to.

'Would you mind?' he asked, passing the bottle over. He grimaced at his hand, but without resentment. It struck her that it was the first time since the fire that he had allowed her to give him any help. She poured the wine and handed him a glass.

He raised it to her. 'To us,' he said, adding, as he searched her face, 'If you'll still have me, that is.'

For one fleeting, panicky moment, she wondered if he could know what she had so nearly done. But then he said softly, 'No one's as important to me as you are, Flora. Not Danny, not anyone. I've come too close to forgetting that, the past weeks. I'll not do it again.'

They would have made love right there, under the willow, if Deefer hadn't decided it was some game he should be joining in, sending the rest of the wine flying as he bounced around them, yapping madly. They were laughing as they hadn't laughed in weeks, as hand in hand they went back into the house, shutting Deefer firmly outside. It was as if Kieran had been on a long journey, and had come back to her.

'I've missed you,' Flora said softly.

And he looked deep into her eyes and whispered, 'I've missed you too.'

They were on the sofa, moving to their own slow, intimate rhythm when the doorbell rang.

'Leave it,' Kieran murmured in her ear, and she entwined him more tightly, wanting nothing to break the moment.

The doorbell rang again, and Deefer hurled himself against the French doors in such fury that the glass shivered in its frame.

For the second time that day, Kieran rolled away from her. But this time, he was laughing as he struggled one-handed into his trousers. He bent and kissed her. 'Don't forget where we'd got to. I'll be right back.'

Flora heard him open the front door. She heard the laughter leave his voice, as he called to her, 'We've got a visitor, Flora.' She jumped to her feet, straightening her clothes just in time as Kieran came back in.

'I'm really sorry to disturb you both,' Greg said, his face mercifully expressionless as his glance strayed to the rumpled sofa. 'But I think I must have left my glasses when I came round earlier.'

Chapter Twenty-Four

Whitelaw pushed his empty plate away from him, leant across the table to plant a peck on Val's cheek, then got to his feet.

'You're not going out again?' Val asked, swallowing the last of her cottage pie and looking up at him with something as close to reproach as she ever got. 'I've made a rhubarb crumble!'

'Sorry, love.' Whitelaw was tempted, but even his favourite pudding couldn't deflect him. 'I shouldn't be too late back. Stratford-on-Avon tomorrow, remember!' he added by way of consolation.

'Don't be,' she retorted with mock severity, then broke into a grin. 'What time shall I say we'll pick Millie up?'

'Eight o'clock sharp! We'll stop and get breakfast on the way.' He knew how much Val was looking forward to the trip; her pleasure made him realise just how long it had been since they'd had a day out. He just wished he could share her excitement.

He went out to the car. One of the neighbours was having a barbecue. The smell of charcoal and grilling steak wafted on the warm early-evening breeze. Whitelaw could hear the clink of glasses, the muted buzz of conversation, a sudden burst of laughter. Who in their right minds, he asked himself, would choose to be a copper?

He stopped to examine a colony of greenfly that had settled on one of the fat rosebuds on the bush by the front door. The buggers seemed to be thriving on the eco-friendly pesticide the bloke from the garden centre had talked him into. Greenfly friendly, more like. He squashed the sticky bodies between thumb and forefinger until the bud was clean, regarded his handiwork with satisfaction, and then got in the car for the drive to Oultonshaw Manor.

He had reluctantly decided against a patrol vehicle this time. He suspected that the visit itself would ruffle enough feathers with his superiors; no need to be deliberately provocative. And the impact of a marked car would have been lost anyway, he realised as, some twenty minutes later, he drove through the high ornamental gates. The Denstones were far too up-market to have the neighbours to worry about.

He had also decided against divulging that Danny Nolan's body had been found. The information had not, as yet, been released to the press, and they would be able to stall Sid Barker for a further day or two with the 'until the next of kin' routine. This fish was too big to risk losing it by jerking the line too soon; he was going to play Denstone in slowly, inch by inch; make sure the hook was firmly in before he struck. He had rung earlier to announce the visit, asking to speak not to Henry Denstone, but to Tricia. Whitelaw had wanted her to know he was coming; wanted her there so that he could gauge her reaction to what he had to say. Henry's poker-face would, he suspected, be more difficult to read.

Once again, he was shown into the living room, but this time both Henry and Tricia were waiting for him. He wondered briefly as to the whereabouts of Penelope; being wined and dined somewhere by Medlock, most probably. Whitelaw felt a moment's entirely unworthy glee at the prospect of Medlock's reaction to the family's fall from grace. One look at Denstone's pinched, self-righteous expression, however, brought him back to the purpose of the interview.

Tricia, dressed in floating floral silk, was already going into lady bountiful mode, offering first a seat, then wine, coffee, home-made lemonade from the silver tray already set out on the coffee table. Whitelaw, who was partial to home-made lemonade, declined. He didn't want this to appear a social visit.

'I assume this is about the theft, Inspector?' Denstone said testily, when Whitelaw had finally convinced Tricia that he wasn't going to change his mind.

'Indirectly, sir.'

'Which means you haven't yet apprehended the person responsible?'

'Not yet, sir,' Whitelaw said pleasantly. 'But I think we're getting closer. Do you have any photographs of the event, by the way?'

'Why?' Denstone asked coldly.

Whitelaw gave a self-deprecating shrug. 'I'm not really sure, sir. Just making certain that we turn over every available stone, as it were.'

Tricia went over to the rosewood writing desk, returning with a large manilla envelope containing a sheaf of prints. Some were of the various groups of performers: rows of grinning school kids in identical tee shirts, a solemn-looking group of musicians, a bunch of teenagers, some of whom Whitelaw recognised from his visit to St Saviour's. Others were less formal: knots of guests in conversation, or beaming into the camera, champagne in hand. He asked Tricia to identify those who had sat on the reserved front rows in the marquee.

'Is this of any relevance, Inspector?' Denstone snapped impatiently.

Tricia ignored him. 'Edna Brassington,' she said, handing Whitelaw a picture of an anxious-looking, mousy woman. She was standing beside a thin, balding character who so looked archetypically an accountant that Whitelaw had guessed he was the Denstone finance director before Tricia got to him.

The next shot was of Penelope, the daughter. Looking even plainer and lumpier than she had at Lambert's do, she was standing alone, gazing wistfully at a tall figure nearby, his back towards her.

'And I dare say you recognise this gentleman,' Tricia said with an arch smile as she passed quickly over her daughter's picture to one showing the same tall figure in profile: Greg Farrell, deep in conversation with Flora.

Whitelaw gave a brief nod as he noted Flora's animated expression and the way Farrell was leaning towards her to catch what she was saying.

The last person she pointed out was a heavily built man whose utter boredom was all too evident from his photograph, and whom Tricia identified, with more than a hint of antagonism to her tone, as Stanley Brassington.

'Your colleague on the Bench, I believe, sir?' Whitelaw looked across at Denstone. Brassington had already been checked out. He'd taken over at Northern Motors less than a year before. He had no previous links with Blackport, let alone Denstone Park.

'Correct.' Denstone smiled sourly. 'Hence the young hooligan's precipitate departure.'

Whitelaw didn't respond. 'Thank you, Mrs Denstone,' he said, handing the envelope back. 'Most helpful.' He wondered whether to bring Perotti's name into the conversation, but decided to wait.

'I really can't see why you are still wasting time on pursuing this boy,' Tricia observed, arranging herself elegantly on one of the sofas, wine glass in hand. 'Greg made it perfectly clear that he didn't want to press charges. I would have thought that was an end to the matter.'

'I'm afraid it isn't quite as simple as that, Mrs Denstone.'

Her husband said, with an acid smile, 'It's gratifying to know that theft is still taken seriously, Inspector. One sometimes wonders, when one reads the statistics.'

Whitelaw, realising that the man was trying to wind him up, played the comment with a dead bat. 'I couldn't agree more, sir. I sometimes ask myself what the country's coming to. Oh, by the way, I believe congratulations are in order.'

Denstone blinked. 'I beg your pardon?'

'Your honorary degree, sir. I was delighted to read that the university is going to recognise your contribution to the community. Next week, I understand? You must be very proud.' He beamed and added with anticipatory malice as he thought of what might have hit the fan in the intervening period, 'Yet another honour to add to the family reputation.'

'Maybe you could get to the point, Inspector.' Denstone did not return the smile.

'Quite right, sir. Mustn't waste your valuable time.' Whitelaw leant forward, hands on knees, and took aim. 'Might I ask why Nicholas Perotti is on the payroll at Denstone Automotive Engineering?'

The effect of the sudden change of pace was extraordinary. Had Denstone been a batsman, he would have been on his way back to the pavilion; stumped. His papery face flooded with colour, his thin mouth flew open like a trap door, but no words came out.

'What?' It was Tricia who spoke first. She had spilt some of her wine and it spread, unheeded, like an additional crimson petal across the fabric of her skirt as she looked from one of them to the other with a display of incredulity that suggested either rather greater acting skill than Whitelaw remembered, or genuine amazement.

'A thousand a month, from memory. Am I right, sir?'

Whitelaw would have expected a man like Denstone to have covered his tracks more carefully; at least to have an explanation readily at hand, but it was clear the man had been caught entirely off guard. He swallowed several times, his Adam's apple bobbing convulsively, before clearing his throat and saying in a barely recognisable croak, 'It was by way of a retainer.'

'A retainer, sir?'

'It was . . .' Denstone cleared his throat again. Whitelaw could practically hear the frantic ticking of his brain. 'It was payment to ensure that he was available. For when my wife opened the new centre.' Denstone's glance flitted momentarily to Tricia, then as quickly away again.

As an explanation it wasn't just lame, it was paraplegic. But it fed Whitelaw his next line nicely.

'Of course,' he beamed. 'Mr Perotti was employed at Denstone Park, wasn't he?'

Denstone nodded, but did not speak. Again, his gaze flitted to Tricia.

'He must have been an outstanding teacher,' Whitelaw went on. 'To have merited such a generous retainer, I mean.'

'Maybe you could explain what this is all about, Inspector?' Tricia asked.

'We are investigating certain matters that date back to Mr Perotti's period of employment at Denstone Park,' he said blandly. 'I was curious to find out why he was currently on the company payroll. But, as Mr Denstone has now explained—'

'If there is any irregularity involving Denstone Park, your questions should be directed towards me, not my husband,' Tricia cut across him. 'I administered all its affairs, and appointed Nicholas Perotti myself.'

She must have found it a useful weapon over the years, Whitelaw thought admiringly; that disconcerting contrast between the empty-headed, rich-man's-wife appearance and the formidable will that lay behind it.

'Oh, it's a little early to be talking of irregularities, Mrs Denstone,' he said airily, one eye still on Henry. The man's hand, he noticed, was trembling so uncontrollably as he reached for the glass of lemonade beside him that he was forced to abandon the manoeuvre. 'At the moment, we're merely undertaking some routine enquiries.'

'And what exactly is the nature of these enquiries? I trust you're not following the *Echo*'s example by raking up the arson attack at the school?'

'I'm afraid I'm not at liberty to say at present, madam.'

'I can assure you that Nicholas was questioned along with the rest of the staff. The fire was no more than an act of senseless vandalism, and I very much regret the attitude of those journalists who have seen fit to attempt to manufacture a mystery where none exists.'

Whitelaw found himself suppressing a smile at the image of Tricia Denstone and Sid Barker squaring up to each other. It would be a contest worthy of a front-row seat. He turned to Denstone, who was silent, hands clamped together in his lap as though in prayer, his face rigid and unreadable. 'There was a security firm guarding the premises, I believe, sir.'

'That's correct.' The words were barely more than a whisper. Denstone stared at his questioner with an expression reminiscent of a startled rabbit. Then, as if making a conscious effort to pull himself together, he added in a firmer voice, 'With hindsight, it was clear that the grounds were far too extensive for a single guard to monitor efficiently.'

Tricia breathed in sharply. Whitelaw had the impression that the subject of security was yet another potential flash point, so it was to her that he addressed his next question. 'I assume you organised the security, as you ran Denstone Park?'

'No, Inspector, I did not.' She shot her husband a look that made it abundantly clear who had.

'Maybe you can help me then,' Whitelaw turned back to him. 'Can you recall the name of the firm?'

'We are talking of an incident that took place ten years ago, Inspector,' Denstone appeared to have regained control of himself. 'I'm an extremely busy man. Surely you do not expect me to—'

'No, of course not, sir.' Whitelaw smiled apologetically. 'Not to worry. It will be on the file.'

Denstone's mouth tightened, but he didn't reply.

'Just what is this about?' Tricia demanded.

'As I said, madam, I'm not at liberty—'

'There were extensive investigations at the time,' she cut across him. 'Both of the fire and of . . .' her voice wavered slightly, '. . . and of my son's death.'

Whitelaw noted it was 'my', not 'our'. He also noted the slightest flicker of what could have been pain on Denstone's face.

'It was a very difficult period,' Tricia continued. 'It has taken me nearly ten years to get to the point where I can contemplate starting again.' Denstone's eyes were fixed upon her, but it was to Whitelaw that she was speaking. 'Do you have any idea how much this project means to me? To my son's memory?'

Whitelaw said nothing.

She leant forward and laid a slim hand on his own. 'I do hope that whatever you're questioning Nicholas about need not be made public, Inspector. I'm more than willing to dispense with his services, if you consider it appropriate.' She scanned his face pleadingly, then realising from his continued silence that playing the femininity card wasn't going to work, she jumped to her feet in a rattle of heavy gold bangles. 'I will not allow Nicholas Perotti, or anyone else,' she said with a venomous glare at her husband, 'to jeopardise its success.'

The passion, Whitelaw was certain, was uncontrived.

'As I say, these are just routine enquiries.' He got to his feet. 'I do appreciate you sparing the time to see me.'

Denstone looked surprised, as though expecting further questions. But Whitelaw had the feeling that, more than ever, he should stick to his original plan. Panic in the ranks. He would very much have liked to be a fly on this particular wall once the Denstones were alone together.

Another little tug on Perotti's line would be his next move, he decided. He could almost have enjoyed it, had the stakes not been so high.

Chapter Twenty-Five

Being a pessimist by nature, Whitelaw had expected the weather to break, but Sunday had dawned fine yet again, and even at eight thirty, he was warm in his shirtsleeves. Whistling along to the car radio, he wound down the window, his nostrils filling with the powerful scent of the rape seed that covered the rolling fields on either side of the road in great acid-yellow carpets. Despite the fact that his mission was not a happy one, he was grateful to be getting away from Blackport, and he couldn't help feeling in holiday mood as he headed towards the M6 and the Midlands the following morning, Millie and Val chatting happily together behind him.

If thirty years in the force had taught him anything, it had taught him to grab such respite when he found it.

Even three hours on the motorway, one of them spent crawling in a solid line of caravans and lorries over and under and round the soulless sprawl of Spaghetti Junction, didn't entirely dent his good humour. He was still whistling as they finally meandered through the last few miles of Warwickshire countryside.

It wasn't until they reached the outskirts of Stratford-upon-Avon itself that he could no longer put the purpose of the visit out of his head. 'We'll have a bit of a drive around before we stop,' he said, ignoring the municipal car park on the edge of the town; more as a delaying tactic than in the interests of sight-seeing. He nosed the car into the creeping traffic that stretched back from the town centre, asking himself, as they edged around the narrow streets, what the place would have been like if Shakespeare *hadn't* lived there. Everything was half-timbered, upper storeys jutting at crazy angles above the modern plate glass of burger bars and mobile phone stores at street level. Every restaurant, café and fish and chip bar seemed to be named after the Bard. Even the bank on the corner of the High Street had a florid mosaic of Shakespeare's head above its portals. Several Japanese tourists were solemnly videoing it, clearly imagining the building to be of some arcane cultural significance. Medlock would no doubt have had something fancy to say about Art and Mammon.

'Nice petunias,' Whitelaw commented, nodding at the riotous hanging baskets and tubs that filled every available corner. He wasn't sure why, in the back, Val and Millie burst out laughing.

It didn't take long to realise that there was no hope of finding a parking space. After half an hour, they arrived back at the vast car park they had passed on the way in, where they left the car and set off again on foot. Val wanted to walk down to the theatre, so they turned their backs on the shops, and headed instead for the grassy banks of the river. The square, brick-box building that dominated it was a disappointment to Whitelaw; he had expected something more in keeping with the prevailing air of antiquity.

Val shook her head at him, when he said as much. 'It was built in the thirties. It's the Globe you're thinking of.'

'Right,' Whitelaw nodded, trying to sound as if he knew what she was talking about. The only *Globe* he knew was the one that the *Echo* had been before it had changed its name back in the fifties.

By way of changing the subject, he bought ice creams, and they sat on a low wall outside the theatre to eat them. The brilliant sunshine lent the scene a carnival atmosphere. Families picnicked on the river bank, squealing youngsters rowed past in hired punts, a group of ducks waddled down to the water's edge like a procession of pompous academics. Tourists craned and pointed at the theatre from the top of an open-topped bus. Whitelaw was glad that he had arranged to meet Flora and Kieran at Greg Farrell's cottage, rather than here. He watched a pair of swans glide past under the tendrils of a willow tree as the sun caught and spangled their gentle bow waves, and tried not to think of the contrast with the murky, litter-strewn wharf where Danny Nolan had been found. He glanced at his watch, and reluctantly swallowed the last of his ice cream. Then, arranging to meet up with Val and Millie again in an hour, he set off.

Consulting the directions Flora had given him, he followed a side street that led away from the river and took him back across the High Street, where he struck off into a maze of narrower lanes. Within a couple of minutes, he was away from the drone of traffic. The microphones of the open-topped buses, the splashes and shrieks of the boaters, were replaced by birdsong and the distant sound of a church bell.

It didn't take him long to find the address: a small, inevitably half-timbered cottage complete with rambling roses over the porch and a dovecote in the garden. Almost too perfect to be real, Whitelaw thought sourly, as he tugged the wrought-iron bell pull. It was like something out of one of Farrell's films. But the peaceful idyll was abruptly shattered by the ferocious barking of what sounded like a Rottweiler from behind the studded oak door.

Danny Nolan's dog, presumably.

He heard it being called, its bark becoming muffled but no less furious as it was shut up somewhere inside the house. Finally, Kieran, his hand still heavily bandaged, opened the door. Whitelaw had been wondering how to break the news, but in the event he needn't have bothered. Kieran scanned his face then said flatly, 'You've found him.'

It was Flora who asked the questions, she who wept when Whitelaw told them what he knew of the circumstances of Danny's death. He chose the word 'strangled' rather than the pathologist's 'garrotted'; somehow, he thought, it sounded less brutal. He didn't mention the pathologist's other findings: the savage beating that had fractured the boy's jaw and eight of his ribs before he died; the cigarette burns that had been discovered on his arms.

Kieran sat silent, staring into his untouched tea, lost in his own thoughts. His hand was resting on the head of the big, ginger mongrel that had almost sent Whitelaw flying when it had been let out from the kitchen, but which was now standing subdued, its muzzle in Kieran's lap, as though it understood what was going on.

Whitelaw leant forward and patted the creature's bristly flank. 'About that phone call,' he said cautiously.

If Kieran was going to hurl recriminations, he had every right to do so; Whitelaw almost wished he would. But he simply said in the same, flat tone, 'I didn't speak to him. Flora did.'

She recounted the conversation, her eyes filling again with tears.

'And this was on the Monday, you say?' Whitelaw asked. 'You're absolutely sure it was that long after the gala?'

She nodded. 'If he'd tried earlier, he wouldn't have got through. We . . . I . . .' she twisted the handkerchief she was clutching and glanced in anguish at Kieran. 'I'd left the phone off the hook. No one could get through. Greg was trying all day Saturday too, but he—'

Kieran's head came up. 'You never said.'

'I did.' She coloured slightly, as if realising how sharply she had responded. Softening her tone, she added, 'He rang me at work in the end, don't you remember? To tell us about the stuff going missing.'

'You never told me that before.' Kieran was looking at her closely. 'You never said he'd tried to ring over the weekend.'

Whitelaw cleared his throat. 'If you could just try to remember exactly what Danny said, Flora . . . ?' He was sad to see how much of an issue Farrell still was between them.

She tore her gaze away from Kieran. 'There isn't anything else.

He just said he was in London, and to . . .' she swallowed hard and, looking down at the crumpled handkerchief, said in a small voice, '. . . to tell Kieran he was sorry.'

'And you're sure it was Danny's voice?'

'Of course. I recognised it straight away.' She shook her head as if to clear it. 'I still don't understand. You say you think Danny was . . .' she bit her lip, '. . . he died sometime on the Saturday. So how—'

'Could it have been prerecorded, do you think?' Whitelaw cut across her. 'I mean, was it a two-way conversation, or did he just say what he had to say?'

'I . . .' She looked at him despairingly as she shook her head again. 'I can't remember. But why would Danny go along with prerecording something like that anyway, if he hadn't stolen the stuff? It doesn't make sense.'

Whitelaw recalled the cigarette burns.

Kieran seemed to pick up his unspoken thoughts. 'You can make people do most things, if you hurt them enough,' he said harshly.

It was more than a general observation, and it gave Whitelaw the introduction to the second and even more difficult reason for his visit. He paused before he spoke, then he said, 'Listen, son, all this with Danny . . .' He swallowed. 'Well, I know you had a rough time of it yourself, when you were a—' Start again, he told himself, as Kieran's mouth tightened. 'It's just that I've got a friend with me today. You've met her once before, actually. At the station. She works with people who . . .' He floundered around, trying to find the right words, wondering how the hell Millie managed to do the job she did, when he couldn't even introduce the idea of counselling without making a pig's breakfast of it. 'She might be able to help you come to terms with . . .' He looked down, concentrated on patting the dog again, finding himself unable to meet Kieran's eye. '. . . With what's happened,' he finished vaguely.

'I'm not much for magic wands.'

Whitelaw could hear the scorn in Kieran's voice. He glanced at Flora for support. 'She said she'd wait for us, by the river. Just in case you wanted to . . .'

'Deefer could do with some exercise.' She put her hand on Kieran's.

Whitelaw watched as slowly, the young man's fingers interlocked with hers, then clung to her as though she were all that was stopping him from falling. He could only imagine how far that fall might be, if she were to let go.

'At least let's walk back with Ray,' she said gently.

Val and Millie were sitting on the green beside the Swan. Whitelaw made the introductions. Deefer bounded joyously around the green, disrupting picnics and upending toddlers, until Kieran called him back to heel with a fierceness that dwindled the polite conversation to silence.

'Right, ladies, how about a trip on the river?' Whitelaw put one arm around Val's shoulder, and one around Flora's. 'You don't mind if I borrow your girlfriend for a while do you, son? She probably knows a bit more about boats than I do, coming from the Scillies!' Even to his own ears, the heartiness sounded hideously false as he went on, 'I know Millie gets seasick in the bath. And you're not going to be much good for more than rowing round in circles, with that hand. Maybe the two of you could find a table for us at the pub where all these actors hang out? We'll be gasping for a drink, by the time we get back.'

Millie gave him a long, eloquent stare. Then, turning away from him, she said simply, 'Is that OK with you, Kieran?'

'Sure.' Kieran shrugged, his eyes on Deefer. 'Why not?'

It was a start, Whitelaw supposed.

He found it impossible to gauge, when they met up again an hour later, whether Millie had got anywhere or not. At least the two of them were still together, sitting at a picnic table outside the Dirty Duck, although Kieran got to his feet as soon as the others joined them.

Flora glanced at him, read his message, and said, 'We'd better get off.'

'Take care of yourself, love,' Whitelaw squeezed her arm, as she said goodbye. He was surprised when Kieran held out his hand; was encouraged by the strength of his grip.

'Thanks for coming.' For the briefest moment, Kieran met his eye. Then looking down, he murmured, 'Thanks for telling me about Danny yourself.'

Whitelaw was embarrassed to feel a lump forming in his throat. 'I'll get them, son,' he said gruffly. 'If it's the last thing I do, I'll get the bastards. I promise you that.'

It wasn't until that evening, when he dropped Millie off outside her flat, that Whitelaw asked.

'You know I'm not going to tell you, Ray.' The brisk words were tempered by the warmth of Millie's smile.

'Do you think you helped?'

'Maybe.' He noticed the strain in her expression, and realised what a toll her work must take on her; it couldn't be easy, sharing the weight of such crippling burdens. 'We'll have to wait and see.'

'What did you make of them? As a couple, I mean.'

Millie looked at him in surprise.

He shook his head. 'No, you're right. None of my damned business.'

My goodness,' Val commented when he got back to the car, 'I don't think I've ever seen such a handsome young man as that Kieran.'

Whitelaw had told her very little of the real agenda for the visit to Stratford-upon-Avon. He knew that she had been aware, before they set off that morning, that it wasn't going to be a simple day out. He also knew that Val was quite content to pretend it was, because it made his job easier on both of them; and he loved her for it.

He gave her a sidelong look as he put the car into gear. 'What, not even the famous Greg Farrell?' He was only half-teasing; Val had been beside herself when Flora had casually let slip where she and Kieran were staying. Whitelaw had found his wife's reverential interest in the place inordinately irritating, and Val knew it.

She laughed. 'Ray Whitelaw, I do believe you're jealous!'

'Rubbish! What's a heart-throb like Greg Farrell got that I haven't?' He contrived a laugh of his own, but he knew it wasn't just Val he was thinking about as he added, 'I just don't understand what it is all you women see in the bloke.'

Whitelaw almost beat the blackbird down to breakfast the following morning. By five thirty, he had already pinched the side shoots out of the tomato plants, tied up the runner beans and forked round the courgettes. Sleep had proved elusive, his over-tired brain shuttling between professional worries and his concerns for the young couple he had left behind in Stratford-upon-Avon until he finally gave up the struggle. Leaving Val snoring gently, he had stealthily pulled on his old clothes and retreated to the sanctuary of the garden for a couple of hours' hard thinking before he went in to work.

He had arranged to see Lambert at nine. It was a sad indication of how things were, in Whitelaw's opinion, that he had to make an arrangement at all; time was when he would simply have wandered up the corridor to discuss whichever case was uppermost in his mind. These days, Lambert was out of the station more than he was in it, attending functions here, there and everywhere. The only certain way to catch him at all was via his secretary's appointment book.

The meeting, he suspected, was not going to be easy. Getting the OK to go for access to Perotti's bank account had been one thing; to examine the Denstones' financial affairs was likely to be a different story. He wanted to present his case as cogently as he was able. Hence the gardening.

Nicholas Perotti was as bent as a kirby grip. There was no doubt at all in Whitelaw's mind that the smooth bastard had been an active participant in the abuse that had taken place; had taken his pick of the youngsters at Denstone Park like a kid let loose in a sweet shop. But was he bright enough or cold-blooded enough to have orchestrated three deaths that had, as the police surgeon had pointed out, all the hallmarks of well-planned contract killings? Was he rich enough, for that matter?

Henry Denstone was.

With a force far greater than necessary, Whitelaw smashed his spade into a clod of soil as he summoned up Denstone's self-righteous face, and tried to put out of his head the chilling idea that had been elbowing its way to the front of his mind since the early hours. It was too far-fetched even to consider, he told himself each time it surfaced. It was going to be hard enough to sell Denstone as a suspect as it was, without wandering off into the realms of fantasy. And yet . . . He leant on his spade and allowed himself to examine the notion properly.

Freddie Denstone had been killed after a row with his father; that much, he could recall from Lightowler's potted biography of the family. What if that row had been sparked off because Freddie had somehow discovered what was going on? Was it conceivable that Denstone had actually been cold-blooded enough to have organised a hit-and-run accident for his own son? Whitelaw recalled Kieran's claim, so glibly written off at the time as delusion, that he had nearly been the victim of a similar incident.

Coincidence?

Or history repeating itself?

Resolutely, Whitelaw pushed the theory aside. He suspected

he had a quite sufficient excess of questions over answers, without the addition of filicide.

He was right.

Lambert heard him out, his arms folded, his legs stretched out under his desk. Whitelaw had promised himself he would be succinct; purposeful. Even to his own ears, he was waffling in the face of his superior's prolonged silence. At last he talked himself to a standstill, and still Lambert said nothing.

'So . . . I'll go round to the Crown Court, shall I, sir?' he hazarded at last, as Lambert put down the pencil with which he had been tapping his teeth.

'Just let me be quite sure I haven't missed something, Inspector.' Lambert looked up. His tone was so pleasant that Whitelaw knew for sure that he wasn't going to like what was coming next. 'You are intending to apply to judge in chambers for access to Henry Denstone's bank accounts, yes?'

Whitelaw nodded cautiously.

Lambert smiled at him benignly, like a school master encouraging a particularly dense pupil. 'And what do you need to do before the judge grants leave?'

'Lay the evidence?' Whitelaw ventured, wondering if it was some kind of a trick question.

'Precisely so.' Lambert nodded again. 'And can you see any problem with that? Putting to one side for the moment the fact that Henry Denstone is Chairman of the Magistrates' Court.'

'With respect, sir, I don't think that's relevant.'

'Quite right, Inspector. And I have no doubt the judge would find it of no relevance either.' Lambert, to Whitelaw's intense surprise, was still smiling. He leant forward and said in a confidential whisper, 'But, you see, to lay evidence assumes that you *have* some evidence. Does this Volvo belong to Denstone? No, it does not. Have your inquiries regarding the arson attack at Denstone Park led anywhere?' He overrode Whitelaw's attempted protest. 'You make great play of the fact that Pioneer Security looked after not only the Chemico plant, but also Denstone Park. But as one of the biggest such firms in Blackport that is less than surprising, isn't it? Have you come up with any but the most tenuous evidence to link Henry Denstone with the victims? No, you have not. Do you, in fact, have any shred of proof that he is guilty either of murder or sexual abuse?' He brought his fist up suddenly and banged it down on the desk, scattering papers as he bellowed, 'No, you do not. You're a policeman, not a bloody crime novelist. Policemen deal in facts, not "ifs" and "maybes". If the judge in the Crown Court wants fiction, he'll go down to Waterstone's and buy the latest Reginald Hill.'

'But the proof might be there, mightn't it? In Denstone's bank accounts,' Whitelaw persisted, relieved that he had thought better than to air his suspicions about Freddie Denstone. 'Someone's had to be paying for a hit man, and where better to find one than in an organisation like Pioneer Security? Just about every psychopath in the North-West's worked there at one time or another. Some of the bouncers they employ—'

'So what are you expecting to find, exactly?' Lambert snapped. 'A standing order to Rent-a-Thug?'

It was going to be just as Whitelaw had anticipated. If he'd come in requesting a warrant for some old lag off the Eden Rise Estate, it would have been granted with barely a second glance. But try the same thing with one of the city elders . . . He could feel his anger boiling up as he remembered Jason's charred corpse, Sunil's mutilations, Danny's broken bones. 'Henry Denstone's up to his neck in this shit,' he shouted, jumping to his feet, 'and I, for one, am not prepared to stand by and let him get away with it just because—'

'For God's sake, man, pull yourself together!' Impatiently, Lambert motioned him back into the chair he had just vacated.

Whitelaw sat down, breathing hard as he tried to control his temper. Outshouting Lambert, he knew from long years of experience, was unlikely to help his cause.

Lambert regarded him in silence for a moment, then said quietly, 'I do hope this investigation isn't turning into a vendetta, Whitelaw. I understand that your visit to Oultonshaw Manor on Saturday evening caused a great deal of distress to Mrs Denstone. Not that she has put in a complaint, I should add. Her daughter simply made her concerns known to DS Medlock.'

Whitelaw could imagine. 'Very considerate of her, sir.'

'This is not a laughing matter.'

'I didn't suggest it was.' Whitelaw's face was stony. 'Nothing about this investigation makes me want to laugh. In fact, much of it makes me want to vomit.'

'Yes, well . . .' Lambert aligned his pencil with the neat stack of mail in front of him. It was several moments before he spoke again, then he looked up and said, 'You didn't see fit to mention that two key parties to this inquiry were known to you from a previous investigation?'

Whitelaw had wondered how long it would be before that one came up.

'No, sir. I did not.'

'You didn't, in view of the particularly sensitive nature of that previous investigation, think it relevant?'

'I thought, and still think it entirely irrelevant, sir,' Whitelaw said firmly.

'And you don't feel you have given undue weight to what Henshall has to say? I ask, because it has been brought to my attention that he appears to be in a highly unstable mental condition at present.'

'Might I point out, sir,' Whitelaw struggled to keep his voice calm, 'that Kieran Henshall was entirely accurate both in believing that Danny Nolan was in danger and in suspecting the phone call was bogus. My only regret is that I didn't listen to him sooner.'

'Hmm.' Lambert looked at him hard. 'Well, just be sure that it's kept professional.'

Whitelaw wondered what his superintendent would have

made of the trip to Stratford-upon-Avon. 'Is that all, sir?' he asked, getting to his feet.

'No, Inspector. I regret that it is not. Sit down, if you will.' Lambert regarded him over the top of his spectacles. 'Word has got back to me that some of the junior officers on the case are less than happy about the way in which you have been conducting yourself recently.'

'Let me guess,' Whitelaw snorted. 'Lightowler. I wanted to have a word with you about him.'

'Yes, well, he wanted to have a word with me about you too.' Lambert retrieved the pencil and pointed it at Whitelaw like a pistol. 'When you're at work, you keep your personal prejudices to yourself, is that clear?'

'Eh?'

'You do not spread rumours about a fellow-officer's sexual orientation. Our code of practice quite clearly states—'

'Now listen.' Whitelaw leant forward. 'I don't care if he fancies men, women, or the Chief Constable's goldfish. What I won't have is—'

'Lightowler feels he is being victimised. In fact, he was so concerned that he approached DS Medlock, who very sensibly advised him to come and speak to me.'

Whitelaw shook his head. He said nothing, but his expression must have said it for him.

'It is precisely that attitude which brings me back to my original point,' Lambert said coldly. 'I can't help thinking that your obsession in implicating the Denstones in this unpleasant business has at least an element of personal spite.'

'If you really think—'

'You will extend me the courtesy of hearing me out,' Lambert snapped. Whitelaw recognised the tone; it was the one that said negotiation was not an option. He glared at his superior, but kept his mouth shut, as Lambert went on, 'You came to me some days ago accusing DS Medlock of . . . let us say a lack of objectivity in this case. He has concerns, and I have to say that I am inclined to share them, that your own motivation is not entirely without self-interest. As it seems impossible to keep personal involvement out of the equation, I have decided to at least balance it out. Medlock is back on the investigating team, as from now. You can either work with him in a professional manner, or you can hand over the reins to someone who can. Is that quite clear?'

The anger was swelling inside him, throbbing through his veins, beating a tattoo in his temples, but Whitelaw knew that to lose his temper would be fatal. Push matters to the point where he was removed from the case, and Medlock would have won completely.

'Quite clear, sir,' he said grimly.

Chapter Twenty-Six

Medlock had evidently anticipated the outcome of the meeting; his immaculate leather briefcase was already sitting on the second desk in Whitelaw's office. Lightowler's clutter had been swept into a cardboard box that stood by the waste bin. Whitelaw suspected that Lightowler himself would be as carelessly discarded, now his purpose had been served. Of Medlock himself there was no sign.

Whitelaw went along to the incident room and told Crutchlow that he would be out for the rest of the day. 'Go through it again,' he said, nodding at the computer printout of registered keepers that had so far yielded no more information than that neither Henry nor Tricia Denstone owned a Volvo T5R. 'And when you've done that, you can start on this lot.' He indicated the stack of files relating to the fire. 'There's a witness statement from the guard on duty in there somewhere. I want his name. It's on the tip of my bloody tongue, but I'm buggered if I can remember it.'

Without waiting for Crutchlow to reply, he made for the car park. Lambert had presented him with two options. But it was a third that Whitelaw had in mind: that of being seen to be toeing the line, while doing everything in his power to keep Medlock on the periphery. Which meant having as little communication with him as possible. Making sure that his mobile was turned off, Whitelaw threw it into the glove compartment and headed away from the station. He decided to drive out to Denstone Park, more to clear his head with some country air than with any hope of discovering anything that hadn't been found out already. His meeting with Lambert had set off the sort of headache that threatened to linger for days if he didn't take the necessary evasive action, which included a couple of quiet pints in a decent country pub.

His spirits lifted as he left the sprawl of the city behind him. He drove to Hepton Magna, the nearest village to Denstone Park. Fifteen miles to the south-east of Blackport, the place had in recent years become a sanctuary for the city's élite band of barristers, bankers and hospital consultants. Range Rovers stood outside the King's Arms, where once pack horses might have been tethered. The pub had the air of a lovingly preserved, if historically inaccurate museum; not Whitelaw's sort of place, but by the time he got there he was too thirsty to argue. He stuck his head in the lounge bar, all horse brasses and hunting prints, and headed for the snug, which was empty apart from half a dozen elderly men sitting in a corner.

He bought himself a pint of best, and sat at a nearby table. The men were dressed in working clothes; their accents proclaimed them as locals, rather than newcomers. Whitelaw guessed they might have come from the clutch of ugly council houses on the edge of the village; probably original residents from the days before the village's gentrification, now working as gardeners and odd job men to the occupants of the cottages they could no longer afford to inhabit.

One of them nodded to him good-naturedly, and he took the opportunity to ask for directions to Denstone Park. Having received them, and after a few minutes desultory conversation about the place, he guided his fellow drinkers round to the subject of the fire, hoping that, as locals, they might provide him with some useful snippets of gossip. The general opinion appeared to be that the fire was the best thing that had happened since Tricia Denstone had got her hands on the place. Views on its transformation to a school for the performing arts ranged from scepticism to downright hostility. But as to the cause of the blaze, Whitelaw left them an hour later none the wiser, apart from a passing suspicion that any one of them might have set a match to Denstone Park.

Neither did his visit to the house itself prove any more enlightening. A large board at the entrance announced that restoration was in progress. The extensive grounds were a mass of bricks, timber and builders' vans; the charred carcass of the house itself swathed in scaffolding. He spoke to the foreman and some of the site workers, but none was local, and in as far as they were interested in the place at all other than as a temporary source of employment, it was in its future, not its past.

By the time Whitelaw left, it was getting on for three o'clock. He was tempted to take the rest of the afternoon off. The pint had done nothing to relieve his headache, and his limbs felt heavy with an unaccustomed fatigue that made him fear the onset of flu. He prayed that he was wrong. The last thing he needed was to be laid up just as Medlock came back on to the team; there was no telling what stunts he'd pull, left to his own devices. Squaring his shoulders, he turned the car back towards Blackport. It was time to bring Nicholas Perotti in for questioning, he decided.

He called in at the station just long enough to pick up the keys to a patrol car. He didn't go up to the office. He would have to encounter Medlock sooner or later, he knew. Later suited him fine. He was walking across the car park when he heard a voice calling his name. Crutchlow was running towards him.

'I've been trying to get hold of you all afternoon, Guv,' he panted.

'Well you've got me now,' Whitelaw snapped, guiltily remembering his mobile, still in the glove compartment.

'That Volvo. I went through the list of registered holders again, like you said.' Crutchlow's voice was excited. 'One of them was a Lawrence Fieldgate. Who just happens to have been the guard on duty at—'

'Lol Fieldgate?' As soon as Whitelaw heard the name, he remembered. But the image of the belligerent, cocky young thug he'd interviewed at the time of the fire wasn't the only memory the name sparked, Whitelaw realised with a lurch of excitement. 'I've seen Fieldgate recently,' he said slowly. 'He was at Oultonshaw Manor the day after the gala. Cheeky sod mistook me for one of the cleaners.' He banged the bonnet of the patrol car. 'I *knew* I recognised the face.'

'That figures. I mean, that he was there, Guv, not that he mistook you for . . .' Crutchlow flushed, and went on quickly. 'Fieldgate's been in charge of security at Denstone Automotive Engineering for the last ten years.'

'Has he indeed?' Whitelaw's mind was already racing. 'Have you given anyone else this information?' he demanded, thinking of Medlock.

'No, Guv.' Crutchlow looked worried. 'I thought I'd better—'

'Good,' Whitelaw interrupted him, grateful that there were still young constables around who could use their heads. 'Let's keep it that way for the time being. I'm going to pull Perotti. In the meantime, find out everything you can about Fieldgate. Discreetly.'

Perotti's house was empty when Whitelaw arrived; no car in the drive, and post sticking from the letter box. He wondered fleetingly if maybe he had allowed the softly-softly approach to run on for too long. Creating panic was all well and good, but by delaying, he realised, he had also given Perotti ample time to do a runner.

He pulled the post out and glanced at it: a gas bill and a couple of junk items, then peered through the letter box to see if any more had accumulated behind the door. To his relief, the hall floor was empty. A copy of the morning paper neatly folded on the telephone table confirmed that Perotti wasn't far away. Which meant that all Whitelaw had to do was sit and wait.

Windows rolled down to ensure everyone heard the babble of the two-way radio, he observed the dog-walkers, counted the flotilla of cars on the school run as they returned at four o'clock with their squabbling cargoes, and watched the elderly man on the corner mow the front lawn. The man was more interested in the police car than he was in the mowing, and spent a long time peering at Whitelaw each time he emptied the grass box. Whitelaw settled back in his seat, making the most of the enforced inactivity to go over the latest developments.

They had been looking for a hit man, and now it looked as if they could have found one. Even ten years ago, Lol Fieldgate had been a nasty piece of work: the sort who was always on the make; always spoiling for a fight. What if Denstone had bribed him to start the fire at Denstone Park? And if so, was it such a leap to ask if the man could also have been paid to deal with Jason, Sunil and Danny? Far-fetched on the face of it. But hardly more far-fetched than the notion that it was pure chance that had provided Fieldgate with the job at Denstone Automotive Engineering; chance that had brought him to Oultonshaw Manor at the time that Danny disappeared. For a moment, Whitelaw glimpsed how things must have been for Denstone as he attempted to hold his beleaguered world together: blackmailed by Perotti, leant on by Fieldgate, trying desperately to keep a lid on his terrible secret. Maybe, after ten years, he had even begun to think he was safe. And then Jason Morrissey had turned up . . . Whitelaw's small spark of sympathy was instantly snuffed out. What sort of a monster would order not just one death, but three – four, count-ing Norah Bateman – simply to save his own skin? Lol Fieldgate might turn out to have been the one who had metaphorically pulled the trigger, but it was Denstone who had master-minded the murders; Whitelaw was certain of that beyond any shadow of a doubt. All he had to do now was to prove it. And Nicholas Perotti, the weak link in the ungodly trinity, was his best hope.

*

As the afternoon drew into early evening, more of Perotti's neighbours appeared, ostensibly to tend their front gardens. Hanging baskets all along the road were treated to more water than was probably good for them. The police car was causing a discreet stir, which was just what Whitelaw wanted.

It was after seven by the time Perotti drove up, and there were plenty of spectators. He didn't appear in any rush to relieve their curiosity. He removed his sunglasses and adjusted his hair in the driver's mirror before he got out and walked over to where the patrol car was parked. Whitelaw wondered what was going through his mind.

'What is it this time, Inspector?' Perotti's expression was one of mild irritation, mingled with resignation.

Whitelaw found it less than convincing. Beneath it, he sensed fear. Leaning out of the window, he answered equably, 'Just a few more questions.' He took his time going through his briefcase, finally coming up with the bank statement. He made sure Perotti had sight of it before he said, 'Perhaps you would like to come down to the station, sir?'

Perotti breathed in sharply. 'Is that entirely necessary?'

'Not at all.' Whitelaw got out of the patrol car, still holding the statement. He glanced towards the elderly man, who was trowelling an already immaculate border of busy Lizzies. 'I'm happy to proceed in front of an audience, if you are. Can't think it'll do much for house prices, of course. Not once word gets around that you're being questioned about your involvement with a murdered rent boy.' He allowed the volume to rise as he hit the final three words of the sentence.

Perotti blanched; his carefully cultivated urbanity already beginning to slip. Beads of perspiration were breaking out on his forehead. Whitelaw could almost feel the downdraught from the ears of the elderly neighbour, who had by now given up any pretence of weeding and was staring, trowel in hand, with naked curiosity. Perotti must have felt it too. Glancing at the man with a nervous half-smile, he hissed. 'Do you want me to follow you?'

'No, no!' Whitelaw held open the rear door. 'Don't want to waste your petrol, do we? Allow me to give you a lift, sir.'

The neighbours were gathering outside the house to chew the fat before the patrol car had reached the end of the road.

Perotti didn't speak on the way back to the station. Whitelaw observed him in the rear-view mirror. The man fiddled nervously with his watch strap, studied his fingernails, massaged his lower lip between thumb and index finger. Once, while they were waiting at traffic lights, he caught Whitelaw's eye in the mirror and attempted a smile. Whitelaw stared back, deadpan, until he looked away.

'Am I under arrest?' he asked, as Whitelaw led him past the front desk.

'Oh, you'd know if you were, sir.' Whitelaw punched in the security code and held the door open for him.

'Just "helping with your enquiries" then?'

If it was Perotti's feeble attempt at a joke, Whitelaw wasn't laughing. He let the door slam behind them, thrust his face close enough to smell the acrid underlay of sweat beneath the other man's aftershave, and said in a low voice, 'I'd be offering all the help I could, if I were in your shoes, Nicholas.'

Perotti swallowed, then said tremulously, 'Are you threatening me?'

Whitelaw stepped back. He looked Perotti up and down, telling himself that he must keep things impersonal. The bastard was innocent until proven guilty, he reminded himself. Too many investigations fell at the last hurdle because someone forgot that golden rule, and couldn't resist a bit of summary justice. And with Medlock in the wings just waiting for him to foul up, he couldn't afford any slips.

'Just giving you my considered advice,' he said blandly. 'And I assume that as an upright member of the community, you'll be willing to help us in any way you can.'

Perotti, as he was shown into the interview room, looked no more reassured than Whitelaw had expected him to. He decided to give him a few moments to ponder on his predicament, and leaving him alone in the stuffy, windowless room, went along to the incident room.

Crutchlow was still at his desk, poring over a sheaf of papers. He jumped to his feet as Whitelaw entered the room. 'Lawrence Fieldgate, Guv,' he said. 'He's dead.'

'Dead?' Whitelaw echoed.

'You remember that pile-up on the bypass last week? Well, Fieldgate's Volvo was the car that triggered it. Apparently went out of control and hit the central reservation. Fieldgate was badly injured. He died at the General yesterday afternoon, without regaining consciousness.'

'Shit,' Whitelaw muttered, sitting down heavily. Not only had the crash wiped out a prime suspect, he realised, abruptly drained, it had also wiped out any possible forensic on the car.

'And listen to this, Guv,' Crutchlow went on. 'I've just got the mechanic's report across. He reckons the Volvo had been tampered with. Pinch bolts on the steering coupling had been loosened, if that means any more to you than it does to me.'

'No, it doesn't,' said Whitelaw grimly. 'But I imagine it would to the head of an automotive engineering company. Denstone must have decided it was time to start getting rid of his accomplices.' With effort, he pulled himself to his feet and grabbed the lab photographs. 'Good job we pulled Perotti when we did, then. Come on, Constable,' he threw over his shoulder as he set off down the corridor. 'Let's go and tell him what a lucky boy he is.'

Perotti was slumped in a chair, head in hands, when they returned. He raised red-rimmed eyes to stare at them, but said nothing.

'Right, then.' Whitelaw shut the door. He looked down at the other man speculatively, arms folded, and said, 'Now listen to me very carefully, Nicholas. I'm going to stick my neck out. I'm going to say that I don't think you had any part in the deaths of Jason Morrissey, Sunil Doshai or Danny Nolan.'

'Danny . . . ?' Perotti looked up.

'And what's more,' Whitelaw went on, 'I'll go so far as to say that I don't think you knew anything about Lol Fieldgate's so-called accident either.'

'Who?' Perotti's uncomprehending stare confirmed Whitelaw's words.

Whitelaw took a seat and leant across the table. 'But if I'm going to try to convince my superiors, not to mention the CPS, that you're not an accessory to murder, you're going to have to tell me everything you *do* know.'

Perotti had begun to cry. Whitelaw watched him in disgusted silence for a moment before nodding to Crutchlow, who switched on the tape machine and recorded the usual details of time, date and who was present.

'Come on then, Nicholas,' Whitelaw said, impatient to get on with the questioning. 'You'd better start at the beginning. Just what was going on at Denstone Park?'

Crutchlow glanced across at Whitelaw, paused as if expecting him to say more, than asked quietly, 'Do you want your solicitor present during this interview, Mr Perotti?'

Which, Whitelaw knew, was the first question he himself should have asked. He had promised himself he would do things by the book, and in his haste to get started, he had nearly messed up already. 'You're entitled to the duty solicitor, if you haven't got one of your own,' he said evenly, when Perotti shook his head. 'It's your right.'

Perotti, his face still covered with his hands, whispered, 'I don't need a solicitor. I haven't broken the law.'

Whitelaw's head was pounding. Rubbing his hands across his eyes, he said, 'You quite sure about that, are you?'

Perotti took a shaky breath then looked up and said, 'You have to understand that I loved Jason. Truly loved him. He was the most beautiful boy . . .' His eyes filled with tears.

'Right. And you showed your love by sexually abusing him, did you? Very moving.'

Perotti was sobbing.

Whitelaw swallowed. He'd never suffered from claustrophobia, but suddenly he felt he had to get out. He wasn't sure whether it was the distasteful nature of the questions, the heat, or Perotti's aftershave, but the interview room seemed to be closing in around him. He clenched his fists, digging his nails into his palms in an effort to regain control of himself. With effort, he relaxed his fingers and said, 'Go on.'

'I never touched him,' Perotti lifted his tear-streaked face. 'Not then. I wanted to, God knows, but I didn't.' He buried his head in his hands again, his shoulders heaving. 'I swear to you, I didn't. I thought I was helping him. Jason had so much talent . . .'

'Oh, he was a natural, was he?' This time, Whitelaw's fists were clenched in anger. 'I suppose you're going to tell us he enjoyed being—'

Perotti's head shot up 'No! As an actor. I thought he was interested in Jason because—'

'You thought *who* was interested, Nicholas?' Whitelaw leant forward, everything else forgotten as he scanned the man's face, saw in his eyes the conflicting emotions raging inside him: the need to expiate his guilt warring with the fear of reprisal. And with so many people brutally silenced already, that fear must be real enough. Whitelaw could see it gaining the ascendancy, as Perotti lowered his eyes. He knew he had to go for broke. Gripping the man's wrists he said, 'Come on, Nicholas. Get it off your chest. We already know it was Henry Denstone. All we need is for you to confirm it.'

He had anticipated a reaction from Perotti, and he got it.

'Henry Denstone?' the man repeated. '*Henry?*'

Then throwing back his head, he began to laugh hysterically.

Chapter Twenty-Seven

The combination of the heat, the headache and the cackling laughter was enough to make Whitelaw lose what fragile grip he had been maintaining on his temper. Slapping the lab photographs of the three corpses, Jason, Sunil and Danny, one by one on the table, he thrust his face in Perotti's and snarled, 'Let us all in on the joke, Nicholas. Have a look at these and tell us what's so fucking funny.'

The laughter halted as abruptly as it had started. Unlike the previous interview, Whitelaw noted, Perotti's attention was not on Jason as he stared at the images in front of him. The man's expression changed from slow recognition, through disbelief, to an ashen-faced, unfeigned horror that demonstrated beyond any shadow of a doubt that until that moment, he had had no idea that Danny Nolan was dead.

'Oh, sweet Jesus,' he whispered. 'That's the boy, isn't it? The boy who ran away?'

'Yes, it is.' Whitelaw snatched the photograph from him; even to have the man's hands on that much of Danny was offensive. 'Or rather it was. So why don't you tell us just exactly what or who it was Danny Nolan was running away from that night at the gala, if it wasn't you?'

'It could only have been . . . No, it's not possible,' Perotti muttered, shaking his head as if to clear it.

'What's not possible, Nicholas?'

It was as if Whitelaw hadn't spoken. Still white-faced, Perotti stared into space, as if making a genuine effort to understand whatever thought process was going on inside his sick brain. 'The only one who . . .' he started, then stopped again, his expression clearing. 'The tee shirts,' he said slowly. 'The boy was standing on the stage . . .' He nodded, recreating the moment in his head, speaking more to himself than his questioners. 'That must have been it.' He refocused on Whitelaw with an expression bordering on triumph. 'He must have seen the tee shirts!'

Whitelaw wondered momentarily if whatever guilt the man had been harbouring had finally tipped him over the edge and into insanity.

'What tee shirts?' he snapped.

'The tee shirts with Freddie's photograph printed on them. The ones the children were wearing.'

With dawning comprehension, Whitelaw recalled the photographs Tricia had shown him, the row of grinning young-sters in their identical tee shirts.

'I think it's time you told us everything you know about Freddie Denstone,' he said.

Perotti was almost pathetically willing to oblige. Freddie had been the apple of his mother's eye from the moment he was born, he told them. As handsome as his younger sister was plain, as charming as she was dull, he had sailed through childhood and adolescence, attracting nothing but adoration from all around him. A golden boy.

And, like most golden boys, utterly spoilt.

Tricia could deny him nothing. From the time he was a toddler, anything that Freddie wanted, Freddie had. And Freddie wanted everything. But as he got older, as he moved from expen-sive toys to designer clothes and then on to fast cars, he grew restless. It was all just too easy. As he got older, he moved from spoilt to wild.

Perotti was starting to remind Whitelaw of Terry Lightowler. He considered choking him off; telling him to get to the point.

But as the man continued, he began to realise that this *was* the point.

Freddie's precocious sexual awareness had been indiscriminate from the start, Perotti said. By the time he was in his late teens, there was little he hadn't tried.

'And how come you knew what he'd tried?' Even as Whitelaw asked the question, he knew the answer. Again, he was reminded of Lightowler; the day he had caught him at the computer. Perotti's expression was identical. Just talking about Freddie Denstone was turning the perverted bastard on.

Perotti looked him straight in the face. There was no mistaking his meaning as he said, 'Oh, I knew.' He even managed a thin smile.

Whitelaw stared at him with contempt, temporarily lost for words. After a moment, he said, 'Go on.'

Perotti told them that Freddie had always wanted to go into films, like his mother; had had his heart set on drama school in London. 'His exam results weren't good enough to get him a place. Tricia had to lean on a few of her old contacts.'

Whitelaw could imagine. 'So Freddie went off to London?'

Perotti nodded.

'He kept in touch?'

Perotti gave a bitter laugh. 'Oh yes, he kept in touch.'

He had been relieved, he said, to see Freddie go. The boy had begun to make the odd indiscreet comment about their relationship; and Perotti had known that if word of his own sexual preferences got back to Tricia, let alone of his liaison with her precious son, he would have been out of Denstone Park in seconds. But then Freddie had come back.

'His father was beginning to kick up about the amount of money he was getting through down in London. I suppose I was the easiest way for him to top up his bank balance.' Perotti's face contorted briefly as he added, 'It wasn't until later that he discovered more lucrative means.'

'Such as?' Whitelaw demanded.

Perotti looked down, biting his lip. It was a moment before he spoke, but when he did so, his voice was firm. 'Such as putting his talents to the production of pornographic videos.'

Whitelaw closed his eyes. The nausea that he had been attempting to keep at bay for the hour or so that Perotti had been talking swept over him with renewed strength. He loosened his tie and ran a finger inside his collar, then said, 'For which he needed a constant supply of fresh meat. Which you provided for him.' His own voice was so hoarse that he barely recognised it.

Crutchlow cleared his throat and said quietly, 'Would you like a short break, sir?'

Whitelaw glared at him, then turned his attention back to Perotti. 'You sold him those little boys to save your own miserable skin.'

'It wasn't like that.' Perotti was crying again. 'I loved Jason. I would never have . . .' He pressed his eyes with his palms; struggled to squeeze back the tears. At length, he said in a shaky voice, 'Freddie came down to Denstone Park over the summer. He seemed . . . calmer. More in control. He said he had got into film-making, and wanted to enter some competition at college. He asked me if any of the boys on the summer school had caught my eye. I thought he was talking about their acting talents, God help me. So I told him about . . .' His voice cracked. 'I told him about Jason.' In a barely audible whisper, he added, 'They went back to London. Together.'

'And it was when Jason returned that you realised what Freddie had really been after?' Whitelaw prompted.

Perotti shook his head. 'I'd no idea. It wasn't until nearly a year later that I found out. I had thought about Jason often.' He glanced up. 'I don't expect you to understand, but it's the truth. I had had no contact with him. I realised that was out of the question. Then, one night when I was driving down by the docks—'

Whitelaw snorted. 'No need to ask you what you were looking for there, I suppose?'

This time, there was defiance in Perotti's glance. 'I've made no secret to you of my sexual preferences, Inspector. In those pre-AIDS days, one took one's pleasures where one could find them.'

'OK,' Whitelaw said wearily. 'You were cruising the docks. Then what?'

'I saw Jason hanging around on one of the street corners. I stopped the car, told him to get in. And he asked me if I wanted business. I was horrified. It was then that he told me what had happened to him in London. And how Freddie had paid him to get other boys down there too. He seemed to think it was some kind of a joke.'

'And you told Henry Denstone.' It was all beginning to make sense. Whitelaw leant towards the tape recorder and said, 'The suspect nods his head.'

'I went down to London first, to confront Freddie,' Perotti said at last. 'I threatened to go to the police, expose him for what he was. He laughed at me. Asked me why I thought anyone would believe a sad, jealous old queer like me.' He glanced up at Whitelaw. 'I realised he was probably right. So I went to his father instead.'

'Who *did* believe you.'

Perotti shook his head. Staring into space, he said, 'I didn't think so at the time. He threw me out. But a few weeks later, after Freddie's accident . . .' He ran his tongue over his dry lips. 'Henry came to see me. Offered me money to say nothing.'

'Which you accepted,' Whitelaw said scornfully.

'Freddie was dead. What would have been the point in dragging the family through the mud?' Perotti looked up pleadingly. 'I gave Jason half of that money, every month. Right from the start.'

'Oh, I'm sure you did,' Whitelaw spat. 'For services rendered, you perverted bastard!'

Perotti jumped to his feet. 'Why are you making me go through all this again? I've done nothing illegal. The other officer said everything would be all right, as long as I—'

'Other officer?' Whitelaw grabbed Perotti's arm and forced him back down onto his chair. 'What other officer?'

Perotti stared at him in real fright. 'Sergeant Medlock. He came to see me yesterday. He told me—'

Whitelaw was out of the door before the sentence was finished. Turning back into the interview room, he jabbed a finger at Crutchlow. 'You. Keep an eye on him. I'll be back.'

Crutchlow winced as the door reverberated shut. Then, clearing his throat, he said into the tape machine, 'Inspector Whitelaw leaves the room. Interview suspended at nineteen fifty-three.'

Whitelaw tore into the office, grabbed Medlock by his jacket collar and jerked him to his feet.

'What the fuck do you think you're playing at?' he bellowed.

Medlock pulled free of his grasp. He regarded his superior coolly then said, 'If you give me a clue as to what you're talking about, I'll try to tell you.'

'You know bloody well what I'm talking about!' Only the very greatest effort of self-control prevented Whitelaw from punching the other man's teeth in. 'How long did you think it would be before Perotti told me what was going on? Long enough for you to warn Denstone, I suppose. Long enough for him to—'

Medlock, unfazed by Whitelaw's outburst, resumed his seat and said with enraging patience, 'Calm down, for God's sake. You'll give yourself a heart attack. I did try to contact you yesterday, but you were—'

'Don't give me that crap.' Whitelaw slammed his fist on the desk, dislodging a pile of paperwork. 'I know your game. You spotted Denstone's daughter as a career opportunity the minute you clapped eyes on her. Well, if you think I'm going to stand aside and let you get her father off the hook—'

'You know my game? You haven't got a clue. Do you really

think I'd jeopardise my career to save Henry Denstone's skin?'

'Don't think you're going to bluff your way out of this one, Medlock. Why else would you be interviewing Perotti behind everyone's back? Why else would you tell him—'

'Not everyone's back.' For the first time, Medlock raised his voice. '*Your* back. You think I'm stupid enough not to have cleared it with Lambert first? You're so bloody set on bringing the Denstones down, and me with them, that you'd go in mob-handed, slinging accusations around like confetti, without enough evidence to do him for parking on a double yellow. It didn't need me to make Lambert see it.'

'Not enough evidence?' Whitelaw jabbed a triumphant finger at him. 'Well, that's where you're wrong. Ask your girlfriend's precious father about Lol Fieldgate. Ask him how he's going to explain—'

'You're losing it, Whitelaw.' Medlock straightened his lapel and stood up. 'If anyone's going to foul up this investigation, it's going to be you. That's why I went behind your back.' He got as far as the door, then paused. 'If you've got a complaint, go to Lambert. See which side of the fence he comes down.'

Whitelaw slumped down in his chair. The outburst had drained the last glimmer of his energy. He reached for his cigarettes, more to stop his hands shaking than because he wanted one. He knew exactly what Medlock was trying to pull. And he felt powerless to stop him. He couldn't pin anything on Perotti; there was no law against what had gone on inside the sick bastard's head, as long as it had stayed inside his head. And although the circumstantial against Denstone was overwhelming it was just that: circumstantial. The only ones they had anything on were Lol Fieldgate and Freddie Denstone. Both of whom were dead. He fumbled to strike a match, suddenly so exhausted that even that simple task seemed beyond him. The evidence against Denstone was all there; it had to be. But he couldn't seem to get his head round it. His brain felt as if it had been turned to jelly. The acrid smoke, when he inhaled, filled him with such violent nausea that he stubbed out the cigarette after one drag.

He looked up as the door was tapped cautiously and Cyril Turner appeared, a cup of tea in one hand, a large brown envelope in the other.

'Medlock said you could probably do with—' He broke off. 'You all right, Ray? You're not looking too good.' He put the cup down on the desk. 'You want to watch you're not coming down with—'

'I'm fine,' Whitelaw snarled.

'Suit yourself.' Turner shrugged good-naturedly. 'This was delivered while you were out this afternoon, by the way.' He put the envelope down next to the tea.

Whitelaw glanced at it without interest. 'What is it?'

'Private and personal, it says.' Turner pointed to the neatly printed lettering at the top of the envelope and winked. 'Thought it might be something you'd rather I didn't see. Oh, and that lad Henshall's rung a few times. Said could you get back to him a.s.a.p.'

'What did he want?'

'Didn't say. Just asked if you could—'

'Yeah, yeah.' Whitelaw nodded wearily. 'I'll just have this first.' He hadn't realised how parched he was, until Turner had brought the tea.

'You sure you're OK?'

'Just knackered.' He managed the ghost of a smile. 'Go on, sod off, Florence Nightingale. I'll give you a buzz if I need the kiss of life.'

Turner went out, closing the door quietly behind him. Whitelaw reached for the cup, but somehow his arm didn't seem to be obeying instructions. He gazed down at it, trying to work out what was going on, deciding that his early-morning digging must have trapped a nerve. Abandoning the manoeuvre, he used his other hand to tear open the envelope. It contained a typed sheet of paper, and a bundle of photographs. Whitelaw scanned the letter first.

Dear Whitelaw, *it read,*

I address this letter to you because it appears to me that you are a man of integrity and will know how best to deal with what I am about to tell you. I write it in sound mind, and in the full knowledge that by doing so, I am destroying not only my own life, but the lives of those around me. I only wish the destruction could have stopped at that. In my defence, all that I can say is that with my son's death, I imagined the matter was closed. Events have proved me wrong.

If Nicholas Perotti has not already told you what he knows, I am sure that he will be only too willing to do so. Payments will not be made to him out of my estate, and he therefore no longer has cause to keep silent. In that knowledge, I see no reason to repeat the sordid facts in this letter.

I take full responsibility for the deaths of Jason Morrissey, Sunil Doshai and Danny Nolan. Had I been less concerned with my family name, and shown more regard for the law that I have spent a large part of my life seeking to uphold, they would be alive today. My only hope is that their deaths are avenged by due recourse to the courts. For my son's death, I hold myself less to blame, although my dear wife, Patricia, will not, I know, forgive me. My only culpability was that I loved him dearly, and saw no fault in him until it was too late.

I also take responsibility for the eradication of Denstone Park. My dishonourable hope was that in destroying what had for generations been my family's home, I might also destroy the memory of Freddie's terrible wrongdoing and preserve our good name. My accomplice in the matter, Lawrence Fieldgate, is now dead. I have given much consideration as to whether I should name him. But I have come to believe that his involvement may go beyond the fire itself.

The enclosed photographs will, I think, provide you with all the evidence you require as to the identity of Fieldgate's more recent paymaster. I found them in my son's bedroom on the night of his accident. I wish with all my heart that I had done with them at the time what I am doing now, but regret is a self-indulgence that achieves nothing.

Use them well, Inspector Whitelaw. Give those boys the justice that I, by my pride and cowardice, have for so long denied them.

The letter was signed 'Henry William Denstone, OBE, JP'.

Whitelaw reached clumsily for the sheaf of photographs. The first two were copies of those he already had: Jason and Danny in the sunlit gardens of Denstone Park. But there were more. Many more. Whitelaw's sight blurred as his gaze shrank from one obscenity after another. Freddie and Jason. Freddie and Danny. Jason and Danny. And then another man, tantalisingly familiar, his features concealed as he bent over Danny's small body. Whitelaw peered at it more closely, then turned to the next. He stared at it in disbelief, the skin on the back of his neck prickling.

He went to speak, to call out the name so that all the world could hear it. But all that came from his mouth, as his head gave up the unequal struggle to remain upright on his shoulders, and smashed forward onto the table as the chair clattered from under him, was a howl of strangled, inarticulate rage that sounded barely human.

The linoleum was blessedly cool against his cheek. The photographs lay scattered around him where they had fallen. He tried to reach them, but his limbs were made of stone. For a wild moment, he wondered if Medlock had spiked the tea, until he remembered that he hadn't managed to drink any of it.

After what could have been minutes, could have been hours, the door opened. Whitelaw heard Medlock's voice calling his name. Saw Medlock's expensive shoes approaching, caught a glimpse of the man's face, as he bent down, then straightened up again. Heard his voice receding into the corridor, shouting for assistance. Saw Medlock's face again, this time in double vision, peering into his own. Then, in the moment of peace before several pairs of feet were running along the corridor towards them, watched him gather up the letter and the photographs and slip them quietly into his inside pocket.

Chapter Twenty-Eight

Kieran was already up when Flora awoke the following morning. She could hear him speaking quietly on the phone. She wondered who he was talking to. He had said very little since Whitelaw's visit. Flora wasn't sure whether it was the news of Danny's death that was preoccupying him, or his conversation with Millie D'Sousa. Or something else altogether. The only subject that punctuated his long silences was Greg Farrell.

By the time she had dressed, Kieran was sitting out in the garden, his head bent over a note pad, pen in hand, Deefer by his side. His expression, when he looked up, was troubled.

'What did Greg say when he saw I was drunk?' he asked without preamble.

Flora sighed. They had been over and over it; how Greg had turned up at Sephton Street at the same time that she had; how they had found Kieran, unconscious, upstairs; how she had agreed to go out for dinner with Greg anyway. And now they were going over it all over again.

Kieran hadn't asked her how Greg's glasses had come to be down the back of the sofa, and she had offered no explanation, but she knew that the incident could be the only reason for his sudden interest.

'Who were you ringing?' she asked, in an attempt to divert him.

'Ray Whitelaw. He wasn't there,' he answered dismissively,

and went straight back to his theme. 'So what did you do then? Get changed? Have a shower?'

'I wasn't going to turn up at the sort of place he'd arranged to take us to in what I'd travelled up from the Scillies in, was I?'

He didn't answer her smile.

'What did you expect me to do, Kieran?' she asked, unable to keep the irritation from her voice any longer. 'Just how many times do you expect someone with Greg Farrell's clout to walk into your life and offer you a chance?'

He was looking at her keenly. After a moment he said slowly, 'Have you ever stopped to ask yourself why anyone that famous would bother? Why he would let two people he barely knew use his house?'

'Because he cares what happens to you! He's seen how good you are, and he wants to help.'

She knew she was trying to convince herself as much as she was Kieran. Nothing had happened between them, she told herself firmly. And nothing was going to happen. Ever.

She could feel herself blushing, as he said, 'I don't think it's as simple as that.'

She hated the deception that was worming itself between them. She longed to come clean; to confess the ill-judged kiss. But how could she tell him that not only had he every right to suspect Greg's motives, but that also, for a moment at least, her own had hardly been beyond reproach? How could she do that to him when he had so much else to cope with? He had been trying so hard to pull himself back from the edge. She wasn't about to push him back towards it.

'Listen,' she said, avoiding his eye, 'I've been thinking. Maybe it was a mistake to come down here. Why don't we go down to Scilly, like Simon wanted us to? Get right away from everything for a few days?'

'I've been thinking too.' The way Kieran said the words made her heart sink, the more so when he went on, 'I want you to listen to what I've got to say, Flora. Hear me out through to the end, before you say anything. Because I know you're going to try to tell me . . .'

The rest of his words were drowned, as Deefer jumped up and began to bark furiously. Greg Farrell was standing in the French doors. Neither Flora nor Kieran had heard his approach.

'Hope I'm not disturbing anything,' he said. 'But I thought you'd want to know straight away.' His expression, as he came closer, was so sober that Flora's discomfort at the interruption turned immediately to concern.

'Know what?' she asked. 'What is it, Greg?'

Kieran had got to his feet without a word, his hostility as clear to Flora as the raised hackles on Deefer's back.

Greg looked solemnly from one of them to the other. Then, extending his hand to Kieran, he broke into a grin. 'I've managed to fix up that audition,' he said. 'Looks like your luck's about to change at last. Congratulations!'

He had arranged it for later that same morning, he went on. 'Best way. Less time to get yourself worked up. Or pissed,' he added with another grin.

Flora looked anxiously at Kieran, but his face was expressionless, as Greg went on, 'Now, what I thought might be a good idea was if I took you round backstage, gave you a chance to familiarise yourself and get the feel of the place. There's a rehearsal for one of the other shows, but it doesn't start until eleven, so that should give us plenty of time.' He paused, clearly surprised by Kieran's lack of response. 'OK?' he prompted, with a quick glance towards Flora.

She saw Kieran's sharp eyes follow the look; waited for him to reply; had no idea what that reply might be. She realised that she wasn't even sure what she wanted it to be. It was the opportunity he had been waiting for all his life; and it was being given by someone he mistrusted, had more right than he knew to mistrust. Except, of course, that reading her as he could, he *did* know.

Before he spoke, Kieran turned and scanned her face. Then he made his decision. With a smile that Flora could see was forced, he said, 'Thanks, Greg. Thanks a lot. That would be great.'

She felt an obscure sense of loss.

'Come on then!' Greg clapped him on the back. 'Don't let's hang around!' He turned and smiled warmly at Flora. 'How about we all meet up for a coffee in a couple of hours? See you at the stage door, OK?'

'Fine.' She had the feeling that they had done some kind of deal. And that she was the merchandise. She looked past Greg and spoke directly to Kieran. 'You want to cancel our earlier conversation, I take it?'

He held her gaze. There was an expression in his eyes that she couldn't fathom; that made her nervous.

'Not cancel,' he said. 'Postpone. Just for now.'

Flora told herself that her uneasiness was simply nerves on Kieran's behalf. She wandered around the garden when they had gone, feeling increasingly apprehensive. She made herself a coffee, and tried to read the paper; amazed, when she glanced up at the kitchen clock, that only ten minutes had passed. The two hours before she was due to meet up with them again stretched ahead of her like an eternity.

To calm herself, she made a desultory attempt at weeding one of the borders. Deefer watched, his head on one side.

'Tell me I'm being stupid,' she commanded, sitting back on her heels and glaring at him after no more than a couple of clumps of chickweed had been half-heartedly uprooted.

Deefer whined, his tail wagging tentatively.

'You're right,' she said, throwing down the trowel. 'I'm going to find out what he's up to.'

There was no sign of Kieran or Greg when she got to the theatre. So vibrant later in the day, at that time in the morning the place was largely deserted, the foyer doors still locked.

Flora found her way round to the stage door. She stood un-
certainly in front of it for a moment, then pushed it open on to
a cramped room dominated by a cluttered reception desk. The
woman behind it was busy on the telephone, so Flora occupied
herself by gazing around. The small room was lined with overflowing pigeon holes and notice boards bearing scribbled
messages for cast members. As she read one famous name after
another, Flora began to feel her confidence ebbing away. She
hadn't the slightest idea what she hoped to achieve by barging in
like this. She glanced at the monitor on the far wall, which showed
the main stage, deserted apart from the two shadowy figures
standing together in the wings, and wondered what was going
through Kieran's mind.

'Can I help?'

The woman's voice made her jump. 'Flora Castledine,' she
announced, hoping she sounded more assured than she felt as
she added, 'Greg Farrell's expecting me.'

Before the woman could reply, a small, pretty blonde whom
Flora recognised from the television pushed open a door at the
back of the room, and asked, 'Has Nick been in?'

'Not yet, dear.' The woman shook her head.

'Sod. Well, tell him I'll be in the green room, will you?' said
the blonde, and disappeared back through the door.

'Sorry about that, Miss Castledine.' The woman turned back
to Flora with a smile more friendly for the mention of Greg's
name. 'Mr Farrell did say to expect you.' She glanced up at the
monitor, then reached for a microphone. 'I think he's busy at
the moment. Do you want me to tannoy him?'

'No, that's OK. I'm a bit early,' Flora said hastily.

'Perhaps you'd like to wait in the green room?' The woman
got to her feet. 'I'll show you . . .'

'Don't worry.' Flora flashed her a smile and headed for the
door through which the blonde had disappeared. 'I know where
it is.'

Once on the other side of the door, she found herself faced with a confusing labyrinth of passages crowded with pieces of scenery and rails of costumes. A muted clatter of crockery suggested the direction of the green room. Flora hesitated. Maybe she should simply do the sensible thing; buy herself a coffee and wait. But she was too uneasy to do the sensible thing; too worried by what Kieran might be saying to Greg.

Or what Greg might be saying to him.

For a moment, as he stepped out onto the stage, Kieran forgot everything.

He stared out across the footlight. Stalls. Circle. The gods, where he had sat all those years before when he had visited the theatre on a school trip, and for the first time had glimpsed the magical possibilities beyond the boundaries of his own nightmare existence. He imagined the rows of seats not empty, but filled with the enraptured audience he had dreamt of ever since. And in that imagined moment, all thought of Flora, of Danny, of everything except the fulfilment of that dream, deserted him.

'Good feeling, isn't it?'

Greg was by his side. He put his hand on Kieran's shoulder, and Kieran saw the moment for what it was: naked, dangerous ambition. And was ashamed.

'Come on!' Greg had already darted to a small, spiral staircase off to one side of the stage and was climbing nimbly up the steep, narrow rungs.

A warning sign forbade entry to unauthorised personnel. Greg ignored it. But then Greg Farrell *was* authorised, Kieran thought bitterly. Greg Farrell could go anywhere he chose.

'I'll stay down here, thanks,' he said.

'What, feet firmly planted on the ground?' Greg looked down at him and laughed. 'That's not your style, is it, Kieran? You're a risk-taker, the same as I am!'

Kieran recognised the edge of mockery in the tone; knew that he shouldn't rise to the bait. He had almost been beguiled into forgetting his purpose once; he mustn't allow it to happen again. But as he felt the anger welling inside him he knew he was unable to resist Greg's challenge. For days, he had been thinking about the way Greg Farrell had come into their lives. Day and night, the evidence had taunted him as Greg was taunting him now. He had tried to tell himself he was mistaken. But slowly, inexorably, the pieces had slotted themselves together in his head until he was convinced that it wasn't a delusion; that what he suspected was, inescapably, the truth.

Wordlessly, he followed.

'Come and have a look at this!' Greg stepped on to a platform on the other side of the small gate at the head of the stairs, and then out on to the flimsy gantry that ran above the stage, suspended from the vault of the ceiling by metal wires. Spotlights hung from under it like sleeping bats. 'Imagine it, Kieran!' He stretched out his arms, setting the gantry swaying as he encompassed the vast auditorium. 'Imagine controlling the emotions of every single member of that audience. Making them laugh. Making them cry. Making them believe anything you want them to believe. Imagine the power of that! Come on, you're not afraid of heights, are you?'

Kieran's mouth was dry as he joined Greg on the gantry, but his trepidation had nothing to do with vertigo. He swallowed and then said quietly, 'That's what you think it's all about then, do you? Deceiving people?'

Greg's arms dropped back by his sides. He looked at Kieran quizzically, then gave a half-smile. 'Not deceiving.' He shrugged. 'Bewitching, maybe.'

Kieran glanced down at the stage, some thirty feet below, and felt a fleeting moment of fear as he recognised the foolishness of confronting Greg in such a place. He took a step back towards the platform and reached for the fly rail to steady himself, wincing as its hard edge bit into his still-healing burns. Involuntarily, he loosed his grip. But he welcomed the pain. It strengthened him to go on. Now, he told himself; do it now, up here where Greg would be forced to hear him out. He positioned himself to block Greg's exit from the gantry and took a deep breath, trying to calm himself. Then in a low voice, he said, 'I know what you've done.'

'What I've done?' Greg's smile had faded.

'You rang Flora at work, didn't you?' Kieran heard and despised the unsteadiness in his own voice. He cleared his throat, and went on, 'The Monday after Danny disappeared. You told her you'd been trying to get through on the Saturday. You did tell her that, didn't you?'

'Hey,' Greg held up his hands. 'Just hold on a minute. What is this?'

'How did you know where to ring?'

Greg stared at him. 'I'm not sure I know what you're getting at, but . . .'

Kieran could feel the sweat prickling his palms. He focused on Greg's face, willing himself to continue. 'How did you know our phone number? It isn't in the book; we've only just moved there.'

'I'm sorry? Look, I really don't have the first idea . . .' Greg gave a wary laugh. 'Listen, Kieran, if this conversation's going where I think it's going, then all I can say is that Flora wouldn't be the first girl to imagine—'

'You got it from the note I left in Danny's room, didn't you?'

'What is all this? I rang to let her know . . . to let you *both* know about the theft. Now, if you've got some hare-brained notion that I—'

'It was you killed Danny, wasn't it?' Kieran cut over him.

'*What?*' Greg stood stock-still, staring at him with an expression of such incredulity that Kieran experienced a panicky stab of self-doubt.

'You waited for Danny to come round to see me,' he pressed on, before he completely lost his nerve. 'You or your henchman. Then you—'

'Shit, Kieran,' Greg took a step towards him, 'I knew you'd been having some problems lately, but—'

Kieran backed away. 'Danny was coming to me for help when he was lifted. You had him disposed of, the same as the others had been disposed of. And to make his disappearance more convincing, you pretended he'd stolen your stuff. Then you simply waited for everyone to forget him. Only I messed things up for you, didn't I? Because I wasn't going to forget him. Even after you faked the phone call. So you tried to get rid of me too. That bloke who drove his car at me – it was your hit man, wasn't it? And when that didn't work, you had another go yourself, the night I was plastered. You lit the gas under the chip pan before you took Flora out to dinner, and left me to fry.'

Greg had heard Kieran out in silence. Now, he shook his head and said coolly, 'I'm sorry, mate, but you're seriously in need of some help.'

'That's what you'd like everyone to think, isn't it? But once the police know—'

'Now just a minute!' Greg's mouth tightened. 'You seriously believe the police are going to listen to any of this crap?'

For the first time, Kieran felt he might be getting under the other man's skin. 'I'll make bloody sure they do,' he said.

'What possible fucking reason would I have for wanting you dead?' An angry flush was spreading up from Greg's throat. 'Or Danny Nolan, for that matter? I'd never even set eyes on him until half an hour before he took off! For Christ's sake, pull yourself together, before you make a bigger fool of yourself than you already have.'

'It was you had Danny taken down to London, wasn't it?'

It was no more than guesswork; but Kieran knew instantly that he had hit the mark. There was a moment's utter silence, then Greg said, 'You don't know what you're talking about.'

Kieran held his gaze. 'You reckon?'

Greg glanced down at the empty stage; rubbed the back of his hand across his mouth as if trying to reach a decision. Then he shrugged, and said lightly, 'Everyone's got their price, Kieran. So what's yours?'

Kieran clenched his teeth, fighting the almost overwhelming urge to make a lunge for the bastard, send him crashing on to the stage below. Every sinew in his body was crying out to do it. But that would be too simple.

Greg had taken the silence for hesitation. 'I've got a lot of contacts. Think about it. Within twelve months you could be a household name. Be richer than you could imagine.'

Still Kieran did not speak.

'Your choice,' Greg said, moving closer. 'Listen, I never meant for any of this to happen, believe me. Those boys . . . I'd never have got involved in any of that if Freddie hadn't talked me into it. I needed the money. I didn't realise they would be so young, I swear I didn't.'

He paused, waiting for a response that didn't come.

'And let's face it,' he added quietly, 'we've all done things when we're young that we've regretted later, haven't we?'

Kieran breathed in sharply, his knuckles white on the rail.

'One session,' Greg whispered. 'One mistake. Don't you think I've suffered for it? Been terrified ever since that one of those kids would recognise me in the papers and come back to haunt me? How do you think I felt when Jason Morrissey turned up demanding money?'

'Are you expecting sympathy?' At last, Kieran spoke; spat the words out. 'You *murdered* him!'

'Not *me*, Kieran! I didn't know any of that was going to happen, I swear. I was at my wits' end. I tried to get out of the gala; Blackport was the last bloody place on earth I wanted to be. I made up a story about threats from religious cranks to get Tricia off my back, but she's like a fucking pit bull terrier once she gets her teeth into you. The next thing I knew, Fieldgate had been detailed off as bodyguard. He came down to London the week before the gala to meet me. Anything I needed, he said. Nothing too much trouble. There was something in the way he looked at me as he said it that got me thinking. Morrissey was getting more and more pushy. All I wanted was someone to put the frighteners on him. No problem, Fieldgate said. He'd take care of things. Can't you understand? Hundreds of thousands of pounds had been sunk into *God's Only Son*. What do you think the press would have made of—'

'Oh, sure, I understand. What were a few lives, compared with your career?'

'It wasn't like that! I didn't realise the maniac was going to kill him. And then it was too late.'

'And you gave me a lift back to Danny's out of the goodness of your heart, did you?' Kieran's face was white with rage. 'Don't try to make out you didn't know what was going to happen to him, you bastard. You went along with it every inch of the way.'

'I recognised Nolan as soon as I saw him. I thought I was in the clear at first; even when I spoke to him, it was obvious he hadn't made the connection. But the way he reacted when he saw Freddie plastered over those fucking tee shirts . . . can't you understand? I just couldn't take the risk.' Greg's face contorted briefly; suddenly, he was no longer pleading. 'Do you think I was going to give up my career, everything I'd worked my guts out for, without a fight? For the sake of some snivelling little kid who'd have been selling himself to all-comers in a few years anyway? Don't look so shocked! I've seen the ambition in you, Kieran. I've seen how hungry you are for success. Don't tell me you wouldn't have done the same thing, in my place.' He put out his hand. 'Use your head. I can make good things happen for you, if you'll let me.'

Kieran shook him off. 'I'll see you in hell first, you bastard.'

Greg stepped back. For a long moment he looked at Kieran in speculative silence. Then, as if coming to a decision, he sneered, 'Go and fuck yourself, my friend. No one's going to believe you.'

'They'll believe the photographs.'

Kieran hadn't expected the same stunt to work twice, and it

didn't. Greg shook his head derisively. 'You haven't got the photographs. You wouldn't be here, if you had.'

'I've got enough to go to the police, bring everything out into the open . . .'

'There's nothing you can do to me. There's nothing to tie me in with the murders.'

'How about your henchman? How much loyalty do you reckon you'll have bought from him, once the police pull him in?'

'Fieldgate?' Greg threw his head back and laughed. 'Fieldgate got greedy. I was no better off than I'd been before. And let's face it, he wasn't even all that good at his job, was he? Couldn't even aim a fucking great estate car at you without missing. So you see, there's no one who's still alive to link me with Morrissey or the Nolan kid. Only the word of a jealous no-hoper with a mental problem. Not to mention a criminal record. I think I can cope with that.'

Kieran flinched. Then he said savagely, 'If you're so fucking invulnerable, why all the "I'll give you anything you want" crap?'

It was clear from Greg's lazy smile that he knew he was getting back in control. 'Because I'm *bored*. I just want you off my back. You and your silly bitch of a girlfriend.'

'I'll not let this go.' Kieran's voice was shaking. 'You think you can buy anything, don't you? Well, you can't buy me. If the police won't listen to me, the tabloids will. Since when have they been interested in proof?'

'I'd be careful, before you go throwing threats like that around.' Greg's face hardened. 'You're not exactly in the best bargaining position up here.'

'So what are you going to do? Push me off?' Kieran said with improvised bravado. 'Take a bit of explaining, wouldn't it? Seeing as you invited me here for an audition.'

'Audition?' Greg laughed. 'Oh, please! Give me some credit for forward planning.'

'Shame you told Flora about it, in that case,' Kieran glanced down at the deserted stage and edged closer to the platform as he spoke.

'You were too nervous to go through with it?' Greg shrugged. 'I don't I'll find it too difficult to think of something that will satisfy Flora.' Another lazy smile. 'I've always found her quite . . . receptive.'

Kieran breathed in sharply, struggling to remain focused, as Greg went on, 'And in any event, she's all too aware of how unstable you are. Or should that be "were"? I tried to stop you jumping, of course . . .'

He made a sudden lunge forward – but not quite sudden enough. Kieran grasped the fly rail with his good hand, flung himself sideways and set the gantry swinging.

Greg cried out as his legs went from under him and, as if in slow motion, fell forwards onto his knees. He tried to scramble up, but the momentum of the gantry unbalanced him. Making a futile grab at Kieran's legs, he slipped towards the edge, his own legs dangling into space, his body flung across the gantry's narrow width. The gantry swung back; more gently this time, but enough to slide him inexorably closer to the edge. Greg looked up, his face bloodless with terror. The fingers of one sweating hand were hooked under the gantry; the other flailed desperately as it tried to make contact with anything that might save him.

'Help me,' he whispered.

For a second, Kieran hesitated. Then, still hanging on to the fly rail, he reached out and gripped Greg's free hand.

The pain was excruciating. It was all he could do not to cry out, as Greg clutched the raw flesh beneath the bandages like a vice. It was only Flora's voice echoing up from the stage below, calling to him to hang on, that prevented him from blacking out.

The few seconds that it took her to reach them, and help support Greg's weight, lasted an agonising eternity. Kieran's shirt was soaked in sweat as gradually, between them, they hauled Greg back to safety, and collapsed, gasping for breath, onto the gantry floor.

It was Kieran who spoke first. 'Don't think this changes anything,' he rasped, cradling his damaged hand. 'You're going to do this properly. Police, courts, prison . . . I want to see you treated for the rest of your life like the scum you are. That's the only reason you're not splattered all over that stage.' His voice was shaking with rage. 'I let one bastard off the hook by killing him. Death's too good for you.'

Flora had got herself back to her feet. She offered Greg her hand as he pulled himself up, his face ashen. 'Oh God, I'm so sorry about this.' She looked down at Kieran, her eyes filled with tears. 'I thought he was getting better, but—'

'What the hell are you saying?' Kieran stared at her in dawning horror. 'It was him. Flora! He killed Danny. And the others.' His voice was rising as he scanned her face. 'He tried to push me . . .'

'I can't take any more of this.' Flora turned away from him and covered her face with her hands. 'I'm sorry, Kieran,' she sobbed, 'I really can't.'

'I was trying to stop him jumping,' Greg said quietly. 'I'm not sure if he was trying to kill us both, or just himself.'

'You bastard . . .' Kieran lunged at him, setting the gantry swinging again as Flora let out a scream.

Greg grabbed his arm, twisting it viciously behind his back as he bundled him on to the platform.

Others had gathered on the stage below.

'Is everything all right, Mr Farrell?' someone shouted.

'Everything's under control,' Greg called back. 'We're bringing him down now. No need to fuss.' His pressure on Kieran's arm increased, as he turned to Flora and said, 'You've got to get him some help, before he harms himself. Or someone else. If you'd like me to arrange a psychiatrist . . .'

She blew her nose, shook her head with the determination Kieran loved so well. 'No, I'll take care of it.' She glanced across, not meeting his eye.

Kieran strained towards her, his arm still pinioned. 'You've got to believe me,' he cried desperately, as she flinched away from him.

Flora led the way down the narrow stairs. Greg, with a final, malicious jerk that all but ripped Kieran's arm from its socket, shoved him down behind her.

'I'll get him back to Blackport,' she said, when they reached the bottom. 'There's someone up there he's seen before. She'll know the best way . . .'

'I'll drive you up.'

She shook her head. 'We've put you to enough trouble already.'

'Nonsense,' Greg said firmly. 'I'm due up there tomorrow anyway, for the degree ceremony.'

Kieran struggled to free himself. 'You think they're still going to give you a degree, once they find out . . . ?'

Greg's voice was calm. 'I really don't think it would be sensible for you to attempt the journey without help, Flora.'

They were talking as if Kieran didn't exist, and there was nothing he could do to stop it. Whatever he said would simply tighten the trap of insanity into which Greg Farrell had led him. He watched, powerless, as Flora bit her lip and said, 'Well, if you're quite sure . . .'

'That's settled, then.' Greg smiled. 'I'll pick you up first thing in the morning.' Once more Kieran murmured Flora's name, but she refused to meet his eye. Putting her arm around his waist as if he were an invalid, she guided him through the onlookers on the stage. All he could do was to be led, head down, aware of the dozens of curious eyes boring into him. Any further commotion, he was sure, and he would find himself sectioned to the nearest psychiatric unit.

'Will you be safe on your own with him until the morning?' Greg asked, when they got to the stage door.

Flora nodded. 'The doctor at the hospital prescribed some tablets for when he was really bad. They'll knock him out for the rest of the day.'

'You're absolutely certain you don't want me to come back with you?'

'Best not.' Flora's eyes flicked towards Kieran.

Greg followed her glance, then dropped his voice to a whisper. 'Look, I don't want to make things worse than they already are, but I have to tell you that he was making some pretty wild accusations up there. I realise that it's all part of his mental condition, but I have my reputation to consider.' He gave a small smile. 'You do understand? I really can't have him going round . . .'

Kieran clenched his jaw. The bastard was giving the performance of his life.

'Of course.' Flora returned the smile. 'Don't worry. He won't be out of my sight for a moment. You have my word on that.'

'Until tomorrow, then.' Greg leant forward and kissed her cheek; a warm, lingering kiss. He shot Kieran a look of pure triumph as he said to her, 'You've got my number. Ring me when you've got him off to sleep.'

'I will.'

Taking Kieran's arm, she propelled him towards the pavement. He turned to her, desperate, now they were away, to make her see the truth, but her fingers tightened, and she whispered fiercely, 'Don't.'

It wasn't until they were well away from the theatre that, still looking straight ahead, she murmured, 'Don't say a word. Just keep acting mad. It's our only chance.'

Chapter Twenty-Nine

Flora and Kieran didn't stop to pack. They called back at Greg's cottage for just long enough to pick up Deefer and order a taxi to the nearest hire car garage, and then they drove. Or rather, Flora drove.

'Are you sure you don't need to call into a hospital and get that seen to?' she asked, when they were on their way.

Kieran, who had been surreptitiously flexing the fingers of his damaged hand, now let it fall back into his lap. 'No, it'll be OK.' He looked across at her. 'So how much did you hear?'

'Enough.'

'It was you should have been having the audition back there.' He glanced at her again. 'You had me fooled.'

'That's all it was, acting.' She didn't take her eyes from the road. For the moment, the rest of the conversation remained unsaid.

After a while, she asked, 'Do you think Ray Whitelaw will believe us?'

'He's got to, hasn't he?' Kieran replied simply.

It was late afternoon by the time they reached Blackport, and they drove straight to Central police station. Flora cut through the university campus to avoid the traffic.

'Weird, isn't it, to think this was where we met?' she said, as they passed the students' union building.

Kieran gave a tight smile. 'I bet you wish sometimes that we hadn't.'

Flora jerked the car to a standstill in the middle of the road. Pulling him towards her, she kissed him, hard, on the lips. Then she said fiercely, 'You're an idiot, Kieran Henshall.'

A group of lads sitting on the union steps raised their glasses in salute and cheered.

They were both grinning, as she drove on, past Senate House and then the vast neo-classical Assembly Hall. Several vans were parked outside. Two young women were unloading an elaborate floral decoration from the back of one of them. A small army of porters was carting stacked chairs up the sweeping steps, in readiness for the degree ceremony the following day.

'Put your foot down, Flora.' The grin had vanished from Kieran's face. 'We've got to see Whitelaw today.'

'I've told you, he isn't here,' the desk sergeant repeated. 'Now, if you'd like to—'

'We've got to speak to him. It's urgent,' Kieran cut across him.

The sergeant looked him up and down, his expression speaking volumes as he took in Kieran's crumpled clothes and grubby bandages. Kieran couldn't imagine that Deefer, who it had been too hot to leave in the car, was doing much to improve their image. He also a nasty suspicion that it was the same officer who had been on duty the night he had been brought in for stealing his own car. In which case, the fuss he's kicked up then would be doing their present cause no favours either.

As if reading his thoughts, Flora said with her most winning smile, 'We really do need to speak to DI Whitelaw personally, Sergeant.'

The man's expression was very different as he transferred his

attention to her. 'If you would just like to take a seat, miss, I'll
see what I can do,' he said.

With a quick wink at Kieran, she gave their names, and the
man spoke into the telephone on the desk.

Kieran looked at the notice boards, trying to control the
jumpiness he always felt in police stations. He wondered if he
would ever be able to see a uniform without immediately going
on the defensive.

Eventually the door opened. Kieran's heart sank. It was the
bastard who had interviewed him after the fire.

'Where's Whitelaw?' The words came out more aggressively
than he had intended, as the man introduced himself as DC
Lightowler.

'Acting Inspector Medlock has taken over from DI Whitelaw,
but he isn't available at the moment.' There was a distinct glint
of malice in Lightowler's eyes as he went on, 'So you'll just have
to make do with me, won't you?'

Flora had come to stand by Kieran's side. 'What's happened
to Ray Whitelaw?' she demanded.

'I'm not sure that's any of your concern, miss.' Lightowler
smiled at her blandly. 'Now, how can I be of assistance?'

Kieran turned to her despairingly and muttered, 'We can't tell
him.'

'We've got to,' Flora replied. 'We've got no choice.'

It was only with some reluctance that Lightowler allowed Deefer
to accompany them into the interview room. The dog did
nothing to endear himself by growling softly each time
Lightowler made a move. Eventually, they were settled, and
Kieran embarked on his story. The tape machine, he noticed,
wasn't running, and at the first mention of Greg Farrell's name,
Lightowler put his pencil down. Even as he spoke, Kieran knew
he was wasting his time.

'If I remember correctly, Miss Castledine, you and Mr Farrell arrived at the scene together.' Lightowler turned to Flora as Kieran attempted to explain the cause of the fire.

'That's right,' said Flora, evenly.

'Been somewhere nice? You were wearing a very smart outfit that evening, if I might say so.' Lightowler was making no secret of what he was insinuating.

'We were having a business meeting.'

'Business?' Lightowler nodded sagely. 'What *business* would that be, then?'

'Listen!' Kieran jumped to his feet. 'Do you mind telling me what bloody relevance—'

'Your girlfriend was out for the evening with a gentleman you are now accusing of arson, amongst other things. Every relevance, I'd say.' Lightowler turned back to Flora. 'What sort of business?'

'Greg . . . Mr Farrell had offered to help Kieran in his acting career,' she answered, tugging at Kieran's sleeve to get him to sit down.

'Ah,' Lightowler smiled, as if all had suddenly become clear. 'Acting, is it?' He picked up his pencil and turned it between thumb and forefinger for a moment, before looking at Kieran and commenting drily, 'And no publicity's bad publicity, isn't that what they say? You don't like Mr Farrell very much, do you Kieran?'

'You expect me to, in view of what I've just told you?'

'He seems to be a lot more forgiving than you are. Maybe he's been taking his work home with him!' Lightowler smiled broadly at his own joke. 'Turning the other cheek, and all that.'

Kieran looked at him blankly.

'He rang here earlier. To inform us that the pair of you had scarpered without paying your rent. Says he doesn't want to press charges because of your recent . . . mental problems. But he did warn us you might try to cause some trouble.'

'Oh, the bastard,' Flora breathed.

'Mind you, on reflection, I'm not so sure he got it right about the mental problems,' Lightowler mused. 'I guess slinging accusations at someone as famous as Greg Farrell is one way to get your name known, especially when the press are all up here covering the degree ceremony.' He tapped the pencil against the side of his nose. 'Maybe you're not as barmy as you look, sunshine.'

Kieran, who throughout Lightowler's monologue had been struggling to control his temper, was on his feet again, pushing the chair out from under him with such force that it clattered to the floor. Deefer sprang up, barking.

'You fucking moron!' Kieran shouted over the racket. 'If you seriously think——'

Lightowler didn't reply. He simply hit the panic button behind him. Within seconds, two uniformed men piled into the room and had Kieran on the floor, still shouting.

'What the hell are you doing?' Flora cried, yanking on Deefer's lead to prevent him from joining the fray.

'Threatening a police officer is a serious offence, Miss Castledine,' Lightowler said, as Kieran was dragged back to his feet, his wrists handcuffed behind his back.

'But he wasn't——'

'And perjury is even more serious. So if you don't want to find yourself in the cell next to his, I suggest you leave peacefully and take that animal with you.'

'I knew we should never have trusted you bastards,' Kieran shouted.

'Keep calm. I'll get it sorted.' Flora darted forward, planted a kiss on his cheek, and whispered, 'Plan B.'

Still restrained by the two constables, and struggling against the cuffs, Kieran watched her go.

As far as he knew, there was no plan B.

Flora had wondered if the man at the seedy bed and breakfast would question the name 'Anne Smith', but he didn't so much as look up from the doubles match that he was watching on the portable television on the reception desk. He just took her money and pushed her key across to her, his eyes glued to the screen.

The level of subterfuge, she told herself as she turned the key in the lock and glanced into the shabby room, was probably wildly over the top in any event. But too many people had died during the past weeks for her to take any chances. She had been shocked to read, on a newspaper hoarding on the way from the police station, that Henry Denstone was one of them. Pulling from her bag the paper that she had stopped the car to buy, she reread the article. 'Tragic Accident' was how the headline described his death. Flora wondered nervously just what kind of 'accident' had befallen her employer. The details in the paper were sketchy. The quoted police spokesman, she noted, was Acting Detective Inspector Neville Medlock.

She went back out to the car, which was stifling and smelt overpoweringly of dog. She longed for a shower and a change of clothes, but the meagre possessions she had accrued since the fire were still in Stratford. She glanced down at her short denim skirt. That would have to be replaced at any rate, she decided. There was no way she would be allowed in the following day wearing that.

Getting back into the driving seat, she set off for the shops.

She had withdrawn all the cash her cards would permit while Kieran had been organising the car hire; cash was anonymous, cheques weren't. She had enough in her wallet to buy a simple navy dress and some more suitable shoes than the open sandals she had on. She caught the chemist's just as it was closing, and hastily selected soap, toothpaste and shampoo. She paused by the hair colours. If anyone were to come looking for her, her waist-length auburn hair would be a dead giveaway. She shuddered at the phrase she had unconsciously chosen, reached for a bottle of dye, then changed her mind. Paying the impatient shop assistant, she carried her purchases back to the car, and drove to St Saviour's, where she walked quickly across the deserted yard, let herself into the storeroom, and started to sort through the props.

Back at the B & B an hour later, showered and changed, she examined herself critically in the bedroom mirror. The wig she had chosen gave her a plain, dark brown bob. With her own vivid hair crammed out of sight beneath it, and a pair of wire-rimmed spectacles perched on the end of her nose, she decided that even Kieran wouldn't recognise her, let alone Greg Farrell.

She slipped the dress off, lay down on the creaky, unyielding bed, and for the first time, allowed herself to go back over everything she had heard on that stage in Stratford. A tiny part of her brain still refused to believe what Greg had done; the cold-blooded cynicism with which he had planned and manipulated; his utter lack of compassion. She recalled with revulsion the evening she had spent with him in the restaurant, the contrived sincerity with which he had talked about wanting to help when, even as he was speaking, he must have believed Kieran to be already dead. How could she so willingly have allowed herself to be deceived?

Shivering, she drew the thin counterpane around her shoulders. Her longing for Kieran was a physical ache. But he was locked up in the overnight cells at Blackport Central. She was on her own. All she could do now was to wait.

And pray.

White. Walls, ceiling, everything was white.

The fluorescent strip above him flickered like a nervous tic. He seemed to have been staring at it all his life.

A young woman's face appeared briefly above his own. Soft voices murmured somewhere over his head.

He tried to look up, but his head flopped sideways. He was like a marionette with its strings tangled.

He tried again to speak, to tell them what he knew; what everyone had to know. Carefully, he unpicked some words from the jumble inside his brain. But once inside his mouth, they got snarled up again; wound themselves around his tongue; refused to come out.

'Just relax, Mr Whitelaw.' Cool fingers on his cheek.

How could he relax?

Firm hands lifted his head like a football to realign it on the pillow. Tucked him into the snowy sheets like a letter in its envelope.

A letter no one could read.

A sudden splash of colour into the whiteness; a strong, familiar smell. Sweet peas, from the garden. Greenfly on the petals. Buggers had got at those, and all. Must tell Val . . .

Must tell . . .

'He's a bit restless, Mrs Whitelaw.' The same soft voice. 'Quite normal in stroke patients . . . The brain's still swollen . . . We won't know the extent of the damage . . .'

Val's face. Brave smile pinned over the strain.

He wanted to reach out with his finger and trace the single tear she hadn't noticed. Wanted to tell her not to worry.

Wanted to tell . . .

Chapter Thirty

The lawn outside the Assembly Hall was already milling with students, when Flora arrived. Students as they were rarely seen. Jeans and tee shirts had been swapped for demure frocks and soberly cut suits. Spiky hairstyles had been tamed to accommodate mortarboards. Cameras were flashing everywhere, as proud parents captured the moment for posterity.

Other, larger cameras were in evidence as well. Several outside broadcast crews had arrived, Flora observed, and were setting up on a cordoned-off section of grass in front of Senate House. She remembered, from her own graduation, that this was where any newsworthy honorary graduates were interviewed after the ceremony. And they seldom came more newsworthy than Greg Farrell.

There was also, she noticed nervously, a substantial police presence.

'What are that lot doing?' she asked a girl who, despite her ankle-length black dress, still contrived by virtue of several nose-rings and a good deal of kohl pencil to look anything but conservative.

'The pigs?' the girl shrugged. 'Some religious cranks threatening a demo or something, I heard. Probably just hoping for an autograph, dozy bunch.' Her face became more animated. 'Do you realise, Farrell earned more for his last bloody film than the annual GNP of Sierra Leone? Now that would be worth demonstrating about.'

Flora nodded. She could imagine who had started the rumour about a demo. Police protection would suit Greg Farrell very well.

After a while, ushers began shepherding the students into the hall. The degree ceremony was scheduled to begin in half an hour, at eleven a.m. Flora made her way over to the gym, which was doubling up for the day as a robing room. Heaps of gowns lay strewn around on trestle tables. Flora went to take one.

'Cutting it a bit fine, aren't you, love?' The elderly man behind the table shook his head reprovingly. 'Let's have your ticket, then.'

Flora had forgotten that in order to hire a gown, students had to pay in advance, and produce a ticket on the day.

Her dismay must have shown on her face. The man rolled his eye and said, 'Not another one!'

Flora made a show of searching in her bag. 'I had it a minute ago.' She looked at him imploringly.

'I don't know,' the man grumbled cheerfully. 'You're the fifth this morning. If you lot are our future captains of industry, God help us, is all I can say.' He handed the gown over with a wink. 'You'll get me shot, you will! Got the right hood?' he enquired, as Flora snatched one at random from the colourful stacks on the next table.

She nodded, and flashed the man a grateful smile.

'And for God's sake bring it back afterwards,' he shouted after her as she flew out, dragging it around her shoulders as she went.

The chaos that always ensued when too small a number of ushers tried to organise the movements of too large a number of students was well established, by the time Flora got back to the Assembly Hall. It was relatively easy for her to slip in without the second of the two tickets that she was missing. She squeezed in at the end of a row of others with the same azure hoods as the one she had taken, and realised with some amusement that she had awarded herself an M.Sc.

The amusement didn't last long. Suddenly, the hall was filled with the majestic opening chords of Charpentier's *Te Deum*, and everyone rose to their feet as the procession entered. Flora craned to see the mace-bearer in full regalia, followed by the Chancellor, the Vice-Chancellor and the senior academics resplendent in their velvet caps and gowns. She picked out several that she knew, and was grateful for her disguise. Her heart hammering, she heard the rustle of recognition as Greg, stunning in the scarlet robe of a Doctor of Letters, filed gravely past, eyes straight ahead, and took his seat with the other dignitaries at the front.

The last notes from the organ died away. The congregation sat. Flora was aware that all around her, heads were craning for a better view of the famous Greg Farrell. She glanced behind her. Ushers lined the sides of the hall. In addition, a number of uniformed policemen flanked the massive pillars of the entrance.

Plan B had not been complicated – she had intended simply to stand up, as Greg was presented to receive his degree, and accuse him before the assembled company. Taking stock of the situation, she realised how hopelessly naïve the notion had been. The instant she made a sound, she would be bundled out of the hall before she had a chance to say a word. Just another student protester. She doubted Greg would even register that the outburst was aimed at him.

The Chancellor was on his feet. His voice echoed around the hall as he announced in sombre tones, 'Before I open this Degree Congregation, I would like us all to remember our second honorary graduand, Henry Denstone, who was so tragically and suddenly taken from us earlier this week. Our condolences go to his family. His name, synonymous for so many years with the prosperity of this town, will be remembered with gratitude and pride. Will you please stand.'

Everyone got obediently to their feet.

'There will now follow a minute's silence.'

Flora closed her eyes, thinking not just of Henry Denstone, but of the others who had died. She looked up. Greg Farrell was standing alongside the Chancellor, head bowed, hands clasped in front of him as if in prayer.

She wasn't finished yet, she promised herself.

Somehow, she sat through the oration, during which a syco-phantic professor from the English department eulogised on Mr Farrell's contribution to the British film industry and his achieve-ments in popularising the classics by his skilful character interpretation.

'To what greater honour could we at this fine university aspire, than to offer an honorary degree to God's Only Son?' the professor rounded off, to a ripple of respectful laughter.

Greg, beaming modestly, got to his feet, as the Chancellor intoned, 'By the authority vested in me . . .'

It was only with the very greatest difficulty that Flora was not physically sick.

As soon as the main business of the morning was underway and the rows of graduands began to shuffle up to receive their degrees, she put her lingering nausea to good effect. She wasn't going to achieve anything inside the Assembly Hall; she had realised that within minutes. Clamping a handkerchief to her mouth, she scurried to the back, mumbled, 'Need some fresh air,' and emerged into the blinding sun, where she leant against one of the pillars, breathing deeply, her faintness not affected. Then, slipping quietly down the steps, she made her way towards the press enclosure.

A thin, smartly dressed woman, whom Flora recognised as a news presenter from *North West Today*, was talking to one of the cameramen, and dragging on a cigarette. She looked up as Flora approached.

'Fuck, they're not coming out already, are they?' she demanded in celebrated crystal tones as she ground the cigarette into the lawn and smoothed her hair.

Flora shook her head.

'Thank Christ for that. The woman rolled her eyes heaven-ward. 'Any idea how long?'

The conversation had attracted the attention of one of the policemen who, with nothing better to do for the moment, were standing around, enjoying the sun. He checked his watch.

'Better get into position,' he said to one of his colleagues. 'It's going to be bedlam when that lot pile out. Move along, love,' he added to Flora. 'You can't stand there. Sorry.'

A patrol car was parked in front of Senate House, together with several police vans. Two plain-clothes officers were standing beside it, deep in conversation. One was a tall, blond-haired man, vaguely familiar. The other, she realised, was DC Lightowler. He stared at her as she moved to one side, said something to the other man, and began to walk towards her.

Flora felt a stab of panic. What if he had recognised her? But why should he? In any event, to make a run for it would be the surest way to break her cover, she told herself, feeling a prickle of sweat between her shoulder blades. Moving as briskly as she could without actually breaking into a trot, she headed towards the gym, not slackening her pace until she reached the entrance. She glanced fearfully back, but the man had stopped by the barrier.

She decided to ditch the gown; Kieran had always claimed the police were suspicious of students, and the damned thing was so hot she felt as if she were going to melt at any minute. With a mental apology to the ticket man, she took it off and bundled it under one of the benches in the entrance lobby, then stood in the doorway, her eyes trained on the Assembly Hall, until finally the doors were flung open and the procession filed down the steps.

Immediately, the police formed a guard around Greg, and he was hustled into the enclosure, as the main body of students began to surge out of the hall. A considerable number of them headed after him, in the hope of catching a glimpse of the celebrity while he was being interviewed. Flora joined them, edging her way to the front. A couple of dozen policemen, facing out into the crowd, ringed the enclosure, despite the fact that the threatened demo had, unsurprisingly, failed utterly to materialise.

The crowd was at its thinnest in the place where she was standing; not many were interested in Greg Farrell's backview. Only a couple of policemen were guarding the section, but that, while an advantage, was not Flora's primary aim in choosing the spot. By positioning herself just behind Greg, she ensured that when the cameras were on him, they would be on her as well.

A makeup girl was adjusting Greg's hood. The thin woman was standing beside him, microphone in hand, her profiled face already set into a bright, attentive smile. The man with the clapper board did his bit, as everyone else scuttled out of shot.

Flora's heart was hammering furiously. She held her ground, realising that there was no point in making a move only to find that it was an abortive take. She would only have seconds; she was well aware of that. Her only hope was for the cameras to pick up enough of the confrontation to set the ball rolling. The idiot policeman standing on the far side of the lawn with his blond sidekick might reckon that no publicity was bad publicity. Flora could only pray that he was wrong.

It took three attempts before, finally, the sound engineer was satisfied. Greg glanced at his watch, managing to convey, with the utmost charm, that this would be the final take. The crowd was once again motioned to silence. The woman started her introduction. Greg ran a hand through his hair and smiled as he prepared to answer her inane query as to whether he was pleased to be receiving the degree.

Flora took a deep breath. To her horror, she saw that Lightowler and the other policeman, who had been standing at a distance and murmuring into their radios, were moving directly towards her; which could only mean that they had somehow guessed what she was planning. It was now or never, she told herself.

Throwing herself forward, she yelled at the top of her voice, 'Greg Farrell is a child-molester and a—'

It was over in seconds. The breath was knocked out of her as the bulky policeman to her right leapt forward and brought her to the ground, clapping his hand over her mouth and knocking off her wig so that her auburn hair spilt out on to the grass around her.

Greg whirled round, his eyes registering an instant of shock before professionalism took over. 'I'm afraid this young woman has been making a nuisance of herself for some time,' he informed the bemused presenter gravely. He glanced down at the policeman and said, his voice more irritated, 'Can you at least get her out of shot, please?' Flora, doubled up and winded, was barely able to draw breath with the policeman's meaty hand still clamped over the lower half of her face. Greg looked her in the eye, then turning back to the cameraman said, 'Do we really need to see all this on television, for God's sake? The poor girl's mentally disturbed. She probably has a perfectly respectable family, somewhere.'

A murmur of assent went round the crowd. A smattering of people clapped. The presenter was listening into her earpiece, but before she could respond, the blond man stepped forward, warrant card in hand.

'No, sir,' he said. 'I think we should keep them rolling for the moment.'

'Would someone mind telling me what's going on?' Greg snapped.

The man didn't answer him. Instead, he looked directly into the camera. 'Acting Inspector Neville Medlock, Blackport Constabulary,' he said. Then turning back to Greg, he went on over the rising babble of the onlookers, 'Gregory Richard Farrell, I am arresting you in connection with the deaths of Jason Morrissey, Sunil Doshai, Daniel Nolan, Norah Bateman, Lawrence Fieldgate and the attempted murder of Kieran Henshall. You do not have to say anything . . .'

As he proceeded with the caution, and the police cordon moved in to control the surging crowd, Flora was hauled roughly away, still gasping for breath, towards the police van. A couple of reporters got as close as her police escort would permit, shouting questions, but their attention was quickly deflected as Greg was hustled past, surrounded by the rest of the press pack. Flora watched as he was bundled into the back of the waiting patrol car and driven off at speed. Medlock, she noticed, had not gone with him. With a brisk 'No comment', which none the less allowed time for a battalion of flash guns to go off, he turned his back on the press and got into the yellow sports car that was parked alongside.

As he roared off up University Boulevard, Flora could see that he was smiling.

Chapter Thirty-One

Whitelaw had been moved from intensive care, and on to the general ward. It seemed like the first small step back into the world. Somehow, just being away from the monitors, the monotonous bleeping of the machinery that had been registering every surge of blood around his veins, made him feel infinitely more optimistic.

The move was celebrated by a seemingly constant stream of visitors.

First Val, calling in on her way to school. 'They say you're making wonderful progress, Ray,' she said. She was so clearly delighted at the overnight improvement in his condition that after a couple of minutes she refrained, much to Whitelaw's relief, from using the hushed, sepulchral voice she had employed ever since he had been brought in, and was soon chattering away as normal.

Her main topic of conversation was the same as that of the porter who had wheeled him down from intensive care, the nurse who had washed and shaved him, and the lady who had brought the tea: Greg Farrell's spectacular arrest.

Val was beside herself. Whitelaw would have liked to tell her that the news had come as a bit of a shock to him as well. In fact, had he been able to talk, he would probably have been speechless, he told himself as Val rattled on. The thought pulled the good

319

side of his face into a semblance of a grin. Was laughing at his own jokes progress?

After Val came the heavy squad: the sharp-suited Head of Neurology and his entourage of registrars, housemen and medical students. Whitelaw was prodded, poked, had pins stuck into him and lights shone in his eyes. He was asked to grip the fingers of an extremely pretty young girl, and to his enormous satisfaction was able to persuade his recalcitrant right hand to make contact with hers, if only feebly. That *was* progress.

But even greater was to come.

Just before lunch, a short, dumpy woman with heavy eyebrows and the makings of a fine moustache woke Whitelaw from a dream in which he was digging the garden, as fit and able as he had ever been. The image was so utterly mundane that when he came to and found himself lying immobile in the unfamiliar room, it seemed for a moment that he had not woken from a dream, but had slipped into a nightmare. Then, gradually, he remembered where he was; what had happened. It dawned on him that this, from now on, was reality. To his acute embarrassment, Whitelaw realised that he was weeping.

'Side effect of stroke, I'm afraid. You'll find yourself doing it at the drop of a hat for a while.' The woman's ugly features were transformed by her compassionate smile. 'You're beginning to improve already, Mr Whitelaw,' she went on in a light Irish lilt entirely at odds with her stolid appearance. 'In the next few weeks you'll get better and better.' She patted his hand. 'You will. In the meantime, I want you to concentrate on the half of your body that does work. Start with the little things. The big things will follow, I promise you.'

She showed him how to hitch himself up the bed using his left arm and leg. Rearranged the bedside table so that everything was in reach. Shakily, Whitelaw reached for a tissue and blew his own nose.

Progress indeed.

'The speech therapist will be along later,' the woman said. She laid her hand lightly on his and looked earnestly into his face. 'It will come back. It'll be hard work, the hardest you've ever done, but it will come back if you want it enough.' With a smile, she pulled a notepad and pencil from her pocket. 'In the meantime, there are other forms of communication.'

She helped Whitelaw sit up in the bed. She pulled the bed-table across in front of him. Then, putting the pencil in his left hand, she said, 'Off you go. Get writing!'

He had taken his handwriting as much for granted as he had his own face. The childish, wobbly script that was all he could manage left-handed, as the woman looked on, was utterly un-familiar. It was frustrating. Whitelaw felt as if he were back in the infants as laboriously, he printed the letters. It was also exhila-rating. He could connect again, however clumsily.

It took him almost five minutes to complete his first epistle to the world, and when he had finished it, he felt as exhausted as if he had done a day's work. He flopped back onto the pillow as the woman picked it up, read it, and laughed.

'You'll make a good recovery, Mr Whitelaw,' she said, getting to her feet. 'You've the right mental attitude.' She passed the pad back to him.

'BUGGER THIS FOR A GAME OF SOLDIERS', was what he had written.

He spent the afternoon practising. He tried to think of what his first message to Val should be. That he loved her? She knew that already. That with her help, he was determined to pull through? Everything that he thought of sounded too . . . heroic. It would only make her cry; probably make him cry too. In the end, he settled for: 'SPRAY THE SWEET PEAS.' He handed it over as soon as she came in after school.

They both cried anyway.

He was just finishing his first session with the speech thera-pist when Medlock arrived, bearing a huge basket of fruit.

Everyone knew Whitelaw hated fruit.

Medlock treated the therapist, a stylish, long-limbed blonde, to his most dazzling smile as he said apologetically, 'I hope I haven't come at a bad time.'

The girl blushed prettily. 'No, we were just finishing.'

They were quite similar-looking, Whitelaw noticed; they could almost be brother and sister. But there was nothing fraternal in Medlock's expression as he said, 'I'll have to remember what time you're around.'

'Usually about this time.' The girl looked down at Whitelaw, her smile becoming professional again. 'Just keep practising those sounds, Ray. B-b-b. D-d-d. remember?'

How could he forget? He'd spent the last half an hour doing nothing else but try to coax his uncoordinated lips and tongue into playing ball. He was beginning to think that being sick was harder work than being fit. Especially when it meant that he had to endure the company of the likes of Medlock.

Having finally dragged his attention away from the speech therapist's legs as she swung off down the ward, Medlock dumped the fruit down by Whitelaw's right side, where he couldn't have reached it even had he wanted to, and drew up a chair.

'Sorry about all this,' he said, waving vaguely at Whitelaw. 'Mind you, you were asking for it. Fags, beer, bacon sandwiches . . . And you were letting yourself get far too personally involved at work, if you want my opinion.'

Whitelaw didn't, but before he could reach for the notepad, Medlock shook his head, then said brightly, 'Still, bit late for the lectures now, eh? I thought I'd cheer you up with the latest on the Farrell case.'

He handed over the day's edition of the *Echo*, thoughtfully folded so that the photograph of Greg Farrell being taken into custody was the first thing Whitelaw saw. The headline, in massive capitals, read: 'SAINT OR SINNER?'

Sid Barker would be having a field day, Whitelaw thought sourly. There were enough clichés in the situation to keep him going until retirement.

Beneath the photograph, ran the caption, 'Captured on Camera: Blackport's DI Medlock makes his move.'

'Nice to see us getting some favourable press coverage for a change,' Medlock said complacently. 'Sorry if I pissed on your bonfire, as it were.'

This time, Whitelaw did reach for his pad, the full frustration of the situation hitting him again as he fumbled with the pencil. The words were there, clamouring in his brain, clogging his mouth, but he wasn't about to risk making an exhibition of himself by spewing them out, half-formed and unintelligible, in front of Medlock. Humiliated by his slow, wavering pace, he printed out, 'WHAT ABOUT DENSTONE?'

Medlock took it from him. 'Poor bastard hanged himself,' he said with a slight lift of the shoulders. 'Well, it was quite clear from his letter that that was what he had in mind, wasn't it? I suppose the thought of going through the charade of that degree ceremony with Farrell was just the last straw.' He leant back in his chair, stretching luxuriously as he broke into a grin. 'Perhaps Tricia will call it the Henry Denstone Memorial Fund now, what do you reckon? Let's face it, she's not going to raise much cash with young Freddie's name to it, once everything hits the fan. Poor old Henry! All those years trying to protect her from the truth, paying off wankers like Perotti, keeping a thug like Fieldgate in employment, watching Farrell's career take off and knowing there was nothing he could do about it without bringing everything down on her head. No wonder he was such a sour-faced old git! The funny thing is, if Farrell hadn't fabricated the theft, I doubt Denstone would ever have connected him to the murders. Why should he? But when he did . . . My God, that must have been some dilemma for a man like him.' Medlock shook his head, appearing, for the moment, genuinely moved at the thought of Denstone's plight.

The moment didn't last. 'Still,' he went on cheerfully, 'the timing couldn't have turned out better from our point of view, could it?' He gave a small, self-deprecating laugh. 'Well, from my point of view, at any rate. Although that idiot Henshall and his mad bitch of a girlfriend very nearly succeeded in screwing things up. It must have been one of the few unaided intelligent decisions Lightowler's made in his life, running him in.'

Whitelaw tried to drag himself up in the bed, his mouth working frantically. In a gesture as ridiculous as it was futile, he shook his fist, because he didn't know what else to do.

Medlock gazed at him sadly. 'Poor old Whitelaw. You still don't get it, do you? Well, let me spell it out for you. That first time we went to Oultonshaw Manor to investigate the theft, didn't it all seem a bit odd to you? Henry so keen to get Nolan found? Farrell not wanting us involved? It set an alarm bell ringing. Then, as the evidence started to come through, it set off a few more. It didn't add up, not when all the other odds and ends were thrown into the equation: the son's death; the fire at Denstone Park . . . Too many coincidences. And as you always told me, Guv,' he gave Whitelaw a patronising smile, 'a good policeman never trusts coincidences. So I decided to do a bit of investigating from the inside, as it were; get friendly with the Denstones' daughter. Desperate for affection, of course; I realised that as soon as I set eyes on her. It was quite obvious she was ripe for anyone who offered her a bit of TLC. Which I did. And it wasn't long before she was telling me all about the dear departed Freddie and the things that he'd got her to do to him in the name of sisterly devotion.' He shook his head. 'What a thoroughly perverted little bastard he must have been.'

Whitelaw closed his eyes. It wasn't only the dispossessed whose lives had been destroyed.

Medlock resumed his monologue. 'So that put Freddie nicely in the frame. But as he'd been dead for ten years, it wasn't going to advance the investigation very far, was it? Penelope had mentioned Greg Farrell, and how he and Freddie had been at drama school together, but I have to admit it was a while before I made the connection. Ironic, really, that it was Penelope who fitted the final piece into the jigsaw for me. Unwittingly, of course; I get the distinct feeling she's always had a bit of a soft spot for our Greg. Imagining him as Christ must really have given her the hots. She's heavily into religion.' He grinned. 'Well, I suppose with a face and figure like that, you'd have to put your hope in the spiritual, wouldn't you?' Leaning forward, he asked, 'Sorry, Guv? Were you trying to say something? No? Well, let me know, if I'm going too fast for you. Now, where was I?' He nodded. 'Ah, yes. While you were off on Sunday to see your little friend from the funny farm, I was in church with Penny. And very uplifting it was too. You should try it. In fact . . .' He got up and walked round to the bedside locker.

Whitelaw followed him with his eyes, wondering what the hell was going on, as Medlock opened one of the drawers, and produced a New Testament.

'Amazing,' he said. 'You can find these things everywhere, and yet it was the one place none of us thought to look.' Perching on the side of the bed, he flicked through the pages. 'Ah, here we are. The reading for last Sunday. The gospel according to St Mark, chapter ten, beginning at verse fourteen. "Suffer the little children to come unto me."' He shook his head admiringly. 'Clever, that. I mean, we knew Jason Morrissey got religion for a while when he was in his teens, but who would have expected the little shit to have such a well-developed sense of irony?' He gazed at Whitelaw expectantly, head on one side. 'Oh dear, you still don't get it, do you?' He held the page in front of Whitelaw's face. 'Mark, 10:14. Or, as Morrissey wrote it, MARIO, 14.'

With a small smile of triumph, he tossed the Bible onto the floor, beside the fruit. 'Academic, in view of Henry's little epistle, as it transpired. But it was gratifying to have got there before it was spelt out so clearly that even you realised Farrell was our man.'

He looked across at Whitelaw, then threw back his head and laughed. 'Dear God, did you seriously believe for one minute that I'd have *married* that dreary bitch? Just because Denstone had a bit of influence in this one-eyed town? You really *don't* know what makes me tick, do you?' He got to his feet. 'Well, take care of yourself, Whitelaw. As I say, I'm sorry about the stroke.' He bent down and retrieved the newspaper, pausing to admire his picture, before adding with a chuckle, 'But if you have to have one at all, I'm so glad it wasn't a couple of days later, or who knows, it might have been your ugly mug all over the front page!'

Whitelaw watched as Medlock strolled up the ward, whistling softly. Then, putting together all the treatment he had received during the day, he hauled himself up the bed, clamped his lips together as the speech therapist had taught him, and with the force of someone vomiting out a gobbet of poison, bellowed, 'Bastard!'

It wasn't perfect. But it was good enough to break Medlock's stride. Like the woman said, start with the little things. The big things would follow.

The last visitors of the long day were Kieran and Flora. They came down the ward quickly, Flora casting an anxious glance over her shoulder towards the nurses' station in the corridor beyond. For a wild moment, Whitelaw wondered if they had escaped from custody and were on the run, the more so when Kieran hastily slipped under the bed the rucksack he had been carrying, and whispered as he took a seat, 'We can't stop long.'

'Millie told us what had happened.' Flora bent and quickly kissed Whitelaw's cheek. 'We're off to Scilly overnight, but we wanted to call in and see you first.'

They were looking so furtive, the pair of them, that it had to mean trouble. Whitelaw gripped Flora's wrist, as she straightened up, and gazed at her questioningly. He reached for his pad. As he did so, a muffled squeak came from under the bed.

'Quick, draw the curtain round.' Kieran hissed. He bent down, pulled the rucksack out, and sat it on his lap.

Whitelaw blinked. His eyesight was playing up again; the rucksack seemed to be moving of its own accord.

'We checked it out with Val first,' Kieran said as he undid the straps. 'Seeing as she's going to have to look after him until you're fit. She thought you'd like to meet him straight away.'

From inside the rucksack, he produced a small black and white bundle. A Border collie pup. For a moment, his eyes met Whitelaw's, and Whitelaw felt the sting of tears. Bloody stroke. He hadn't blubbed since he was a toddler, and here he was doing it three times in the one day.

'You'll have to get better now, won't you?' Kieran said gruffly. 'He'll need too much exercise to have you sat around here on your backside for long.'

The puppy yapped. Stifling a giggle, Flora popped it back inside the bag. 'Listen, we're going to get thrown out in a minute,' she whispered. 'We'll come in to see you again next week. We'll have to be back up then. There'll be more statements.'

'And funerals,' Kieran added soberly.

Flora drew back the curtain. A staff nurse was heading down the ward towards them, frowning.

'Oh, by the way.' Kieran wrapped the heaving rucksack inside his jacket, trying for nonchalance and, for such a good actor, failing miserably. 'Val said to ask what you wanted to call him.'

'I hope you haven't got what I think you've got in that bag, young man.' The staff nurse glared ferociously at Kieran's wriggling jacket.

'Sorry,' he said contritely. 'We're just off.'

Whitelaw shook his head; the first time since the stroke that it had given any hint of obeying his instructions. He pointed to the rucksack. Tested the name in his mouth. But it was too important to risk getting it wrong. He had to be sure they understood.

He picked up his pencil instead, and inscribed a single word. 'DANNY'.